Of their own volition, her fingers moved from his shoulders to curl in the wavy silkiness of his hair. His mouth was a searing flame that stole her breath. Helplessly, Aurora pressed closer to him, longing for something she couldn't name.

She felt boneless, on fire. . . . She felt as if she were falling. . . .

It was only Nicholas, nudging her onto her back on the soft mattress.

Her eyes fluttered open, and she stared up at him. She was trembling, her cheeks hotly flushed, her senses spinning.

His eyes watched her as his hand moved to the empire-waist bodice of her gown; she felt herself drowning in their shadowed depths. When his fingers curled over the low décolletage, she tensed, but he bent to her again, his mouth hovering just above hers, heating her lips. "Don't be afraid to feel, angel. Tonight, just let your senses rule. . . ."

By Nicole Jordan

The PASSION

A Novel

Nicole Jordan

BALLANTINE BOOKS • NEW YORK

2010 Ballantine Books Mass Market Edition

Copyright © 2000 by Anne Bushyhead
Excerpt from *To Desire a Wicked Duke* by Nicole Jordan copyright © 2010 by Anne Bushyhead

BALLANTINE and colophon are trademarks of Random House, Inc.

Originally published in mass market in the United States by Ivy, an imprint of The Random House Publishing Group, a division of Random House, Inc., in 2000.

This book contains an excerpt from the forthcoming book *To Desire a Wicked Duke* by Nicole Jordan. This excerpt has been set for this edition only and may not reflect the final content of the forthcoming edition.

ISBN 978-0-345-52338-9

Printed in the United States of America

www.ballantinebooks.com

9 8 7 6 5 4 3 2 1

To four wonderful writer friends:
Rosemary Edghill, India Edghill,
Donna Sterling, and Deborah Smith.
I hope you realize how special you are.

Prologue

Journal entry, July 16

I take up my pen once more, aching with the struggle in my heart. I must escape this passion that consumes me, but I know not how.

You came to me tonight. I felt your presence, your warmth, before hearing your footfall, my senses are so highly attuned to your nearness. The spell you cast over me has made me your slave more surely than any shackles.

You murmur my name and I turn to you. Your dark eyes are intense, questioning. I stare back, entranced. You have only to look at me and a rush of pleasure fills me.

I move into your arms, aching with love and desperation. Your touch is like a balm, your hand on my breast at once soothing and arousing.

I close my eyes, feeling your maleness, your strength, against my fragility. You know so well how vulnerable I am to you, to your fierce passion. I feel my body flame with it. I tremble at the caress of your lips, your heated breath, your deft fingers as you undress me.

Your robe falls to the floor. In the light of musk-scented candles, your nude body shimmers with grace and power, the master of any woman's fantasies.

Your hand brushes along my loins and I feel myself shudder. In turn I stroke the thickening swell of your hardness. I feel no shame. You have taught me desires of the *flesh, sensitized my body to pleasure, burning away all inhibition.*

I am already flowing, my center hot and throbbing, turning liquid with your touch, as you lie with me. Your eyes filled with challenge and desire, you move over my body and glide within me, thrusting deeply. My cry is hoarse with delight as I arch in surrender.

You command my senses. I am desperate, hungering to taste you, drugged with your opiate, with the need to fill and be filled.

You flood me in your passion. I am drowning and I draw you down with me.

Afterward, we lie close, our harsh breaths mingling, our damp skin clinging. I feel you grow still as you taste the salt of my tears. Rising above me, you stare into my eyes and see the ache in my heart I cannot hide.

Your fierce kiss is meant to soothe, but it only deepens the conflict tearing at my heart.

The choice is mine, you say. You offer me freedom, a precious gift. Because my happiness means more to you than your own, you will let me go.

But can I bear to live without you?

And is the choice truly mine to make?

PART I

Bonds of Desire

Chapter One

At first glimpse he seemed infinitely dangerous, even barbaric. And yet something in his eyes called to me. . . .

British West Indies, February 1813

The scene was pagan—the half nude man bound in chains, his sinewed torso bronzed by the Caribbean sun. Silhouetted against the ship's tall masts, he stood defiant, unbowed.

For a brief instant Lady Aurora Demming felt her heart falter as she stared up at the frigate's railing.

He might have been a statue carved by a master sculptor, all rippling muscle and lithe strength . . . except that he was flesh-and-blood male, and very much alive. Sunlight warmed the hard contours of his body, gilded the dark gold of his hair.

That tawny shade of gold was heart familiar. At first glance Aurora had flinched with the memory of another face forever lost to her. But this brazen, nearly naked man was a stranger, possessing a raw masculinity quite unlike her late betrothed.

He was stripped down to breeches, but though he wore the chains of a prisoner, he remained unbroken, his gaze fierce and remote as he stared out over the quay. Even from a distance, his eyes seemed to glitter dangerously, giving the impression of simmering anger tenuously controlled.

As if he felt her gaze, his focus slowly shifted and locked on her, riveting her in place. The bustle and noise of the waterfront faded away. For a fleeting moment, time ceased and only the two of them existed.

The intensity of his stare held her motionless, yet Aurora felt herself tremble, her heart suddenly drumming in a painful, almost wild rhythm.

"Aurora?"

She gave a start as her cousin Percy recalled her to her surroundings. She stood on the harbor quayside of Basseterre, St. Kitts, before the shipping office, the warm Caribbean sun beating down upon her. The pungent smells of fish and tar permeated the salt air along with the raucous cries of seagulls. Beyond the busy quay stretched brilliant blue-green waters, while in the distance rose the lush, mountainous island of Nevis.

Her cousin followed the direction of her gaze to the prisoner on the naval frigate. "What has you so fascinated?"

"That man . . ." she murmured. "For a moment he reminded me of Geoffrey."

Percy squinted across the quay. "How can you possibly tell at this distance?" He frowned. "The hair color is similar, perhaps, but any other resemblance must be superficial. I couldn't imagine the late Earl of March as a convict, could you?"

"I don't suppose so."

Yet she couldn't tear her eyes away from the fair-haired prisoner. Nor could he from her, it seemed. He still watched her as he stood at the head of the gangway, prepared to disembark. His hands manacled, he was guarded by two armed, burly seamen of the British navy, but he gave no notice of his captors until one jerked viciously on the chain that bound his wrists.

Pain or fury made his fists clench, but he offered no other sign of struggle as he was herded at musketpoint down the gangway.

Once more Aurora heard her name called, this time more firmly.

Her cousin touched her arm, his look full of sympathy. "Geoffrey is gone, Aurora. It will do you no good to dwell on your loss. And your grief can only prove detrimental to your upcoming marriage. I'm certain your future husband will not appreciate your mourning another man. For your own sake, you must learn to quell your feelings."

She had not been thinking of her loss, she was ashamed to admit, or the unwanted marriage her father was forcing upon her, but she nodded for her cousin's benefit. She had no business showing an interest in a barely dressed stranger. A criminal, no less. One who evidently had committed some heinous crime to warrant such savage punishment.

With a small shudder, Aurora forced her attention away. The primitive display was no sight for a lady, much less a duke's daughter. She had rarely seen so much naked male flesh at one time. Certainly she'd never been *shaken* by a man, as she had been moments ago when he caught her eye.

Chastising herself, she turned to allow her cousin to hand her into the open carriage. She'd come to the docks with Percy to confirm her passage to England. Because of the conflict with America and the danger of piracy, there were few ships leaving the West Indies. The next passenger vessel was scheduled to depart the island of St. Kitts three days hence and was only waiting for a military escort.

She dreaded returning home and had delayed as long as she dared, months longer than originally planned, using the excuse that travel was dangerous while a war raged. But her father was adamant that she present herself at once to prepare for her wedding to the nobleman he'd chosen for her. In his last letter he'd threatened to come and fetch her himself if she failed to honor the agreement he had made on her behalf.

Aurora had one foot on the carriage step when a disturbance across the quay made her pause. The prisoner had reached the end of the gangway and was being harangued to climb into a waiting wagon, obviously a difficult task because of his chains.

When he moved too slowly, he was given a savage shove

that sent him stumbling almost to his knees. Saving himself by clutching the wagon's rear gate, he drew himself up and turned to eye his guard with a contemptuous stare.

His cool insolence seemed to infuriate his tormentors for he received a musket butt to the ribs, which doubled him over in pain.

Aurora's cry of protest at the vicious attack lodged in her throat when the prisoner swung his chains at the guard. It was a futile gesture of defiance, for he was bound too tightly to effect any real damage, but apparently his rebellion was the excuse his guards wanted.

Both seamen set upon him with the stocks of their muskets, driving him to the cobblestones with cries of "Scurvy dog!" and "Bastard sea scum!"

Aurora recoiled in horror at seeing someone treated so viciously, without mercy. "For pity's sake . . ." she murmured hoarsely. "Make them stop, Percy!"

"It is a naval matter," her cousin replied in a grim tone, speaking in his role as lieutenant governor of St. Kitts. "I have no justification for interfering."

"Dear God, they'll beat him to death. . . ." Without waiting for a reply, she picked up her skirts and ran toward the commotion.

"Aurora!" She heard Percy curse under his breath, but she never slowed her steps nor paused to consider the danger or the madness of intervening in the violent dispute.

She had no weapon at hand and no clear plan beyond attempting a rescue, but when she reached the guards, she swung her reticule at the nearest assailant and managed to hit the side of his face.

"What the 'ell . . . ?"

When the startled seaman flinched at the unexpected attack, Aurora left off her flailing and pushed her way between the fallen prisoner and his assailants. Hiding her own fear, she sank to her knees, half covering the nearly unconscious man with her own body to shield him from being struck again.

The guard swore a vulgar oath.

Coldly furious, Aurora lifted her chin and stared up at him, silently daring him to strike her.

"Ma'am, ye've no business 'ere," he declared angrily. "This man is a vicious pirate."

"You, sir, may address me as *my lady*," she replied, her normally serene voice almost fierce as she called upon the power of her rank. "My father is the Duke of Eversley and claims the Prince Regent and the Lord High Admiral among his close acquaintances." She could see the sailor assessing her and her attire; her fashionable silk bonnet and walking dress were the gray of half mourning, with only a touch of lilac trim on the lapels of the spencer to relieve the severity.

"And this gentleman," she added as Percy hurriedly reached her side, "is my cousin, Sir Percy Osborne, who happens to be lieutenant governor of Nevis and St. Kitts. I would think twice before challenging him."

Percy's jaw tightened at her declaration, and he murmured in disapproval, "Aurora, this is quite unseemly. You're causing a spectacle."

"It would be more unseemly to stand by while these cowards murder an unarmed man."

Ignoring the guard's glare, she glanced down at the injured prisoner. His eyes were closed, but he seemed to be conscious, for his jaw was clenched in pain. He still looked half savage—his skin glistening with sweat and blood, a growth of dark stubble shadowing his jaw.

His head seemed to have suffered the worst damage. Not only was his temple bleeding profusely, but his sun-streaked hair, a much darker gold than her own, was matted black with dried blood, evidently from an earlier injury.

Aurora tensed as her gaze dropped lower, yet even so, she felt her heartbeat quicken. The raw masculinity that had unnerved her at a distance was even more obvious this close, the sinewy hardness of his body unmistakable. His sun-bronzed chest and shoulders rippled with muscle, while the canvas breeches hugged his powerful thighs.

Then he opened his eyes and fixed them on her. His gaze was dark, the rich hue of coffee flecked with amber. His intent stare gave her the same jolting sensation she'd felt earlier: the feeling of being totally alone with him, along with a keen awareness of her femininity.

Nearly as strange were the tender feelings of protectiveness his injuries engendered. Gently Aurora reached up to wipe the smear of blood from his forehead.

Chains jangling, he grasped her wrist. "Don't," he muttered hoarsely. "Stay out of this . . . you'll be hurt."

Her skin burned where his fingers touched, but she tried to ignore the sensation, just as she disregarded his entreaty. At the moment she was less interested in protecting herself than in saving his life. "You don't expect me to watch your murder, do you?"

The pained smile he gave her was fleeting as he released her wrist and struggled to push himself up on his elbows. For a moment he dizzily shut his eyes.

"You need a doctor," Aurora said in alarm.

"No . . . I have a hard head."

"Obviously not hard enough."

She had forgotten they weren't alone, until her cousin leaned over her shoulder and gave an exclamation of dismay. "Good God . . . Sabine!"

"You know him?" Aurora asked.

"Indeed, I do. He owns half the merchant ships in the Caribbean. He's an American. . . . Nick, what the devil are you doing here?"

He grimaced in pain. "An unfortunate encounter with the British navy, I fear."

Aurora realized his speech was much softer and flatter than her own clipped sounds as her cousin turned to the guards and demanded an explanation.

"What is the meaning of this? Why is this man in chains?"

The guards were spared having to reply when their commanding officer joined them. Aurora remembered having met Captain Richard Gerrod at some polite government function a few weeks before.

"I can answer that, your excellency," Gerrod said coolly. "He is bound in chains because he is a prisoner of war, condemned to be hanged for piracy and murder."

"Murder, captain? That is frankly absurd. You must have heard of Nicholas Sabine," Percy insisted, pronouncing the American's name Sah-*bean*. "He is a hero in these parts, not a murderer. Obviously you have mistaken his identity."

"I assure you I have mistaken nothing. He was recognized by one of my officers on Montserrat, where he was reckless and arrogant enough to visit a woman in the midst of a war. He most certainly *is* the notorious pirate Captain Saber. Not only has he commandeered at least two British merchantmen since the war began, but he sank the HMS *Barton* just last month."

"It was my understanding," said Percy, "that the *Barton*'s crew was saved from drowning by that same pirate and deposited on the nearest isle."

"Yes, but a seaman died in that engagement and several more were injured. And Sabine nearly killed one of my crew yesterday while resisting arrest. He has indeed committed acts of war against the Crown, Sir Percy. Acts punishable by death."

Percy turned to the fallen man. "Is this true, Sabine? You're a pirate?"

Sabine's half smile held cold anger. "In America we use the term *privateer*, and we've never yielded the right to protect our own ships. The *Barton* was attacking one of my merchantmen and I intervened. As for commandeering your vessels, I considered it a fair exchange for the loss of two of my own."

Aurora wasn't as horrified as perhaps she should have been at the accusation of piracy. With their two countries at war, Britain considered any armed American ship culpable. And Sabine should indeed have a right to defend his own ships. She knew her cousin would agree. Though such political beliefs were disloyal to the Crown, Percy considered the war a mistake and Britain primarily at fault for instigating it. The charge of murder, however, disturbed her greatly. . . .

"Pirate or not," Percy said to the captain, obviously troubled, "there will be ramifications for taking this man prisoner. Are you aware Mr. Sabine has any number of connections to the Crown? Including several island governors as well as the commander of the Caribbean fleet?"

The captain scowled. "His connections are all that stopped me from hanging him out of hand. But I doubt that will save him. When Admiral Foley learns of his crimes, I'm certain the order will be given to execute him." Grimly Captain Gerrod looked down at Aurora. "My lady, you would do best to keep away. He is a dangerous man."

She suspected the American was indeed dangerous, but that hardly justified the guards' vicious brutality.

"Oh, indeed," she said scornfully, rising to face the captain from her full height. "So dangerous your crew must beat him senseless, even with him trussed up like a Christmas goose. I quite fear for my life."

Gerrod's lips tightened in anger, but Percy quickly intervened.

"What do you intend to do with him, Captain?"

"He'll be turned over to the garrison commander and imprisoned in the fortress until he can be executed."

Aurora felt her heart clench at the thought of this vital man losing his life. "Percy . . ." she implored, gazing at him.

"I'll thank you, excellency," Gerrod said darkly, "not to interfere with the performance of my duty. Get to your feet, pirate."

Sabine's lip curled, his simmering hatred of the captain evident in the blistering heat of his dark eyes. But his fury remained tightly controlled as he struggled to his knees.

Aurora helped him stand, lending support when he swayed, and felt her pulse quicken as his hard body momentarily leaned against her. Even bruised and bloodied, the overwhelming maleness of him affected her.

Her cousin must have been reminded of the impropriety, for Percy gently grasped her arm and drew her away. "Come, my dear."

Obviously stiff with pain, Sabine moved toward the wagon. Aurora flinched when she saw the bloody lacerations marring his broad shoulders and muscular back, and again when one of the burly guards grasped his arm and urged him into the wagon.

Helpless, Aurora bit her lip to keep from crying out in protest.

Captain Gerrod gave her a stern glance as both guards climbed in after the prisoner, but he addressed her cousin. "I hadn't planned on escorting the prisoner to the fortress— I should be preparing my frigate to sail for the American seacoast to join the naval blockade. But I see I must, to ensure my orders are carried out to the letter."

"I intend to visit the fortress myself," Aurora threatened rashly, fearing what they would do to their prisoner once they were alone. "If you dare beat him further, I promise you will regret it."

She felt her cousin's fingers tighten on her arm in warning and barely refrained from shaking off his grasp.

The captain gave a stiff, angry bow, and then climbed into the front passenger seat and ordered the elderly black driver to drive on. Aurora and Percy watched as the pair of draft horses drew the wagon away.

"You will *not* involve yourself further, Aurora," Percy muttered under his breath.

Stubbornly she freed her arm from his tight grip. "You don't condone such vicious treatment, I'm sure of it. If Mr. Sabine were an English prisoner in American hands, you would expect him to be dealt with humanely."

"Of course I would."

"What will happen to him?" she asked, her voice suddenly hoarse.

Percy didn't respond at once, which confirmed her worst fears.

"Surely there will be a trial," Aurora protested. "They wouldn't hang someone of his consequence at once, would they?"

"It may not come to hanging," her cousin answered grimly. "The admiral might very well show leniency."

"And if not? Can you intervene?"

"I have the authority to overrule an admiral's commands, but doing so would perhaps mean the end of my political career. My views on the war are frowned upon as it is. And setting free a condemned prisoner would likely be considered treason. Piracy and murder are grave charges, my dear."

Aurora gazed back at Percy bleakly. "You must at least send a doctor to see to his injuries."

"Of course. I'll speak to the garrison commander myself and see that Sabine receives proper medical care."

She stared into his blue eyes that were so much like her own and could read the concern there—as well as the comment he didn't voice.

What did it matter if Nicholas Sabine's wounds were treated if he shortly was to hang?

Percy's wife was alarmed by the bloody condition of Aurora's gown, but less appalled by the reason than might be expected.

"I don't know that I would have had the courage to intervene," Jane said thoughtfully when she'd heard the tale.

The two women were alone in Aurora's bedchamber. After Percy had escorted her to his plantation home and then left to fulfill his promise regarding the prisoner's medical treatment, Aurora's maid had helped her change her gown and then took it away for cleaning. Lady Osborne remained to get a more detailed, private accounting of the morning's events.

"I don't think it particularly courageous to stop a man from being beaten to death," Aurora retorted, still outraged by the morning's incident. "And my intervention seems to have done little to change his fate."

"Mr. Sabine has prominent family in England," Jane said more soothingly. "The Earl of Wycliff is his second cousin. Besides possessing enormous wealth, Wycliff has always commanded a great deal of power in government circles. He could very well intercede on his cousin's behalf."

"They may hang him long before news of his imprisonment reaches England," Aurora replied darkly.

"Aurora, you haven't developed a *tendre* for Sabine, have you?"

She felt herself flush. "How could I? I met the man only this morning, and just for a moment. We were not even formally introduced."

"Good. Because frankly he isn't at all a proper sort of gentleman, despite his connections. Indeed, I suspect he is rather dangerous."

"Dangerous?"

"To our sex, I mean. He's an adventurer and something of a rake—and an American, besides."

"Percy called him a hero."

"I suppose he is. He saved the lives of some two hundred planters during a slave revolt on St. Lucia a few years ago. But that hardly makes him acceptable. Common gossip says he is the black sheep of his family who spent his adulthood traveling alien lands and engaging in any manner of wild exploits. Only after his father died did he become the least respectable—and only because he inherited a fortune and took over the family business interests."

"You haven't accused him of being much worse than half the wild young bucks in England."

"He is indisputably worse, I assure you. Otherwise he

would never have been accorded membership in the notorious Hellfire League, despite being sponsored by his
cousin, Lord Wycliff."

The Hellfire League, Aurora knew, was an exclusive club
of the premier rakes in England, dedicated to pleasure and
debauchery. If Sabine was a member of that licentious as-
sociation, he was indeed wicked.

"And you cannot dismiss the fact," Jane added pointedly, "that he is a condemned pirate, with blood on his
hands."

Aurora looked down at her own hands. One of her dearest friends, Jane was both attentive and shrewd enough to
evaluate a situation objectively—attributes that made her
an ideal politician's wife. Percy quite rightly adored her, a
sentiment that was wholly reciprocated.

"Aurora," Jane said, "is it possible you've become absorbed with this man to escape your own concerns? Perhaps you are trying to ignore your own plight by involving
yourself with a stranger's fate."

Aurora laced her fingers tightly together. Quite possibly
her sympathy for Sabine was greater because of her own
difficult situation. She could identify with him; she knew
what it was like to be powerless to effect her own future, to
have her life not be her own. He was at the mercy of his
captors, while she was subject to her father's dictates—
and was soon to be ensnared in a supremely distasteful
marriage.

Jane must have read the truth in her expression, for she
said gently, "You have more important worries than a pirate's fortunes. You would do far better to forget this incident entirely." She rose to her feet with a soft swish of silk
skirts. "Come down to luncheon when you are ready. You'll
feel better when you've eaten, I daresay."

Aurora, however, did not feel better, nor did she have
any appetite. She merely toyed with her food as she anxiously awaited word from her cousin.

When the message did finally come from his offices in

Basseterre, Percy's note said little other than to reassure her that he'd spoken to the garrison commander, who promised to have the fortress physician examine the prisoner's injuries.

Aurora shared the note with Jane and pretended to dismiss any further thought of the matter. A short while later she excused herself, claiming she needed to contemplate her packing for her return to England. But she made absolutely no headway. Instead she found herself staring down at the floor, remembering a pair of dark eyes gazing at her intently, and the trembling way it had made her feel—

For mercy's sake, stop thinking of him, Aurora scolded herself.

Logically she agreed with Jane. It was far wiser to put the notorious pirate out of her mind. She would be leaving St. Kitts in a matter of days. And she had her own serious troubles to deal with—namely her imminent engagement to a domineering nobleman some twenty years her senior. A man she not only didn't love but actively disliked for his imperious, overbearing manner and his strict, almost puritanical adherence to convention. A public announcement of the betrothal would be made upon her return to England.

For a moment Aurora felt the same jolt of panic the thought of her impending marriage always engendered. Once they were wed, she would be a virtual prisoner to decorum, indeed would be fortunate to be permitted even an original thought of her own. But as she'd done for months, she forced her disquiet away.

Abandoning the notion of planning for her voyage, she picked up a book of poetry. But when she tried to read, she was unable to focus on the page. Instead she saw the blood-stained features of Nicholas Sabine as he lay helpless at her feet, half naked and in chains. When she tried to push him out of her mind, she failed miserably.

She didn't have to close her eyes to picture him lying in a prison cell, wounded and in pain, perhaps even near

death. Would he even have a blanket to cover his near nakedness? Despite the warmth of the Caribbean sun, it was still
winter. The brisk ocean breezes blowing off the Atlantic
side of the island could make the nights quite chilly. And
Brimstone Hill Fortress, where he had been taken, was
perched high on a cliff, exposed to the elements.

More alarming, a condemned prisoner could disappear
forever in the vast, sprawling warren of dark chambers and
narrow passageways of the fortress. Its massive citadel
was defended by seven-foot-thick walls of black volcanic
stone that had taken decades to construct.

She'd once attended a military reception at Brimstone
Hill with Percy and Jane and found even the officers' quarters unwelcoming. She shuddered to think what the pris-
oners' accommodations were like.

It was no consolation to remind herself that she'd done
all she could for him. No use arguing with herself and demanding that she be sensible. She had never been able to
walk away from anyone in such a vulnerable position.

The past years would have been easier had she been
capable of simply ignoring her conscience, of controlling
her protective urges. If she could have maintained a proper
detachment when her father vented his wrath on his hap-
less dependents. But she could never be so unfeeling.

And now all she could think of was Nicholas Sabine,
vulnerable and helpless, at the mercy of his brutal captors.

Perhaps if she paid him a brief visit, just to make certain
he was being cared for, she would be able to ease her mind
enough to forget him. . . .

Feeling her anxiety lessen for the first time since the
disturbing incident on the quay, Aurora quietly set down
her book. Her heart took up an erratic rhythm at the prospect of seeing the American again, yet she repressed the
forbidden feelings as she went to the bell pull to ring for
her maid.

She would be defying propriety with a vengeance, perhaps even risking scandal, to visit a condemned pirate in prison, yet this could well be one of the last acts of independence she would ever make.

Chapter Two

I should have trembled in fear, but his touch held me spellbound.

He was dreaming again. Of her. The savage throbbing in his head eased as she bent over him. The tender brush of her fingers on his feverish brow was gentle and soothing, but her touch roused a worse throbbing in his loins.

She was the essence of every male fantasy—angel, Valkyrie, goddess, sea siren. She was golden temptation and primal torment. He wanted to draw her down to him and drink of her lips. Yet she held back, just out of reach—

"You there!"

He awoke with a start, memory and pain flooding him with brutal intensity. Woozily Nicholas lifted a hand to his aching head and felt the bandage there. He was lying on a bare cot, no longer bound by chains. The musket butt prodding his sore ribs, however, was regrettably familiar, as was the burly guard hovering over him.

"You there, bestir yerself!"

His blurred vision steadied. He'd been taken prisoner, he remembered, and brought to the fortress on St. Kitts, where he would probably hang for piracy and murder. At first he'd paced his cell like a wounded animal, his frantic thoughts on his half sister and the debacle he'd made of his promise to protect her. But exhaustion and pain had finally forced him to lie down. He'd fallen into a tortured slumber, only to begin dreaming of the golden-haired beauty who had defended him so valiantly on the quay.

What the devil was he doing? Nick swore at himself. Lusting after a strange woman, no matter how beautiful or courageous, was completely mad under the circumstances. Instead he should be focusing on his sister and ward, trying to think of a way to ensure her safety once he was dead. . . .

"I said bestir yerself! There's a lady to see you."

Nicholas slowly raised himself up on his elbows. Beyond the guard, the cell door was partway open. . . . His gaze shifted and his heartbeat seemed to stop.

She stood there just inside the dim chamber, tall, slender, regal as a princess. Even with the hood of her black cloak casting her exquisite features in shadows, he knew her. Yet unlike the avenging angel he remembered from the quay, she appeared hesitant, uncertain. Wary.

"I'll leave the door ajar, milady. If 'e gives you a 'int of trouble, you just call out."

"Thank you."

Her voice was low and melodious, but she said nothing else, even when the guard had left the cell.

Wondering if his vision was an illusion, Nicholas slowly sat up. The watery beam of sunlight filtering through the tiny barred window highlighted dust motes dancing around her dark skirts, but did little to illuminate her features.

Then she pushed back the hood of her cloak, uncovering her bright hair, which was coiled in a smooth chignon, giving Nick a jolt of sexual awareness. Her uncommon beauty seemed to light up the dark stone cell.

She was quite real, the living fantasy of his dreams . . . unless he had died and this was his version of heaven. Followers of the Muslim faith believed a blessed man would be surrounded by beautiful maidens upon reaching Paradise. The pain from his injuries, however, made Nicholas suspect he was still in temporal form.

She was gazing at him in surprise, studying his face. Then, as if she realized she was staring, she flushed a little and shifted her gaze to the bandage that wrapped his head.

"I see they at least summoned a doctor. I was afraid they wouldn't. No, please don't get up on my account," she added when he tried to rise. "You are in no condition to stand on formality."

"What . . ." His voice came out too hoarsely, so he cleared his throat and began again. "Why are you here?"

"I wanted to make certain you were all right."

Nicholas frowned, trying to sort out the confusion in his aching head. Perhaps the blows had indeed rattled his brain.

No lady would risk her reputation to enter the bowels of a prison on behalf of a stranger. And she was every inch a lady, he knew—blue-blooded to the core. In fact, hadn't she claimed to be a duke's daughter when she'd dressed down that seaman this morning?

Nicholas stared at her, wondering if he'd missed some vital clue to the enigma she presented. Then a sudden thought struck him.

Was it possible she was here to deceive him? Was that bastard Gerrod up to some sort of trickery, using her to ferret out information?

Nick's eyes narrowed in suspicion. His ship was still at large in the Caribbean, for he'd gone alone to Montserrat to fetch his sister—aboard a Dutch fishing ketch—not wanting to risk the lives of his crew on his own personal mission. But Captain Gerrod was fiercely set on determining the American schooner's whereabouts.

It could greatly advance the captain's naval career to capture an enemy ship—which was a likely reason, Nick suspected, that he'd been spared immediate hanging. That, and the fact that Gerrod hadn't wanted to make any political missteps by offending his prisoner's illustrious connections.

Grimly Nicholas contemplated his beautiful, unexpected visitor. Was she somehow in league with Gerrod? Her compassion had seemed entirely genuine this morning, and so had her animosity toward the captain. But perhaps she'd somehow been persuaded to work with Gerrod against him.

Had she been sent here to torment him? To tempt a condemned man as if holding out the promise of water to a man dying of thirst in a desert? The stark possibility that such beauty and kindness could be a ruse stabbed Nick with anger.

His jaw tightened. He would do well to remember their nations were at war. As an Englishwoman, she was his enemy, and he had to be on his guard.

She seemed uncomfortable with the way he was watching her, and when he deliberately dropped his gaze lower to linger on her breasts, he thought he saw her flush in the dim light.

"I don't believe we were properly introduced, madam," he prodded.

"No. There wasn't time. I am Aurora Demming."

An appropriate name, he thought irrelevantly. Aurora was Latin for dawn. "*Lady* Aurora. I remember. You made mention of it on the quay."

"I wasn't certain how conscious you were of your surroundings."

At the reminder of the assault, Nicholas raised his hand to feel his bandage. "You find me at a disadvantage, I fear."

An awkward silence stretched between them.

"I brought some items you might need," she said finally.

When she took a tentative step toward him, he focused on the bundle she held in her arms. She seemed oddly nervous as she set her offering down on the cot and glanced around the dim, spartan cell. "I should have brought candles. I didn't think of it. But here is a blanket . . . some food."

Her gaze met his briefly and then slid away. "I also borrowed a shirt and jacket from Percy's overseer. You seemed larger than my cousin . . ."

It was his state of undress that was tying her tongue, Nicholas realized. If she was like other gently bred ladies of her station, she would hardly be accustomed to visiting a half-nude man or estimating the size of his physique.

"How did you get past the guards?" he asked cautiously.

She seemed grateful for the change in subject. "I prevailed upon the garrison commander, Mr. Sabine." Her smile was fleeting. "Actually I resorted to a slight deception. I implied that my cousin Percy sent me."

"And did he?"

"Not exactly."

"I thought Gerrod would have forbidden me any visitors."

"Captain Gerrod has no authority over the fortress garrison, nor is he much liked here on the island."

"Then he didn't send you to question me?"

A look of puzzlement drew her fine brows together. "No. Why would you think so?"

Nicholas shrugged. If she was dissembling, he would be much surprised. But if she had an ulterior purpose for coming here, he couldn't fathom what it was. Did she want something from him?

When he reached for the bundle she had brought him, she retreated a step, as if fearing his proximity. He withdrew the shirt and carefully pulled it on, wincing at his aching muscles.

"Forgive me, my lady," he mused aloud, "but I fail to understand your reason for championing me, a stranger, and a condemned prisoner, at that."

"I didn't care to see a man murdered before my eyes. It seemed the captain was far too eager to find an excuse to kill you. At the very least his men would have beaten you senseless."

"That still is no reason for you to play Lady Bountiful, bent upon kindness and good deeds."

The cynicism in his tone made her chin lift a degree. "I wasn't satisfied that you would be cared for."

"And you wish to make my final days more comfortable? Why?"

Why indeed? Aurora wondered. It was impossible to explain the affinity she felt for him. Even harder to deny. He was a privateer at the very least. A violent man. One with blood on his hands.

And now that he was no longer defenseless, his effect on her was even more forceful. He'd been given a chance to wash off the blood, and his handsomeness was astonishing, even with the stubble on his jaw. That rough growth along with the strip of muslin wrapping his head gave him a rakish appearance, making him look very much the lawless pirate.

She could well see why her cousin called him dangerous with the ladies. He had the sinful allure of a fallen angel, with hair the color of amber, and a face whose planes and angles were beautifully sculpted. The brazen sight of his bronzed shoulders and hard-muscled arms, too, had stirred an odd fluttering in her stomach.

Yet his face could have been carved in stone now, and the cold insolence of his stare took her aback. He seemed highly mistrustful of her motives—which was not so surprising, since she wasn't certain of them herself.

Her reaction to his beating this morning had been purely instinctive, perhaps because intervening in violent disputes had become an ingrained habit with her. More times than she cared to count she had stepped in to shield defenseless servants in her father's household from his irrational fury.

But that didn't explain the urgent need she'd felt to reassure herself of his well-being. Perhaps her affinity for this stranger—this inexplicable familiarity—was simply because his coloring so closely resembled that of her late betrothed, a man she had loved dearly.

"I expect I came because you remind me of someone who was very dear to me," Aurora replied rather lamely.

When he raised a skeptical eyebrow, she averted her gaze from the expanse of sun-warmed flesh on his bare chest where his shirt remained open.

She stood stiffly as she felt his eyes moving down her body, touching her breasts in insolent perusal. He seemed to be assessing the gown beneath her cloak, a severely cut day dress of charcoal gray bombazine.

"You wear half mourning," he observed. "Are you widowed?"

"No. My betrothed was lost at sea some eight months ago."

"I don't recall seeing you on St. Kitts before."

"I arrived last summer. My cousin and his wife were visiting family in England shortly after the tragedy occurred. They thought a change of scene might help me to forget my grief and so invited me to return with them to the Caribbean. We set sail before word reached England about America's declaration of war. Had I known, I never would have come. And in fact, I will be returning in a few days."

Aurora was aware her voice had dropped and knew he must have heard the bleak note of reluctance she couldn't hide. The last thing she wanted was to return to England and face the fate that awaited her there.

Nicholas Sabine was still studying her, as if trying to determine her veracity. "You don't seem particularly eager to go home, my lady. I should think you would be impatient after all this time away."

Her smile was pained. "I suppose my lack of enthusiasm stems from the marriage my father has arranged for me."

"Ah," he said knowingly. "A cold-blooded contract. The British upper class are so very fond of selling their daughters into marriage."

Aurora stiffened at his presumption. She had not meant to share personal confidences with Mr. Sabine, nor did she care for the intimacy of this conversation. "I am not being *sold*, I assure you. It is more a matter of social expedience. And my father wishes to see me well settled."

"But you are not exactly willing, either?"

"His would not be my choice for a husband, no," she admitted quietly.

"I wonder that you haven't considered rebelling. You don't strike me as the meek type. On the quay this morning you were a veritable tigress."

"Those circumstances were hardly ordinary," Aurora said, flushing. "I am not in the habit of challenging convention."

"No? And yet you are here. It was rather unwise to risk your reputation like this, you must admit. Where I come from, ladies don't visit convicts in prison."

"They don't in England, either," Aurora replied, forcing a wry smile. "I am entirely aware of the impropriety . . . and normally I am quite sensible. But my maid accompanied me, at least. She is waiting outside in the corridor . . . along with the guard."

The pointed reminder of the guard seemed to have no effect on Mr. Sabine. He buttoned his shirt slowly, regarding her from under long dark lashes.

When he stood, she took a wary step back. She was tall enough that he didn't dwarf her with his broad-shouldered, long-limbed body, but this close his masculinity was almost overwhelming, his nearness threatening.

"You aren't afraid of me?" he asked, his silken tone sending shivers down her spine.

Unsettled, Aurora fought for control of her rioting senses as she stood her ground. She *was* afraid of him. Of his intensity. Of the way his raw virility made her heart pound. "You don't seem the sort of man who would hurt a woman," she replied uncertainly.

"I could take you hostage—had you thought of that?"

Her eyes widened as her uneasiness rose. "No, I hadn't. Percy says you are a gentleman," she added, suddenly doubtful.

His smile flickered as he closed the distance between them. "Someone should have taught you not to be so trusting."

Reaching out, he captured her wrist in a light grasp. His fingers seemed to burn her skin, yet she was determined not to show how unnerved she was by his touch.

"Someone should have taught you better manners," she retorted coolly, adopting her most regal air. When he didn't release her, she stared him down. "I did not necessarily expect gratitude, Mr. Sabine, but neither did I expect to be manhandled in this fashion."

The hardness in his dark eyes abated a degree as he let go of her hand. Several heartbeats later he lowered that taunting gaze. "Pardon me. I do seem to have misplaced my manners."

Absently she rubbed her wrist, where his touch had branded her. "I understand you have had a difficult time. And you are an American, after all."

His smile was mocking. "Ah, yes, a heathen Colonial."

"You must admit you are very . . . direct."

"And you must realize condemned men are given to desperate acts."

Her expression sobered as she remembered he was to be hanged. "Percy means to exert his influence on your behalf, but he might very well lose his post were he to demand your release. He is already suspect for sympathizing with the American cause. He believes the war is absurd, and that we British are more at fault than you Americans."

Nicholas stared down at her beautiful upturned face. If she was innocent of duplicity, he had greatly wronged her. He felt a savage anger toward many of her countrymen, but he should never have taken his fury and resentment out on her.

"Forgive me," he said grudgingly. "I am indeed in your debt. If I can ever repay the favor . . ." He let the comment slide, knowing he was unlikely now to be in a position to repay her kindness.

A sudden sadness filled her eyes. "I wish there were more I could do."

"You've done enough already."

She bit her lip. "I suppose I should be going."

Nicholas found himself staring at her mouth. "Yes."

"Is there something else you need?"

He flashed a wry smile that held grim amusement.

"Aside from a key to my cell door and a fast ship to make my getaway? A bottle of rum wouldn't go amiss."

"I . . . shall try."

"No, don't. I was jesting."

He reached up to brush her cheek lightly with the back of his knuckles. Her lips parted and he heard her soft intake of breath. Nicholas felt his loins stir.

"You shouldn't be here," he said quietly. "For your own good, you should stay away."

She nodded and took a step back, her blue eyes misting. As if unable to speak, she turned without another word and fled the gloomy cell.

With a clang the door swung closed behind her, no doubt drawn shut by the prison guard. Nick bit back a curse at the grim reminder of his imprisonment.

For a moment he stood there, breathing in the faint scent of lilacs she'd left behind and wanting to hit something. He wished to hell she hadn't come. Whether intentionally or not, she had set his blood on fire.

Amazing, considering the sort of woman she was—blue-blooded, proper, straitlaced. The exact opposite of the women he was usually drawn to. Yet if he were free, he might very well have pursued her.

If he were free . . .

His jaw clenching at the reminder, Nicholas glanced up at the high, barred window of his cell. Damn it to hell, he had to get out of here—or at the very least find a solution to his crisis.

Turning, he began to pace the narrow confines of his cell, his thoughts once again caught up in turmoil. What would happen to his sister once he was dead? He'd sworn a solemn oath to his father to see to her welfare, but because of his blundering miscalculation, he'd been taken prisoner and rendered powerless to help her.

His unaccustomed helplessness left him seething, filled with a furious need to take action, no matter how futile. His pacing became more agitated . . . until suddenly, he came to an abrupt halt. Nicholas stared unseeing, a wild notion invading the back of his mind.

He had never feared death, although he'd always taken immense pleasure in living his life to the fullest. If he were hanged, his chief regret would be his failure to honor his promise. There might still be a way, however, for him to discharge his responsibilities, albeit from beyond the grave.

Lady Aurora Demming.

She could be the answer.

Or was he insane?

He started to rake a hand through his hair but stopped when he encountered the bandage—a bandage that had been her doing. He'd been mistaken about her, obviously. She was kindhearted, caring; her concern for him was evidence of that. She wasn't in league with Gerrod, or anyone else for that matter. She was indeed an angel of mercy.

Angel and siren, Nicholas thought, remembering her eyes that were the color of sapphires. She was also younger than her regal, aristocratic manner suggested, perhaps barely twenty. Yet despite her recklessness in first coming to his rescue and then visiting him in prison, she was no doubt well bred and virtuous . . . and high ranking enough to command respect, if not awe, among the beau monde. As a duke's daughter, she would have entry into the loftiest echelons of British society.

Recklessly Nick flung himself on the cot, ignoring the angry protest of his bruised body. His thoughts spun furiously as he stared up at the grimy ceiling overhead. He had no desire to drag the lady into his concerns, but if it meant protecting his sister, he would use the Devil himself. He would utilize Lady Aurora to help his ward, take advantage of her prominent standing in English society . . .

His mouth curled in a grim semblance of a smile. He must still be reeling from the blows to his head if he was entertaining such fantasies. It was highly doubtful a duke's daughter would lend herself to a mad proposal admittedly

conceived in desperation. He intended to make her sacrifice worth her while, of course, yet even so she might
refuse.

Well then, he would simply have to convince her.

He had no choice. If there was the slightest possibility
of fulfilling his promise, he had to seize it.

Chapter Three

When he summoned me to his chamber, my heart lodged in my throat.

It was irrational, Aurora knew, to brood over a stranger she had met for a brief moment and would never see again. Yet even in sleep she could not forget him. Aurora tossed and turned the entire night, her dreams dark with images of Nicholas Sabine struggling to break his chains while she was powerless to help him.

When the hangman's noose tightened around the strong column of his throat, she woke with a start, her heart pounding in fear. Unable to bear the grim visions any longer, Aurora hurriedly dressed and went downstairs, where she found Percy eating breakfast before he left for his offices. She joined him at the table but declined anything but coffee.

"Will you go to the fortress today?" she asked, trying to keep her tone casual yet knowing she failed.

Percy gave her a concerned look. He hadn't approved of her visiting the prisoner yesterday, even on a mission of mercy for a man who was his friend. Indeed, he'd been a bit startled to hear of her boldness.

"This is not like you, Aurora. I know you must be aware of the impropriety of your behavior. Normally you show more consideration to your position in society."

Aurora lowered her gaze, knowing her cousin was right. Yet she hadn't been herself since she first laid eyes on Nicholas Sabine. She couldn't explain her desperate concern even to herself, let alone to her cousin.

"I simply abhor seeing anyone treated in such a terrible fashion," she prevaricated.

Percy's gaze held sympathy. "My dear . . . you should prepare yourself for the worst. Word was sent to Barbados yesterday, asking the admiral's permission to hang Sabine. We may learn the answer today."

She felt her stomach clench with fear. She had hoped he might be spared that dire fate, if only because of his prominent connections.

"I promise I will let you know the verdict as soon as I hear," Percy assured her.

Aurora nodded, not trusting herself to speak with the ache in her throat.

She was glad when Percy turned the subject to more mundane matters, and gladder still when he took his leave. When she was alone, she rose and went to stand at the breakfast room window, gazing out, unseeing, at the sun-swept lawns with their tall, swaying palms and splashes of scarlet bougainvillaea.

She was mistaken to have visited Nicholas Sabine in his prison cell, she realized. Not simply because of the impropriety, but because she'd only gained more vivid images that made him harder to forget. It was impossible to stop thinking about him. She could still feel his overwhelming presence—the forbidden sight of his bare, sun-bronzed skin, his quiet touch on her cheek, the tenderness in his dark eyes. . . .

Aurora bit her lower lip, chastising herself for her foolishness. Hadn't she learned it was better not to care too deeply for anyone?

She had lost the two people who were most dear to her. Her mother several years ago. Then, more recently, her betrothed, Geoffrey Crewe, Earl of March.

Her long-planned future had shattered when Geoffrey perished at sea. She'd been engaged to him practically from the cradle. As her father's nearest though distant male relative, Geoffrey was next in line for the dukedom and the vast Eversley estates. And Father was determined to keep the title for his grandsons, since an ignoble physical condition had left him unable to sire any more children.

Aurora understood why he so badly wanted a son to continue the line of inheritance that had been unbroken since the reign of Henry II—and why she had always been his biggest disappointment.

She would have been happy to have been born male, for then she could have avoided the fate her father had determined for her. She hadn't even recovered from the tragic news of Geoffrey's death when her father quietly accepted on her behalf the suit of a noble crony—the illustrious Duke of Halford. No matter that she could scarcely bear to contemplate marriage to such a man, or that he had already outlived two young wives, losing one to childbirth and one to a bizarre drowning accident. Halford was wealthy enough to buy a duke's daughter, and his lineage went back even farther than Henry II.

Her father didn't see the union as punishment. He claimed he merely wanted to see her settled and well provided for, safely wed to a title and fortune when the Eversley title passed out of their direct family at his death. With a bitter sigh, Aurora wondered if in truth he simply wanted her off his hands, so he would no longer be reminded of his failure.

When Percy and Jane had invited her to visit their home in the West Indies, she'd accepted gratefully, not only hoping her grief would heal more readily in fresh surroundings, but also wishing to delay her unwanted marriage as long as possible. The intervening months, however, hadn't diminished her revulsion at the necessity of becoming Halford's bride. She dreaded returning to England now, where her illustrious suitor was reportedly growing impatient to publicly announce their betrothal, but she'd run out of excuses to tarry.

Clenching her hands into fists, Aurora turned away from the window. Ordinarily she would have gone riding to work off her feelings of frustration and helplessness or joined Jane in making her weekly round of charitable calls, a responsibility Jane took very seriously as the lieutenant governor's wife. But Aurora didn't want to be away from the house if word came about the American prisoner.

Instead she fetched a shawl so that she could pace the grounds in view of the front drive. It was hard, though, to remain passive, to sit idly by while the world was ruled by men.

How different her life would be were she a male, Aurora reflected fiercely. How much more freedom she would have. She would have relished possessing a measure of control over her existence. Were she a man, she would have had the power to influence her own future . . . and others' as well.

Perhaps then she could actually have helped Nicholas Sabine, instead of being forced by propriety to accept a woman's lot and wait impotently at home for word of his fate.

The afternoon was well advanced by the time Percy returned home. Aurora had been watching for him anxiously from the drawing room and so was able to meet him at the front door.

"I am glad to find you here, my dear," Percy said quietly. "I thought you might have accompanied Jane on her calls."

"I wanted to hear the news."

Waving off the footman who stood ready to take his hat, Percy met her gaze with reluctance. The grim expression on his face told her without words the news she dreaded hearing.

She pressed a hand to her mouth to hold back a cry.

"Aurora, I'm sorry," he said simply. "The admiral was disinclined to be merciful."

For a moment her cousin remained silent, as if giving her time to compose herself. Then he took her hands in a gentle grasp. "My dear, this is obviously a wretched time, but I have a serious matter to discuss with you."

Still numb with shock, Aurora scarcely heard what her cousin was saying.

"There has been an unanticipated turn of events." He paused, a troubled look on his face. "Nicholas Sabine has a . . . request to make of you."

"A request?" she repeated hoarsely.

"I spoke with Nick after the admiral's decision became known," Percy explained in a low voice, "and he sought my opinion of a rather wild notion. I did not refuse him outright, for I thought you should hear him out and decide for yourself. It *is* an extraordinary proposal . . . but then these are extraordinary circumstances."

"I . . . don't understand. What does he wish to ask of me?"

"He would like your help, actually. It seems he has a duty he must fulfill, yet now he will no longer be alive to do so."

"What duty?"

"Sabine has a ward, a half sister who lives on Montserrat. The young lady urgently needs the protection of someone of your consequence, as well as an escort to England. And since you are planning to return there shortly . . . Well, there is more, but I don't want to influence you unduly. You should hear the proposal directly from Sabine himself. If you are willing to listen, I will accompany you to the fortress at once."

"You mean now, at this moment?" Aurora asked in confusion.

"Yes, now." He released her hands. "Time is growing short, I'm afraid. The hanging has been put off until tomorrow, but after that . . ."

His voice trailed off, yet Aurora was grateful that he failed to put the rest of his sentence into words.

She had never again expected to see the bold American who had touched her life so fleetingly. Thus it was with a heavy heart that Aurora returned to the fortress prison. She felt a hollowness in the pit of her stomach as she preceded her cousin into the dim cell.

Nicholas Sabine stood with his back to her, a shaft of sunlight gilding his fair hair. He was fully clothed this time, she noted absently. Someone—perhaps Percy—had provided him with a coat and a pair of Hessian boots, so that he more closely resembled a gentleman of means than a savage pirate or a condemned prisoner.

When he turned slowly to face her, however, he still had the same powerful effect on her; she felt her heart quicken in her chest as she met the dark intensity of his gaze.

"Thank you for coming," he said in a quiet voice. He glanced at her cousin. "Might I presume further upon our friendship, Sir Percy, and ask that you allow us a few moments in private? Lady Aurora will come to no harm, I give you my word."

Percy nodded, although reluctantly. "Very well. I shall wait outside in the corridor, my dear."

Her cousin withdrew, leaving the door partly ajar. Sabine's half smile was fleeting, almost ironic, as he noted the precaution.

Returning his gaze to Aurora then, he gestured with his hand, indicating the cot. "Would you care to sit down, Lady Aurora? I think you might want to be seated to hear what I have to say."

"Thank you, but I prefer to stand," she replied politely.

"As you wish."

His dark gaze was riveted on her as he contemplated her in silence. Aurora withstood his piercing assessment with uncertainty, wondering what he intended to ask. When he didn't speak, her gaze went to the bandage at his temple. It seemed clean and a bit smaller than yesterday, as if it had been freshly changed. She was about to inquire how his head wound was faring when he spoke.

"What has Percy told you?" Sabine asked.

"Only that you need my help for your sister."

"I do." He eyed her speculatively another moment, then turned to pace about the small cell like a caged cat—lithe, graceful, on edge. "You may call me mad, but I ask you to hear me out fully before you decide."

His sense of urgency communicated itself to her, making her uneasy. "Very well, Mr. Sabine," Aurora prodded. "I am listening."

"I suppose I should begin by telling you a story—a love story, if you will. But I fear it may shock a lady of tender sensibilities. Are you game to hear it?"

"Yes," Aurora murmured doubtfully.

He continued to stalk the floor, keeping his voice low as he spoke. "There once was a man—an American—who went to England and fell in love. The lady returned his affection, but any union between them was doomed from the start. Not only was she quite young, but her family would never have permitted her to wed beneath her class. Even more damning, he already had a wife and a young son, with another child expected shortly.

"Refusing to dishonor her or his marriage vows, he left England, determined to vanquish his feelings and never see the young lady again. But business concerns required his return a few years later, and he discovered her nearly in despair. She was to wed an older gentleman whose physical deformities rendered him a monster in her eyes. As his bride, she would reside on her husband's remote estate, away from everything she held dear.

"She couldn't bear to be imprisoned in such a marriage and believed her life was at an end, without her ever having lived, or ever knowing passion. And so she begged the man she loved to show her what true intimacy was. Unable to resist her plea or deny his feelings any longer, he became her lover."

Sabine paused in his tale and glanced at Aurora, as if to gauge her reaction. When she managed to keep her expression noncommittal, he went on. "Their illicit affair lasted only a few months, for he had to return to his family and to his responsibilities. Shortly afterward, however, the young lady discovered she was with child."

Aurora winced inwardly. She could well imagine the scorn an unwed young woman would face if her *enceinte* condition became known. "What happened?" she murmured.

"Not surprisingly the lady's engagement was promptly dissolved. To quiet any scandal, she was married off to a younger son of an Irish nobleman and banished to the Caribbean to live, while her outraged father washed his hands of her. The lady died last year, without ever being reunited with her family. She left behind an only child, a daughter."

"Your sister," Aurora said gently.

Sabine drew a slow breath. "Yes. My half sister, to be exact. As you've guessed, the lady's lover was my father."

"Did he know about the child?"

"Not at first. But she wrote to him when her husband passed away, telling him what had happened. My father supported her financially for years, even though he couldn't publicly acknowledge the child. He felt it necessary to keep the secret from his family, to spare my mother the shameful knowledge of his love affair. He died four years ago, but on his deathbed, he told me about his daughter and exacted a promise from me to take care of her."

Again Sabine flashed that ironic half smile that tugged at Aurora's heart. "I could hardly refuse to honor his dying request, could I? Truth tell, I was never the ideal son. Our relationship was always . . . strained because I had no serious interest in taking over the shipping firm he had built. My father, you see, was a nephew of the sixth Earl of Wycliff, but with little prospect of inheriting the title. Before the war with the Colonies, he immigrated to Virginia to make his fortune. And he far exceeded even his own dreams, building a formidable empire from almost nothing. Yet I preferred the life of an adventurer to following in his footsteps. When he died, though, I felt compelled to assume the responsibilities I had always neglected."

"Did you meet your sister then?"

"Indeed. My first act was to visit her on Montserrat. She bears the name of Kendrick, the Irishman her mother wed, but she's always known the story of her birth. Her mother wanted her to understand she was a child of love."

"Captain Gerrod said you went to Montserrat to see a woman," Aurora remarked thoughtfully.

Sabine's mouth curled at the mention of his nemesis. "Yes, my sister. She is almost grown up now—nineteen— and actually quite a beauty. She's also my ward. Her mother succumbed to a fever last year, shortly before the war started, and left Raven's wardship to me."

"Raven? That is an unusual name for a young lady."

"Perhaps, but it fits. She was born with hair black as a raven's wing, a throwback to one of my family's Spanish ancestors, apparently. And she is unconventional in more than just appearance. When I first met Raven, she was a complete hoyden, more at home in a stable or in a beach cove playing pirate. But lately she's made an earnest attempt to conform and conduct herself as a proper English lady. She's determined to realize her mother's dream for her—to be accepted by her English relatives and take her rightful place among the nobility. And one major obstacle has been overcome. Raven has been invited by her grandfather to live in England."

"Her mother's father?"

"Yes. He is Viscount Luttrell, of Suffolk. Perhaps you're acquainted with him."

Aurora searched her memory. "I've met him, but I never realized he had a daughter."

"Because Luttrell disowned her twenty years ago. But recently he had a change of heart. When he learned of his daughter's death, he regretted never attempting to reconcile. His health is failing now as well, and he wants to meet his only granddaughter and see her established in society. Raven's aunt has agreed, albeit reluctantly, to formally present her, but it's questionable how readily Raven will be received by the ton, given the dubious circumstances of her birth. She's anxious—passionate, even—to make a good match so she will be welcomed by the society that shunned her mother. Her path would be far smoother, certainly, if she had someone of elevated social status to befriend and advise her."

"And you wish me to be that person."

"Yes." His dark eyes met hers with unwavering intensity. "I don't care much for being a supplicant, Lady Aurora. It doesn't set well with me. But I would be grateful if you would extend the same kindness to my sister that you showed me yesterday."

Nicholas Sabine was obviously a man accustomed to getting his own way, Aurora thought. Helplessness would not be a sensation he would welcome. Yet she had no difficulty answering his entreaty. Her heart would have to be hard indeed to be unmoved by the girl's situation. "Of course, Mr. Sabine. I would be happy to do whatever I can to make her entry into society successful."

His face softened only a degree. It surprised her that his relief wasn't greater until she remembered his other concern. "Percy mentioned that your sister needs someone to accompany her to England, as well."

"She does." He resumed his pacing, his movements tightly controlled. "Before the war began, I had planned to transport Raven to England on one of my own ships. But as an American, I would hardly be welcome there now. My cousin Wycliff is too occupied trying to defeat the French to fetch Raven, and it could be years before you Brits finally prevail against Napoleon. I have a cousin on my mother's side, but he's American as well."

Sabine started to rake a hand through his hair, stopping when he encountered the bandage. "I had arranged with Wycliff to utilize a ship from his Caribbean fleet while I merely provided Raven armed escort across most of the Atlantic. In fact, I went to Montserrat to arrange the final details of the voyage with her. Unfortunately I was set upon by Gerrod's crew. And now that my fate has been settled . . ."

Aurora felt her throat tighten at the thought of this vital man losing his life.

"Well," Sabine continued with a hard smile, "despite this setback, I intend to do everything in my power to fulfill my promise to my father and ensure my sister's welfare. Which is why . . ." He paused again, this time studying her from beneath his thick lashes. ". . . why I would like to make you a formal offer of marriage."

Aurora simply stared, not comprehending. After the space of a dozen heartbeats, she realized she had indeed heard him correctly. She drew an uneven breath. "Are you serious?"

"Deadly serious." His beautiful mouth twisted without amusement. "I assure you, I do not take the prospect of matrimony lightly. I have never before proposed marriage to a woman—and would not be doing so now, if the circumstances were not so dire."

Still stunned, Aurora could only stare at him. She opened her mouth to say something, then shut it again. Moving over to the cot, she sat down as he had first suggested, needing the support after all. Her mind was racing with shock, bewilderment, as she tried to form a reply. "Mr. Sabine, I don't . . ."

"You said you would hear me out before you gave me an answer."

She lifted her gaze to his. "Yes, but . . . Are you not aware that I am expected to marry when I return to England?"

"So Percy informed me. You are promised to the Duke of Halford. But I understand the engagement is not yet official."

"No. We could make no public announcement while I was in mourning for my late betrothed. But my father is set on the match."

"But what about you, Lady Aurora? I gathered that you were reluctant to wed your father's choice. Was I mistaken?"

"No, you weren't mistaken," she admitted in a low voice.

Sabine moved to stand before her, holding her rapt attention. "Then consider the advantages of a union between us. You wouldn't have to wed Halford. That alone should prove a strong incentive. I remember the duke from my last visit to England three years ago. He must be more than twice your age, and as arrogant and puffed up with his own consequence as any nobleman I've ever had the misfortune to meet. Is that what you want, a lifetime of imprisonment as his wife?"

When she didn't answer, he continued. "There are other advantages as well. I assure you, I would make the inconvenience to you financially worth your while. I am a wealthy man, Lady Aurora, with a fortune that probably exceeds Halford's. I took the liberty of discussing the possible particulars with your cousin, and he's satisfied that the settlement I'm prepared to make would leave you a wealthy woman. You would have complete financial independence from your father. Just think. You would no longer be obliged to remain under his thumb or wed his choice of suitors."

The thought of no longer being subject to her father's dictates was vastly appealing. Even so . . .

"I suspect," Sabine pressed, "that you would find me a more agreeable husband than Halford. But even if not, it isn't as if you would be tied to me for life— Or actually you would. But our marriage would last only a few hours, a day at most. After that you would be my widow."

Aurora flinched at his casual reference to his intended hanging. He was making light of his desperate situation, clearly. But when she searched his strong, masculine face, she realized he did not want her pity. His entire focus was only on seeing to his sister's welfare.

"I realize I would be taking advantage of your kindness," he murmured, reaching down to take Aurora's hand in his larger, more powerful one, "but I am lamentably short of options."

Unnerved by his touch, she withdrew her hand and rose, moving past him to pace the floor herself.

"I've told you, Mr. Sabine," she said with what she thought was reasonable calm, "I would be happy to help your sister . . . without any formal arrangement between us. Surely it isn't necessary for us to wed."

"Perhaps not, but it would greatly improve the odds of securing Raven's future. If you are related to my ward through marriage, you would have every right to guide and influence her foray into society. In fact, if you were willing, I could turn her wardship over to you." Sabine let that sink in before adding, "That might be impossible if you marry Halford. I imagine he would object to his duchess associating with a . . . an unusual young woman like Raven. He's a stickler for propriety."

"So he is," she agreed absently.

"As your husband, he could forbid your having any connection with my sister."

Aurora raised a hand to her temple. Halford not only could forbid her, but no doubt *would*. "Even so . . . marriage to you is such a drastic step. . . ."

Visibly schooling his impatience, Sabine forced his mouth into a semblance of a smile. "Perhaps you might be more amenable if I took a different approach. If I attempted to flatter you and cosset your sensibilities."

She stiffened defensively and shot him a glance. "My sensibilities do not require cosseting, Mr. Sabine."

"No?" For the first time his smile reached his eyes. "I didn't think so." Then he sighed and dropped his voice to a murmur. "I do regret having to propose to you under such distasteful circumstances. Ordinarily I would try to employ all my powers of persuasion, but I'm afraid I haven't the time to try to charm you. I wouldn't be lying, however, if I claimed to be utterly besotted by your beauty."

Aurora found herself staring at him, wondering if his admission was mere cajolery. Doubtless Nicholas Sabine had a ruthless charm that he could wield to lethal effect.

Taking a deep breath, she returned to the conversation at hand. "I cannot simply agree to marry you, Mr. Sabine. There are other practicalities I must consider."

"Such as?"

Such as the fact that Nicholas Sabine was not the kind of man she would ever willingly choose as her husband. She had never met so compelling a man, or one who had made such a forceful impact on her. There was a sense of danger about him, an intensity that was intimidating, if not frightening . . . although his ferocity now might be driven by his concern for his sister. "If I were seeking a husband, a pirate—an American one—would not be my first choice. By your own admission, you are a violent man."

"I don't recall ever making such an admission."

"What of the man Captain Gerrod mentioned? He said you nearly killed one of his crew while resisting arrest."

Sabine's jaw hardened, but he met her gaze unflinchingly. "A man was wounded, true, but at the hand of his own crewmate. I was unarmed when I was set upon by some half dozen seamen. When I fought back, one drew a knife, and in the melee, another fell against the blade. I saw what happened just before I blacked out. I suppose I was struck over the head with a bottle."

He raised his hand to his head wound, indicating the damage the bottle had done. Then his expression softened. "I understand why you would be reluctant to accept my hand. I'm a man about to be hanged as a pirate—not at all the sort a lady like you should be associating with." He laughed softly to himself. "Indeed, if you were my sister, I would not allow you within a mile of me. But in my own defense, whatever acts of privateering I committed, I did to save my father's legacy. Your countrymen are set on destroying everything he worked for, and I swore to him I would keep his empire flourishing under my direction."

His dark eyes were intense as he gazed at her. "My fatal mistake was in thinking I could elude the British navy on Montserrat. I was careless. It's ironic, actually. I had taken a room at a tavern and was preparing to call on Raven when I was recognized by one of Gerrod's officers. The same lieutenant whose life I'd spared a month earlier when I saved the *Barton*'s crew from going down with their ship."

Aurora frowned. It had been a noble gesture to save an enemy crew, certainly, but that did not make Nicholas Sabine a saint. "Gerrod called you Captain Saber. That is hardly the title of a gentle man."

"Saber is a nom de guerre, merely that. Calculated to make the enemy consider twice before attacking my ships."

Her expression troubled, Aurora searched his face. "But you were charged with murder as well as piracy," she murmured.

"Regrettably men die in war, Lady Aurora," he returned coolly. "I make no apology for my privateering. And I assure you, Gerrod and his ilk are hardly innocents themselves. Any number of Americans have been killed by the British navy, some of whom were my friends. I've had crewmen, illegally taken by your press gangs, who were savagely beaten like animals, some who died in service—" Sabine stopped himself and took a slow breath. His anger under control, he moved to stand before her. "My own past is not entirely spotless, but I have never been guilty of murder. And I have never shown violence toward any woman, ever. I promise you solemnly, you have nothing to fear from me."

No, Aurora reflected. Nothing to fear but what he made her feel. His mere nearness made her pulse race, made her skin warm and her body feel flushed with awareness.

"And keep in mind," he pressed, "the short duration of our union. Even if I were the kind of man you claim, you wouldn't have to suffer my company for long. I certainly can refrain from acting the savage pirate for the brief term of our marriage."

Aurora felt an ache in the vicinity of her heart. She

couldn't believe this man would soon die. He radiated vitality and vibrant life. . . .

"What you are proposing sounds so . . . cold-blooded," she said finally, grasping at straws.

He shook his head. "Think of it as a business arrangement. Ladies of your class commonly enter into such agreements."

It was *not* common for ladies to marry only to lose their husbands the next day, Aurora thought in dismay. "So you wish this to be a simple business arrangement?"

"Not precisely." She heard him draw a slow breath. "I should make my meaning clear, Lady Aurora. Our marriage would not be in name only. To be legitimate, it must be fully consummated."

Her gaze locked with his, searching. His fathomless eyes were steadfast, unwavering in their intensity.

"I want no question of the legality of our union," he said levelly, "or the possibility that it could be set aside. Your father is a powerful man, as is Halford. I don't care to see my efforts to secure my sister's future go for naught."

Her heart faltered in its rhythm as she understood his meaning: they would share a bed as husband and wife.

Taken aback, Aurora stared at him. She had seriously been considering his desperate proposal until he added that disturbing condition. The possibility of physical intimacy with this man unnerved her. The thought of giving herself to a stranger— But was that not what she would be required to do when she wed Halford? This man, no matter how intimidating, was infinitely more appealing than the aging duke. She felt her pulse quicken dangerously.

Sabine was still watching her. Holding her gaze, he took her hand and raised it to his lips. But instead of kissing her fingers, he turned her hand over and kissed the tender inside of her wrist. His lips on her sensitive skin felt like a brand and sent hot and cold shivers through her.

"Will you consider becoming my wife for a night,

sweetheart? I think I can safely promise that you would not find your introduction to the marriage bed onerous."

Her breath caught in her throat at the images his promise conjured in her mind. That and the seductive sensuality in his eyes held her so spellbound, she couldn't reply.

His gaze dropped to her lips. "I regret I'm not able to court you as you deserve. A woman as lovely as you should have an equally lovely setting . . . moonlight, roses, whispered promises . . ." He leaned toward her, his breath fanning her lips. . . .

When Aurora stiffened instinctively, however, he stopped. Instead of kissing her, he spoke in a velvet-edged voice. "I cannot believe you truly fear me, Aurora. Not a woman of your rare courage. I saw the fascinating change in you yesterday, from proper lady to avenging angel."

Warily she searched his face. Stubble still shadowed his jaw, giving his handsome features a dangerous aura. He might claim not to be a pirate, but he still resembled one. She was not often intimidated, but this man disturbed her with his vital masculinity. She was even more unsettled by the forbidden sensations he aroused so easily in her. The raw, powerful sexuality emanating from him was palpable, the tension between them very real.

"Give me your hand, sweetheart. Touch me . . ." Taking her hand, Sabine guided her fingers to his face. "I am flesh and blood, just like you. Not so very threatening."

He was indeed threatening. He made her breathless, fluttery inside. And yet there was something warm and tender in his eyes that allayed true panic.

"This doesn't frighten you, does it?" he asked, drawing her fingers to his lips, letting her touch him there.

"No . . ." she murmured truthfully.

"What of this?" When he brushed her mouth with his, his lips were warm and soft—soft as the caress of a butterfly's wing. An unmistakeable yearning flooded Aurora, along with an unfamiliar hunger she could only call desire.

She stared at him, dazed, as he drew back.

The husky texture of his voice stroked her as brazenly as the hand that rose to graze the line of her jaw. "Have you never been kissed before?"

"Yes . . . By my betrothed."

"But not a true kiss, I imagine. A true kiss is more than a meeting of lips. It's a mating . . . of mouth and tongue and breath . . . An intimate knowing." His fingertips traced the line of her mouth. "I want to truly kiss you, angel."

His delicate touch made her shiver. "I . . . You shouldn't. . . ."

His smile was soft, indulgent, tender. He had a beautiful mouth, especially when he smiled.

"In circumstances such as these," he replied, "it is not improper for a man wooing his lady to claim a kiss. This is my sole opportunity to persuade you to become my bride. Perhaps the last time I will ever see you, ever touch you. Will you deny me my last chance to fulfill my father's dying wish?"

"No," she whispered, helpless to resist.

This time when he bent his head, she didn't stiffen or pull back. She let him draw her into his arms, let him hold her as a lover would.

His kiss was like nothing she had ever experienced. His mouth was hot, wet, open against hers, bold and unexpectedly intimate. Her nostrils filled with his scent, her mouth with his brazen flavor, as shocking pleasure assaulted her senses. . . .

Her wanton response dismayed her, yet to her surprise, he was the one who abruptly ended the kiss.

"Perhaps this was a mistake," he said, his voice unsteady as he leaned his forehead against hers. "I thought I would have more control. . . ."

Drawing a deep breath, he slowly drew away to capture her gaze. "No," he said with more composure, "judging from your response, I wouldn't say you feared me. You felt the same fire I did. The signs are all there. Your pulse has quickened, your skin is flushed. . . ."

Her heart racing, Aurora stood mutely, torn between dismay and desire as he so perfectly described the sensations that were overwhelming her. She shouldn't be feeling this way, experiencing these powerful, forbidden feelings for a stranger. Never had she had such a primal reaction to a man, a reaction no lady would acknowledge.

"And that is only the beginning, sweetheart. There is much more I could show you. Give me that right, Aurora."

His eyes had darkened with sensuality and were as fathomless as midnight, Aurora saw. Captivated, she stared into them.

His voice dropped lower. "Your cousin believes he can secure a special license in time for us to wed tomorrow evening. I would consider myself the most fortunate of men if you would do me the honor of giving me your hand in marriage."

Aurora shut her eyes, struggling to recover her dazed senses. Her mind was spinning, and she felt a similar chaos in her heart, a tumult of hope, fear, doubt. Did she dare consider his mad scheme? It was so very tempting, and yet undeniably daunting as well.

"You are my best hope, angel. My only hope. One night. Can you give me that?"

She swallowed thickly.

"Must . . . I answer this moment?" she said at last. "The decision you are asking me to make is a profoundly serious one. I need time to consider."

"Of course." His gaze held sympathy. "But however much I dislike pressing you, perhaps I should remind you that time is running short."

"I know." Her tone was bleak.

She stepped back, out of his embrace, and was unsurprised to discover how feeble her knees were. She didn't need Mr. Sabine to remind her of the urgency. He was to hang tomorrow—unless she consented to become his bride.

Then his execution would be delayed long enough for them to wed.

Her eyes were burning as she gazed up at him, her throat tight. So tight that she couldn't manage another word.

Turning blindly, she made her way outside the cell, where she leaned weakly against the stone wall. A shudder passed through her as she thought of him dying—

"Aurora, are you unwell?" Percy's concerned voice asked. She had forgotten entirely that he was awaiting her in the corridor.

Unable to speak, she shook her head.

"Come, we must get you out of this dungeon and find some fresh air."

She was grateful when her cousin took her arm and led her along the dim passageway and up a narrow flight of steps. When she reached the open air, she drew a deep breath, trying to contain the turmoil of emotions that were tearing at her inside.

Percy waited patiently while she struggled to regain her composure. "So," he said finally, "I take it Sabine proposed?"

"Yes." Her voice held an edge of bleakness she couldn't hide.

"And did you give him an answer?"

"Not yet. I couldn't . . . not so quickly. I told him . . . I needed time to consider such a drastic step."

"Well, of course you do. I can only imagine what a difficult decision it must be for you—to defy your father and wed a stranger. Perhaps we should go home and discuss it with Jane."

She gave him a forced smile. "Yes."

Percy led her to the waiting carriage and handed her inside, then took his place beside her. Aurora sank back against the squabs and stared blindly out the window.

She shuddered to think how her father would react, the rages she would have to endure . . . Yet it wasn't only withstanding her father's inevitable explosion or marrying a stranger that made her decision so difficult. *She was being asked to wed a dead man.*

Still, it was the thought of Nicholas Sabine dying that was breaking her heart.

Chapter Four

I cannot comprehend the power he holds over me. How is it possible when I have known him such a brief time?

"So he has proposed a marriage of convenience to safeguard his illegitimate sister's future?" Jane asked thoughtfully when she'd heard the tale.

The three of them were in the drawing room—Percy on the settee beside Jane, relating the particulars of Sabine's proposal, while Aurora stood at the window, too restless to be seated.

"Yes," Percy replied. "Except the girl isn't considered illegitimate, nor is her illicit conception common knowledge. The affair was hushed up long ago."

Jane pursed her lips in contemplation. "I can understand the advantages to Mr. Sabine's sister, but how would Aurora benefit by marrying a pirate?"

Percy answered readily. "Financially the marriage could be quite attractive for Aurora, since he means to settle a large jointure on her. His mother and two sisters in Virginia will inherit part of his fortune, and his shipping empire will go to an American male cousin. But Nicholas hopes to provide for his half sister without his mother ever learning of the girl's existence—or of his father's infidelity. Nick proposes to leave a substantial sum to Aurora, a portion of which she will hold in trust for Miss Kendrick. And he would ask Aurora to assume the wardship. If she's his wife, such arrangements would be unexceptional."

"True," Jane agreed, "but if he is hanged for piracy . . . Marriage under such a cloud would prove socially difficult for Aurora, if not impossible."

"Her standing in society should shield her somewhat. And remember, Nick is not without noble family of his own. His cousin, the Earl of Wycliff, will be a formidable ally."

"Yet she would return to England a widow, have you considered that?"

"Which could be a decided advantage. I've never liked the thought of her having to marry Halford. If Aurora is a widow, it wouldn't be proper for her to wed until a decent interval had passed, and Halford would have to look elsewhere for a bride. Of course then she would not become a duchess, which *is* a drawback."

Aurora didn't care for the way they were discussing her future as if she weren't present. "Am I to be given a say in the matter?" she asked.

Jane looked contrite. "Forgive me, dearest. I suppose we became carried away because we care so much. But Percy is right. You should give Mr. Sabine's proposal serious consideration."

"I thought you said he was dangerous," Aurora replied, frankly surprised by Jane's endorsement. "You called him a notorious adventurer, did you not?"

"Most certainly. Any man with his reputation would be dangerous to young, *single* ladies. But an offer of marriage changes the circumstances altogether. Matrimony can render even the worst sort of rakehell respectable. And this could very well be the answer to your dilemma, Aurora. I know how you dread having to wed Halford. As your husband he would be as controlling as your father, and you'll find it repugnant, being forced to live under his domineering thumb and to bear his children." Jane gave a delicate shudder. "Sabine is the lesser of two evils by far."

Aurora managed the ghost of a smile. "That is hardly a glowing recommendation for a husband."

"He isn't an ideal choice, I grant you. But his wealth can compensate for a multitude of sins."

"Do you realize how mercenary that sounds?"

"I am only being practical, Aurora. A generous jointure would allow you a vast measure of independence. You could not only escape your father's demands that you marry, but you could set up your own household as well."

"You would condone defying my father?" she asked skeptically, not quite believing Jane's seditious counsel. "He will be incensed if I am unable to wed Halford as I agreed."

Percy answered for his wife. "You were compelled to agree to your father's choice under duress, Aurora. He would never have permitted you to accept our invitation here had you not promised to wed Halford when you returned to England. In any event, I would be more deserving of his wrath than you. I gave him my word that I would look after your welfare. I believe, however, that by championing your marriage to Sabine, I would be acting in your best interests. Just not in the manner your father expected."

Aurora fell silent, thinking grimly of her stern, illustrious father. Not even Percy realized how violent the Duke of Eversley's temper could be. For the most part, she had been a dutiful daughter; rightly or wrongly, she possessed a strong sense of family loyalty and obligation due her rank. But she would be crossing her father with a vengeance by making such a scandalous marriage.

Jane rose and went to her, putting a comforting arm around her waist. "Perhaps I'm callous to say so, Aurora, but it isn't as if the union would be permanent. You could even look at it as if Sabine were merely lending you his name. Once you leave here, you will never see him again. You wouldn't have to spend your life tied to a man you don't love."

Reminded that Nicholas Sabine was to lose his life, Aurora squeezed her eyes shut.

"I know how much you loved Geoffrey, my dear," Jane murmured, apparently mistaking the reason for her despair. "But it will only compound your misery to be locked in a loveless marriage to Halford. You've had enough sorrow in your life."

Aurora looked down at her clenched hands to hide her reflections. She had loved Geoffrey deeply, but not in the way Jane supposed. Theirs had been a comfortable alliance rather than a grand passion. Geoffrey had been a gentle soul and one of the kindest men she had ever known, with a sharp mind he preferred to engage in scholarly pursuits.

His quiet, complacent nature was what had made the prospect of marriage to him so appealing, Aurora knew. She had cherished him for his temperament as much as anything—because he was so completely unlike her father. He would never try to rule her or dictate her every action or fly into rages at the slightest provocation, as her father did. As Geoffrey's wife, she would be free to live her own life, to control her own future. Indeed, Geoffrey was perfectly content to follow her lead in all matters, so long as he could keep his nose buried in his books. She had grieved at his death, but she'd loved him more like a brother than lover.

Her throat tightened with guilt and regret that she hadn't felt a greater passion for him, but she banished the bittersweet ache his memory always engendered and swallowed past her dry throat.

"Mr. Sabine," she said finally, "wants more than a marriage in name only. If we wed, he will insist on . . . on consummating our union, so no one can question its legitimacy."

That gave Jane pause, while Percy looked grave. He made none of the objections Aurora expected, however.

"Your father would indeed be unable to challenge the marriage then," Percy asserted. "And everyone knows Halford's preference for schoolroom misses. He will undoubtedly give up his pursuit of you if you're truly a widow and no longer a virgin bride."

Aurora couldn't help flushing at such plain speaking, even though she should be accustomed to it by now. The frank honesty and openness in the Osborne household was uncommon but admittedly refreshing compared to the stifling mores under which she'd been raised.

Seeing her discomfiture, Jane frowned at her husband, but then nodded slowly in agreement. "Mr. Sabine is injured, Aurora. He is not likely to be much of a husband to you. And you would only have to submit once. Furthermore . . . pray forgive me for being immodest, my dear, but I daresay Mr. Sabine has enough expertise to make the experience not . . . unpleasant for you."

It was Percy's turn to frown, but Jane forestalled his comment by asking him about the nuptial arrangements. "You can't possibly allow your cousin to be married in that dismal prison, Percy," she said emphatically.

"I doubt Nicholas would be allowed to leave the fortress, but the Brimstone chapel is quite adequate. The ceremony could be held there tomorrow evening, which would allow enough time to secure a special license and arrange for a solicitor to write out a new will."

When Aurora remained silent, Percy went to stand before her and take her hand. "You know, my dear, you don't have to accept Sabine's proposal, or Halford's either, for that matter. You are welcome to make your home with us for as long as you wish. You needn't return to England."

"Thank you, Percy," Aurora said quietly. "But my life is there, with my family, my friends."

"Well, don't let us browbeat you into making a decision you will regret."

She smiled briefly. "I won't." This was too important a matter to allow herself to be pressured even by her loving, well-meaning relatives. "I am profoundly grateful for your concern—grateful to you both," she said, including Jane in her glance. "But will you forgive me if I say I need some time alone to consider?"

"Of course we'll forgive you," Jane said warmly, giving her a gentle hug.

"Certainly," Percy agreed. "But I'm afraid you will have

to make up your mind quickly. Nicholas Sabine is running
out of time."

"I know," Aurora said bleakly.

After fetching a pelisse, she made her way outside to walk
beneath the palms. The Caribbean sun was setting, sheen-
ing the distant ocean horizon a glittering copper rose, but
Aurora scarcely saw the beauty. Instead she saw a lean,
bronzed face with dark, fathomless eyes gazing at her
intently.

There were any number of reasons marrying Nicholas
Sabine would be madness. He was a rake and adventurer
and accused felon. They were enemies, their countries
caught up in an interminable war. Her father would be outraged. Society would be aghast. Yet it was her own emotions that she feared most. Could she bear the turmoil of
losing a husband to the gallows so soon after vowing to
love and honor until death parted them?

She had already lost too many people she cared for,
including the man who was her long-intended husband.
And as irrational as it might be, she already grieved for
Nicholas Sabine, when she'd known him for barely a day.
Her emotions were far too deeply involved—and she would
only compound her involvement by becoming his wife.

After Geoffrey's tragic death, she had vowed never to let
herself care deeply for anyone again. She'd had more than
enough of bereavement.

Coming to the edge of the palm-lined path, Aurora turned
blindly back toward the house, grappling with her conflicting emotions. How had she come to this difficult choice?

Before Geoffrey's death, her future had been well established. As the Earl of March's wife she would have had
everything she wanted out of life. Tranquility. A comfortable marriage. An agreeable husband for whom she held a
strong affection. A large measure of independence. The
hope of children.

After the tragedy of Geoffrey's disappearance at sea,

she had tried to forget her grief, but her father had only compounded her misery by forcing her to accept another suitor. At least there was no chance of her being hurt by giving her heart to Halford.

Her lips curved in a bitter smile as she paused beside a palm tree.

She seemed destined to make a cold-blooded marriage. For her, true love was something only to be longed for and imagined. She would never know the kind of grand passion that poets spun legends about, the kind of intense, overwhelming love Raven's mother had known with Nicholas Sabine's father. . . .

Nicholas Sabine. Aurora shut her eyes, remembering how he had kissed her earlier. The caress of his lips had been ardent yet restrained—and more arousing than any kiss she'd ever known.

He was nothing like Geoffrey. He was an adventurer and privateer, a man of violence rather than intellect. Bold and brazen rather than gentle and studious. Dangerous. His touch set her blood racing. His dark eyes promised pleasures she had never even dreamed of . . .

And yet he had honor. What other man would go to such lengths to fulfill a deathbed promise to his father? Would risk his life to see a sister he scarcely knew safely settled?

Aurora leaned against the thick trunk of the palm tree. How could she possibly refuse his plea? Her heart contracted painfully as she remembered the dim cell where he was imprisoned. Her predicament at being forced into wedlock couldn't compare to his desperate plight, but she knew what it felt like to be trapped. And she was his only hope.

She took a steadying breath. If she had to marry coldheartedly, she would prefer to choose the candidate herself. And despite the drawbacks, there were excellent reasons to wed Mr. Sabine. Foremost was that she could escape a lifetime sentence as the Duchess of Halford. She would be in charge of her life for the first time since she could remember. She would be free of her father, of his rages.

Freedom. She hadn't realized how desperately she craved it until Sabine had offered it to her. She had come to the Caribbean seeking a haven, anxious to get out from under Father's tyrannical thumb. These past months had been like a balm to her ravaged heart, without the grim reminders of her lost loved ones or the strain and tension of living in her father's household.

It was unlikely she would ever have another opportunity like this. Marrying Nicholas Sabine was the only way she would have true independence. As his widow, she would have the tranquility she longed for.

Of course, the marriage vows would have to be consummated. *One night. Can you give me that?* He had implied that he could show her passion she never dreamed of, and she didn't doubt him. Yet she would have to surrender her innocence to him. . . . Her mind sheared away from the thought of carnal intimacy with the dark-eyed adventurer.

Aurora exhaled slowly, ignoring the knot coiling in her stomach. The intimacy of the marriage bed would only make her emotional conflict worse. But if she could manage to get through one night without letting herself grow even more dangerously attached . . . If she forced herself to maintain a rational detachment, treating her marriage simply as a business proposition, to be concluded as swiftly as possible. If she simply did what had to be done . . .

Steeling herself, Aurora pushed away from the tree trunk, willing herself to calm. She might be making a very great mistake, but her decision had been made.

She would agree to become Nicholas Sabine's bride.

Tomorrow would be her wedding day.

"She accepted my suit?" Nicholas repeated, wanting to be certain he hadn't misunderstood his visitor's announcement.

"Yes," Percy assured him. "And furthermore, Commander Madsen has agreed to defer your sentence for another day so that your nuptials might go forward. You and Aurora are to wed tomorrow night."

Nick let out his breath slowly, releasing the tension that had knotted his gut ever since his capture. "You have my sincerest gratitude, Percy, for allowing me to present my case to your cousin, and for helping persuade her."

"I didn't have much of a hand in persuading her. Aurora made up her own mind."

"I imagine you underestimate your influence." Nicholas walked over to a table that now held a decanter and several glasses. "Will you help me celebrate my good fortune with a glass of wine?"

"Wine?" Percy frowned slightly as he glanced around the dingy prison cell. "I see you even have chairs now. Your accommodations seem to have improved since I was here last."

"Compliments of Commander Madsen, to express his regret at having to imprison me," Nick said dryly.

"Ah, yes. He said he owes you a debt of gratitude. I understand his brother's wife was one of the many people you ferried to safety during that uprising on St. Lucia six years ago."

"So he says. I'm afraid I don't precisely recall her."

"Madsen remembers it clearly enough. It's why he agreed so readily to delay your execution." Percy smiled faintly as he accepted his glass from Nick. "In fact, he seemed delighted to oblige. I think he's frankly angry to be left with the responsibility for carrying out such distasteful orders. And there is no love lost between him and Lord Admiral Foley, either. Madsen mentioned that he would much prefer to ship you to Barbados and let Foley deal with you."

"I'll have to see that the commander receives some significant token of my appreciation after I'm gone."

"A case of good French brandy would do nicely, I expect," Percy said with little humor. "As allies of the Frogs, you Americans have greater access to the necessities of life than we do." He glanced at the sleeping cot with distaste. "It would be even better if Madsen could be persuaded to find other quarters for you. My cousin deserves more suitable accommodations than the fortress dungeon for her bridal bower."

"She does indeed," Nicholas said with quiet grimness. "Don't worry. I'll make certain Madsen is persuaded."

"Good. But he may be willing to do it for Aurora's sake as well as your own. He's become rather smitten by her."

"I doubt he's alone in that—a woman as lovely as she is," Nicholas replied.

"Yes, but he would never have approached her while she was in mourning. Fortunately or not, her circumstances have shielded her from normal modes of courtship. In England she would have been much sought after for her rank if not her beauty, but her longstanding betrothal to Lord March kept any other suitors at bay, as did her father. I doubt Aurora is even aware of her effect on men. . . ." Percy frowned. "Which reminds me, I feel I must speak up, Nick. My cousin is very much a *lady*. I hope you will go gently when you make her your bride."

Nicholas returned a cool glance. "I assure you, I have never mistreated a woman in my life."

"I don't believe you would intentionally harm her. I just meant . . . restrain your lust . . . keep your customary wildness under control. Aurora is nothing like your usual paramours. She's a complete innocent, with no experience in carnal matters."

"I will be considerate, I give you my word," Nicholas swore solemnly. "Now, perhaps we should discuss financial arrangements. The war will make it difficult for Lady Aurora to access my funds in any American banks, but I will write a letter for her to present to my cousin Wycliff in England. I'm certain Lucian will honor my wishes and provide her marriage settlement immediately. He can reconcile the amount with my estate once the war ends."

The two men spoke for a time about business matters— Aurora's jointure and what portion she would hold in trust for his sister and how the will should be written.

When Percy was satisfied the main contingencies had been accounted for, Nick changed the subject once again by saying gravely, "I would ask one more favor from you, my friend. Make certain Lady Aurora leaves St. Kitts before my sentence is carried out. I don't want my wife to see me die."

"That might be more difficult than all the rest," Percy replied slowly. "Aurora may very well refuse to leave you until the bitter end. She has a strong loyal streak, you see. She could feel obligated to stay until it is over."

"You cannot let her see me hang, Percy."

"No, I agree."

"Get her to Montserrat, by force if necessary. Wycliff's schooner should be docked there waiting to take my sister to England. They can embark directly from there."

"I shall see to it," Percy said earnestly. He met Nick's gaze. "I should be doing more to help you out of this damnable situation."

Nicholas grinned and reached out to shake his friend's hand. "You've already done more than I have any right to ask. Believe me, if I can see my sister safe, I will die at peace."

When Percy was gone, Nick lay down on the cot, his mind at ease for the first time since being taken prisoner. An odd sentiment, considering that tomorrow was to be his wedding day. Matrimony was an institution he had always ardently avoided, deploring any shackles that would restrict his much-cherished freedom. Ordinarily the prospect of taking a bride would have him rebelling, resisting with all his might. But his circumstances were anything but ordinary.

As was his bride.

Aurora Demming was a contradiction—surprisingly tough for a lady of her class and upbringing, with a stunning combination of regal elegance and allure.

Was he asking too much of her? She was the privileged,

pampered daughter of a duke. Proper. Innocent. And enchanting enough to send blood rushing to his loins at the mere thought of touching her.

She was a beauty, the kind of woman to haunt a man's dreams, with pale gold hair and deep blue eyes and lush lips made for kissing.

When he remembered tasting those lips, another fierce stab of desire pierced him. Nicholas swore softly at himself. How would he manage to restrain himself? He'd had countless women. Passionate lovers who could wring a man dry. Bold, exciting ones who challenged his expertise and stressed the limits of his control. Tender ones who could satisfy his male hunger in a surfeit of pleasure. But he suspected making love to Aurora would be an experience unlike any he'd known. When he'd kissed her earlier, he'd glimpsed the fire of long-suppressed desire in her eyes.

He shut his own eyes, letting himself fantasize about his wedding night. He drew a sharp breath as he imagined having her cool beauty beneath him. The thought of rousing her to passion brought an ache to his body that had nothing to do with his injuries. A man could die happy after being in her arms.

Nicholas exhaled slowly, feeling his rigid muscles slacken.

Wedding her was no mistake. If tomorrow was to be his last night on earth, he wanted it to be in the arms of a siren whose hair glittered with sunlight.

Chapter Five

He took my body with surprising gentleness, treating my innocence as a precious gift.

The ceremony took place as planned in the fortress chapel, with Jane and Percy and Commander Madsen in attendance. Yet when Aurora first laid eyes on her intended husband, she felt an unexpected shock. He had recently bathed and shaved, and the clean, chiseled angles of his face revealed a stunning handsomeness that made her breath catch.

He was dressed as a gentleman of means rather than a condemned prisoner, in a bottle green coat and pristine white cravat that contrasted attractively with his golden skin, while his sun-streaked mane had been tamed to an almost fashionable style.

Both the fresh bandage wrapping his brow and his unsmiling face, however, emphasized the somber nature of the event. A wedding should have been a joyous occasion, but no one in the bridal party experienced any joy, including the bride and groom.

Aurora chiefly felt numb. This strange ritual was not what she'd envisioned when as a girl she had imagined her wedding day. The heavy gold ring Nicholas Sabine presented her—his own, engraved with the emblem of a masted ship—was too large for her slender finger. And the light brush of his lips on hers when he sealed their troth was almost cold. But it was the grimness in his eyes that made her heart sink.

The dinner given afterward by the commander in his quarters was slightly less solemn but still awkward, for no

one could forget what was to happen the following day.
There were no toasts to long life or happiness for the bridal couple, and Colonel Madsen made no secret of his
anger about being forced to carry out such a distasteful
duty. He took his leave shortly after the sweets had been
cleared away, brushing off Aurora's attempts to thank him
for his hospitality and merely wishing the company a good
evening.

Percy and Jane lingered a while longer and embraced
Aurora fondly when they said farewell. It had been arranged for Aurora's maid to attend her, but when Jane
wanted to summon the girl, Nicholas intervened, saying he
would see to his bride himself.

He ignored Jane's frown of disapproval and Aurora's
questioning look, but in a few more moments her cousins
were gone, leaving her alone with the man whose name
she now shared.

"I trust you will forgive me if I'm not eager for company," he murmured, throwing the bolt on the door and
securing them inside.

"Of course," Aurora answered unevenly, not quite certain how she should behave or what he expected of her.

"Would you like some wine? Or perhaps something
stronger?"

She started to refuse, but then changed her mind, realizing wine might help ease the tension that had suddenly
seized her. "Yes, thank you, I would."

The commander's quarters were neither large nor particularly sumptuous; the chamber they occupied was both
a dining room and parlor. But they were the best the grim
fortress had to offer.

Aurora had been surprised to learn the colonel had leant
his rooms for their wedding night at Nick's request. Even
in prison her new husband was not completely powerless
at influencing his fate.

When Nicholas went to the sideboard, Aurora absently
toyed with the overlarge ring on her finger.

"You don't have to wear it," he said, observing her action.

"I am just concerned that I will lose it. Perhaps I should put it away for safekeeping."

"That might be wise."

She slipped it into her reticule, then clasped her hands together to keep them steady.

Nicholas poured a snifter of brandy for himself and a glass of sherry for Aurora, which she accepted gratefully. Then he raised his glass in mock salute before taking a long swallow of brandy.

Unable to meet his gaze, Aurora sipped her wine more slowly. She felt her heart skip a beat when her new husband indicated the adjoining door with a polite sweep of his arm.

"Shall we retire, my lady?"

Reluctantly she preceded him into the bedchamber. The room was dim, lit only by a bedside lamp and a low-burning fire. Aurora eyed the bed warily. The frame was rather narrow, yet the covers had been turned down invitingly and her nightdress had been laid out with evident care. Her mouth suddenly went dry.

She felt his gaze survey her as she stood frozen. After watching her a moment, though, Nicholas went to the hearth and stirred the coals, rousing a more lively flame. "My manners are remiss again," he said casually. "I haven't thanked you yet for accepting my proposal."

"It . . . seemed the most sensible course," she replied, fighting to keep her voice from sounding weak.

"And are you always sensible?"

"Usually, Mr. Sabine."

"Why don't you call me Nicholas? After all, we are husband and wife now."

Aurora shivered slightly at the reminder.

He turned to her, his gaze locking with hers. "Bridal nerves are not uncommon, I understand."

"I suppose not."

"I have told you before, Aurora. You have nothing to

fear from me. You needn't look as if you are going to the guillotine."

She took a deep breath, chastising herself for being such a mouse. She had agreed to become his bride, and she would uphold her end of the bargain—or die trying.

"Do you know what is supposed to happen between us?" he asked when her chin lifted in determination.

"I have an idea. Jane told me generally what to expect. I am prepared to submit as your wife."

His eyes softened. "I am not interested in your submission, Aurora. I want you to enjoy this as much as I do. In fact, I think you'll find lovemaking quite pleasurable."

"Jane said . . . it might prove so with you."

His faint smile held more than a hint of charm. "I shall do my utmost to justify her faith in me."

When Aurora remained immobile, Nicholas raised an eyebrow. "Come and sit by the fire, sweetheart. I won't ravish you, I promise."

Aurora searched his compelling eyes, finding a tenderness there that amazingly reassured her.

Two wing chairs were arranged before the hearth, with a small cherrywood table between them. Aurora chose the one closest to the door. Nicholas remained where he was, one booted foot on the hearth fender. His tone was thoughtful when he next spoke. "Did you ever consider that this marriage business might be terrifying for me as well?"

"You?" Aurora responded in surprise.

"Yes, me." His mouth twisted in a wry, self-deprecating smile. "I've never taken a bride before. Truthfully, I've hunted man-eating tigers in India with less trepidation."

She stared at him, not believing this man with his bold vitality had any conception of fear. She studied him a moment, unconsciously admiring his ruthless good looks— the strong jaw, the slashing brows, the sensual eyes with their long, dark lashes.

She wasn't genuinely afraid of him, although she didn't

know why. A man with his history of violence should have frightened her. But he was still unnerving.

There was a leashed energy in his lithe, powerful body that was intensely male. An intensity that was sexual—there was no other way to describe it. All her senses came alive in his presence, her feminine instincts acutely aroused. That was what unnerved her, she realized. His powerful sexuality . . . and the dismaying effect it had on her.

"I expect we should discuss the arrangements regarding our marriage," he said after another moment. "I spent most of the day with the solicitors, trying to foresee various difficulties and making every legal provision I could think of. Financially at least you will be comfortably situated."

"Thank you," she murmured, suspecting he had introduced the subject now to give her something to think about other than the consummation to come.

"Raven, however, could prove a possible problem to my plan," Nicholas mused. "She won't be eager to accept you as her guardian—a total stranger. Nor is she likely to suffer the confining strictures she'll encounter in England, either from her family or society in general. Although she claims to have every intention of conforming in order to make a good match, she has an aversion to rigid rules. She's something of a rebel, I fear. Much like me."

His crooked smile was meant to put her at ease, Aurora suspected, but the sensuality of it had just the opposite effect. "I'm certain we will work something out," she said gamely.

"Good. I've written Raven a letter, telling her how our marriage came about and explaining how she stands to gain, but you may have to persuade her to accept you as her ally. I think she will, once she understands the lengths you've gone for her."

He hesitated. "I will be relying on you to guide her, Aurora. I believe we discussed the support she'll need from you once you reach England, but there is another matter I forgot to mention. Raven's mother reportedly left something in her personal effects for me to hold in keeping . . . a rare book, I understand. It was a gift from my father years ago. He told me about it before he died, but he wasn't certain what happened to it. He would have been gratified to know Elizabeth Kendrick kept it all this time. She told me she wanted her daughter to have it—but not until Raven is old enough, after she is wed herself. Now that you have charge of her, you will have to be the one to judge when to give it to her. I have no doubt you will act in her best interests."

"Of course," she murmured, wondering what kind of book inspired such concern.

He shifted his gaze to look down at the hearth. Firelight played over his beautiful features as he stared at the flames. "There is one other thing I would ask of you, Aurora. Will you promise me something?"

"What?"

"I want you to leave tomorrow for Montserrat."

"Tomorrow?" Aurora felt herself frown. "Must it be so soon?"

"I would rest easier, knowing Raven's welfare is in your hands."

A chill settled about her heart. He was to die tomorrow. How could she deny him this simple request?

"Will you promise me?"

"Yes," she said, her voice suddenly hoarse.

He gave a brief nod of satisfaction. "There should be a ship at Montserrat ready to take you both to England. Your cousin will escort you to the island and see you safely aboard. I regret the inconvenience, but there is good reason for haste. By now Raven no doubt has learned what befell me, and by going tomorrow, you may reach her in time to prevent her doing something totally rash—like setting out to rescue me."

"Very well." Aurora hesitated before murmuring, "It won't really be inconvenient. Most of my packing has already been done. Before . . . I met you, I had planned to leave for England the following day."

"Before I intervened in your life, you mean," he responded with a twist of his sensual mouth.

There was little she could say to that. Truthfully she was glad he had intervened in her life and spared her a repugnant marriage, but this hardly seemed the appropriate time to discuss her feelings.

Firelight etched his profile as he took another swallow of brandy. "Well," he added, rather easily for a man who was about to die, "at least it will all be over for you tomorrow."

She shuddered, not wanting to be reminded of the fate that awaited him.

Almost absently, he bent to stir the coals again, and a lock of tawny hair fell over the bandage wrapping his forehead. When he raised a hand to rake back his hair, she noticed the red stain seeping through the white muslin.

"You are bleeding," Aurora said, rising to her feet in alarm.

He touched the bandage gingerly, and a smear of blood came away on his fingers. "So I am. The gash must have opened when I washed earlier."

"May I look?"

He raised an eyebrow but made no objection when she reached up to probe beneath the dressing. "Please, will you move over to the light so I can see?"

When he complied, Aurora set both their wine glasses on the bedside table and turned up the lamp. Nicholas sat on the edge of the bed, watching her as she carefully unwound the strip of muslin from around his brow. She could feel his intent gaze on her as she inspected the wound beneath the pad.

"I doubt this is what you planned for your wedding night," he said in a low voice. "I'm sorry."

No, this was not what she had planned. Had Geoffrey survived, this night would have been far different for her.

She would not be preparing to give herself to a stranger, nor would she have been so unnerved by her husband's nearness the way she was with Nicholas Sabine. *Or so strangely excited.*

Aurora mentally chastised herself. She should not be thinking of Geoffrey or comparing the two men. Geoffrey was gone, and soon so would this man be.

Her sadness must have shown on her face, for he asked quietly, "Your betrothed . . . did you love him a great deal?"

She flushed, realizing he had mistaken the cause of her sorrow. "Yes."

Making an effort to shrug off her melancholy, she went to the washstand and wet the corner of a towel before returning to her new husband. "Your wound bled a little. The blood should be wiped away so it won't mat your hair."

"Please do."

"Forgive me if I hurt you."

"You won't." He didn't seem inclined to change the subject, however, as she gently cleaned his scalp. "You said I bore a resemblance to your betrothed."

"I thought so at first because of your fair hair. But I was mistaken about any real resemblance. You really are nothing alike."

"How so?"

"Geoffrey was a . . ."

"A proper gentleman?"

"A proper, *gentle* man."

"Do you not think I can be gentle?" Nicholas queried solemnly.

Her heart gave a fluttering leap. "This is not what you expected either, was it?" she asked, trying to ignore the sensations he aroused in her.

"To be truthful, I never gave matrimony much thought."

"You never wanted to marry at all?"

His brows drew together thoughtfully. "I suppose I had a vague notion that someday I would marry and sire an heir. But I was too busy sowing my wild oats to entertain any serious thought of settling down." The half smile that flashed across his mouth was fleeting, before he gave a graceful shrug of his shoulders. "It's too late now for recriminations or deliberations on what might have been."

"I regret you were trapped into an unwanted marriage," Aurora replied, her voice rough with emotion.

Nicholas reached up to close his strong hand around hers, commanding her attention. "I don't mean to spend my last night dwelling on regrets." His dark eyes held her spellbound. "Do you think we could make a pact, sweetheart? For tonight we forget everything else that has happened?"

"I would like that."

"So would I." His voice was hushed. "Very well, this is our night. Nothing exists, before or after this moment. Tonight we live only for the present."

"Yes," she whispered.

He reached up and slid his fingers behind her nape. Time suddenly seemed suspended as he drew her head down. He meant to kiss her, she realized, her pulse leaping in an erratic rhythm.

His mouth was amazingly soft and tender when it touched hers briefly, yet it stirred a riot of unruly emotions within her. She wanted to turn and run, but when he drew back slightly, his fathomless gaze locked with hers, imprisoning her as surely as any chains.

Aurora felt her heart hammering as Nicholas leisurely took the towel from her limp grasp and let it fall to the floor. Hooking his arm around her waist, he urged her closer, between his spread legs, till her breasts brushed his chest. A tremor rippled through her.

With some futile thought of self-preservation, she pressed her palms against his broad shoulders, staring at him. His eyes, dark and sensual, told her clearly he didn't intend to stop at a kiss.

"Your wound . . ."

"Will survive. But I might not if I don't taste you soon." Still holding her lightly, he slowly lay back on the bed,

drawing her with him. Heat spread in her, catching hurt-
fully in her stomach as she found herself stretched fully on
top of him, cushioned by his powerful body. She trembled
at the stunning intimacy of this simple contact, the unfamiliar hardness against her softness, the warmth of his
frame beneath her thin silk gown.

"Open your mouth this time, lovely Aurora," he murmured as he delicately teased her into parting her lips.

The intrusion of his tongue was slow and sensual, more
erotic than anything she had ever felt before. For a long
moment she remained rigid, experiencing the foreign sensation of his open mouth tasting deeply of hers. He was
drinking of her, savoring her. It was tantalizing, the warm
stroke of his tongue inside her mouth.

She could feel herself softening, her breath quickening
in steady arousal, but her simple pliancy still was not
enough for him.

He left off kissing her long enough to murmur in a husky
voice, "Kiss me back, sweetheart," before his mouth found
hers again.

Dazed, she let her tongue shyly move to meet his and
was rewarded by his low, guttural sound of approval.

The pressure on her mouth deepened. A heavy ache
began forming in her lower body as his intoxicating lips
and tongue taught hers about kissing. His hands stroked
down her back, bringing her hips even closer to his, exciting her further.

For long moments they lay together, tasting each other
in the heated silence. Aurora lost any perception of time,
any sense of herself. There was only the captivating awareness of Nicholas, of his raw masculinity and his sensual,
drugging kisses, of his hard-muscled body beneath hers.

Eventually his caresses became more ardent; he claimed
her mouth fully, dragging her into his kiss and sending delicious liquid sensations flooding through her defenseless
body. Of their own volition, her fingers moved from his

shoulders to curl in the waving silkiness of his hair. His mouth was a searing flame that stole her breath.

Helplessly she pressed closer to him, longing for something she couldn't name. She felt boneless, on fire . . . She felt as if she were falling. . . .

It was only Nicholas, nudging her onto her back on the soft mattress.

Her eyes fluttering open, she stared up at him. She was trembling, her cheeks hotly flushed, her senses spinning.

His eyes watched her as his hand moved to the empire-waist bodice of her gown; she felt herself drowning in their shadowed depths.

When his fingers curled over the low décolletage, she tensed, but he bent to her again, his mouth hovering just above hers, heating her lips. "Don't be afraid to feel, angel. Tonight you can abandon reason and just let your senses rule."

When she made no protest, he gently tugged on the neckline of her bodice, then drew down the edge of her chemise over the top of her corset to expose the swell of her breasts that were pushed up by the stiffened fabric. With expert skill, he bared her nipples to the night air, making her shiver. When his bold fingers found one hardened bud that quivered there, she moaned involuntarily at the delicate-sharp sensation that shot through her.

"Has no one ever touched you like this before?" he whispered in her ear, his breath warm.

"No . . ." The word was a breathless gasp as his thumb moved slowly over the sensitive crest, circling and teasing.

Aurora shut her eyes, giving in to the pleasure he was determined to rouse in her. His warm, commanding mouth returned to claim hers as he gently tormented her aching breasts, leaving her whole body fiery with shame and excitement.

She was scarcely aware when he slowly drew up the hem of her gown or when he reached beneath the edge of her chemise. But then his stroking palm moved higher, brushing the soft, swollen flesh at the apex there, lingering.

Aurora went rigid. When she tried clamping her knees together, he insinuated his hand even deeper between her thighs.

He was breathing deeply, his lashes a dark sweep against his tanned face as he cajoled in a husky voice, "Open your legs for me, siren, and let me touch you."

Unable to deny him, she did as she was bid. Coaxing her further, he stroked the soft curling thatch of her womanhood. A moist, aching weakness pulsed to life in the secret place between her legs. She felt so strange, melting, throbbing . . . Instinctively she whimpered and arched her back, longing for some fulfillment that seemed to elude her.

Yet he seemed to know exactly what she wanted, needed. With exquisite care, his finger slipped between her cleft lips and penetrated her.

She gasped into his mouth, but he continued his tender assault, exploring, probing, learning her secrets. He was wooing her, his fingers sheathed in her pulsing warmth while the rough pad of his thumb brushed the now slick bud of her femininity.

She clutched at his shoulders, not certain she could bear any more, but he went on stroking, surging and withdrawing rhythmically, driving her on to greater heights, until instinctively her hips lifted and sought to match his pace.

Almost desperate now, she moaned and twisted under his hand, the coiled tension inside her growing more urgent with every stroke that rubbed against the bright center of sensation. All she knew was the devastating heat of his mouth on hers, the hot pounding of her blood, the fierce delight of what he was doing to her.

Suddenly the pleasure was too keen, too fierce to be borne. Frantic, she writhed beneath his possessive hand, yet the glowing spark grew till it seemed to shower her with burning embers. Aurora felt wave after wave of hot, shameful sensation wash over her helpless body.

His hand rose to cradle her throat, soothing her thundering pulsebeat, while his mouth feathered kisses over her flushed face.

A long moment passed before the sensual reverberations waned. Her limbs felt weak, limp, her senses dazed by the bewildering surge of fire through her body.

Opening her pleasure-hazed eyes, Aurora stared up at him. Nicholas was lying on his side, supported on one elbow, watching her. She was sprawled inelegantly on the bed, her legs dangling off the edge, her skirts hiked up to her hips, totally exposed above her stockings and garters. His heated gaze drifted over her—her bare breasts with their peaked nipples, and lower, to the juncture of her naked thighs.

Her face flushing with awareness, she reached down to put some order to her dishevelment, but Nicholas stopped her by covering her hand with his own.

"There is no need for shame or shyness between us, angel."

She averted her gaze. "I behaved like a wanton. I am not usually so . . . licentious."

"Only because you never before had the opportunity. I suspect you are quite a passionate woman at heart. There is a fire inside you that you keep hidden. . . ." When she remained silent, he raised his fingers to her chin and forced her to look at him. "A man finds an aroused woman incredibly desirable."

Her flush deepened. "I never imagined . . ."

"How pleasurable lovemaking could be?"

"Yes."

His half smile was indulgent. "That was only a taste, sweeting. There is more—much more—for you to learn about carnal desire. And with your permission, I intend to spend the rest of the night showing you."

Aurora returned his gaze solemnly. She wanted Nicholas to teach her about passion. She wanted to feel that bewildering fire again. Tonight could be her only opportunity, this her sole experience with lovemaking. She might

very well never marry again. If so, she would never again
know a man's touch, or know what it was to be a woman.
Yet there could be complications. . . .

"Jane said . . . there could be a child from our . . . union."

His gaze never wavered. "Jane is very practical, it
seems."

"Yes. She wanted me to know the possible consequences
of being with you."

"There are ways to prevent conception, but it is possible
a child could result from our union. Would that be so very
undesirable?" he asked.

A strange longing filled her at the thought. "No." She
would want his child, she realized. To keep some part of
him after he was gone. "It wouldn't be undesirable in the
least."

His expression softened. "Then there is nothing for you
to fear."

Nothing except losing my heart. But the thought fled
when Nicholas surprised her by sitting up.

"I suppose we should begin by shedding all these unnecessary layers of clothing."

When he reached down to help her, she reluctantly
accepted his assistance. "The light," she murmured self-
consciously, rearranging her bodice to cover herself. The
lamplight was too bright to be merciful.

Nicholas hesitated a moment, but then obligingly turned
down the lamp, leaving only firelight to illuminate the
room. "Is that better?"

"Yes, thank you."

He took her hand and brought it to his cravat. "You may
do the honors, love."

"You want me to undress you?"

The faint curve of his lips was devastatingly sensual.
"That seems a fitting place to begin if we are to conquer
your nervousness. It's only unfamiliarity that makes you
apprehensive, sweetheart. When you become accustomed
to me, you'll find you have nothing to fear." His compelling

eyes held hers while his husky voice cajoled. "You may take the lead, set the pace. I won't force you to do anything you don't wish to do. You are in complete command."

Reassured in some measure, she tentatively did as she was bid, removing first his cravat, then his coat and waistcoat and linen shirt. His boots and stockings he removed himself. When she hesitated, he followed with his breeches and drawers.

When he stood before her, his tall, nude body lean and hard and well-muscled, she stared spellbound.

"I am your husband, Aurora," he said, his voice a velvet murmur. "You needn't fear me. I am just a man, flesh and blood like you."

He was not at all like her, she thought skeptically, viewing his naked, sun-bronzed flesh and taut sinews. He possessed a broad chest and narrow hips and powerful thighs, like the statues of Greek gods she'd seen. And the alien hardness springing from the curling, dark gold hair at his groin made her heart beat erratically. She didn't fear him exactly, but neither was she in the least at ease.

"Now your turn," he murmured. When she hesitated, he smiled. "Of course you are accustomed to a lady's maid. Would you like my assistance?"

"Yes."

"It will be my pleasure."

He began with her hair, pulling out the pins and letting the pale gold mass cascade down her back.

"You have beautiful hair," he murmured, his fingers gliding through the silken tresses. "Like spun gold."

After a moment, his hands slid beneath her hair to the fastenings at the back of her gown. Well-bred and shy about her body, Aurora stood silently as he dispensed with her gown and corset and stockings. Her chemise was the last to go. Feeling the cool night air caress her nakedness, Aurora shivered.

"Your body is exquisitely lovely as well," he said,

turning her to face him. "I intend to show you all the pleasures it was made for."

When instinctively she moved her arms in front of her
body to hide from him, he gently pushed them aside.

"No shyness between us, siren." He ran a finger along
her throat to the tip of her breast, the erotic feel making her
draw a sharp breath. "What does it matter if I see your
charms? Whatever secrets you share will be safe with me."

Her vision clouded at the reminder. Come tomorrow, he
would be gone. Whatever intimacy they shared would go
to his grave. But tonight was what mattered now. Tonight
he was her husband, her lover. She could give herself to
him without fear or shame. She could abandon her inhibitions, her natural reserve.

She reached up to touch his sensual mouth with her
fingertips. "You said you wanted to forget," she reminded
him, her voice soft. "Nothing exists, before or after this
moment."

"So I did." Tender flames warmed the depths of his eyes.

He had beautiful eyes. Eyes that took possession of her
wherever they touched.

He took a step closer then, bringing their skin in contact.
The heat from his body leapt into hers, shocking, scalding.

Aurora trembled at the erotic sensation, feeling her breasts
graze his chest, and below, the hot, throbbing maleness of
him press against her stomach.

"Have you never wondered what it would be like to lie
with a man? To feel his hard flesh deep within you?" Nicholas bent his head, his lips kissing a path along her cheekbone.

Yes, she had wondered, Aurora reflected dizzily. In the
most secret corners of her heart, she had dreamed about a
nameless lover who could rouse her to passion—

"But if you had," he answered his own question, "you
could not properly admit it."

That brought a faint smile to her lips. "No. A lady
would never admit to such things."

"No, never. But if you ever have wondered . . . now is the

time to indulge your curiosity." Capturing her trembling hand, he enfolded it around the throbbing shaft of his manhood. "Touch me, love. Feel my flesh. . . ."

Holding her breath at the alarming size of him, she accepted his bold guidance, learning the unique feel of him. The smooth velvet skin of his phallus. The granite hardness. The swollen marble head. The soft curling hair and heavy sacs beneath. He really was not so frightening. Not any longer. If she were honest, she would admit she found the differences in their bodies thrilling. His sheer masculinity called out to everything feminine in her.

His hands rose to her breasts then, cupping their lush swells. Aurora closed her eyes and sighed. How expert he was, she thought dazedly. His hands were a murmur against her body, his fingertips gliding over her flesh, fanning over her breasts in deepening strokes.

"You are enchanting."

He was the one who was enchanting, Aurora thought, unable to resist the exquisite languor that had stolen through her limbs. He had bewitched her.

Voluntarily her mouth sought his while she moved closer, straining to feel his flesh against her. A gratified murmur sounded deep in his throat.

He kissed her for the space of a dozen heartbeats, his lips at once soothing and arousing. After a while, though, he lifted her in his arms and settled her on the bed, then followed her down to lie beside her.

His eyes half shut, his gaze sensual and compelling, he began to stroke her aching breasts again, his palms rubbing the tautened globes, his fingers kindling arrows of impossible rapture in her tight nipples.

Aurora surrendered fully to him. It was magical to lie in his arms like this, to breathe in the warm, masculine scent of him, to feel his incredible touch. Then he bent his head, savoring her stiffened nipple with his mouth, and her breath lodged in her throat.

She wanted him, she realized. Wanted to experience the

spark and fire between a man and a woman that he had shown her once before. His tongue flicked over the rosy bud, rasping slowly, before his lips closed to suckle the swollen crest. Aurora arched against the scorching heat of his mouth, her hands blindly seeking his hair.

He wanted her also, she knew it. She could sense it even before his erect manhood stirred heavily against her soft belly.

And then his wonderful, teasing fingers slid down once more between her moist thighs.

"You're wet for me." His voice was husky. "Your body is flowing with honey."

It was true. Her feminine cleft was sleek with wetness, her body aching shamelessly for him. She said his name, in a voice that sounded shaky, as he stroked the soaked bud. She should have been scandalized by his brazen passion, by her own wantonness, but all she could focus on was the magical caresses of his fingers and mouth.

She was trembling with desire by the time he left off arousing her breasts and shifted to cover her with his body. Sparing her most of his weight, he settled between her thighs and began kissing her again, holding her attention. She was hardly aware of his intentions until he began easing the velvet smooth head of his manhood inside her.

When she tensed, he kissed her more deeply, his tongue penetrating her mouth like his shaft was doing. Not allowing any resistance, his powerful thighs kept her own thighs parted as he slowly, slowly sank lower, pushing forward with inexorable pressure.

Aurora stiffened, gasping for breath. She felt sure she could never accommodate his enormous size, and yet her body was opening for him, stretching painfully, his alien hardness filling her. . . .

She squeezed her eyes shut and tried to catch her breath.

He was not moving now. "Look at me, sweet siren." There was tenderness in his eyes as he gazed down at her.

She lay rigid, feeling excruciatingly full of him. "It . . . hurts."

He kissed her temple. "Only the first time. The hurt will go away and all you will feel is pleasure." His gaze plunged deeply into hers. "Trust me."

Incredibly, she did trust him. He lay completely still, waiting for her to grow accustomed to his impalement and the feel of his thick member deep inside her. Eventually she felt a blurring of the edges of her pain.

He brushed back a tendril of hair from her cheek. "Better now?"

"Yes." It wasn't unbearable now. The burning had lessened.

After another long moment, she stirred her hips, tentative, testing. The discomfort was definitely fading.

He feathered a kiss at the corner of her mouth as he withdrew, but when he carefully slid upward once more, she felt the rise of heat in her again. He kept up the slow, deliberate rhythm, coaxing her with his hard body, until hot, urgent longing began to clamor inside her.

The hunger was as timeless as man and woman. She whimpered feverishly, her nails digging into his shoulders as she instinctively matched his rhythm. He squeezed his eyes shut like a man in pain, his breathing rough as he moved inside her, thrusting gently into her melting flesh.

When she was on the brink of climax, he reached down between their bodies to find the engorged bud of her sex. Stunned, she arched against him, straining, crying out as the shattering, burning tumult broke within her.

Nick captured her wild moans with his mouth but never stopped, using all his skill to prolong her ecstasy as wave after wave of rapture convulsed her slender body. When she bucked and writhed against him, he clenched his teeth, striving for control, trying desperately to keep his savage need in check as he lay buried deep inside her.

It was too much. A great shudder moved through his frame as Nicholas at last let himself fill her with the hot desire that he'd felt for her from almost the first time he saw her. A hoarse moan ripped from his throat as he plunged into an endless raw pleasure so intense it seared.

Finally it was over. He was shaken as he lay there in the darkness, yet eventually consciousness returned. When he felt her trembling beneath him, a fierce tenderness engulfed his heart.

Easing his weight to the side, he pulled the covers up over them and drew her into his arms. His body wrapped around her, warming her, calming her.

They lay there together, weak in the aftershocks of pleasure. After a long moment, he lifted his head.

In the firelight, she looked like a wanton angel, with her tangled cloud of hair, her pale ivory skin, her lush lips swollen and wet from his kisses.

It was amazing that she should have such an effect on him, Nicholas thought absently. She was physically inexperienced, totally virginal, and yet making love to her had created a tumult of feelings inside him that were entirely unexpected. The fierce sweetness of it had possessed him totally.

Perhaps the marriage vows they had spoken meant more than simply a cold business arrangement, bonding them together in ways he had never intended.

Wife. The word was strange, engendering even stranger feelings of longing and need. He wondered if he would leave an heir, if they had made a child. A son ... or a daughter. The thought brought an odd ache to the vicinity of his heart.

As if she could sense his bewildered reflections, the woman in his arms stirred. She was watching him, Nick realized, her luminous blue eyes searching. Desire knifed through him again, sharp and insistent, but he clamped down on his lusts, reminding himself of her virginal state.

"Are you all right?" he murmured, pressing a kiss on her forehead.

"Yes." A sigh whispered from her. "That was . . . wonderful."

A smile touched his mouth as a fresh wave of tenderness flooded him. "I'm gratified you think so."

"Was that . . . was I . . . a disappointment for you?"

He lifted an eyebrow in surprise. "Quite the contrary, siren. I've never experienced lovemaking quite so delectable." At her slight frown of skepticism, he gave a soft laugh. "It's true. Perhaps you're too inexperienced to recognize the fierce control I had to exercise, but it was all I could do to keep from ravishing you." He leaned forward to brush a kiss on her nose. "I could make love to you all night long . . . but I suppose I must show some consideration for your innocence and let you sleep."

A look of sadness passed over her face, and she reached up to touch his mouth with her fingers. "I really don't want to sleep. If this is my only night with you, I want it to last as long as possible."

He gazed at her, wanting to chase away the shadows in her beautiful eyes. She was thinking of the morning to come, he knew.

Shifting his position, he eased over her.

"So do I, angel," he whispered huskily as his mouth lowered to find hers. "So do I."

Chapter Six

In his embrace I discovered the wonder and the anguish of desire.

Confusion was Aurora's first reaction as she slowly stirred awake. Her body felt unusually sensitive, her lips and breasts tender, while an unfamiliar discomfort throbbed between her thighs. Blinking at the sunlight filtering through the chinks in the shutters, she tried to place the strange, spartan bedchamber. More bewildering, she was pressed against a hard, warm, male body that was decidedly nude. . . .

Memory came rushing back full force. Her marriage. Her husband. Nicholas Sabine.

For a moment she lay in his arms remembering, her cheek against his shoulder, their limbs entwined. For much of the night he had made love to her with exquisite tenderness and passion. What she had expected to be a brief, obligatory bedding had become a true wedding night. Nicholas had awakened her to desire, given her her first taste of ecstasy, leaving her trembling and shaken.

And she had surrendered to him completely, responding with an abandon verging on desperation. Despite their pact, the dire future he faced had added a primal urgency to their lovemaking.

Aurora bit her lower lip hard. Last night he had made her forget her sadness, but the dreaded morning had come. Today he would die.

She squeezed her eyes shut. She couldn't allow herself to care for him. He was a condemned man. . . .

Yet it was already too late. She had begun to feel a deep

affinity for her new husband, which made it all the harder to think of him dying.

The tears she'd been fighting started slipping down her cheeks and onto his bare shoulder. When she felt him stiffen, she realized he was awake.

Determinedly, she drew a shaky breath, trying to stem the flow of tears.

"I don't want you to grieve for me, Aurora," he said in a low voice.

"I c-can't help it."

"God, please don't cry . . . I would rather face a brigade of charging cavalry than one weeping woman." His hand came up to caress her cheek. "Your tears are the worst possible torture for me."

"I . . . I'm sorry."

She closed her eyes while his thumb carefully wiped the tears away. After a while she drew another shuddering breath, determined not to weep. Yet she could no longer bear to remain idle while he went to his death.

"This cannot be allowed to happen," Aurora vowed, her own voice low and fierce. "*I* won't allow it. I intend to visit the governor at once and compel him to stay your sentence. Sweet heaven, how could I have been so blind not to think of it before now?"

Disentangling himself from her nude form, Nick sat up, turning his back to her. "Might I remind you of your promise to help my sister?" he said quietly. "Your cousin has arranged to escort you to Montserrat today—this afternoon."

"I can't leave here as long as there is a chance your life could be spared."

Nicholas raked a hand through his hair. He had feared this very response from her. She wouldn't abandon him to his fate, not now. Not after the incredible night just past. The passion that had blazed between them had shocked them both, creating an emotional bond that would be hard to break.

With a silent oath, Nick glanced down at her to see tears

glistening wetly on her lashes. It made him ache to see her crying, yet he couldn't allow his fate to come before his sister's. He couldn't take the risk. Somehow he had to sever the bond between them.

She was gazing up at him, her eyes intensely blue, her hair a golden cloud, her lush lips swollen from his kisses. She was as beautiful as anything he had ever seen. And as vulnerable.

Reaching for her hand, he raised it to his lips, pressing a kiss on her knuckles. "I thank you for making my last night a pleasant diversion, sweetheart, but it is over now. Since our marriage has been consummated, there is no longer any need for a pretense of affection between us."

When the color drained from her face, Nicholas locked his jaw. He wanted to take back the cruel words making light of the searing passion they had shared. But he couldn't allow himself to be swayed by the hurt in her eyes.

He forced himself to hold her gaze, even when she pulled back her hand and drew the covers to her breasts in a defensive gesture.

Schooling his features to impassivity, he rose and went to the washstand to clean away the results of the night's passion. He could feel her watching his naked back, but when he turned to dress, she averted her face.

"We had a bargain, you will remember," Nicholas said coolly as he drew on his drawers. "Your financial independence in exchange for supporting my sister. I trust you will honor our agreement."

Her chin came up at that, as if he had stung her pride. "Certainly I shall."

He was glad to hear the edge of anger in her tone; that was far more bearable than tears.

He donned his breeches, then sat in one of the wing chairs before the hearth to pull on his boots. "Your cousin Percy has all the documents you will need, and my letter to Raven as well. Show it to her when you reach Montserrat, along with my ring as proof of our marriage. She will recognize the ship emblem—"

Just then a thudding noise sounded in the outer room. Nick froze, while Aurora flinched. Someone was pounding on the parlor door. The garrison soldiers, no doubt.

"Sir, we have orders to return you to your cell," a brusque voice called out.

"One moment, if you please," Nicholas responded. "I have yet to finish dressing."

He drew on his second boot, then his shirt. Without haste he tied his cravat and donned his waistcoat and coat. All the while, Aurora remained silent, still stunned and hurt by his sudden coldness.

"So this is farewell," he said when he finally turned to her.

"I suppose so," she replied, her voice barely a whisper. She stared back at him, searching for any sign of the passionate, considerate lover she had known last night. There was none. He was a stranger again, his lean face beautiful and hard.

"I am counting on you to care for my sister," he repeated.

"You have my word," she forced herself to say tonelessly.

"And you will set sail for Montserrat today as you promised?"

"Yes."

"Then I can rest in peace."

When she put a hand over her mouth to hold back a sob, he took a step toward her, then stopped abruptly. A muscle tightened grimly in his jaw, but he remained silent.

He gave her one long last look before turning away. As she watched, Nicholas left the bedchamber without another word, shutting the door softly behind him.

Aurora stared after him numbly, wondering how he could have turned so cold after his exquisite tenderness last night. Wondering how she could bear the feelings of dread and anguish that were gnawing so relentlessly at her.

But there was still time, perhaps, to save him. . . .

She had just thrown off the covers when a tentative rap

sounded on the bedchamber door. Her heart skipped a violent beat, her first thought that Nicholas had returned. But the voice that called out softly was female and belonged to her personal maid.

"My lady, 'tis I, Nell. The gentleman . . . your husband . . . bid me see to you."

"Come in, Nell," Aurora said, hiding her fierce disappointment as she rose and went to the washstand.

Nell blinked to see her normally modest mistress entirely unclothed. "I . . . I've brought your traveling dress for the journey this afternoon, my lady, and ordered hot water for your bath—"

"No." Aurora shook her head. Soaking in a hot bath might have eased the unfamiliar aches of her body, but there wasn't time. "Thank you, Nell, but I will make do with wash water. And then you must help me dress quickly. I must pay a call on the governor at once, and there isn't a moment to lose."

She had to try to save Nicholas, even if it meant defying his wishes and breaking any or all of her promises to him.

Aurora found the governor, Lord Hearn, at his plantation home, where she pleaded fervently with him to intervene with the navy and spare her husband's life. It took all her powers of persuasion to convince him simply to consider such a politically damaging step. Even then, his lordship insisted on discussing the matter with his lieutenant governor first.

She wasted precious time searching for Percy, making a fruitless trip home. By the time she tracked him down at his offices, nearly three hours had passed since she had said farewell to Nicholas in their bridal bower, and the day had turned chill gray, with dark storm clouds threatening to the south.

When she met Percy coming out of his offices, his expression looked as grim as she had ever seen it. He greeted her tersely, saying he was just on his way home to find her. And when she began telling him about the governor's possible willingness to intervene, Percy shook his head. "Aurora, I am afraid it is too late."

"Too late? What do you mean?"

"I received a message from Commander Madsen only moments ago. He has already acted. Nicholas is gone."

Aurora felt herself turn white. "No . . . that can't be true."

"I'm sorry. It is."

"He can't be dead," she whispered hoarsely. She pressed her hand to her mouth, trying to stem her cry of despair as pain lashed through her.

After a moment, Percy reached out to take her other hand. "Aurora, you know Nicholas would not want you to grieve for him. He wished you to forget about him and move on with your life. . . . Indeed, we should be leaving shortly to find his sister. Not only did I promise Nick I would escort you there this afternoon, I don't like the looks of the sky. A storm is brewing, and we should make haste if we hope to outrun it. My yacht is waiting to take us to Montserrat—"

"I want . . . to see him."

He frowned. "I told you he is gone."

"I want to see his body. Please, Percy . . . I cannot go without saying good-bye."

He gave a heavy sigh. "I feared you might feel this way, that you wouldn't be convinced to leave until his fate was final. Very well. I will take you to see his grave, if you insist. He was buried at the fortress."

She stood over the freshly dug grave in stricken silence, her heart as heavy as the dismal sky, while tears slipped relentlessly down her face. There was no headstone or marker. Only bare, pungent earth to indicate the passing of the man whose vital presence had touched her life so briefly . . . and so powerfully.

Aurora bowed her head, fighting to hold back a sob. She felt cold, sick inside. And along with the salt of her tears was the bitter taste of guilt. Guilt for not trying to do more to save him.

Nicholas, I'm sorry.

"Come now," her cousin murmured at her elbow. "You have a promise to fulfill."

She nodded mutely, the muscles of her throat locked tight.

Percy understood why she'd had to come here. Only seeing Nicholas's grave could convince her that he was truly gone.

Only now could she accept the finality of his death.

She donned widow's weeds for the journey to Montserrat—a traveling dress of black bombazine that she'd originally worn to honor the memory of her late betrothed. No sooner had Aurora and Percy boarded his yacht, though, when the dark sky opened up. They were forced to wait nearly an hour before the rain diminished enough to permit them to set sail.

Aurora was glad for the storm, for the weeping sky and lashing winds mirrored her mood exactly. She watched dully from the captain's stateroom as the storm spent its fury outside.

The worst of the squall bypassed them to the south, but choppy seas made the short voyage to the nearby island rough. However, by the time they arrived, the angry clouds had turned to scudding fleece, with the sun making an occasional appearance.

Because of its rugged green hills and considerable Irish population, Montserrat was known as the Emerald Isle of the Caribbean, and after the rain, it glistened like a jewel in the sun. When the schooner dropped anchor, the passengers were rowed ashore. Percy hired a carriage, which swept them past rich flatlands planted in sugar cane toward gentle, tropical-forested mountains. The climb offered a magnificent view of the sea, yet Aurora scarcely noticed. She was grateful for her cousin's silence, for she wanted to be alone with her own dark thoughts.

Eventually the driver brought them to a halt before a plantation home. The house had a certain charm, boasting the arched stonework and shaded balconies of the West Indies, brightened by colorful bougainvillaea and hibiscus. But it had seen better days, as evidenced by fading whitewash and peeling green paint on the shutters.

No grooms or footmen came to greet them, and when Aurora and Percy climbed the front steps to wield the knocker, a long wait ensued before they heard the sound of movement from within.

A young woman opened the door. She was dressed in a plain blue muslin gown and held a pistol in her hand.

Aurora blinked to find the weapon aimed at her heart, while at her back Percy muttered an oath and roughly drew her aside, out of direct range.

The young woman lowered the pistol with a murmur of apology. "Forgive me. I expected someone else. We've had trouble lately. . . ." Her voice trailed off.

"What sort of trouble?" Aurora asked, recovering from surprise.

"Some rather unpleasant visits by the British navy." Her mouth curled in derision, before she schooled her features to politeness. "What may I do for you?"

"We're here to see Miss Raven Kendrick," Aurora replied, although she knew this must be Raven. A rebel and a beauty, Nicholas had said. This young woman was certainly that, with her ebony hair and blue, blue eyes and her deadly looking pistol.

"I am Miss Kendrick," Raven answered. "And you are . . . ?"

"Lady Aurora . . . Demming. And this is my cousin, Sir Percy Osborne. We are here on behalf of your brother."

A look of alarm crossed her face. "What do you know of my brother?"

Aurora swallowed, momentarily made mute by the ache in her throat. She felt Percy's hand at her elbow, supporting her.

"He was taken prisoner, that much I know," Raven declared. "Is he all right?" When Aurora's eyes blurred with tears, the girl's mouth went white. "He's dead, isn't he?"

"I . . . I'm afraid so."

Raven's eyes filled with grief. After a moment she turned away, bowing her head as she struggled for composure.

Finally, though, she turned back. "What happened?" she whispered hoarsely.

"It is rather complicated," Aurora answered in a low voice. "May we come in?"

"Yes . . . yes, of course." Squaring her slender shoulders as if bracing for a blow, she stood back to give her visitors admittance.

Three days later Aurora stood at the stern of a two-masted brig with her new ward, watching the island of Montserrat fade to a green speck on the horizon. It had been harder than she expected to say good-bye to Percy—everything had been harder with her heart so heavy. She would miss her cousin and Jane dearly.

Fortunately the past three days had been a whirlwind of activity, offering little chance to grieve. Aurora had spent the interval helping Raven make final preparations for her relocation to England: packing up her worldly possessions and closing the house, bidding farewell to the last few servants, and selling the last-remaining livestock, including a mare Raven was inordinately fond of. They both shared a passion for horses, it seemed.

During that time Raven had singlemindedly thrown herself into her tasks. She'd spoken little about her half brother, but Aurora suspected the girl mourned his death with a surprising intensity. Though Raven hadn't known Nicholas long—only a few years—during that short time she had apparently grown quite attached to him. Aurora thought it fortunate that she and Percy had arrived on Montserrat when they did, for Raven was indeed planning to leave the next day and go in search of her brother.

The girl had been shocked by his death and taken aback to learn about the change in wardship. But once she read Nicholas's letter, she offered little protest to the arrangement—confiding that she saw the benefit of having someone like Lady Aurora guide her in society and claiming to be glad for Aurora's consoling presence.

Aurora thought Raven showed remarkable courage in leaving behind the only life she had ever known. It couldn't be easy, traveling partway around the world to live in a strange country with scornful relatives she had never met, attended only by her maid and a faithful Irish stablehand named O'Malley, who apparently had appointed himself Raven's personal guardian.

Now, standing beside Aurora at the ship's railing, Raven kept her chin lifted and stubbornly set as she watched her home disappear.

"You have always lived on the island, have you not?" Aurora murmured in an effort to distract the girl's sorrow.

"The whole of my life."

"I know you will greatly miss it."

Her mouth quivered momentarily, making her seem younger and more vulnerable than her nineteen years. But she quickly controlled it. "It doesn't matter. This is what my mother always wanted for me." Taking a deep breath, Raven pointedly turned to face the bow of the ship. "And I have no family left now."

"You have me," Aurora said gently.

"I'm glad." She managed a tremulous smile. "I'm glad Nicholas found you."

Repressing the shaft of pain that pierced her at the remembrance, Aurora faced forward as Raven had done. "You shall make a new life in England, Raven. We both shall."

"Yes." Clenching her jaw, Raven slipped her hand in Aurora's.

Inspired by the young woman's courage, Aurora raised her gaze to the endless sea, where home beckoned. She, too, would have to leave the past behind and look toward the future. A future without Nicholas.

"A new life," she vowed in a fierce whisper.

Sleepless, Aurora lay curled beneath the covers of her bunk, watching as dawn spread rosy fingers of light through the shipboard cabin. The brig belonged to the Earl of Wycliff, and the cabin she shared with her maid was comfortably if sparsely appointed.

There was no reason to rise early. The voyage to England would last seven or eight weeks if good weather held, and this was but the first morning. Except for their servants, she and Raven were the only passengers on board, and they both made poor company at present.

The cabin was quiet except for the steady slap of waves against the hull and the breathing of her maid, who had finally fallen asleep in the opposite bunk after feeling ill much of the night.

Too quiet, Aurora thought regretfully. She could not be grateful for the solitude, her first since leaving St. Kitts. For the most part, she had managed to bury her own sorrow, avoiding thoughts of Nicholas above a dozen times a day, refusing to allow herself to dwell on her loss. At least until now. Now, in the quiet of dawn, the pain came rushing back with renewed force.

Closing her eyes, she fingered the ring he had given her, which she wore now on a gold chain around her neck. The metal was warm from her body and reminded her acutely of Nicholas and the searing passion they had shared on their brief night together.

Unable to bear the solitude of her dark thoughts any longer, Aurora rose and braced herself against the sway of the ship as she silently began to dress. Even though she would have been glad for the companionship, she had no wish to wake poor Nell. Perhaps if she went above deck, she might find the captain or one of his officers to bear her company.

She was extricating a shawl from her valise when she came across the parcel wrapped in layers of tissue paper. Her fingers traced the name written in a weak hand: Nicholas Sabine. The parcel had been left for him by Raven's mother among her possessions.

Aurora felt her heart twist strangely as she opened the wrapping. Inside was indeed a book as he'd expected, although not just any book. Aurora caught her breath at its stunning beauty.

The cover was inlaid with gold leaf and adorned at the four corners with clusters of semiprecious stones. Embossed into the gold was the title: *Une passion du coeur— par une dame anonyme.*

A Passion of the Heart—by an Anonymous Lady.

Curious, Aurora opened the jeweled cover. The book was a journal, she realized, written nearly a hundred years ago, though it had been published more recently.

The first entry, also written in French, was dated September 3, 1727:

It has been seven months since I was captured by Turkish corsairs and sold as a slave in Constantinople into the harem of a prince. Seven months since my gradual conversion from despair to desire, to unwilling love.

Only today was I allowed pen and parchment to set down my thoughts about my captivity.

I remember vividly the day I was brought before him as his concubine. I was so innocent then, a Frenchwoman of good family, unprepared for the mysteries of passion that awaited me at the hands of my new master. I could not know how profoundly he would affect me, awakening a woman's tender longing and hungry desire.

At first glimpse he seemed infinitely dangerous, even barbaric. And yet something in his eyes called to me . . .

Aurora shut her eyes, reminded so poignantly of the first time she had seen Nicholas on board the naval frigate.

Then, he had been a captive, bound in chains, and yet he had seemed just as dangerous, just as compelling, as the prince in the journal.

She moved on, turning pages that seemed worn and obviously well read. Nicholas had said the book was his father's gift to the woman he loved. Raven's mother had evidently loved him in return, if the condition of the pages were any indication. Numerous passages had been underlined, one of which drew Aurora's eye.

His hand on my breast was at once soothing and arousing, his skilled fingers stroking my taut nipple, a torment to my sensitized flesh.

A flush of embarrassment stung Aurora's cheeks at the explicitness of the text. She had promised to read the journal and decide whether it would be appropriate to give to Raven, but she could answer that question with one glimpse.

Nicholas could not have known the scandalous nature of the journal's content. She herself had never read anything so openly licentious. And yet she couldn't deny its forbidden allure. The Frenchwoman's erotic descriptions had a poetic, lyrical quality about them that was at once powerful and fascinating.

Her gaze settled on another passage at random: *His bold touch inflamed my innocent senses, driving me to greater heights of pleasure, kindling the burning need in me.*

Nicholas, oh Nicholas. She closed the cover, unsure she could bear to read something that brought back such tormenting memories.

Wrapping her shawl about her to ward off the dawn chill, Aurora hesitated a long moment before picking up the journal and leaving the cabin.

Above deck, the crew was scurrying over the brig, climbing the rigging and adjusting the innumerable sails. Not wanting to be in the way, Aurora went to stand at the rail.

After the dimness of her cabin, the bright sunrise blurred her vision. Or perhaps it was tears. She could barely see the vast ocean stretching out before her. The brilliant blue-green waters of the Caribbean had become the gray of the Atlantic, while a chill breeze buffeted the ship, making the canvas snap overhead.

Shivering, Aurora wrapped her arms around herself and lifted her face to the wind, glad for the numbing effect.

She stood at the railing for a long while, her heart aching as she remembered Nicholas. He had been so vital, so larger than life— *For mercy's sake, stop thinking of him!*

Somehow she had to force her memories of Nicholas out of her mind. That brief chapter in her life was closed. When she reached England, she would make a fresh start. She would begin a new life for herself, one free of emotional tumult. She would be her own woman, with no domineering father or commanding husband to control her or make her life a misery.

Faith, she should be counting her blessings rather than wallowing in sorrow for a man she hardly kr.ew. Logically she should be grateful their marriage had lasted such a short time. She could never have been comfortable with Nicholas as a husband. His intensity, his passion, his raw virility, were too overwhelming. . . .

Whatever bonds they had formed were physical. Bonds of the flesh, not of the heart. Their marriage had been a purely cold-blooded business contract, nothing more. And she would have to bury his memory with the same cold-blooded detachment.

With renewed determination, Aurora swallowed the ache in her throat and forcibly turned her thoughts to the journal she clutched in her hand. The lady had been captured as a slave but found passion in the arms of a magnificent stranger. What was her tale? How would her story end?

Anxious for the distraction, Aurora found a keg to sit on out of the direct force of the wind. Then, her heart taking up an unsettling rhythm, she opened the jeweled cover to the first page and began to read.

At first glimpse he seemed infinitely dangerous, even barbaric. And yet something in his eyes called to me. . . .

PART II

Dance of Passion

Chapter Seven

Against my will, he haunted my dreams.

London, June 1813

The masquerade was a grand success if the size of the crush was any indication. The ballroom overflowed with shepherdesses and princesses, armored knights and mythological gods. Even the Prince Regent had made an appearance earlier, assuring a triumph for the ball's hostess, Lady Dalrymple, who was Raven's aunt.

Behind her satin mask, Aurora kept a watchful eye from the sidelines as her ward moved through the lively steps of a country dance with a Cupid. Raven was dressed as a gypsy and fit the role to perfection, with her flowing ebony hair and bright skirts and gold bangles.

More than one gentleman obviously admired both the costume and its wearer. Standing beside Aurora, the Earl of Clune eyed the vivacious gypsy with interest.

"Your ward appears to be enjoying her success," Clune remarked. "But I'm surprised her aunt condoned her attendance at a masquerade."

"There is no harm in it," Aurora replied mildly. "Lady Dalrymple would never allow any scandalous behavior in her own home. And it would have been cruel to keep Miss Kendrick imprisoned upstairs in her bedchamber and deny her the experience of her first masquerade. Besides, she has made her come-out, and she is older than most debutantes—and decidedly more mature."

The earl turned to regard Aurora, probing her mask. "It

is also surprising to think of you as her guardian. You cannot be much older than she."

"Two years. And I am more friend than guardian to Raven. I do, however, take my responsibility for her quite seriously." Aurora returned Clune's gaze steadily. "If you are thinking of pursuing her, my lord, I feel I must warn you against it. I'm certain you would not suit in the least."

His rakish smile was all charm. "Indeed. Chaste young debutantes are not my style. I have a decided partiality for lovely young widows, however. If you find yourself in need of consolation, Lady Aurora, I would be delighted to oblige."

Aurora repressed a smile behind her mask. Jeremy Adair North, nicknamed "Dare" for his outrageous exploits in the bedrooms and ballrooms of Europe, was one of the premier rakes of the beau monde. It was hard to dislike him, no matter how wickedly or scandalously he behaved, for he possessed a seductive charm that was infectious. His wealth and rank also served to excuse his notoriety in the eyes of the ton. In addition to an earldom, he was reportedly soon to become the Marquess of Wolverton, for his grandfather's health was failing rapidly.

Aurora had known Lord Clune for some years. He'd never paid her the least attention until now, undoubtedly because she was considered fair game in her widowed state. The moment he had spied her across the room, he'd sought to discover the woman behind the mask, claiming that he relished a mystery. He hadn't stopped quizzing her until she revealed her name.

"Must I remind you I am in mourning, sir?" Aurora asked, deliberately adding an edge of sternness to her tone.

"And yet you are here this evening. It is hardly considered proper to attend a public function so soon after suffering a bereavement."

"My husband did not wish me to grieve for him. And until tonight I've taken care to follow proper conventions of mourning. Even now my deviation is not so egregious. I am not dancing, and I've made every effort to conceal my identity. You did not recognize me, you must admit."

Clune eyed her with amusement. Her costume, consisting of a silver domino and a headdress encrusted with crystal beads, was rather plain compared to the other guests' extravagant attire, and extremely modest, covering her head to toe, while her mask hid all of her face but her mouth and chin.

"On the contrary," Clune responded in mock offense. "I would never fail to recognize the most alluring beauty in the room."

Aurora bit back a wry reply. She had no intention of engaging in a flirtation with the most notorious rake in London. She was highly conscious of the need for circumspection, for Raven's sake, as well as her own, and knew the risk she'd taken in coming here.

"My sole reason for attending tonight," she explained patiently, "is that Miss Kendrick asked me to provide her support. She does not yet have so many friends that she feels comfortable in society."

"She is not lacking for admirers now, certainly," his lordship commented, shifting his gaze to the ballroom floor. "Witness the gaggle of besotted young bucks flocking around her." The dance had ended, and a laughing Miss Kendrick was completely surrounded by a dozen young gentlemen, all vying for her attention.

Aurora was gratified to see Raven so much sought over. She was fitting in to the British social whirl amazingly well. Indeed, with her vivacity and frank outspokenness, she had earned a reputation as an "original."

To Aurora's delight, Raven had proven a joy to befriend. Despite her unconventional beliefs and hoydenish ways, her manners were extremely agreeable, and she could be graceful and poised and articulate when she chose to. She primarily needed to polish her social skills and her understanding of the intricacies of etiquette.

It was her attitude, particularly her tendency toward recklessness, that was most likely to land her in trouble. But

she was trying very hard to repress her natural high spirits. Except for her early morning gallops in the park with
Aurora—gallops that Aurora admittedly was guilty of
encouraging—Raven had made a staunch effort to conform to convention, so that none but the highest sticklers
could find fault.

She listened carefully to every utterance Aurora made,
for she was adamant about fulfilling her mother's lifelong
wish—making an excellent match by wedding a title and
fortune. Having grown up in the limited society of a small
Caribbean island, shunned by her haughty relatives because of her conception, Raven was determined to join the
elite realm of the British aristocracy that had repudiated
her mother.

She might very well reach her goal of having a half
dozen offers of marriage by the end of the season, Aurora
suspected. It was a coup that earlier this evening Prinny
had pronounced Miss Kendrick "charming."

"A pity you must refrain from dancing," Clune mused
aloud. "But I suppose you cannot afford the slightest indiscretion after your disastrous marriage." When Aurora
sent him a sharp glance, he smiled lazily. "I say that in jest.
Doubtless I'm one of few people who don't consider it
shocking that you wed a notorious American. I remember
Nicholas Sabine from his visit here a few years ago—
quite an impressive man. The first and only Yank to be welcomed as an honorary member of the Hellfire League."

Clune was the nominal leader of the club of wicked
rakes called the Hellfire League. He, along with Nicholas's English cousin, the Earl of Wycliff, had been the subject of sensational gossip for years, and deservedly so.

"I remember being green with envy," Clune admitted,
"listening to Sabine tell about his adventures. . . . Exploring foreign lands, searching for hidden treasure, battling
bandits . . . He once narrowly escaped being skewered by
an angry warlord's scimitar on the Barbary Coast, were
you aware?"

"I hardly find that cause for envy," Aurora replied dryly.

"Perhaps not, but his courage was admirable. To hear Wycliff tell it, your Nick was a hero countless times over. In India once, he tracked down a man-eating tiger that had been preying on villagers for months. Took the animal down with one shot. They renamed the village after him."

Wycliff had told her similar tales about her husband's exploits. Nicholas reportedly had once saved the life of a Russian prince while hunting wolves. When the nobleman's troika went through the ice into a lake, Nicholas had pulled him out and carried him more than a mile to shelter. He'd been rewarded with enough priceless jewels to ensure a luxurious life for years—which, added to the fabulous pirate treasure he'd discovered beneath the Caribbean in his youth, had made him a wealthy man long before he assumed control of the Sabine shipping empire.

Aurora felt her gaze blur momentarily at the bittersweet thought of Nicholas. Without question, he had often risked his life simply for the thrill of it, but he had also saved a number of lives in the process. It was one of the reasons she felt such guilt over his death; she'd done nothing to save him until it was too late. If only she had insisted on speaking with the governor sooner . . . If only . . . But it did no good to dwell on the past.

And she preferred to remember Nicholas as the tender lover he had been on their wedding night, rather than the reckless, dangerous man she knew he was at heart.

"I understand," Clune observed, "your father was not over-joyed that you wed during your sojourn in the Caribbean."

"No," Aurora murmured. The ton had been scandalized by her marriage, as expected. Even for a duke's daughter, it was anathema to marry a brazen pirate who'd met an ignominious end on the gallows. But her father had been *livid* at her transgression, lashing out at her in a convulsive fury that had left her shaken—although publicly he'd maintained a chill pretense of indifference, unwilling to add more fuel to the sensational fire her highly improper marriage had caused.

Thankfully his vow to cut her off without a shilling had had no teeth, since her marriage settlement had made her quite wealthy. Nicholas's cousin, Lucian Tremayne, Lord Wycliff, had attended to the complex financial details at once—when he could have made it extremely difficult for her to secure any part of her claim to her late husband's fortune. Then, when she was treated with disdain by certain high-browed members of the ton, Wycliff had entered the fray, proving her strongest defender and providing her the protection of his exalted name and position, warmly welcoming his American cousin's bride into his family.

Her path was far smoother after that, for few people would dare slight a man of Wycliff's consequence.

For the most part, however, her acquaintances had stood by her. She was still received except in the most rigid of circles. Her closest friends called upon her at her new home with regular frequency, allaying her loneliness. And in some respects, ironically, she had become more of a matrimonial prize than before. A wealthy widow who needed consoling was prime game for fortune hunters—or rakes, Aurora thought with a glance at the handsome, licentious, fair-haired lord standing solicitously beside her.

"I imagine," Clune commented obliquely, "there were others besides your father who didn't welcome the news of your marriage." He gestured along the sidelines toward a tall, stately gentleman dressed as Henry VIII. The Duke of Halford stood there stiffly, eyeing the crowd with his quizzing glass in apparent disapproval of the gaiety. "His grace would not have appreciated your jilting him."

"But I did not jilt him," Aurora replied.

"No? Rumor has it that you were to wed Halford."

"My father favored the match, but we were not betrothed."

"Still, a man as proud as Halford would have taken your sudden marriage as an insult."

"Actually, he was rather understanding," Aurora said,

greatly shading the truth, "when I confessed that I fell hopelessly in love with my husband."

"Well," Clune remarked with a sardonic smile, "his grace has evidently given up pursuing you if he's here looking over the season's crop of debs. You are fortunate to have escaped, in my not so humble opinion."

Aurora could not agree more, although it would have been impolite to say so. She shuddered to think what her life would have been like as Halford's duchess, being forced to follow his counsel and accept his dictates.

When they met upon occasion now, Halford treated her with frosty politeness. For Raven's sake, though, Aurora swallowed her dislike and tried to remain cordial. There was no point in antagonizing him further or making an outright enemy of a nobleman who was a respected figure in the ton.

"Yes, a fortunate escape," Clune added with uncustomary seriousness, "yet you are not so fortunate in love apparently. It is regretful that *two* of your betrothals should end so unhappily."

Aurora swallowed the sudden ache in her throat and merely nodded. It hurt to remember losing both Geoffrey and Nicholas.

"You must be lonely, with no one to console you. I could easily remedy that, my sweet. I understand Wycliff is to be away on business for some time. Doubtless Lucian would wish me to look out for you in his absence."

"You are too kind, my lord," she murmured wryly. "But there is no need for you to concern yourself with my welfare—or to remain at my side all evening. You should be dancing yourself."

One elegant eyebrow arched. "Do I detect a dismissal, Lady Aurora? I am wounded."

She smiled, doubting she had hurt the practiced libertine in the least. "Surely you realize my dilemma, my lord. It will only arouse comment for me to be seen in your company."

"Very well. I am astute enough to take a hint. I shall look for you on your morning rides in the park, then." With an engaging smile, Clune gave her an elegant bow and turned away in search of more willing prey.

As she watched him go, Aurora found herself reflecting on his comments about her marriage. It was true that most of society thought she had ruined her life. Perhaps her action *had* been socially disastrous, but she couldn't regret wedding Nicholas Sabine. No matter how gravely he had jolted her life, he had given her a means for independence that she cherished, one she could never have hoped to attain on her own.

And he had changed her in intangible ways as well—more than she would have thought possible after such a fleeting acquaintance. She had never been the daring sort, except perhaps on horseback. Rather she was sensible and proper, suitably conscious of the duty owed her rank and family name.

Yet since her experience with Nicholas, she had become less patient with society's shallow strictures and rigid rules, less willing to be governed by others' expectations. Tonight was a prime example. Before her marriage, she would never have attended a masquerade while in deep mourning, even in disguise.

There was something liberating about thumbing her nose at convention, albeit from behind a mask. And social prestige seemed so unimportant now compared to the life-and-death issues she had faced a few short months ago. While once she had been a respected figure in society, she didn't much lament her loss of stature.

She was now Lady Aurora Sabine. She had kept her title, since it accorded her a certain deference, but she had set up her own household in a small but elegant residence in Mayfair. Raven was staying at her Aunt Dalrymple's town house for the Season, although come summer she would remove to the country to spend time with her grandfather, who was something of a recluse.

Aurora treasured the freedom her own establishment gave her, even if she was ordinarily confined to its small boundaries. Except for her obligation to guide Raven in society, she lived quietly as a bereaved widow. She rode early in the morning when only the most avid horsemen were about, rather than at the fashionable hour of five when the park was crowded with the cream of the ton. When she accompanied her ward shopping—Raven had required an entire new wardrobe to make her come-out—she wore black and kept her face veiled to honor her husband's memory.

Her display of mourning, however, wasn't all pretense. She wanted to accord Nicholas the respect due a beloved husband. She couldn't forget the tender lover who had swept her into unexpected ecstasy and made her a woman, or deny her gratitude for saving her from an unbearable marriage and from her father's dictatorial rule.

Escaping her father's anger and iron control had felt like a heavy yoke being lifted from her shoulders. She was so very grateful for her liberation. Truthfully, she hadn't realized how badly she craved freedom until she'd tasted it. And now that she had, she would never again allow herself to be so thoroughly dominated by any man. She owed Nicholas for that realization and for her newfound strength.

The Frenchwoman's journal, too, had influenced her indefinably. She was no longer the virginal innocent she'd been on her wedding night. The journal had taught her much about the mysteries of passion and helped her to understand the powerful feelings Nicholas Sabine had aroused in her so effortlessly.

For a moment as she remembered him, a poignant ache tightened her throat. It had been four months since Nicholas's death. Four months that she had tried to put him out of her mind. Thoughts of him would intrude at odd times, but each day it was becoming easier to bury her sorrow. Sometimes long hours went by when she didn't think of him at all.

It was the nights when he haunted her dreams. . . .

Aurora squared her shoulders. She would not allow herself to be tormented by memories. She had vowed to make a new future for herself, and she would not look back.

Her life was on an even course now. There was no turmoil, no grief, no dread. No strife stemming from disputes with her father or his violent rages.

She couldn't remember when she had last felt such equanimity. She was content, even happy now. A quiet, uneventful, peaceful existence held a vast appeal after the upheavals in her past.

She did not have to answer to anyone but herself now. She alone was in control of her fate. Finally, *finally* her life was her own. And that was precisely how she wanted it.

It was perhaps an hour later when Aurora lost track of Raven. Searching the crowd, she finally spied her charge across the ballroom.

Raven was not dancing but stood on the sidelines, conversing with a swashbuckling pirate who sported an eye patch and a sword hanging from his waist sash. Her face was flushed with excitement, and she was laughing and talking animatedly.

Aurora felt her heart catch when she saw the pirate. She didn't actually recognize him, but the sense of familiarity was uncanny. He had the lithe, athletic form of her late husband—the same broad shoulders and narrow hips and long, sinewed limbs. The same aura of danger, of vitality. When he laughed in amusement at something Raven said, his teeth flashed white against his bronzed complexion.

His coloring was quite different from Nicholas's, however. His hair, half hidden by a rakish headscarf, was ebony instead of dark gold.

Aurora raised a hand to her brow. Her mind was playing tricks on her, obviously. Her tender remembrance of Nicholas was making her imagine his ghostly presence.

Just then Raven glanced over her shoulder, as if searching for Aurora. The pirate turned his head slowly, and their gazes locked.

Aurora felt the color drain from her face. For an instant, time ceased to exist, and she was back again in her marriage bed with Nicholas, drowning in his dark, fathomless gaze.

With a whispered oath, Aurora turned and fled.

She found herself in the library, where a lamp had been lit to chase away the gloom. Dizzily she moved toward the sofa and leaned against the high back. Her face felt flushed with perspiration, her pulse erratic.

Pulling off her mask, Aurora bit her lip hard, wondering if she was going mad. She had been unable to forget Nicholas, but she had never before so vividly conjured his image—

"Aurora." The low murmur came from behind her.

She went completely still, memory slicing at her heart. It couldn't be his voice. The man she remembered so poignantly was gone.

"Aurora, look at me."

Slowly she turned around. The pirate was standing there, just inside the room. Dear God, he looked so much like Nicholas . . . despite his black hair and marauder's attire.

Her fingers gripping the back of the sofa, she squeezed her eyes shut, but when she opened them again, the image was still there.

"No . . ." Her denial came out in a hoarse rasp. "You are dead. . . ."

"Not quite, love."

Slowly he removed his eye patch, letting her look fully at his features. She could not have mistaken those eyes. Those dark, beautiful eyes. *Nicholas.*

"Oh, my God," she whispered.

His mouth curved in the faint semblance of a smile. "Aren't you glad to see me, angel?"

Unable to answer or even catch her breath, Aurora raised a hand to her temple. She felt faint with shock, her knees so weak they started to give way. She would have sunk to the floor but for Nicholas. In two strides he had reached her side and grasped her beneath her elbows, lending her his strength. His touch felt very real.

"I don't understand. . . . This can't be."

"It can, Aurora. I am truly here, in the flesh."

She stared back, her gaze riveted on his face. "How . . . ?"

"At the last moment Commander Madsen balked at giving the order to hang me because of a service I had once done a family relation. Instead, he had me transported to Barbados so the British navy could carry out my sentence instead."

"But . . . I saw your grave. . . ."

"What you saw was a deception, I'm afraid. Percy believed you wouldn't leave unless you were convinced you could do nothing more to save me, so I asked him to feign my burial. He arranged it with Madsen—although he had no notion of the commander's change in plan."

The grave was a deception? Stunned, she searched his face, trying to take in the enormity of the revelation. Nicholas wasn't dead. For a dozen heartbeats she remained unable to speak, her emotions a turmoil of shock and bewilderment . . . anger at his deceit . . . joy at seeing him again.

Still not quite believing, she reached up to touch his face. His skin was warm and smooth shaven. His hand closed over hers, holding her palm to his cheek, and for a breathless moment they remained that way, staring at each other.

When another wave of weakness hit her, making her sway, he bent and swept her up in his arms. Aurora suddenly found herself held against a hard male chest. The feel of him was just as startling as his sudden appearance.

She murmured a protest, but Nicholas shook his head. "You should lie down. You've had a shock."

He carried her around the sofa and settled her there, then went down on one knee beside her.

"I'm fine, truly," she murmured as he unfastened the top clasp of her domino.

The further shock of his warm fingers on the bare skin at her throat made her shiver with remembrance. Nicholas seemed aware of it as well, for his hands suddenly went still. He was looking at her breasts, she realized. Abruptly her nipples tightened and pushed against the bodice of her gown in twin, hard peaks.

Her breathing faltered as his heated gaze lifted to her face. "I didn't dream it—how beautiful you are." His voice had fallen to a husky whisper.

Aurora's lips parted, but no sound came out.

Then Nicholas drew an unsteady breath of his own and released her. To her relief, he rose and went to a side table, where he poured her a brandy.

Not wanting to remain in such a vulnerable position, Aurora sat up and smoothed her disheveled clothing. When he returned, Nicholas settled on the sofa beside her and ordered her to drink.

Obediently she took a sip of brandy. The fiery liquor burned her throat, but at least her senses stopped swimming.

"I'm sorry to behave like such a weakling. It's just that . . ."

"I have come as such a shock?"

"Yes." She frowned, searching his face. "It has been months, Nicholas. Why did I hear nothing of your being alive? I cannot believe Percy never wrote me—"

"I doubt he knew at first. The British navy presumed me drowned at sea, and I thought it best to encourage their belief. It's possible Percy heard rumors later and wrote to warn you, but a letter could have gone astray. Mail is often one of the casualties of war."

Reminded of the deception Nicholas had perpetrated with her cousin, Aurora felt a spark of renewed anger surge through her. He had deliberately made her think him dead, letting her weep over his grave. Letting her grieve for him for months . . .

"You might have warned me yourself," she said, fire edging her tone. "How could you put me through that—"

"I'm sorry, Aurora. Perhaps I should have tried to get word to you, but the war made it difficult. And at the time I was rather occupied trying to survive."

Aurora shook her head. How could she be angry with Nicholas when he was really, truly *alive*? Her ire fled as swiftly as it had been born, replaced by a fierce swell of joy. She gazed up at him searchingly, not knowing even where to begin with her countless questions.

Nicholas seemed able to read her mind. "You're curious to know how I escaped hanging?"

"Yes, of course. How did you manage it?"

"I jumped ship during a storm. I told you Madsen changed his mind about carrying out my death sentence and instead had me sent to naval headquarters at Barbados. I was being conveyed there in a brig when a gale blew up. The wind broke the mainmast and left us floundering in the water."

Aurora remembered the fierce storm that had prevented her own departure from St. Kitts the day Nicholas died— or the day she *thought* he had died.

"In the commotion, I managed to break my chains and dove overboard. I wasn't followed. No one believed I could survive in those seas, and it was over half a mile to shore. I was presumed dead."

"How incredible . . . You're alive because the weather turned violent?"

His smile was ironic. "I know. But it's you I owe my life to, siren. Our marriage delayed my execution long enough for fate to shift in my favor."

Aurora bit her lip, recalling anew the long months of sorrow when she had thought him dead. "I wish I had known you were alive. It would have saved me countless hours of grief."

"Did you grieve for me, Aurora?"

"Yes, of course. You were my husband."

There was a short pause. "I still am."

She drew a sharp breath as the import of his comment sank in. Nicholas *was* still her husband. *They were still wed.* Merciful heaven . . .

"In fact," Nicholas added in a low voice, "that's the reason I am here in England. I have a wife here. You."

Once again shock held her speechless. She stared at him, her mind reeling.

"I might have come sooner," he continued, "but it took me weeks to make my way to safety and locate my ship. Then it took more time to arrange for my journey here. Because of the war, I had to commandeer another of my cousin Wycliff's ships and outfit it for the voyage. And I had to hire a British crew with papers that would gain them entry into Britain."

"Entry . . ." Alarmed, she reached out to grasp his hand. "My God, you can't be seen in England. You're an escaped prisoner—"

"Easy, sweeting. I already *have* been seen. I'm here in disguise. As you can see, I dyed my hair. And I've assumed the identity of my American cousin, Brandon Deverill. We bear a strong resemblance, and I don't think he would oppose my impersonation. Brand has his own shipping firm in Boston, and at the moment he is rather occupied with the war."

Aurora's eyes widened. "The war! Nicholas, if your cousin is American, then he wouldn't be welcome here in Britain."

"He would if he were a British loyalist, which is what I'm claiming to be. There are hundreds—perhaps thousands— of loyalists who object to the war and who have sought refuge on British soil, so my story is not at all unusual. I imagine Brand might protest that small detail of my deception, since he despises you Brits after what your government has done to Boston shipping. But I'm sacrificing his reputation for a good cause."

"But . . . if you are found out, you could be hanged. At the very least you would be arrested."

"Most definitely, but I don't intend to be found out." His teeth flashed in an amused smile—an amusement that Aurora could not share. His nonchalance only rekindled her anger.

"You cannot possibly think to remain in England, Nicholas. Don't you understand? You will be *killed*."

"I am rather hard to kill, angel. This wasn't the first time I've escaped death by a whisker."

She could well imagine he had faced death before and no doubt *enjoyed* it. His casualness made her furious, as did his audacity. He had even come to the ball dressed as the infamous Captain Saber, a foolhardy risk that incensed her.

Aurora stared at him, torn between wrath and dismay. Devoid of gentlemanly trappings in his rakish pirate's garb, Nicholas looked the picture of a brazen adventurer, daring fate and laughing in the teeth of danger. Yet Aurora shuddered at the thought of what would happen if he were discovered.

"I am serious, you cannot stay," she pleaded.

"So am I—and I cannot leave just yet. Not when I came all this way just to see you."

"Well, you have seen me, so you may go."

"But we have a dilemma to resolve, sweetheart."

"Dilemma?"

He fixed her with his intense gaze. "What to do about our marriage."

Marriage. An unexpected sense of panic rose up in her. She was overjoyed to know Nicholas was alive, but it didn't necessarily follow that she was pleased to have him for her husband. His presence complicated matters dreadfully—especially since he couldn't even show his face without risking capture and death. Marriage to him would turn her life upside down, would shatter all her hard-won equanimity, would destroy the peace she had finally found. His very nearness sent her senses reeling—

Just then they heard laughter in the hall, and a couple walked past the library door. Aurora froze, deathly afraid Nicholas would be recognized.

"You *must* go," she whispered fiercely when the laughter died away. "Someone might see you. Might see us and perceive your disguise."

"I told you, being seen doesn't concern me."

"It does *me*."

"That is quite evident, faintheart."

"Nicholas . . . !" she said, losing patience.

"Perhaps you're right. A ball is no place for such a serious discussion. But we still need to talk about our marriage."

"Yes, of course. But not now."

"Very well, later." He raised her fingers to his lips and brushed a light kiss there. "I will find you after the ball."

When Aurora nervously withdrew her hand, he reached up to touch her cheek. She shivered with the same warm shimmering sensation his touch always aroused in her. The dark awareness in his eyes told her clearly he knew how he affected her.

She watched as he replaced his eye patch and once more became the dashing buccaneer. He went to the door then, and gave her a final lingering glance before disappearing from the room.

Aurora remained where she was, still feeling the overwhelming impact of his presence, still reeling from his startling revelation.

Her notorious husband of one night was very much alive. And she had no earthly idea what to do about it.

Chapter Eight

His kiss, his slightest caress, left me breathless and trembling.

Nicholas frowned as he sat in the darkened carriage, waiting for his wife to appear. *Wife.* It wasn't a term that sat easily with him. He had escaped hanging, only to find himself fettered by chains of matrimony.

Apparently he wasn't the only one averse to such chains. Lady Aurora hadn't seemed at all eager to acknowledge the legal bond they'd formed under admittedly desperate circumstances. His return had shocked her, but she was clearly more discomfited by the thought of being tied to him for life.

He was just as unnerved.

He'd frankly been tempted to ignore that major complication in his life. He could simply have remained in America and avoided dealing with the issue of his marriage, perhaps for years to come. And yet his conscience hadn't allowed it. For too long he'd evaded his familial responsibilities, Nick reflected. It was more than time to satisfy his obligations, regardless of his own personal desires.

And in all honor, he couldn't simply dismiss the existence of a wife . . . or what he owed Aurora.

It was solely because of her that he was even alive. She'd made it possible for him to honor his solemn oath to his father, which had meant more to him than whether he lived or died. And she'd kept her promise to care for his sister, seeing Raven successfully launched into society. Raven professed to be essentially satisfied with her new life, despite her disdainful, haughty relatives, and claimed Aurora had not only made her stay bearable, but had become a dear friend as well.

He couldn't forget Aurora's sacrifice or pretend it had never happened. Nor would it be fair to her—to either of them—to leave such a volatile powder keg primed to blow up in their faces at some future date.

They were still wed. No matter that necessity had compelled him to make her his wife. The vows they had spoken were real. As was the night of passion they had shared. The memory of it haunted Nicholas mercilessly.

For a moment his eyes narrowed. He'd had ample time during the past four months to convince himself that the golden-haired siren he remembered so vividly was merely a condemned prisoner's fantasy. That the bond he'd felt that night was a primal need for intimacy brought on by desperation. No woman could possibly be as desirable as recollection painted Aurora Demming.

Tonight, however, had proved him wrong. Her cool, regal beauty was as stunning as he remembered, his attraction to her just as intense. Seeing her again was like taking a fist to the gut.

The temptation she presented was very real, if their first encounter was anything to judge by. Just touching her had made him hard in an instant, made him crave the wild sweetness of her body beneath him. . . .

Nicholas tightened his jaw, forcibly reining in his lustful urges. He hadn't expected Lady Aurora to be so set against acknowledging their marriage. She was bound to resist if he tried to claim her as his wife. Yet until that issue was settled between them, he had no business contemplating taking her to bed. He had no business even touching her.

Despite the gaiety of the masquerade, Aurora felt no joy for the remainder of the evening, only dismay and uncertainty and an ever-mounting tension. Nicholas had promised to seek her out after the ball, but she had yet to recover from the shock of seeing him, let alone compose herself enough to hold a rational discussion about their marital status. She could only hope for a reprieve until she'd had time for reflection.

Eager to take an early leave, she found Raven to say good night. They had no opportunity, however, to speak privately about Nicholas's remarkable return from the dead—and barely a moment to exchange promises to meet tomorrow for their usual morning ride—before Raven was whisked away by another dance partner.

By coincidence, Aurora encountered Lord Clune as she prepared to descend the grand staircase to the front door. When he offered to escort her to her carriage, she demurred politely. "You needn't trouble yourself, my lord."

"It is no trouble to enjoy the company of such a beautiful lady."

Aurora knew she should rebuff his casual flattery, but she was too distracted even to respond.

The street was crowded with any manner of vehicles, but the servants leaped to do the earl's bidding, and Aurora's carriage was summoned in short order.

"I have an early engagement tomorrow," Clune said as he handed her into the barouche, "but I hope to see you some morning in the park."

"Very well, Lord Clune," Aurora replied, just wishing to be rid of him.

"Sweet dreams, my dear."

She scarcely heard his courteous behest, for as the door closed behind her, a strong hand reached out to support her elbow and settle her on the seat.

Aurora bit back a gasp, while her heart rose to her throat. In the dim interior she could make out a shadowy figure beside her. *Nicholas.*

She could only stare as the carriage began to move forward. She had not dreamed him. He was truly the man she had wed, and the same sensations quivered through her at his nearness, just as powerful as they'd been four months ago.

His tone, however, lacked any of its previous warmth when he spoke. "Would you care to tell me what that was about?"

"About?" Aurora said rather breathlessly.

"Clune's pursuit of you."

"He is not pursuing me."

Nicholas reached toward her and removed her silver mask, evidently wanting to see her face. "You expect me to believe he feels no interest in you?"

Taken aback by his tone, she gazed at Nicholas warily. "He was simply being kind, accompanying me to my carriage."

"And you are so very appreciative of his kindness." His voice held a hard edge of what could be anger. "Have you forgotten your husband so soon, Aurora?"

"I never forgot you," she replied earnestly.

"No? You are hardly the picture of the grieving widow. Within four months of my supposed death, my lovely widow is attending masquerades and making assignations with noted rakehells."

Aurora's confusion at his unexpected attack melted into annoyance. "I have had enough criticism from my father regarding my conduct, Nicholas. I don't require it from you as well."

"Criticism seems deserved in this instance."

"I assure you," she retorted, "until now I have made every effort to avoid any hint of scandal. I attended tonight's ball for Raven's sake, because she begged me to— But I cannot comprehend why I must defend myself to you."

There was a pause. Aurora could feel Nicholas's gaze searching her. "So you weren't encouraging Clune?" His tone seemed to soften.

"No, not in the least. Our relationship is not what you're implying. He is merely a distant acquaintance. He is also one of the few people who never condemned me for my ill-considered marriage."

Nicholas's pause was longer this time. "Have these past few months been difficult for you, then?"

"You might say so," Aurora replied with an edge of cynicism. "I gained more than a little notoriety when I wed you, a criminal on the gallows. My father was outraged . . ." She bit off the remark, not wanting to dwell on her father's violent reaction. "Suffice it to say that I am no longer received in certain polite circles."

"I regret you had to suffer because of me," Nicholas said finally.

A little mollified, she studied him. Her eyes had adjusted to the dimness of the carriage, and in the moonlight filtering through the window, she could just make out his handsome features. He was no figment of her fevered imagination. He was the same incredibly vital man she remembered, every inch flesh and blood and rock-hard muscle, with the same strong face, the same fathomless eyes, the same sensuous mouth . . . She stopped herself abruptly.

"It has not been so bad, to be truthful," she said. "Your cousin Wycliff was extraordinarily helpful, offering the protection of his name and consequence. And he saw to all the financial particulars, just as you requested of him in your letter. Your settlement was more than generous, Nicholas. It allowed me to purchase a house of my own here in London."

His dark eyes held hers. "But you've come to regret your decision to wed me."

"No." She shook her head. "I don't regret it. You saved me from a repugnant marriage and allowed me independence from my father. It is just that . . . neither of us intended our union to last. We both thought it would end when . . . when you . . ."

"When I died. That still doesn't change the fact that we are legally wed."

A troubled frown creased her brow. "I don't see how we can possibly acknowledge our marriage, even if we wished to. You cannot risk having your identity discovered. Revealing you as my husband would ensure your arrest at the very least, and likely your death."

"I told you, I don't intend to reveal myself. I am here as my cousin Brandon."

"That disguise will be flimsy at best. Even with the change to your hair, you are sure to be recognized."

"I don't think so. I haven't spent much time in England lately. Three years ago I visited for an extended period, but my last trip was very brief."

"Clune remembers you well enough. Just this evening he was recounting tales of your wilder exploits. And he is a very clever man, despite his appearance of indolence."

When Nicholas remained silent, Aurora's gaze raked over his pirate's attire. He wore a black cloak over his tunic now, tied loosely at the neck, but she could see the lethal-looking saber at his side.

"How can you hope to keep your identity secret," she asked, "if you insist on flaunting yourself this way? It was incredibly brazen of you to appear in public dressed as a pirate."

His teeth flashed white in the darkness. "I thought it perfectly appropriate."

Aurora found herself drawing a breath of exasperation at his recklessness. "You cannot be seen with me, Nicholas. I would never be able to explain your presence."

"But you can. You can simply say that I am your late husband's cousin. With such a close familial relationship, our acquaintance will be considered unexceptional."

"You seem to be forgetting one very important matter."

"And what is that?"

"Your sister. You should think of Raven when you contemplate such a rash scheme. If the truth comes out and you're hanged, I, as your wife, would be instantly embroiled in a scandal, and as my ward, Raven would be tarnished by the same brush. Surely you don't want to jeopardize her chances for a good match."

"No. That's the last thing I would want, after going to all this trouble to see her established in society."

She contemplated him for a long moment. "Do you seriously want me for your wife?"

His expression remained enigmatic. "I don't see that I have much choice."

His resignation surprised her. She had expected him to be as eager to find a way out of their dilemma as she was.

"Nicholas," Aurora said slowly, hoping logic would make him reconsider, "we should be sensible about this. There are any number of reasons why a true marriage between us would never work. You are American, and I am English—and our countries are at war. You're an adventurer, one who embraces violence, while I . . . well, I am not adventuresome in the least, and I abhor any sort of violence. And furthermore, we . . . we don't love each other."

She hesitated, finding it strangely unsettling to present this last argument. Whatever she felt for Nicholas Sabine was most certainly not love. "I don't love you—any more than you love me. You only wed me for your sister's sake. Marriage should be about love and commitment, not an act of desperation."

His jaw tensed momentarily when she mentioned the word *love*. But then he relaxed back in his seat with a rueful frown, crossing his arms over his chest and lazily stretching out his long legs. "No, there is no love between us," he admitted.

Unaccountably Aurora winced when Nicholas agreed so readily. It was absurd to feel spurned simply because he disavowed any love for her. A reckless adventurer like Nicholas Sabine was unlikely to give his heart to any woman, particularly one to whom he'd been shackled under duress.

"So you see?" she observed. "There is no point in our trying to remain together. The simple fact remains that I don't wish to be your wife. And you don't truly wish to be my husband."

"There is just one problem," Nicholas said slowly, eyeing her speculatively. "Annulment is not an option, considering that we spent one very passionate night together."

The heated memory of that night flooded Aurora, while her awareness of Nicholas suddenly increased tenfold. His thigh lay alongside hers on the carriage seat; she could feel the heat radiating from his powerful body, seeping into hers.

He must have been remembering the same night, for his intense gaze slowly raked her. She could feel his eyes linger on her breasts, her hips, as if he were imagining exactly what lay beneath her domino and gown.

Aurora flushed, discomfited by the intimacy of his look and by the stark memory it conjured—of Nicholas moving between her thighs, filling her . . . Her breath caught at the unwelcome arrow of pleasure that shot through her.

Then his gaze lifted to settle on her abdomen. "I gather there was no fruit of our union."

"No," she murmured, unable to prevent a strange prick of disappointment that she didn't carry his child. But she shouldn't regret that outcome in the least. Were she breeding, she would doubtless have far more difficulty convincing Nicholas to free her from their marriage as she hoped to do.

"So . . ." he said slowly when she remained quiet, "you're proposing that we simply ignore the fact that we have a legal bond between us? That we live separate lives, pretend as if we aren't actually man and wife?"

"Well . . . I suppose that is what I am proposing. It would be infinitely more satisfactory to us both, more comfortable."

"I think you are forgetting something else, siren," he said softly.

"What?" She looked at him quizzically.

In response he reached out and slid his fingers behind her nape. Slowly, inexorably, he drew her to him, till she was pressed against him, her mouth nearly touching his.

"This . . ." he murmured as his lips found hers.

His kiss was spellbinding, shortening her breath and tightening her body. It was intimate and sexual and incredibly arousing, kindling a hunger in her that she'd never thought to experience again. She felt herself melting against him. . . .

When finally he left off, it was only to move his lips to her ear. "Ours wasn't a love match," he whispered huskily, "but the attraction between us is real enough. You feel the same fire I do, sweeting. How can we pretend it doesn't exist?"

Dazed from his drugging, claiming kiss, Aurora tried to regain her bearings. Her hands were pressed against Nicholas's chest, while she was nearly draped over him, his body supporting her . . . and the carriage had slowed to a halt. Dear God . . .

Alarm rose up in her as she realized they had arrived at their destination, her new home. Any instant now a footman would open the carriage door to help her descend.

Pushing away from Nicholas, she sat up in a panic. "We *cannot* be seen together like this. . . ."

When she reached for the door handle, Nicholas forestalled her by lightly grasping her wrist.

"Let me go!" she exclaimed in a desperate undertone.

"For now I will, Aurora, but this discussion is far from over."

She didn't respond, instead hurrying from the carriage before her servants could detect the presence of the sensual pirate who was also her husband.

Aurora's maid helped her prepare for bed. By the time she dismissed Nell and retired, it was past midnight, yet she was too restless to sleep. She lay in the darkness, staring at the canopy overhead, her mind feverishly occupied with thoughts of Nicholas. Her skin was still flushed from their last encounter, her lips still burning from his kiss.

How was it possible one man could have such a devastating effect on her? How could he wield such emotional power? His mere nearness left her breathless, her senses spinning. His simplest touch aroused her, reminding her of the captivating passion of their wedding night . . . the same incredible passion that filled the journal.

With an oath, Aurora rolled over, throwing off most of the covers. Her bedchamber was too warm, even though the windows had been left open. *She* was too warm.

You feel the same fire I do. She had indeed felt the fire he kindled in her so effortlessly. She had fled the carriage in a state of panic because of it, fearing not only discovery but what Nicholas was doing to her. She had left him to his own devices—

A sudden thought struck her. She had failed even to inquire whether he had somewhere to stay for the night. With his cousin Wycliff out of the country, Nicholas would have no assured welcome— But he was an adventurer, a fearless world traveler. He was quite accustomed to caring for himself without her help. She was *not* responsible for him, even if he was her husband.

Husband. Aurora buried her face in the pillow. Did she have any right to reject him? She was legally bound to him.

Sweet mercy, what was she to do? While she was elated that Nicholas hadn't been hanged, she most certainly did not want him for her husband.

It was alarming to consider such a prospect. She had little doubt he would wreak havoc with her structured, peaceful life, strip away the equanimity she'd finally achieved. Already tonight she had experienced more violent emotion in one night than she'd felt in months—shock, anger, dismay, vexation, fear, joy . . .

Abruptly Aurora crushed that reflection. Her joy at seeing Nicholas again was nothing more than relief that a courageous man's life had been spared. She was glad he was alive. Even so, she deplored the way he made her feel. He set her nerves on edge with his commanding presence and intense vitality. She couldn't even hold a simple conversation with him with any semblance of equanimity.

She shouldn't have to endure such emotional turmoil in her life, not when she had never asked to become his wife. Logically, she had right on her side. Living together forever as husband and wife was no part of the bargain they'd agreed to.

She didn't want to spend her life with a man she didn't love, who didn't love her. A man who could die at any moment. Nicholas had dismissed the danger of his discovery, much to her dismay and exasperation, but the peril was very real. He was risking his life to remain in England.

She didn't want to live in terror that he would be taken from her. She had already lost Geoffrey— Indeed, she had already lost Nicholas once. She would *not* go through that despair again.

No, he couldn't possibly remain her husband. She would simply have to make him see reason.

Nicholas studied his sleeping wife in the faint moonlight, contemplating the vision of loveliness she made.

He shouldn't be here, alone with Aurora, in her bedchamber, but he hadn't been able to keep away. Experience at negotiating a ship's rigging had allowed him to make short work of the oak tree outside her window.

He stood over her slumbering form, drinking in her beauty—the ivory complexion, the delicately arched brows, the full lips that were parted slightly in slumber. Her vivid blue eyes were closed now, but her vibrant hair glimmered like spun silver in the moonlit darkness.

My wife. It was incredible to think of her as such.

In the past he had never willingly considered settling down with one woman. His rootless life had left no room for the encumbrance of a wife. He'd always wanted freedom, always had an insatiable thirst for adventure, with danger and excitement his only mistresses. He had never wished for more—until he met Aurora.

Why was she so unique? He'd encountered countless beauties in his travels, in the lavish and licentious kingdoms of Europe, the exotic lands of Africa, the mysterious realms of the East. But none had ever stirred his senses as this woman had the night they were bound together in matrimony. For months now she had haunted his dreams, as enchanting and beguiling as any siren.

Reaching down, he lifted a treasure of gold strands, letting them glide through his fingers. Aurora was well bred and demure and emotionally wary, yet he'd had a tantalizing glimpse of her hidden fire beneath the layers of reserve, an experience he amazingly wanted to repeat.

Slowly, purposefully, Nicholas tangled his hand in her silken hair. He remembered the taste of her, remembered every inch of her skin, every lush curve and hollow. He remembered himself sinking into the silky fire of her. . . .

Desire, heavy and urgent, tightened his body with startling intensity. A desire he couldn't possibly act on just yet.

Reluctantly Nicholas forced himself to release her hair. He couldn't dispute Aurora. They were altogether wrong for each other. And it was indeed dangerous for him to remain in England. They both might be happier if he simply disappeared from her life.

But although he had listened to her logical arguments with all seriousness, none had convinced him it was right to try to sever their marriage vows.

In the first place, Aurora didn't realize the difficulty of ending a fully consummated union. And in the second . . . the second was the only one that truly counted. His obligation to his father was a stronger reason by far to see this marriage through, Nick acknowledged. He'd sworn he would assume the responsibilities he had neglected for so long, which meant taking a wife and starting a family.

And to be honest, if he had to be shackled to anyone, Aurora was a much more agreeable candidate than most. The physical attraction between them was a stronger basis for a relationship than many wedded couples had. And merely because he was wed didn't mean he had to give up his previous life or cherished freedom entirely.

No, he was resigned to the marriage. He'd had four long months to accustom himself to the idea, while she'd had merely a few hours. Given enough time and persuasion, Aurora would come around to his point of view.

Careful not to wake the sleeping beauty, Nicholas stripped down to his breeches, then joined Aurora on the bed, stretching out beside her.

He wasn't certain if the intimate bonds they'd forged that night were a desperate prisoner's fantasy or something deeper. But it didn't matter. It didn't matter, either, that he would have difficulty convincing Aurora to accept him as her husband.

He had come to England to claim his wife, and he wasn't leaving until he accomplished his goal.

Chapter Nine

His hands on my flesh were magical, caressing and claiming, arousing a fierce desire deep within me.

If this was a dream, she never wanted to wake. The sensual pleasure was so very real . . . Nicholas at her back, her buttocks nestled in the cradle of his thighs . . . his heat and hardness searing her through the thin cambric of her nightdress. His hand had delved inside her bodice to fondle her naked breasts, and she could feel her pouting flesh tightening, swelling, thrusting out to seek his touch.

Aurora moaned, yet he relentlessly continued caressing her, kneading softly, his palm rubbing over the sensitive peaks. When she arched instinctively, pressing with wanton eagerness against his stroking palm, his fingers deliberately closed over one nipple, plucking the taut bud. Her throbbing breasts tightened in an aching rush, while a flaming spark of pleasure flared between her thighs.

The shivery desire inside her built higher as he tormented the swollen crest, and she moved restlessly against him, yearning for release from the mounting tension.

As if knowing what she needed, he withdrew his hand from her bodice and swept it lower, over her rib cage, stroking her belly, his breath hot and moist against her cheek as he whispered soft encouragements in her ear. Drawing up the hem of her nightdress then, he slid his hard, warm palm along her thigh, tantalizing on her bare skin.

When his fingers slid into the tangled curls between her legs, Aurora gasped, incredibly aroused by his erotic caresses. His fingertips moved over her with shocking intimacy, parting the feminine folds. Her body grew moist as his expert touch rasped over her most sensitive flesh, finding the exquisite pressure points, stroking her slick bud of pleasure with tantalizing skill. The fever inside her intensified, and the ragged sound she made was one of savage excitement.

Desperately wanting him to assuage the throbbing ache, she thrust her hips back helplessly against his muscular loins, grinding into him.

She heard his rough whisper in her ear, coaxing her to release. "Yes, siren . . . surrender to the pleasure."

On the verge of ecstasy, she began to writhe, straining toward a mounting, burning frenzy. When his fingers slowly thrust inside her, her deep inner muscles clutched around them. He only increased the rhythm. Frantic with need, she surged against his hand, shuddering and crying out with the powerful, pulsating climax.

Her own sobs woke her. Awash in trembling sensation, Aurora lay dazed and unmoving, her breathing harsh and shallow. For a bewildering moment she was unable to gain her bearings. This was her bedchamber, she could tell in the gray morning light coming through the open curtains. The heat at her back was also very real . . . and very male, as were the warm lips nuzzling her nape. . . .

Nicholas. She went rigid. His hard, muscular forearm was draped across her body, his hand nestled erotically between her thighs, his rigid arousal still throbbing against her buttocks.

Dear heaven, she hadn't dreamed him. He was in her bed, as if he had every right to be there. He had stolen into her room while she slept, brazenly aroused her to ecstasy. . . .

Her cheeks flamed with mortification as she tried to gather her scattered senses. Almost leaping from the bed, Aurora spun around to face him, totally flustered.

Nicholas was lying on top of the sheet, wearing breeches but nothing else. His cloak and shirt and saber were piled on a chair, she realized, his boots on the floor. His ebony hair was tousled from sleep, while the shadow of stubble on his strong jaw made him look very much a disreputable pirate. More discomfiting, his dark gaze was fixed on the swell of her breasts, partially exposed by the open bodice of her nightdress.

With a muttered oath, Aurora straightened her disheveled bodice and began fastening the buttons, appalled not only by the forbidden liberties Nicholas had taken with her, but by her own unwitting, sensual response.

"How did you get in here?" she demanded, not knowing whether she was angrier at him for his devious seduction or at herself for succumbing to it. She had planned to remain coolly indifferent when they next met, maintaining a strict control over her responses. Yet once again he had thrown her equilibrium totally off balance, casting her emotions into chaos.

Casually Nicholas propped himself up on one elbow and nodded toward the open window. "I apprenticed on my father's ships from the time I was ten and learned to negotiate a rigging. I can certainly climb a tree."

Aurora glanced briefly at the window, then shook her head, unnerved. "Well, you can just leave the same way you came."

When he made no move to go, she snatched up the robe lying on the foot of her bed and put it on, buttoning up the high collar.

"I cannot believe your temerity, coming here and . . ." She faltered, unwilling to contemplate how he'd kindled her to passion in her sleep, entirely against her will. It was deceitful, taking advantage of her vulnerability when she was helpless to defend herself. She *hated* being so vulnerable. . . .

Lifting her chin, Aurora made a supreme effort to regain her composure. "You are making," she said, "quite an annoying habit of startling me to death, appearing suddenly and uninvited."

In response, Nicholas sat up and propped the pillows

against the headboard, relaxing back among them. "You left your mask in the carriage when you ran away, so I thought I would return it to you. Like Cinderella's slipper."

Aurora couldn't help but stare at him, unwillingly admiring his bronzed skin and naked, muscled shoulders. She clenched her teeth, vexed at the way his physical attributes made her breathless. His knowing gaze irked her even more. He understood quite well the effect his near nudity had on her.

It was all she could do to keep her tone cool. "That hardly excuses your gall in sneaking into my room like a thief. You seem determined to cause a scandal—"

"I'm only determined to talk to you, love. We never finished our discussion about our future relationship."

"Well, my bedchamber is not the place to do it!"

"I'm not sure I agree with that," he murmured in a velvet undervoice laced with humor. "I can think of few places more enjoyable."

"Nicholas, you *have* to leave. *Now,* at once! Before I have you thrown out."

His expression turned thoughtful. "I must confess, I expected a more cordial reception than this from my wife. On our wedding night you were much warmer."

"On our wedding night, I thought you were about to die. We both thought so."

"You can't deny the fire we both felt that night."

"I can!" Aurora drew a measured breath, striving for control. "If we felt anything at all between us then, it was only an illusion . . . brought on by the despair of the moment."

"No," Nicholas said slowly. "It was very real, sweetheart. I didn't imagine it. And you are the same sensual, responsive woman I remember from that night. I know that now for a certainty."

Heat flushed her cheeks as she recalled just how wantonly she had responded to his erotic caresses moments ago.

She might have argued with him further but for the soft

rap on the door. Aurora froze, watching in horror as her bedchamber door started to open.

In three strides she was across the room, pushing the door shut again.

"My lady," a female voice called through the oak paneling. "I've brought your morning chocolate."

"One moment," Aurora replied, almost frantic as she tried to think what to do. If the maid were to find Nicholas here, she would have no shred of reputation left.

Spinning, Aurora moved quickly over to the bed and yanked the bed curtains closed, concealing Nicholas behind the ivory brocade. She heard his soft chuckle as she returned to open the door, and had to grit her teeth at his misplaced humor. How could he put her in such a vulnerable position and *laugh* about it?

Stepping back, she allowed the maid to enter the room. Her heart hammering, Aurora tried not to glance at the bed curtains as the girl set the breakfast tray down on the bedside table.

"Thank you, Molly. You may go now."

"Yes, my lady."

With a curtsey, the maid left the room, and Aurora firmly bolted the door behind her.

"Is it safe yet?" Nicholas asked, his tone husky with laughter.

"Keep your voice down," she demanded in a fierce whisper. "The servants will hear you." She pulled open the curtains to find him lounging negligently on the bed, his dark eyes dancing. His audacity riled her to no end.

"There is no need for panic, Aurora."

"That is easy for you to say. It isn't *your* reputation that will be in shreds if a strange man is found in your bed."

"If a man were found in my bed, I expect my reputation would suffer no small amount. But there is little chance of that happening, since I am inordinately fond of women."

"Nicholas, this is not in the least amusing!"

"Oh, I think it is. I find it fascinating to see you in a passion. It requires work to make you lose that cool, regal air of yours."

Aurora raised her eyes to the ceiling, struggling for patience. "*Will* you put your clothes on and go away?"

"Where do you expect me to go?"

She controlled her vexation long enough to give him a quizzical look. "Don't you have somewhere to stay?"

"And if I said no? Would you take pity on me and invite me to live here with you?"

"I would have my butler help you to find lodgings," Aurora said repressively.

"You needn't trouble yourself, love."

"Seriously, where are you staying?"

"Aboard ship at the moment. But the docks are too far away for convenience, so I mean to take rooms at a hotel. I thought of staying with Wycliff—Brand claims a slight acquaintance with him—but Lucian is out of town, and the coincidence would only invite suspicion."

"I should think so," Aurora said in a tart undervoice. "You are mad even to be in this country. You are going to get yourself killed."

Ignoring her prediction, Nicholas glanced around the room. "This is a handsome bedchamber—I imagine the entire house is. You said you purchased it with your marriage settlement?"

"Yes." She gave him a questioning look. "You don't mean to go back on your word and nullify the settlement, do you?"

"Not at all. You earned it with your services to my sister."

"Yet you seem intent on destroying all my efforts on her behalf—and on giving me heart failure in the process."

"No, sweeting. I only want to talk. There is still the minor matter of our marriage to be resolved." He patted the mattress beside him. "Sit here beside me."

Aurora eyed him warily. "Surely you don't expect me to trust you after what you just did?"

"I thought you didn't wish the servants to hear. They will, you know, if I have to shout at you across the room."

His amused look suggested a reckless disregard for the consequences of discovery, but she didn't care to put his rashness to the test. With extreme reluctance, Aurora perched on the edge of the bed and crossed her arms over her chest defensively. "Very well, you may talk."

He contemplated her for a moment. "You seem eager to forget that you still have a husband."

"I *am* eager. I never expected this complication in our relationship, you must realize that."

"I do."

"I fulfilled my side of our bargain, Nicholas. You know quite well that lifetime commitment was no part of it. Our agreement was for one night only."

"So it was."

"Ours was to be a marriage of convenience, merely that."

"And it is no longer convenient for you."

"Or for you, either, I'm sure. You never wanted me for your wife."

"I think I could be persuaded to change my mind."

She gave him a startled look.

"We never had the chance to know each other," Nicholas said slowly. "To see if we would suit."

"The answer to that is quite obvious. You know very well we would never suit. You would never be happy with me—nor I with you. I could never fit into your world, among pirates and adventurers, on board a fighting ship. I would never feel comfortable with that kind of existence."

"I was considering settling down after the war ends."

"In America?"

"Yes. My home is in Virginia. My mother and sisters live there."

"What are you saying? That you want me to give up my life and return there as your wife?"

"I expect you would have to, since I obviously cannot remain in England."

Her gaze turned troubled. "This is my home, Nicholas. I have no desire to leave the only life I've known, to live in America among strangers. The war between our countries could last for years, and who knows when I could ever return here, or even see my family and friends."

"I didn't think you were overly fond of your family."

"I am not. But that is not really the issue. What frightens me most is the violent life you lead, the dangerous risks you take. I couldn't bear waiting for you to come home from some far off land, not knowing if I would ever see you again, or if you had been killed. Look at the peril you are in now. You are a condemned man. You could be arrested and executed at any moment." She shook her head. "I have already mourned you once. I won't go through that again."

He remained silent, his dark eyes searching hers.

"There must be another solution," Aurora said finally. "One that doesn't entail us living together as man and wife."

"The only way I know of to dissolve our union is through divorce."

Aurora felt the color fade from her face. Divorce, even if one could be secured—which would be extremely difficult—would ruin her. "A divorce would be disastrous for me. It would brand me a pariah in society. I could never show my face in polite company again."

"Perhaps," he said musingly, "I could try to have an American court declare the marriage invalid. I might have a case, since I was compelled to wed under duress."

"Couldn't we simply go on as if you had never returned?" she asked earnestly. "What would be the harm in leading separate lives?"

He studied her for a moment. "You realize that as long as we're wed, neither of us can ever marry again?"

"I have no desire ever to marry. Once was enough." She

saw his eyebrow lift and bit her lip. "I didn't mean that the way it sounded. It's only that I suffered a great despair when I thought you dead, and I don't wish ever to endure that again. I vowed I would forget my loss and make a new life for myself. And I have thus far."

"I have a question," Nicholas said slowly. "Suppose we do remain legally bound. What happens if either of us should fall in love with someone else? You would certainly want to be free of the marriage then."

"There is little chance of my falling in love again. I loved Geoffrey for most of my life, and I don't believe I could ever love any man but him. But even if I could, I am determined I will never give my heart again. It is too painful to lose someone I care for."

Nicholas clenched his jaw for an instant, but then his mouth relaxed in a faint smile. "Have you considered my perspective? What if I come to love someone else?"

That possibility gave her an unaccountable jolt, but she dismissed it with a skeptical look. A rake like Nicholas Sabine was not likely to fall in love. "I doubt that will happen, but I will make you a promise. If you ever do find someone else to love, I will free you from our marriage. I'll agree to an annulment or a divorce—whatever it takes to end our union."

"So for now we do nothing?"

"Yes," she said, relieved that he intended to be reasonable. "In public we can pretend the other doesn't exist—"

"I am supposed to be your cousin by marriage. It would look odd if we failed to at least speak when we meet in public."

"Well, perhaps we could acknowledge the acquaintance in public."

"What about in private?"

"There is no reason for us to have any private contact." She gave him a stern look. "Or any contact at all. Indeed, I don't know why you are even considering remaining in England. You would do better to leave at once. If you remain, you will only get yourself killed. I couldn't bear that, Nicholas."

"Thank you for your concern, sweetheart, but I don't intend to die any time soon."

"You didn't intend to be imprisoned or sentenced to hang four months ago, either."

Nicholas cocked his head as he regarded her. "There is one other aspect we haven't considered. Carnal relations. If you and I are still wed, we cannot take other lovers without committing adultery."

Aurora felt her cheeks color. He wanted other lovers? Why that should bother her, she couldn't fathom. It would be unnatural for a man of Nicholas's lusty nature to give up carnal pleasures. And she would have no right to demand fidelity from him in any case, not if she asked to be free of their vows.

She forced a smile, attempting to sound worldly. "I understand many married men have affairs. I would have no objection to you seeking out other women or keeping a mistress if you wish."

"And what of you?" His intent gaze held hers.

"You needn't concern yourself with me on that score. I don't intend to take any lovers."

"A lifetime is a long time to remain celibate, especially for a woman as passionate as I know you to be."

She stood up abruptly, uncomfortable with the intimate turn of the conversation. "That reminds me. You entrusted me with another mission. . . ."

She went to her dressing table and drew out the jewel-encrusted journal, which was carefully wrapped in oil-cloth. "Raven's mother left this for you. It is the book your father gave her."

When she handed the package to Nicholas, he opened it curiously. "An expensive gift, obviously," he murmured.

"So it would seem—and rather old."

"What is it about?"

"It is a journal, written by a Frenchwoman who was en-slaved in a Turkish pasha's harem."

After reading the title, Nicholas thumbed through a few pages, then shot Aurora a glance. "You've read this?"

"Yes." She felt herself blushing again. "I wanted to see if it was appropriate for Raven. It most certainly is not."

"I would say not," he observed, giving her a long, vaguely amused look. "I doubt your upbringing prepared you for anything this erotic, either."

"Of course it didn't," Aurora replied. She had been shocked by the explicitness and sensual detail of the jour-nal . . . and yet captivated at the same time. Against her better judgement, her breeding, even her will, she had found herself drawn into the beautiful, erotic recounting of the Frenchwoman's love affair with her master, a tale of smol-dering passion, so vividly told. She had actually read the journal more than once. She knew some passages by heart, although she had no intention of admitting it to Nicholas.

"Now that you are here," she told him, "I can turn it over to you. You can be the one to decide when Raven is old enough to have it."

"I look forward to reading it with great anticipation. Now, where were we in our discussion?"

"We had concluded our discussion."

"Not quite," Nicholas said. "Before you changed the subject, I was remarking on your passionate nature, you will recollect. I was saying that I don't imagine you'll be happy remaining celibate your entire life."

Her discomfort returned in full measure, as did her vex-ation with Nicholas. A discussion of such private issues was wholly out of bounds, despite his apparent belief that he had a right to such intimacy.

Aurora gave him her coolest glance. "I believe that is entirely my concern, Nicholas. I also believe that I have discharged my promise to you, and that we have said all there is to say. It is time now for you to go."

"Not yet."

She tensed. "What do you mean, not yet?"

"Before you take a vow of celibacy, you should consider what you are rejecting. Come here, Aurora."

Her look turned wary. "Why?"

"Because I want to kiss you."

"You must be jesting."

"Not at all. We started off on the wrong foot last night, with my reproaching you for forgetting your widowhood. I would like to make up for it."

Nervously Aurora backed up a step. "There is no need for you to do anything but leave, Nicholas. Immediately. You have no right to be here—"

"Actually, I do. I am your husband. The law gives a husband the right to share his wife's bed."

"You are *not* my husband. In the eyes of the world, I was widowed four months ago."

"Need I remind you how curious your servants would be to find me here?" His half smile irked her almost as much as his veiled threat. "I have only to call out and they will come running."

"You wouldn't dare. You would never risk exposing your identity."

His eyebrow lifted, as if to ask whether she wanted to test her theory.

Resolving to call his bluff, Aurora put her hands on her hips in defiance. "Now that I think of it, I could report you to any number of governmental authorities. I expect the navy would be eager to recapture an escaped pirate."

A gleam lit his dark eyes. "I don't think you will turn me in. You don't want to see my neck stretched on the gallows."

Her frustration reached the boiling point. What she wanted was to wipe that knowing look off Nicholas's handsome face. It was utterly underhanded to use her concern for him as leverage to force her to do as he wished.

She couldn't possibly expose him, though. Not only because she was desperate to avoid the scandal that would ensue if he was found in her bedchamber, but because she couldn't bear to see any harm come to Nicholas. She nearly stamped her foot in vexation.

"You know very well I cannot denounce you," she finally muttered. "I don't want your death on my conscience."

"I knew you were a compassionate woman."

"Well, I thought you were a *gentleman*," Aurora retorted, infuriated by his reckless, irresistible charm.

"I am a gentleman."

"You most certainly are not. A gentleman would honor his promise."

"Which promise was that?" Nicholas asked, a lazy fire in his eyes. "The one regarding our union, where I pledged to love and cherish my bride?"

"The one where we agreed to one night of marriage."

"One night wasn't enough," he said softly.

"It will have to be. I don't intend to play the wanton with you."

Nicholas held out his hand. "Come here and kiss me, Aurora, before I decide to raise my voice."

She glared at him. "This is blackmail!"

"So it is."

"You are despicable."

"And you are as beautiful as I remember . . . more so, since the sadness in your eyes is gone. Come here. I won't claim my marital rights. I only want a kiss."

The velvet edge in his voice didn't reassure her in the least. Yet he might very well reveal his presence to her servants unless she did as he wanted. "One kiss, and then you will go?"

"If you insist."

"You swear it?"

"Unequivocally."

Every muscle in her body stiff, Aurora unwillingly complied. When she moved to stand beside the bed, however, Nicholas made no attempt to kiss her. Instead he took her hand.

Gazing up at her, he drew her forefinger completely into

his mouth and suckled. A treacherous heat radiated suddenly from the pit of Aurora's stomach, and she had to stifle a gasp.

"You said one *kiss*," she said through clenched teeth.

"You can't deny the pleasure you feel," he murmured. "Your heart is beating much too rapidly for you to claim disinterest."

"Will you please just get on with it?"

"So impatient," Nicholas replied lightly.

He drew her down and pressed her back upon the bed, then eased his body over hers. She could feel the strength of him against her—the powerful granite of his thighs, the flat, hard belly, the muscles rippling in his chest and shoulders.

He remained that way for a long moment, gazing down into her eyes, his fingers cradling her cheek.

"Well?" Aurora demanded breathlessly, trying to ignore the temptation of his beautiful mouth.

"Sheathe your claws, siren. I only want to remind you of what you would be missing . . . the pleasure to be found in my arms," he whispered before his lips lowered to cover hers.

Chapter Ten

The strength of his desire alarmed me. Yet I was more frightened of myself, of the fierce desire he stirred within me.

Hunger ran rampant through Nicholas as he drank of Aurora's trembling mouth. Her lips were incredibly soft, her warmth feeding his senses like flame.

When she stirred restlessly beneath him, his hand closed in the silk of her hair, holding her still for his kiss, his tongue thrusting slow and deep, penetrating in a blatant imitation of what he yearned to do between her thighs.

In only moments, she was pressing against his fully aroused body, her hips rocking against his, seeking his hardness. He felt a surge of triumph at her helpless response. When she moaned softly, Nicholas shuddered, so swollen with need he felt near to bursting.

Yet he was the one who broke off the kiss. In an agony of desire, he rolled over onto his back, breathing harshly. He had vastly overestimated his control, he knew that now.

Draping an arm over his forehead, Nick sucked in a deep breath. He was still aching, his hardened shaft cramping beneath his breeches. But he didn't dare continue kissing Aurora. It had been a mistake even to touch her.

Beside him, she unsteadily rose up on her elbow, her hair sliding over her shoulders in an untamed fall of pale gold. She looked shaky, uncertain, as she gazed at him with wonder and concern in her wide blue eyes. She'd felt the same powerful forces that he had, he knew. The pure carnal desire. The raw, primal need that still throbbed through him. The intense, heart-wrenching feeling of intimacy that he'd never experienced with any other woman.

Oh, yes, the bond between them was very real.

"You can't pretend," he murmured, his voice edged with hoarseness, "that there is nothing between us."

"That . . . was only lust."

"Four months is indeed a long time for a man to be without a woman," he said wryly. "But I've endured longer abstinences. And my lust doesn't explain your response, dearheart. Come now, admit it. You wanted more than a kiss from me."

Her hand rose to her lips, still lush and wet from his kiss, and another fierce ache surged through Nicholas. The temptation to take her was so great, he had to lock his jaw against the yearning inside him.

He had best leave, before his resistance shattered, before he gathered Aurora in his arms and ravished her till they were both too exhausted to care about such matters as scandal and mortal danger.

Untangling himself, Nick rose and began to dress, aware that she was watching him warily.

"You really are leaving?" Aurora asked finally as he shrugged into his tunic.

"I said I would."

Evidently she didn't trust him to keep his word about settling for merely a kiss. And she clearly was still troubled about their situation.

"But what about our marriage, Nicholas? You do agree that we should not try to carry on as husband and wife? That we should live separate lives?"

Now wasn't at all a good time to admit he intended to claim her for his wife. "That does seem the best option at the moment."

He could almost sense her relief. His response evidently emboldened her to remark further.

"I do wish you would reconsider remaining in England and return home."

"My business here isn't yet concluded," Nicholas replied—not really a lie; Aurora *was* his business. He started to tie his costume's sash around his waist, but changed his mind. "I will, however, leave my sash and saber in your keeping. A pirate wandering the streets might arouse suspicion."

"It might indeed," Aurora replied with a renewed tartness. "You are bound to be discovered if you insist on this mad impersonation."

He flashed her a bold grin and finished dressing. When he had flung his cloak around his shoulders, tying the cords loosely at his throat, she was still regarding him with disapproval.

Nicholas hesitated. This was the first time in his life he could remember leaving a woman's bed without first finding satisfaction—or fully giving it. And this woman was his *wife*. With her sleep-tousled hair and passion-bruised lips, Aurora was so beautiful it made him ache.

He couldn't help himself. Returning to the bed, he took her face in his hands and kissed her hard.

"Nicholas!" she exclaimed breathlessly, drawing back. "You promised you would leave!"

"Lower your voice, love, or the servants will hear," he warned. "That was only a farewell kiss. It might be days before we even speak again."

He picked up the journal and tucked it inside the pocket of his cloak. Going to the window then, he eased himself up to sit on the sill and swung his legs over.

With one last, lingering look, he disappeared.

Aurora fell back on the bed, relief flooding her, her heart still beating violently from his kiss, her body throbbing with the restless yearning he'd kindled in her.

It frightened her, the tumult of emotions Nicholas aroused in her so effortlessly: exasperation, anger, exhilaration, desire . . .

He was not the kind of man for which a woman could hope to maintain indifference. He was unpredictable, bold, threatening. The kind of man who would overwhelm a

woman with passion, with desire, with need. Who would
command her heart as well as her body.

He demanded my surrender, body and soul.

Aurora shuddered, remembering the passage from the
journal that so perfectly described the danger the Frenchwoman had been forced to face. Desiree had become a
captive in more than physical terms; against her will she
had lost her heart to her strong, vital, compelling prince.

Nicholas was just as compelling, just as dangerous as
the journal's prince. His touch as sensual and magical.

Aurora's hand rose to her breast, the burning memory of
his caresses still vivid in her mind. She was so very vulnerable to him. As her husband, Nicholas had the right to
such intimacies, and more. Yet she didn't dare give him
any further chance to take the brazen liberties he had last
night. She couldn't afford even to allow him near her. She
could no longer trust him. More damning, she could no
longer trust herself.

When they had wed, she'd thought Nicholas an honorable
man, but he obviously had no qualms about subterfuge or
deception—evidenced by his previous ruse where he'd fab-
ricated his burial, or his current fraud, assuming his cousin's
identity. And he had stolen into her room and conducted an
intimate, sensual assault on her while she slept. . . .

A traitorous heat flushed her body at the remembrance,
along with renewed anger at his gall.

She had countless reasons to be angry with Nicholas.
Not only did he lack scruples, not only was he recklessly
endangering his life and courting scandal, but he was acting as if he owned her—and using threats and extortion to
gain his way.

Having lived with her father's black temper for so long,
she *deplored* such violent emotions as anger, but in Nicholas's case, she welcomed it, indeed wanted to nurture it. As
long as she could sustain that dark sentiment, she could
hold any softer feelings for him at bay.

At least she had persuaded him to give up claiming her as his wife. Yet she couldn't congratulate herself. Even though he'd agreed they would maintain separate lives, she was certain she hadn't seen the last of Nicholas Sabine.

The hour was still early when Nicholas reached the mews near Lady Dalrymple's house, where the cream of Mayfair's pleasure and carriage horses were stabled. The cobblestone yard of the livery was bustling—lads grooming and saddling mounts and ostlers harnessing curricles for morning jaunts.

Nick had arranged to meet his sister there, but while he saw no sign of Raven, he soon caught sight of the Irish stablehand who had accompanied her from the Caribbean. O'Malley was leading out a large ebony Thoroughbred and a stockier groom's mount, both saddled for riding.

Intent on testing his disguise, Nicholas paused beside the Irishman. "I would like to hire an equipage for a few weeks," he remarked casually, "and perhaps a hack as well. Can you direct me to the proprietor?"

O'Malley, a hulking, gray-haired brute of a fellow, gave Nicholas a cursory glance. Evidently seeing a gentleman, he tipped his hat politely. "You'll be wanting Mr. Dobbs in that case, sir. You'll find him in the office at the end of the next aisle."

"Thank you." Nicholas hesitated, studying the black horse. "Magnificent animal. Your mistress always did have an eye for good horseflesh."

His gray head snapping up, O'Malley stared at him hard. " 'Tis a ghost I'm seeing, I'll be thinking," he said slowly.

Nick's mouth crooked in a smile. "No ghost, O'Malley. I bear a resemblance to a certain American pirate who wasn't hanged after all."

The look of amazement on his ruddy face turned to one of delight. "Well, I'll be a bleedin'—" He broke off with a sheepish grin. "Beg pardon, guv'nor. I never would have known you with your hair so dark."

"That is precisely my intention," Nicholas said. "I am here in England as Sabine's cousin from Boston, Mr. Brandon Deverill. I calculate that if I can slip by you with your keen eye, I should be able to fool anyone else who might have an acquaintance with me."

"Ah . . . I see. If you say so, sir. Does Miss Raven know the happy news?"

"I surprised her last night at her aunt's ball, but we had only a moment together. She's to meet me here shortly so we can have the chance to speak alone."

Always a clever man, O'Malley understood at once the need for discretion. "I'll be taking Satan back to his stall then, if it pleases you, sir. You can talk there, like you're looking him over for purchase."

Nicholas raised an eyebrow at the horse, who was standing docilely and mouthing the bit. "Satan?"

"He's a handful, aye, but for Miss Raven, he's a lamb. He belongs to Lady Aurora." At Nick's skeptical look, the Irishman grinned. " 'Tis true. Her ladyship prefers a bit of the devil in her horseflesh, too. And she's as fine a horsewoman as I've ever seen."

Nicholas digested that statement with surprise: the compliment was high praise coming from a man like O'Malley, who had practically been born on horseback.

"Lady Aurora," O'Malley added, "chose this fellow for Miss Raven when her aunt wanted to mount her on a plodder. Satan right snorted fire when she first tried him, but you know her. Never was a horse Miss Raven couldn't tame. The London gentlemen are the same way."

"So I understand," Nicholas said with wry amusement.

" 'Tis working just the way she planned—and the way her guardian, Mr. Sabine, wanted."

"Thank you for watching over her so well, O'Malley. I'm certain you have Sabine's undying gratitude."

The Irishman gave a hearty laugh. "Well, you should

know, you being his cousin and all. If you'll please to come with me, sir . . ." He tugged on his cap again and led the horses back to their stalls.

O'Malley made Raven an estimable protector, Nicholas reflected as he followed. His fears regarding her welfare had diminished greatly after seeing how ably the Irishman and Aurora were caring for her.

Raven made an appearance in only a few moments. A trifle breathless, she entered the stall and, without pausing, threw her arms around Nick's neck in a strangling hug.

"No need to choke me, pet," he said, laughing as he pried himself from her grasp.

"It is either that or shoot you," Raven retorted. When she drew back, however, her blue eyes were sparkling. "You *do* deserve to be shot, Nicholas. You have no conception of how I grieved for you—and Aurora, too. I've lived with such guilt, believing I got you killed. Why did you never send us word?"

"I was a trifle occupied at the time, getting out of the fix the British navy had devised for me and then preparing to come after you. And I felt sure you would have learned the news from someone on the islands."

"We never did, Nicholas."

He shook his head warningly. "I'll thank you to practice calling me Mr. Deverill in private, sweetheart, so you won't forget in public. Since Sabine was your guardian, his cousin would be only distantly connected to you."

"Ah, yes, I will have to remember."

"In fact, we should not be seen together in private at all."

A frown creasing her brow, she cast a cautious glance over her shoulder. O'Malley had taken up a position outside the stall's half door along with his mount, screening her and Nicholas from prying eyes.

"I sent my maid home just now," Raven said in a concerned voice, "so she wouldn't see me talking to you, but I didn't consider the danger to you. . . . It is quite dangerous for you even to be in England, isn't it?"

"There is the possibility that I might be apprehended as an escaped prisoner, yes."

"Why ever did you come here then?"

"I wanted to see how my hoyden of a sister fared, of course," Nicholas said teasingly. He surveyed her stylish riding habit of forest green velvet critically. With her vivacity and fresh beauty, Raven didn't look as if she'd risen unfashionably early after dancing half the night away. "From all appearances, you are doing quite well for yourself."

Her smile was wry. "Better than well. You would be proud of me, Nick . . . ah, Mr. Deverill. I recall you once said teaching me to behave with decorum would be like trying to turn a wild filly into a lady's mount. Well, I am quite tame now. Of course, a good deal of the credit goes to Aurora."

"Indeed?"

"I don't know what I would have done without her, truly. She is extremely accomplished and so highly regarded. . . . You couldn't have chosen anyone better to advise me. With her guidance, I've been able to face society's lions without being devoured alive. And if I am not betrothed by the end of the Season to an earl at the very least, I shall be very disappointed."

His amused expression sobered. "You're certain you can be happy with a cold-blooded marriage to an earl?"

Raven's blue eyes turned just as sober. "My happiness is beside the point. Mama wished me to make an advantageous match and marry into the nobility, and I won't fail her, Nicholas. As for cold-blooded, you know I have never wanted love. I won't make the same mistake Mama made, letting passion destroy my life, pining after a man even on my deathbed. And besides, being the mistress of my own household will be far preferable to living under my Aunt Dalrymple's thumb, where I cannot say two words without being reprimanded."

The stubborn set of her jaw gave way to a smile. "Thank heavens for Aurora. She has been so genuinely kind, and she shares my love of horses. I'm to meet her in the park for a gallop in a short while. . . . But enough about me, Nicholas. Tell me, how did Aurora take the news of your reincarnation?"

"She wasn't quite as delighted as you were," he said dryly.

"Only because she doesn't know you well enough yet." Raven's eyes grew wide. "Oh, my word, do you mean to take her back to America with you as your bride?"

Nicholas hesitated. "We haven't worked out our future yet. I imagine Aurora needs time simply to get over her shock at my reappearance."

"But you mean to claim her?"

"That is still in question," he admitted, not wanting to sound overconfident in his powers of persuasion.

"Your marriage was legal, was it not?"

"Entirely. But the issue is more complex than mere legality. Our marriage was supposed to be only temporary. I'm not certain Aurora wants me for a lifetime—or that she thinks I would make very good husband material. I'm known far more for my wild adventures than my stable respectability."

"Yes, but I remember you saying it was nearing time for you to settle down as your father wished. And I think any woman would be fortunate to have you for a husband," Raven declared loyally.

"But then you are prejudiced on my behalf, puss."

"I suppose." She frowned. "Well, you will simply have to persuade her. It shouldn't be impossible. Aurora is quite independent minded, but no one has more ruthless charm than you do. You managed to convince me to forgive my English relatives for the horrible way they treated Mama, when that was the last thing I wanted."

"We'll see," Nicholas said noncommittally.

"I do hope . . . well, I would like to see Aurora happy.

I'm certain she is lonely, being confined to her house for days on end due to her mourning. Your presence here will at least offer her a diversion. How long do you plan to stay?"

"I haven't yet decided. A few weeks, perhaps. The news of my escape will reach England sooner or later, and with a price on my head, the risk of discovery will be greater." His sister's expression grew concerned, but he forestalled her comment. "You had best be off on your ride, Miss Kendrick, before we invite comment."

Raven nodded reluctantly. "Where can I find you if I should need to speak to you?"

"I intend to take rooms at the Clarendon."

She kissed his cheek, then gave him a saucy smile as she accepted the Thoroughbred's reins to lead it from the stall. "Perhaps I will see you in the park some morning, Mr. *Deverill*."

Nicholas found himself smiling fondly as he watched her leave. When he was alone, however, his smile faded. As was her nature, Raven had gone straight to the heart of the matter: whether or not he and Aurora intended to acknowledge their marriage.

For a moment he wondered if he should reconsider his plan to claim her as his wife. He wanted Aurora physically; there was no longer the slightest doubt in his mind. Kissing her this morning had been as stunningly sensual as four months ago, when he'd taken her luscious, virginal body in their marriage bed. The hunger he'd felt for her then hadn't diminished in the least; if anything, the craving was stronger.

The feeling was more than lust, though. It was like a barely banked fire, quietly smoldering, waiting to be kindled to an uncontrollable rage. And though she'd tried to resist it, Aurora had responded to him with an answering fire.

His loins hardened merely at the remembrance.

Nick ran a hand roughly through his now-dark hair. It

had taken an almost superhuman effort to sever their embrace this morning. Yet he hadn't trusted himself to continue touching her without making love to her. And that, to his mind, would cement their marriage.

If they were eventually to dissolve their union, he would damned well have to keep his hands off her. It wouldn't be at all fair or honorable to slake his desire if he only meant to abandon Aurora. And if he were indiscreet enough to be discovered in her bed—or worse, get her with child—the scandal would be unavoidable. He most certainly didn't want to mire her in scandal, or his sister, either.

Nicholas frowned. If he had any sense, he would probably give up the notion of trying to make their marriage work. Aurora was adamantly set against their union. And she had absolved him of any responsibility for her. He needn't feel any guilt over shirking his obligation to her, needn't let his conscience flay him, as it insisted on doing.

Her determined resistance of his advances perplexed him, though. She had surrendered eagerly enough on their wedding night. Since then, however, she had subtly changed from the innocent young lady he had wed. She seemed stronger now, more rigid and self-contained, fiercely determined to close herself off from any emotion that resembled passion.

But she had been hurt before, he had to remember. She'd lost the man she loved, and the experience had left a deep scar. Nick felt himself tense with jealousy each time she mentioned her former betrothed, despite the fact that possessiveness was unlike him. But the man was dead. And he should make allowances for her past grief.

Besides . . . he thought he could make her forget her loss if he put his mind to it. He had never yet met a woman who was unsusceptible to his charm when he chose to exert it. He could overcome her objections to their marriage if he truly wished to.

So, did he wish to?

Was he mad to pursue a woman who was so clearly un-willing to be his wife? Certainly it would be safer to leave England altogether. But then, he had never found much appeal in safety. Since he could first crawl, he had taken risks purely for the excitement of it. He preferred living on the edge, probably because danger made him feel so in-tensely alive. Accepting fate's challenges was a thrill more intoxicating than any opiate.

And winning Aurora would be the most daunting of challenges.

Yet he was more convinced than ever that her cool ele-gance concealed a fire deep inside. Over the years he had learned to trust his gut instincts, for they'd saved him more than once. And every instinct he possessed told him she would be worth the effort.

And then there was his duty. He owed it to his father to shoulder his responsibilities.

Slowly Nicholas nodded. He wouldn't abandon his plan to claim Aurora. He would remain in England for as long as it took, until he convinced her to make their marriage real.

That momentous decision made, Nicholas turned to leave the stall. Feeling a heavy weight press against his hip, he realized he'd forgotten about the book Aurora had given him, which lay in the pocket of his cloak.

Curiously he drew out the jeweled journal. *A Passion of the Heart.*

His mouth twisted in a wicked smile. It was difficult to imagine his regal, well-bred, ladylike wife reading a tale of erotica, yet evidently there were hidden facets to the woman he had wed. Facets he was anxious to discover.

For now, however, he needed to find the proprietor of the livery, so he could hire a carriage and horses for his time in London.

Chapter Eleven

He challenged my heart, daring me to open myself to passion.

Aurora felt a thrill of exhilaration as the ground rushed beneath her mount's thundering hooves. She bent over the gray's neck, calling encouragement to the powerful horse as it strained to best the black Thoroughbred racing along-side her.

The cool wind whipped her widow's veil back from her face and stung her eyes, but she was as reluctant to lose the race as her horse. When the two competitors finally neared the end of the sandy stretch of turf, Aurora's Cronos was ahead of Raven's Satan by a full length.

Aurora pulled up, laughing, while Raven did likewise.

"Well done!" the younger woman exclaimed, a trifle breathless. "I felt sure we would win this time."

As they turned back, Cronos was still snorting and danc-ing with excitement, almost preening at his victory, while Satan shook his head at his rider's firm hold, wanting to set off again.

Murmuring praise, Aurora patted her horse's dappled silver-and-gray neck. "He is most assuredly in high spirits today."

"I suppose that could explain our loss. But I might simply have to admit that you are the better horsewoman."

"I wouldn't give up yet," Aurora said with a smile. "You nearly had us until the very last."

"Oh, I have no intention of giving up," Raven retorted with a grin. "Someday you will eat our dust."

"Perhaps so."

Even though they adopted a far more sedate pace as they retraced their steps along the sandy avenue called Rotten Row, Aurora shared her mount's high spirits. She loved racing the wind on a swift horse—the exhilarating freedom, the excitement of competing and besting a worthy opponent, the sense of power when controlling the mighty animal beneath her, straining as one. The sheer joy of it made her blood sing.

The quiet of early morning in Hyde Park was by far the best part of her day. At present the paths were dedicated to serious horsemen and women, with none of the dandies or stylish ladies in elegant equipages that would congest the park later at the fashionable hour of five.

A fine mist hovered over the Serpentine lake, the dampness glistening on the wide stretches of grass and dripping from the trees that lined the path. By mid-morning when the mist cleared, the park would be filled with nannies supervising their young charges or rambunctious boys frolicking with their dogs, but at this hour, there were only dedicated riders about.

No sooner had she entertained that thought than Aurora saw a blue-coated horseman cantering toward them. Recognizing those broad shoulders even from a distance, she straightened abruptly in her sidesaddle, while her heart took up an erratic rhythm. It had been two days since Nicholas had left the privacy of her bedchamber after his outrageous invasion. Two days during which she had worried about his fate and fretted about his plans regarding their marriage. It vexed her that she'd received no word from him— and vexed her more that he had occupied her thoughts so intensely.

When he reached them, Nicholas slowed to a halt and gave a polite bow. He looked splendid in his exquisitely tailored blue coat and buff breeches and gleaming top boots, the picture of a fashionable gentleman. His eyes, however, glinted with wicked amusement.

"Good morning, ladies. May I compliment you on an excellent race?"

Aurora felt her face warm with color. She was embarrassed to have been caught galloping like a hoyden, especially by this man. Not only had she failed to ensure his sister behaved with decorum, but she'd exhibited precisely the same recklessness she claimed to deplore in Nicholas.

Raven had no such scruples about her conduct, though. "It *was* splendid, wasn't it? Aurora has the most magnificent horses, and she is an angel to let me use them as my own."

"An angel, indeed," Nicholas agreed, his gaze connecting intimately with Aurora's.

When his gaze moved with raking leisure over her dark plum riding habit, she felt her flush rise even higher at the appreciative male interest in his eyes. She was grateful when Raven's groom came trotting up just then, accompanied by her own.

Not by a flicker of an eyelash did the hulking Irishman O'Malley show any recognition of Nicholas. But then Raven had said they'd already met and determined how best to carry out the pretense of Nicholas's impersonation.

As a group, they continued riding down the Row, the two grooms maintaining a discreet distance behind. In keeping with the deception, Raven asked "Mr. Deverill" how he was finding London. And he responded with an amusing but impersonal account of how the wrong baggage had been delivered to his hotel rooms and that he'd been forced to complain to management that the walking dresses were not at all his size.

Aurora thought it fortunate that brother and sister could laugh and converse so easily, for it hid the fact that she herself was dismayingly tongue-tied.

A moment later, however, some other riders caught Raven's attention. In the distance two young ladies were directing their horses onto a narrower path through the grass.

"There are Sarah and Jane," Raven said rather abruptly.

"Forgive me, Aurora, but I must go speak to them." She gave Nicholas a conspiratorial glance. "It was a pleasure seeing you again, Mr. Deverill."

Nicholas tipped his tall beaver hat. "And you, Miss Kendrick."

She turned her horse away, and O'Malley automatically followed, trailing her like a shadow. Aurora could think of no immediate objection to her leaving; there was nothing exceptional in Raven wanting to speak to her friends. Still, Aurora was disconcerted to be left alone with Nicholas. Her own groom was several lengths behind, she realized, glancing over her shoulder.

"She's determined to provide us the opportunity to be alone," Nicholas commented dryly, as if reading her thoughts.

"I cannot imagine why."

"Can you not? Raven considers it romantic that our love has been thwarted and wants us to remedy the situation."

Aurora gave him a quizzical glance. "Raven is not in the least romantic."

"I'm not convinced of that. But in any case, she worries about you being lonely. She thinks we should remain married."

"I see I shall have to talk with her," Aurora muttered under her breath.

"I should talk with her as well about her shameless conduct. Imagine my surprise to see the two of you galloping past like wild Indians." He shook his head disapprovingly, although there was an undertone of laughter in his voice. "I would have expected it of Raven, but you, love . . ."

"Raven isn't to blame," Aurora admitted reluctantly. "The fault is entirely mine. I instigated the race."

"Did you?" His eyebrow lifted. "You mean to say you've been corrupting my sister, rather than the other way around?"

"I should not have, I know, but the horses were fresh, and there were so few people about to see. . . . And, well, the horses did need exercise, after all."

Nicholas regarded her with amusement. "Have I uncovered a secret vice, my love?"

She bit her lip. Riding *was* her passion and her vice. It was her one freedom, her chance to escape her confining upbringing and the restrictive conventions governing widowhood. "As a widow, I am not allowed many liberties," she began defensively.

"So when you come to the park, you allow yourself to go wild."

"It isn't as bad as all that!"

"Oh, I don't think it bad in the slightest. The exercise has flushed your cheeks and brightened your eyes. . . . Amazingly sensual." Nicholas's measured gaze swept over her, while his tone became low and vibrant. "You look as if you've just risen from your bed after a night of passionate lovemaking."

Aurora flushed, hardly knowing how to respond.

"It only confirms what I've suspected all along."

"What do you suspect?" she asked warily.

"That there's a hidden fire smoldering beneath that cool, regal air of yours."

She was flustered by his intimacy, yet she could not look away.

"Your eyes truly are an incredible blue," Nicholas said, his voice taking on a husky note.

Wondering how he could see her eyes, Aurora reached up to touch the brim of her hat and suddenly realized she had forgotten about her widow's veil. Somehow it had blown back, leaving her face exposed. Dismayed, she settled the film of plum lace into place, concealing her features from his penetrating gaze.

"How ungenerous of you to hide yourself away," Nicholas remarked, the laughter back in his voice. "I was enjoying the view."

"What have you been doing with yourself these past two days?" Aurora asked, determined to change the subject.

"Have you missed me, then?"

She gave him an arch look, which she then realized he could no longer see because of her veil. "I was simply worried that you might have embroiled yourself in some kind of trouble."

His smile was pure, unadulterated charm. "Whatever would lead you to think that?"

"What indeed?" Aurora replied wryly with unwilling amusement, struggling to resist his undeniable allure.

"Actually, I've been working on establishing my credentials. With Wycliff out of town, I'm finding it difficult. Your countrymen tend to look down their noses at Americans, no matter how loyal they are to the Crown."

"It would perhaps help if you *were* loyal to the Crown."

"Or if I had more blue blood. I suppose I need to find a sponsor to endorse me, particularly if I hope to move in your elevated social circles. Perhaps I should prevail upon you to introduce me to your highbrowed acquaintances."

She was exasperated by his devil-may-care air. "I should think you would be the least bit concerned about the danger of flaunting yourself about."

"Oh, I won't purposefully flaunt my existence, but I won't hide in the shadows, either."

"I still fail to see why you don't just return home to America."

"Because I don't want to abandon my lovely wife."

Worried both by his statement and that he might be overheard, Aurora glanced over her shoulder and was relieved to find her groom was still a discreet distance away. "You needn't advertise our relationship to the entire world!"

"I am not the one who is railing like a termagant in public, love."

"I am *not* railing."

"No?"

There was a maddening undertone of enjoyment in his voice, and Aurora regretted that she was too well-bred to box his ears and that she held such a strong aversion to physical violence. Instead, she took a deep breath and bit her tongue, vowing not to allow herself to be provoked.

It was hard, however, when Nicholas seemed determined to stir up trouble.

"Speaking of your acquaintances . . ." he said thoughtfully. "If I'm not mistaken, there is one now."

Glancing farther down the Row, Aurora recognized the approaching horseman as the Earl of Clune. Her heart seemed to falter. "Oh, my word . . . Clune. He is one of *your* acquaintances as well. He told me you were once a member of his Hellfire League."

"For a short while I was, during my visit here three years ago. What of it?"

"He is sure to recognize you. You should leave at once, Nicholas, before he sees you."

"I told you, I have no intention of hiding."

"You can't possibly mean to show yourself to him!"

"You will remember that I am Brandon Deverill, your cousin by marriage. There should be no problem. Smile, love, and pretend you are enjoying my company."

It was too late to do anything else, Aurora realized, since Clune was nearly upon them. He flashed his charming rake's smile as he drew his mount to a halt before her.

"Ah, the most beautiful widow in London," he said with a graceful bow. "And the most accomplished horsewoman, as well. The combination is entrancing."

"My Lord Clune," Aurora murmured, acknowledging the acquaintance with a polite nod of her head.

"I don't believe I need ask the outcome of your race this morning, since you always win."

She made a supreme effort not to look at Nicholas as she tried to play down the race. "My horses enjoy the exercise."

"But your competition could be stronger. Perhaps some morning you might prefer a challenger other than your ward. I would be happy to offer my services whenever you wish."

At his wickedly suggestive tone, Aurora felt like squirming in her saddle. His lordship was clearly flirting with her. "Thank you, my lord, but I am quite content riding with my ward."

She had hoped he would move on without noticing Nicholas, but Clune's gaze turned to him next.

"Have we met before? You bear a strong resemblance to someone I know. This lady's late husband, I believe."

Aurora held her breath, while Nicholas smiled coolly. "That is not surprising, since I am Sabine's cousin. Brandon Deverill, at your service, sir."

"The likeness is remarkable."

Nicholas met his gaze directly. "So I am told."

Aurora was unnerved by how closely Clune was studying him. But his lordship merely bowed and offered his condolences. "An excellent sportsman and comrade, your cousin Nick. As game as they come. I was sorry to hear of his death, for I grew quite fond of him during our brief acquaintance. You are an American, Mr. Deverill?"

"By birth, yes. But since my political leanings don't quite coincide with my government's, I thought it judicious to take refuge in England until the war ends."

"You might find your acceptance here rather tricky, especially since your cousin was hanged for piracy."

"I believe Lord Wycliff will vouch for me if you have concerns about my loyalties."

"No, no concerns." Clune's mouth curled in a wry smile. "I have few political leanings at all. But if you find you have need of patronage other than Wycliff's, I should be happy to claim your acquaintance, in remembrance of my late friend Nick."

Nicholas's response was far cooler than Aurora expected. "That is generous of you, sir. I shall keep your offer in mind."

Clune turned and smiled his charming smile at Aurora. "Well, I will let you ride on. You won't want your horse to stand any longer. But I hope you will keep my other offer in mind, my lady. If you care to race some morning, I will be delighted to oblige."

Aurora murmured a noncommittal reply, and felt relief flooding her when Clune spurred his horse and rode past them.

She and Nicholas resumed riding along the Row. Aurora was fuming, appalled by his brazen disregard for his life, but she forced herself to wait until they were out of earshot of the earl.

"What do you call that, if not flaunting your existence?" she demanded, her concern making her sound sharper than normal.

"I call it establishing my cover. Clune knows me better than almost anyone in England. If he didn't recognize me, then I doubt anyone else will."

"I call it barefaced effrontery. You looked him in the eye and *lied*."

"Would you rather I risked telling him the truth?"

Nettled, she lapsed into silence.

"He seems overly attentive to you, my love. Perhaps I should remind you again, you are not a widow—and never were."

She was too vexed to realize Nicholas's good humor had faded. "I do not need reminding."

"I think you do. Clune is one of the premier rakes of England, and he sees you as fair game."

Aurora's chin lifted stubbornly. "I will not allow you to dictate to me, Nicholas. I wed you chiefly so I wouldn't have to endure a husband who prescribed my every action, like Halford. You sound just like him—or my father."

The set of Nicholas's jaw seemed to soften. "I did not mean to pick a fight, Aurora."

"No? You are giving an extremely good imitation of it."

"It's not unreasonable for a man to be possessive of his wife."

"You cannot possibly be jealous?"

"Perhaps I am. But I advise you to keep Clune at a distance."

"I have no intention of letting you choose my friends for me, Nicholas."

He drew his horse to a halt. "Then I had best speak to Clune myself."

She looked startled. "Why?"

"So I can warn him to keep away from my wife."

Aurora stared at him, alarming visions running through her head. She had forgotten that Nicholas Sabine was a dangerous man. By his own admission, he had killed before. Did he intend to threaten Clune? Menacing a peer of the realm was a certain way to jeopardize his own life. He could be caught and hanged. . . .

"You *cannot* harm him, Nicholas."

"Your concern for him is touching, love," Nicholas said coolly.

With a polite bow, he turned his horse around and rode away, leaving Aurora to stare after him, a very unladylike oath trembling on her lips.

Aurora remained in the park far longer than usual, anxiously awaiting Nicholas's return, but she saw no sign of either him or Clune. When she finally gave up and went home, she found herself pacing the floor worriedly.

She was startled when late that afternoon her butler brought her an engraved calling card bearing the name of Brandon Deverill and informed her that Mr. Deverill was delighted to accept her invitation to tea.

It was with both relief and trepidation that she went downstairs to meet Nicholas. She found him in her drawing room, inspecting the collection of portrait miniatures on a side table.

He looked up when she entered, his dark eyes giving her the same sensual jolt she always felt when he merely looked at her.

"Hello, cousin," he said warmly. "How generous of you to invite me to tea."

His amicable greeting was for the benefit of the servant, she suspected, forcing a smile. He was supposed to be her late husband's cousin. Having tea with him in the middle of the afternoon was not too far beyond the pale. It was his audacity that unsettled her nerves.

"How remiss of me, Mr. Deverill. I entirely forgot to tell my staff that you were expected." She turned to the butler, who was hovering at the door, awaiting her instructions. "Danby, we will take tea here, please."

"As you wish, my lady."

When they were alone, Aurora fixed a baleful glare on Nicholas. "I thought we agreed we would not meet in private," she declared, keeping her voice low so the servants wouldn't hear.

"I don't remember making any such agreement, love."

Before she could argue, he picked up one of the miniatures and showed it to her. It exhibited a handsome gentleman with curling dark gold hair and blue eyes. "Is this your late betrothed?"

Crossing the room, Aurora took the likeness from him and set it back down carefully. "Yes, that is Geoffrey, Lord March," she said, running her fingertips gently over the cherished image.

"I can see why I reminded you of him." Aurora shot him a questioning look and found Nicholas watching her. "When we first met, you said I reminded you of someone who was dear to you. I can detect a certain resemblance between us."

She had forgotten she had ever said that to Nicholas or that she'd ever seen a resemblance in the two men. They were as different as the sun and the moon: one bold and vital, blazing with heat and intensity, the other quiet and soothing and gentle.

"I was gravely mistaken. You are not alike in any respect. Certainly not now that you've changed the color of your hair."

"And you're still in love with his ghost?"

"I don't wish to discuss him, Nicholas." It hurt too much to remember. She gazed defiantly at him. "Would you care to explain what you are doing here? You know it is unwise for us to be together."

He studied her for a moment. "Perhaps, but I thought you could use the company. You said you can't get out much because the conventions of widowhood restrict your movements. And since I had a great deal to do with your claim to widowhood, I feel responsible for making amends."

"I told you, I release you from any responsibility or obligation toward me."

"I'm not certain I want to be released. I took a vow to cherish till death do us part."

"Nicholas . . . I thought we had settled this. Death *did* part us, if you will remember? You died and were buried on St. Kitts." Her mouth curved in a mock frown. "Oh, yes, I forgot. That was all a charade, much like the one you are playing now."

Nicholas's lips stretched in a slow smile, but he made no reply. Instead he contemplated her silently with an unsettling, amused gaze.

"What?" Aurora demanded. "Why are you looking at me like that?"

"I am trying to decide if I like this shrewish side of you."

Aurora took a deep breath. She *was* acting the shrew, even after she had vowed she would not allow herself to be goaded by his deliberate provocations. It was quite unlike her to let her temper get the best of her. She'd spent her life maintaining strict control over her emotions. But Nicholas Sabine was so very exasperating. And he had agreed to forget their marriage existed. So why was he still acting as if he were her husband, with the right to rule her? Was he going back on his word?

He was gazing down at her now, giving her the full effect of his lazy smile. Aurora wanted to curse him for his irresistible appeal; he knew perfectly well the impact his sensual charm had on her.

"I believe you are being remiss as a hostess, sweet shrew. Aren't you going to invite me to sit down?"

Aurora raised her eyes to the ceiling, but she willed herself to reply serenely. "Very well, Mr. Deverill. Will you please be seated?"

"Ah, excellent. If you could just refrain from looking daggers at me, I might actually believe you meant to welcome me."

With what she considered admirable control, Aurora waited until he had moved over to the settee before taking the chair opposite him, across the tea table.

"So, what shall we discuss?" she asked, folding her hands primly in her lap.

Nicholas simply watched her. After a moment, his gaze dropped to linger on her breasts. Heat rose in Aurora, and she felt a tingling and a swelling of her nipples that she was helpless to control.

"Do I make you nervous, Aurora?" he asked knowingly.

"Yes," she retorted. "The way you look at me is disgraceful."

"What way is that?"

"As if you're undressing me. It makes me highly uncomfortable."

His mouth lifted in a smile of tempting allure. "Good. I never want you to be too comfortable around me."

Aurora shook her head, torn between fury and despair. "You really deserve to be arrested, you know—before you cause a scandal or drive me to distraction."

"Would you really be glad for my arrest? Clune says you were bereft at my presumed death."

Her alarm returned full measure as she remembered Clune. "Surely you weren't mad enough to actually speak to him?"

"I'm afraid so. I decided a truthful approach would be

most advantageous, so I revealed myself and told him the entire story about my imprisonment and near hanging."

"And how did he respond?" Aurora asked worriedly.

"Once I swore that I wasn't committing treason against your country, he was perfectly willing to assist my deception. I told him I was only here to see my wife, which is the truth."

Aurora eyed him with dismay. "How could you take such a dangerous risk?"

"Actually it was a *calculated* risk. Clune is 'always ripe for a lark,' as he puts it. He also believes in loyalty toward his friends—and he claims me as a friend. He is fond of you, as well. Too fond, in my opinion. He as much as admitted that he'd been bent on your seduction."

Aurora felt Nicholas studying her intently. "I have done nothing to encourage Lord Clune to believe he could succeed."

"So he says. When I warned him to keep away from you, he claimed he had made little progress because you were madly in love with your late husband."

She felt herself blushing. "I had to have some story to explain my abrupt marriage. I thought it best to let people believe I fell in love at first sight."

His flashing smile held a relentless charm. "I rather like that version of the story."

"Yet you and I know the truth. Our union was never a love match—nor was it supposed to last longer than one night."

Nicholas let her comment pass. "You might not have encouraged Clune wittingly, but as a beautiful widow, you are a prime target for men like him. And your resistance only adds to your allure. For a rake like Clune, it's the challenge of the chase that is stimulating."

Her eyebrows lifted curiously. She suspected that while Nicholas might not be as great a libertine as his friend, he knew what drove a rake. "You sound as if you speak from experience. Is that why you still seem to be pursuing me? Because my reluctance to be your wife presents a challenge to you?"

He cocked his head, scrutinizing her with a half-lidded gaze. "Partly, I expect. But it goes deeper than that. As implausible as it may seem, I'm motivated by concern for you."

"Me?"

"Yes, you. It disturbs me to see you so limited by the strict observations of widowhood. That you're forced to lock yourself away from the world. This is not India, where widows are burned alive with their husbands' remains."

The tea tray arrived just then, brought by Aurora's very proper butler. She gave a guilty start, realizing their conversation could have been overheard. Vowing to be more discreet, she fell silent until Danby bowed and withdrew.

After offering Nicholas scones and jam and small finger sandwiches, she hesitated, eyeing him uncertainly. This man was her husband; they had been together in the most intimate way possible. And yet she had no idea how he even liked his tea. "Do you care for milk or sugar?"

"Sugar, no milk. I know," Nicholas said wryly, reading her thoughts. "For a husband and wife we are still practically strangers. Perhaps we should remedy that."

"I see no reason for us to become more closely acquainted."

He studied Aurora as she poured tea from the silver pot into china cups. She performed the task as she did everything else, with a graceful elegance that was the product of a lifetime of training. The perfect lady. And like most gently bred ladies, she had been raised to honor the stifling codes of society.

Yet she continued to surprise him. Aurora was not like so many of her contemporaries—shallow, vain, self-centered, arrogant—although with her breeding and beauty, she could very well have turned out that way. She had unexpected depths, intriguing facets that he found enchanting, sensual. He had been captivated this morning by the glimpse of her free spirit when she'd galloped in the park. And he'd tasted the hidden fire in her embrace more than once. . . .

There was a keenly passionate woman beneath that ladylike exterior, and he was determined to find her, to chip away at her very proper inhibitions. She was too young to bury herself away in a living tomb of celibacy.

It wouldn't be easy to break through her defenses, though. Not when Aurora held such an aversion to risk, when she was so determined to deny any vestige of desire. Like now. When he took the cup of tea she offered, their fingers brushed, creating a frisson of heat. Aurora drew back as if burned. Averting her gaze, she picked up her own cup, clearly intent on ignoring the attraction between them.

Nicholas felt his resolve harden. She needed shaking up, even though she didn't know it.

"So," he said finally. "Do you mean to live the rest of your life hiding behind your widow's weeds?"

Her blue eyes lifted to his. "What do you mean?"

"You've immured yourself in a prison here. Not one of your own making, but a prison nonetheless. You're a captive of convention and decorum, letting society dictate your every action."

"There is nothing wrong with following the dictates of society."

"There is if you let it drain the very life from you."

Aurora pursed her lips together in a frown. "I am not like you, Nicholas. I want a quiet, orderly life."

"I don't think you do, or you never would have come to my rescue and agreed to wed a stranger."

"Those were highly unusual circumstances. I am perfectly content with my situation."

"Are you?"

"Yes. I enjoy a very full life, despite my current limitations. My household may be much smaller than the one I managed for my father, but it still requires effort. I write letters often—actually, I have a wide correspondence. Friends call on me frequently. I read a great deal. I ride daily. . . ."

"Ah, yes, your secret vice. What other hidden desires do you harbor, Aurora?"

She ignored the question. "I have what I have always wanted . . . independence."

"I don't think you can call this independence. You live in constant fear of what others will think. You can't go out in public without hiding your face or out after dark at all. You feel trapped here, you've intimated as much."

"Perhaps, but only because I am determined to avoid scandal. What is acceptable behavior for a man is not at all tolerable in a lady, much less a widow."

Determinedly, Nicholas held her gaze. "Either you're deceiving yourself or you don't know yourself very well. I think there are two sides of you. The woman who bows down to convention, worshiping as if it were an icon. And the one who loves galloping wildly through the park for the sheer joy of it. The same one who gave herself to a stranger in a blazing night of passion."

He could see by the darkening of her expressive eyes that he had hit a nerve. "I think you want to escape that straitlaced prison of yours," he pressed in a low voice, "to let yourself be a sensual woman, but you're afraid to take the risk."

When she didn't respond, he drew the journal from his pocket and set it on the table before her. Aurora stared at it, her eyes very blue.

"I thought of you the entire time I was reading this. You're very much like the anonymous lady who wrote it."

"I cannot see any resemblance," she replied defensively, as if embarrassed by the thought. "Our circumstances could hardly be more different. She was French, enslaved by corsairs and imprisoned in a Turkish harem. She was forced to become a concubine and engage in acts no lady would ever willingly abide."

"She was innocent of carnal knowledge until she met a man who could fire her blood."

"Indeed. And her . . . her lust came to rule her."

Nicholas narrowed his eyes. "Have you never wondered what it would be like to experience that kind of passion? To want someone that desperately?"

Her lips parted, but no sound came out. Nick suspected he'd come close to the truth.

"I've wondered," he admitted. "My father once tried to explain how he felt about Raven's mother. He said that if I read the journal, I might understand."

Aurora lowered her gaze, her ivory skin flushing. "It was a very compelling story," she said finally, "but their love was doomed to fail. Desiree lost her heart to her master and became trapped by her obsession."

"But she never regretted loving."

"That was not the lesson I took from the journal," Aurora murmured, although not as staunchly as before. "I thought she was foolish to allow any man to rule her heart in that manner."

"My father believed it was better to have only one moment of true passion than never to know it at all."

She hesitated. "And look what it gained him. A lifetime of misery, yearning for a woman he could never have." Aurora shook her head, as if trying to convince herself. "It is far better never to give your heart than risk having it torn out."

Nick's gaze dropped to her tempting mouth that had hardened in resolve. A rush of desire swept over him as he thought of transforming her stubborn conviction into melting surrender.

Nicholas drew a ragged breath at the erotic image. "I think you are a woman like Desiree, Aurora. You have the same wild spirit."

She set down her cup unsteadily. "You're mistaken."

His gaze never faltered. "What is it that frightens you about that notion? That you could feel passion that intense? Or that you could be jolted out of that cocoon you've wrapped around yourself?"

She rose abruptly. "I think you should go, Nicholas."

After a moment's hesitation, he set down his own cup and stood. When he closed the distance between them, she didn't back away, obviously determined not to let him intimidate her.

Deliberately he took her hand and raised it to his lips, pressing a kiss on the inner flesh of her wrist. She stood defiantly, unmoving, yet her cheeks flushed, betraying her struggle for control. More revealing, he could see the yearning of long-suppressed desire in her eyes.

She was ripe for passion, for life, Nicholas knew. She desperately needed to be freed from the rigid shackles that bound her, and he was the only man to do it. But he wouldn't fight her just yet. The battle had scarcely begun, and he could be patient.

"I am not mistaken, siren," he said softly. "I've tasted all that sweet fire hidden beneath your layers of cool reserve. There's a sensual, passionate woman waiting to be set free. And I intend to find her."

With a brief bow, he turned and walked away.

Aurora stood frozen, staring after Nicholas's retreating back. When he had left, she let out a shaky breath. Her heart was still hammering in her chest from his nearness, his sheer magnetism.

How did he always manage to overwhelm her that way? How could he make her blood race with a simple touch, turning her knees to water and her willpower to jelly? Why did he kindle such inner turmoil? He brought out the worst in her—dark emotions she didn't want to feel. This time, however, his probing questions had unnerved her as much as his physical presence and his provoking behavior.

Weakly she sank into her chair. Was Nicholas right? Was she like Desiree? Did she have a wild spirit just waiting to be set free?

Certainly she was a different woman since meeting Nicholas Sabine . . . driven by desires she had never known before. She had fought her powerful attraction to him, along with the restless yearning he roused in her so effortlessly, but it was there, simmering below the surface.

Uncertainly Aurora picked up the journal he had left for her. She had been shocked by the explicit sensuality she'd found there, but the love story had captured her imagination. Vulnerable to her master's gentle seduction and exotic temptations, Desiree had been swept up in a storm of passion she never before imagined. . . .

What would it be like to know such incredible passion? To be overwhelmed by the madness of love, the blindness of desire? To experience feelings so powerful they could blot out any vestiges of wisdom and reason?

She'd had a fleeting taste of such passion on her wedding night, Aurora remembered unwillingly.

The book fell open to a well-worn page:

I love the many parts of you. I love your hard flesh so deep inside me. I love the weight and strength of you, so powerful against my softness. I love your feverish hunger, your desire that makes me feel so much a woman.

Aurora shut her eyes. *Nicholas.* He reminded her so very much of the Frenchwoman's lover—bold, virile, vibrantly sensual. Like the prince in the journal, he had awakened a woman's tender longing deep within her.

Against her will, her mind flashed to a vision of their marriage bed, the two of them together . . . Nicholas making love to her with such fierce tenderness, moving inside her, filling her with the pleasure she needed, wanted.

The same pleasure his dark eyes had promised moments ago.

She shivered. She would not allow herself to surrender to the promise in his eyes. She dared not yield to him, no matter how his touch set her blood racing.

Still, she couldn't deny her hungry yearning.

Chapter Twelve

*My resistance seemed hopeless. How could I defend
against the restless yearning he kindled in me?*

Over the course of the next few days, Aurora found herself cursing Nicholas Sabine more and more readily. The
man was dangerous to her peace of mind. By night, he
haunted her dreams. By day, the anticipation of seeing him
filled her with a taut, achy restlessness that would not
leave her.

When she did encounter him, whether on her morning
rides in the park or at some other venue, she always experienced a jolt, the same shivering awareness she'd felt when
she'd first seen him on the quay in St. Kitts. Now, however,
when she met his intense gaze, the heat in his dark eyes
and the unguarded message it conveyed scorched her like
hot coals.

She couldn't avoid seeing him wherever she went, possibly because Nicholas had an ally in his sister; Raven evidently was in league with him, inviting Nicholas on their
various shopping expeditions. He made their meetings look
accidental and innocuous, but Aurora knew his campaign
was carefully planned with the precision of a military
general.

She had no idea how to defend herself against such tac-
tics. She had never before been the object of such single-
minded determination. Nicholas was like a powerful storm
sweeping everything in its path, destroying her equanimity
in the process. No matter how she strove to remain serene
and aloof, to disregard his sensual, ruthless charm, she

found it impossible. He was outrageous, bold, provocative . . . irresistible.

But it was the deeper feelings he roused in her that were the graver threat. He had only to breathe to stir a fierce ache of uneasy emotions inside her.

She considered fleeing London for a time just to escape. Only yesterday she'd received a letter from Geoffrey's mother, Lady March, asking her to visit. Geoffrey's ten-year-old brother Harry was proving a handful, and Lady March claimed Aurora was the only one who could control him.

Yet she couldn't leave London, Aurora knew. She would not act the coward. And she had a solemn obligation to support Raven. Moreover, her father was in Sussex—the Eversley and March estates adjoined—and she had no wish to encounter the duke, even to escape Nicholas.

She thought she understood what drove his pursuit. It almost seemed as if he were wooing her, but Aurora felt certain her appeal stemmed from the challenge she presented. Winning her was a *game* to Nicholas. He was incited by the thrill of the chase.

She began to wonder if resistance was the right course. If she ever actually surrendered to him—if she allowed him to win—perhaps then he might give up the hunt and go home, sparing them both endless grief. She didn't *want* Nicholas running her life, dictating how she should behave, what she should feel. It was the height of arrogance for him to presume to know her mind better than she herself did. He had compared her to the Frenchwoman in the journal, and perhaps there *were* similarities, Aurora acknowledged. But she had no room in her life for wildfire passions raging out of control, nor any desire for the kind of pain such passion could engender.

Clearly she would have to devise a new plan for dealing with Nicholas. There *had* to be some way to turn the tables on him so that she could regain control of her life. She was never going to persuade him to leave her alone otherwise—for his sake as well as her own.

The risk he was taking worried Aurora greatly. She lived in constant fear of his exposure. Lord Clune apparently had taken up his sponsorship and was showing Nicholas about London, squiring him to gaming clubs and indulging in other rakish diversions. She felt sure he would get himself killed if he kept up his reckless imposture.

He was better known in England than he presumed, Aurora believed. But when he was nearly recognized, it was by a French émigré, of all people.

Nicholas had escorted Raven and Aurora into a milliner's shop on Oxford Street. The proprietor, upon seeing him, gave a start and clasped her hands together, exclaiming, *"Mon Dieu!"* under her breath. Then Nicholas removed his beaver hat, fully exposing his dark hair, and the Frenchwoman's look turned to confusion.

She seemed to recall herself and came forward to greet her clientele, but while Raven contemplated fashionable bonnets, the proprietor eyed Nicholas in puzzlement.

"Pardon, monsieur," she said finally in a heavy accent. "I did not mean to stare, but you have the appearance of a man I once knew."

Aurora felt herself tense, yet except for a polite smile, Nicholas kept his expression impassive. "Perhaps you mistake me for my cousin, madame. It happens with some frequency."

"Your cousin is Mr. Nicholas Sabine of America?"

"Yes."

The woman moved forward to clasp his hand fervently. "Oh, monsieur, your cousin is truly an angel. He saved the lives of my entire family. Not only mine, but a half dozen other families as well. Never will I forget him or the debt we owe him."

She was an older woman, with graying hair, but still quite beautiful, with the fine-boned structure and porcelain skin of an aristocrat. Nicholas gave her his most sensual smile, as if she were twenty years younger. "My cousin is a fortunate man, to be remembered so fondly by such a lovely lady."

The proprietor flushed with pleasure and released his hand, almost in embarrassment. But when sometime later they concluded their shopping, she adamantly refused to let them pay for the three bonnets Raven had chosen.

The moment they left the shop, Raven asked the question that had been burning on Aurora's lips. "What did she mean, you saved her family? You were too young to be part of their bloody revolution, were you not?"

"Yes. But I happened to be in France afterward, during one of their gruesome governmental purges."

"And you just *happened* to rescue a half dozen families from the guillotine?" Aurora said dryly.

He shrugged. "Actually, it was only four. And it was a firing squad. The guillotine had been abandoned by then as too 'uncivilized.' "

Raven visibly repressed a laugh at his sarcasm, but Aurora was disturbed to learn of yet another situation where Nicholas could have been killed. She frowned at him over his sister's head.

"I suppose you mean to claim you didn't enjoy playing the hero, courting danger and risking your life?"

Nicholas shook his head. "Danger doesn't trouble me, but I didn't consciously seek the honor. I just seem to have a knack for becoming embroiled in rescues, even when I don't intend to."

"Even so, the problem now," Aurora said slowly, striving for patience, "is that your exploits have made you infamous enough you cannot hope to escape recognition."

"There are few people who know anything of my 'exploits,' as you call them."

"But if someone whom you met *years* ago recognized you, others will as well."

"Then I will just deny the acquaintance as I did just now," he said mildly. "Stop worrying about me, love. It will only give you gray hairs."

His answer dismayed her. Nicholas seemed oblivious to the danger he was in, indeed, seemed to thrive on it.

Giving him a look of frustration, Aurora marched off toward her carriage, leaving him to follow with his sister.

"You shouldn't tease her so, Nicholas," Raven said tightly. "She's worried that you will come to harm and only wants to protect you."

Nick glanced at her quizzically, surprised to hear the anger in her voice. "Was I teasing her?"

"You know you were. If you understood what Aurora has endured, you would not be so unkind."

He raised an eyebrow. "What has she endured?"

"She may be a wealthy duke's daughter, but her father made her life a misery. It must have been wretched for her, living under that tyrant's thumb, having to suffer his rages."

"I trust you mean to explain what you are talking about."

Raven glanced toward the carriage where Aurora awaited her. "There is no time to discuss it now. Meet me at Tobley's Bookshop tomorrow afternoon and I will tell you."

His concern aroused, Nick found himself impatiently waiting for Raven the next afternoon. When eventually she arrived with her maid, he followed her to a rear corner of the shop. They each pretended to peruse the shelves of novels while Raven explained what she had meant about the Duke of Eversley's rages.

"His grace has a vicious temper," she murmured in a hushed voice, "that I had the misfortune to witness shortly after we arrived in England. I was living with my Aunt Dalrymple by then, but Aurora spent the first few days at her family's London house. Naturally she wrote to her father and told him of her marriage to you. She was concerned about his reaction, I knew, but I never dreamed it would be so violent. The duke came to London in a fury, outraged because she had sullied the family name by wedding a condemned criminal. I saw their confrontation myself."

Raven shuddered. "I had just been admitted to their house by the butler—Aurora planned to escort me shopping, you see—when I heard someone shouting. I found Aurora in the drawing room with her father. His grace was standing there, shaking his fists at her and screaming. I could scarcely believe how livid he was. When Aurora tried to calm him, he picked up a heavy vase and threw it at her! Thank God it missed and merely shattered against the wall. It could have killed her."

Nick felt a sudden knot of anger and revulsion coil in his gut at the picture his sister had drawn for him.

"To my shame," Raven went on in a low voice, "I was too stunned to react, but her butler tried to intervene. That poor man is nearly a relic, he's so old, yet even though he was no match for the duke physically, he stepped between them. Eversley shoved him to the floor and went after Aurora, his fist raised. I honestly believe he would have struck her if he hadn't seen me. He stopped only because he didn't wish to commit such an outrageous indiscretion in front of a stranger."

"What happened then?" Nick asked in a hard voice.

"Well, the duke looked as if he would have an apoplectic fit, trying to control himself. He warned Aurora to get out of his sight, in fact, to leave his house entirely—saying that she was no longer his daughter—and then he stormed out."

Raven drew a measured breath. "Aurora was shaking, but she was more concerned for poor Danby, who had struck his head on a table when he was pushed. It was only later, after he had been tended to, that she confessed that sort of violence from her father was not uncommon. I think Aurora was vastly relieved he had washed his hands of her. She wouldn't say anything else against him, but later O'Malley was able to glean more from her servants than she would divulge to me. The tales only confirmed what I saw, that the duke is a terrible tyrant."

"*Tyrant* is obviously too tame a word," Nick said sardonically.

Raven nodded. "From what I gather, Aurora had to keep others safe from his rages for years, at no little cost to herself. That wasn't the first time he had threatened to strike her."

Nick's brows snapped together in a scowl of disbelief. "Eversley beat her? His own daughter?"

"It's monstrous, I know. But his servants paid even more dearly for his temper. Reportedly he took a crop to a groom once and nearly blinded the poor man."

Nick felt his gut tighten, repulsed by the thought of any man taking his anger out on defenseless dependents. And the idea of Aurora being at Eversley's mercy sickened him.

"Every one of her servants," Raven added quietly, "says that Aurora did her best to protect them from her father's fits of violence. More than once she had to physically intervene. And when he turned them out without a reference for the slightest infraction, she found them positions elsewhere. She never forgot them, either. When she set up her own household several months ago, she searched out those who had suffered at her father's hands and offered them employment. At least two of them were nearly destitute and were so pitifully grateful. . . . It is small wonder they think Aurora is a saint."

"No, it's no wonder," he replied tersely, struggling to keep his anger in check. When he'd proposed to her, Aurora had implied her father would be angry at her marriage, but never could he have imagined she would be in actual danger.

"What are you thinking?" Raven asked, eyeing his scowling face.

The smile Nick gave was wintery. "About how much I would enjoy ten minutes alone with the duke."

"I know," Raven said, understanding. "He deserves to be taught what it is like being at the mercy of someone stronger and more powerful. But you cannot reveal yourself to him, Nicholas. You are supposed to be in disguise."

His jaw hardened in frustration at the reminder, but then his tension eased. As Nicholas Sabine, he was severely constrained by the need for secrecy, but as Brandon Deverill, he was under no such restrictions. He could repay the duke for all the grief the illustrious bastard had caused his daughter. . . .

"Now what are you thinking?" Raven asked with a frown.

"That the day will come when the duke receives his just desserts," Nick replied enigmatically.

Apparently satisfied, Raven turned to reshelve the book she had been pretending to read, then added thoughtfully, "I'm certain her father is the main reason Aurora is so concerned about propriety. It is not that she is afraid of defying convention per se, but because the duke threatened her. He vowed that if she caused any further scandal, he would whip her like a stableboy and lock her away where she could no longer sully his name. That is why she is so careful to observe her widowhood, why she doesn't go out in society. She doesn't want to give her father any ammunition to use against her. She knows what he is capable of."

Raven turned back to Nicholas. "But I hope you see now that her concern for your safety is not really irrational at all. It has become second nature for her to worry about others, to try to protect them from harm."

Nick nodded slowly. It explained so much about Aurora. Why she claimed to want a quiet, serene life. Why she seemed afraid of passion. Why she had chosen a reportedly intellectual milquetoast like March to love. After being subjected to her father's fits of temper all her life, she would abhor any emotion that was too intense.

It explained, too, Nick realized, why she had reacted like a mother tigress when she'd seen him being beaten on the quay in St. Kitts; why she had intervened to save a total stranger. And why she had wed him—a pirate and accused murderer—despite all the serious disadvantages. She had wanted to escape her father and his rages.

Her widowhood provided her the safe haven she yearned for, but in reality, she had turned it into a prison, where emotion, desire, passion, had no place.

Scowling, Nick stared unseeingly at the rows of leather-bound volumes before him. He finally was beginning to understand what drove Aurora. Her reserve was far more ingrained and complex than he had first thought, but at least now he could better see what he was up against, and why she resisted him so fiercely. He imperiled her haven, threatened her passionless existence.

His resolve hardening, Nick set his jaw in determination. The task of teaching Aurora to trust him, to open up to him, would be more difficult than he ever imagined. But somehow he would find a way to free her from the joyless prison she had deliberately created for herself.

Chapter Thirteen

*He made me feel intensely alive. He made my heart sing
and set my blood on fire.*

Two evenings later, Aurora received a glimpse of Nicholas's renewed purpose. She had already retired to bed when she heard a soft clink against her window pane, then another. Her startlement quickly turned to dismay when she realized someone was throwing pebbles and trying to get her attention.

Knowing it could only be Nicholas, she went to open the window and peer down. He stood in silver shadow beneath the oak tree, looking up at her.

Her heart did its usual somersault. She hadn't seen him at all today; in fact, she hadn't left the house. A hard rain had prevented her morning ride in the park, and Raven had had an afternoon engagement with her aunt. But the clouds had cleared and now a bright moon drenched the night.

"What are you doing, loitering beneath my window?" Aurora demanded in a whisper.

"I've come to rescue you and take you for a drive," he answered less quietly.

"In the dead of night?"

"It isn't even midnight yet. And you've been trapped inside all day."

"I have already retired for the night."

"Do you mean to invite me up there?"

"Of course not!"

"Then you had best come down here."

"Nicholas, I am in my nightclothes."

"I don't mind," he said with a wicked edge of amusement to his voice. "Get dressed and come down, Aurora. You don't want me knocking on your front door and waking the servants, I'm certain."

His implied threat exasperated her. "I have no intention of being alone with you in the middle of the night."

"I thought that might concern you, so I brought a lad with me. He's holding my horses as we speak. And I have a curricle."

When she hesitated, he called up softly. "Craven. What harm can there be in going for a spin? I can hardly ravish you in an open carriage."

What harm, indeed? Aurora thought wryly. She would be mad to put herself at the mercy of a reckless and charming rogue.

But as usual Nicholas would not take no for an answer. "Come down, love, before I have to climb up there and fetch you. I will meet you at the back entrance."

He turned and disappeared into the shadows, giving her no further chance to protest. Short of shouting after him, she was helpless to try to make him see reason.

With a sigh of exasperation, Aurora stepped back from the window. She could scarcely believe she was actually considering going for a midnight drive in the dark with Nicholas Sabine. And yet she couldn't deny the forbidden appeal of it. What in heaven's name was happening to her? Before meeting Nicholas she'd always been sedate and proper, a model of decorum. But now she was behaving like a wanton.

And what is so wrong about that? a voice in her head prodded. *You have been sensible and proper all your life. You can be a little risqué for once.*

Feeling very much like the Frenchwoman in the journal who had been seduced into sin by her captivating prince, Aurora dressed quickly and drew on a hooded cloak. The house was dark and silent as she crept downstairs and let herself out of the servants' entrance.

Nicholas was waiting for her outside as he'd promised. When he saw her, his smile turned quite brilliant. Aurora drew a sharp breath, suddenly filled with the dizzying pleasure of being near him.

A curricle was waiting at the end of the short drive, and just as he'd claimed, a youth held the pair of horses. Nicholas handed her up into the seat and climbed up after her.

"Wait here, if you please," he said to the boy. "We shall return shortly." With a flick of the reins, he sent the team off at a brisk trot.

Aurora held on to the seat rail while sending him an incredulous look, scarcely believing his audacity.

"I should have known better than to trust you," she said darkly when they were out of earshot. "You led me to believe your tiger would accompany us."

"Only because you would not have come with me otherwise."

"Where are you taking me?"

"Not far. Look around you, siren. Is this not better than being captive in your chaste bedchamber?"

It was a magnificent night, Aurora thought unwillingly. The cool June breeze on her face was exhilarating, the moonlight stirring as it bathed the silent streets. Yet her vexation at Nicholas prevented her full enjoyment. "You cannot make me believe you were thinking only of me when you lured me out here."

"Perhaps I wasn't, but can you fault me for wanting to be alone with a beautiful woman on a moonlit night?"

"Then you don't deny you are bent on seduction."

"There are no laws against seducing my own wife."

She raised her eyes to the sky. "Haven't you anything better to do than drive me to distraction?"

"I can think of nothing better, except for making love to you."

"Nicholas!"

"Actually," he added casually before she could finish,

"Clune did invite me to join his Hellfire colleagues on a tour of the demimonde this evening, but I declined."

Aurora fell silent, disturbed by the image of Nicholas dallying with courtesans in an elegant London brothel. The thought of him making love to any other woman was distinctly troubling—which was absurd, since she had told him he was free to find his pleasures elsewhere.

She glanced up at him, at his strong profile that was chiseled by moonlight. He would have absolutely no trouble finding feminine companionship. He was devastatingly attractive, more sensual and exciting than any man she had ever known. He was also a rake and adventurer, accustomed to living dangerously and breaking hearts. She should know better than to make herself vulnerable this way, being alone with him.

"Why did you decline?" she murmured, not really wanting to hear the answer.

"Because the only woman I wanted was my wife."

She wouldn't dignify his provocative remark with an answer.

"What?" he teased softly when she remained mute. "No sharp rejoinder?"

She gave him a stern look. "I cannot credit that you would prefer me to an accomplished Cyprian."

"Ah, but I do, siren."

"Merely because, like Clune, you only want what you cannot have."

"That isn't why I want you so badly."

"Then why?" Aurora asked, curious in spite of herself.

"I wish I knew," Nicholas replied with surprising seriousness. "I've never been this attracted to any other woman before."

"What you are feeling is simple male . . ."

Nicholas supplied the word she was searching for. "Lust?" His mouth quirked wryly. "It is hardly *simple*, sweetheart. And it is far more than mere lust. It's more like a fierce craving."

"Well, you will just have to control it."

"I am trying my utmost, but I cannot control my imagination. I frequently have fantasies of you naked in my arms, did you know that?"

"Nicholas!"

"Please," he chided, "remember that my name is Brandon."

"If you don't behave," she declared in a fierce undertone, "I will demand that you turn this carriage around and take me home."

His amused expression sobered slightly. "Believe it or not, I do intend to behave this evening. I give you my word, my motives are completely altruistic for once. I only want you to have a moment of freedom."

She didn't know if she could trust him, but when he turned his head to look at her, his gaze was entirely serious. "Raven is worried for you. She thinks you're lonely and in need of company."

"Raven is mistaken. And even if I were in need of company, I would hardly choose you—a bold rogue who's determined to incite a scandal."

"I should think that as a duke's daughter you would find boldness appealing after being accustomed to servility all your life. Surely you don't want me fawning over you and treating you like fragile crystal?"

"I would like you to respect my wishes," she said coolly, "instead of trying to ride roughshod over me. You said I saved your life. For that I think I might be entitled to some measure of consideration."

"I am considering you, love. I'm thinking of your welfare. Admit it, you feel more alive when you're sparring with me, matching wits. My very presence stirs your blood."

"I do not *want* my blood stirred, Nicholas."

"Come now, can you honestly claim you don't enjoy being with me? Or that you would rather be safe in bed than here on a night like tonight?"

It was indeed magical. Aurora tilted her face up to the moon, soothed by its serene spell.

As if by mute agreement, they remained silent for a time, the only sound the clop-rattle of hooves and wheels on cobblestone. When they came to the entrance to Hyde Park, Nicholas turned off the street onto the gravel carriage path.

"I suppose you have a purpose for bringing me here?" Aurora said skeptically.

"You'll see," he replied.

They drove a short distance until the Serpentine came into view. Aurora caught her breath at the stunning beauty of the lake, which resembled a brilliant mirror.

Wordlessly Nicholas pulled off the path onto the lawn and negotiated past a grove of chestnut trees. With a tug on the reins, he drew the curricle to a halt.

Aurora sat speechless for a long moment. "I have never seen the park so peaceful and lovely," she said finally.

"You have never seen a lot of things. Would you care to sit by the water?"

When she nodded, he climbed down and tied the reins to a tree branch, then went around the rig and reached up to grasp her waist. As he lifted her down, Aurora felt his touch like a hot brand, while Nicholas suddenly froze, as if burned by the same scorching heat radiating through her.

"You aren't wearing a corset," he murmured, his voice suddenly husky.

"I had no time to put one on," she replied, flushing.

"I'm going to pretend I never discovered that."

Retrieving a blanket from the boot, he took her by the hand and drew her down past a copse of willows to the water's edge. He spread the blanket on the grassy bank, and when Aurora was seated, settled beside her.

For a long moment she simply sat there, staring in awe at the lovely, shining lake. "It's beautiful."

"Yes."

He wasn't looking at the water, but at her; she felt his scrutiny like a caress.

She wrapped her arms around her knees, looking up at the moon. A silver ring of mist surrounded the rim. Aurora drew a slow, deep breath, drinking in the serene beauty. The night air smelled of damp earth and sweet grass. "Thank you for bringing me here."

"My pleasure." He paused. "I did have an ulterior motive. I wanted to show you how much you're missing by locking yourself away in your prison."

"Indeed?" she murmured, less vexed than usual by his presumption.

"I would bet half my fortune that once you have a taste of freedom, you'll find it hard to return to your dull, proper existence."

She couldn't help but smile at his persistence. "You are still laboring under the misguided apprehension that I am discontent with my life."

"I don't believe it's a misapprehension. I think you are far lonelier than you will let yourself admit."

Aurora winced inwardly at the truth of his charge. No matter how she tried to convince herself otherwise, she couldn't deny the deep ache of loneliness inside her.

Nicholas was still watching her. She could feel his penetrating gaze, probing her secrets.

"You would be happier if you opened yourself up to risks now and then," he said gently. "If you dared to take chances and damn the consequences."

Aurora stirred uncomfortably, wishing she could change the subject. "Like you do? Risking your life simply by being in the country?"

"Even that."

"I hardly think courting danger is the key to happiness."

Nicholas shrugged. "For me it is. Danger makes you feel alive, makes you appreciate living. You should celebrate it, not fear it."

She rested her cheek on her knees and studied him in

turn. She already was risking danger simply by letting him near. Nicholas *was* danger. He was excitement. He was intensely alive. It was what set him apart from other men, she realized: his keen lust for life.

"Have you always been this way? This reckless and daring?"

"I'm afraid so. I was the bane of my father's existence."

"I can well imagine."

"I was rather wild in my youth," Nicholas admitted.

"Far beyond your youth, if the tales are true. Raven says you were the black sheep of your family until only a few years ago."

"Have you been talking to her about me?"

Aurora felt herself flush. "I asked her to tell me more about the stranger I married. It was a way to honor you in death, I suppose."

His smile was charmingly sensual. "I'm gratified."

"So what caused your transformation?"

"My father's death."

Nicholas stretched out on his side, facing her, and propped himself on one elbow. His handsome features looked thoughtful in the moonlight. "I always knew I would inherit the Sabine shipping empire one day. Almost from my cradle my father groomed me to take over his holdings, and I spent much of my youth crewing his ships and learning to sail anything that floated. I relished that part of the business, but I resented being controlled and having my entire future planned out for me in infinite detail. When I was twenty, I finally rebelled and went in search of my own destiny."

Aurora had no trouble imagining a young, restless Nicholas straining to break free of his father's dictates. Fettering him that way would have been like trying to cage a wild tiger.

Nicholas paused, gazing out over the shimmering water. "I rarely saw my father after that, until he lay dying. It was only on his deathbed that I came to realize how much I hurt him by leaving."

She heard the regret in his voice, the sadness, and wanted to offer solace. "It must have been a sacrifice for you to return home to take over the family business."

"Somewhat, but I owed it to my father. I never fully appreciated the sacrifice he made to keep his family intact. He was passionately in love with Raven's mother, and he could have left his wife and children, but he didn't. Besides, it was time I lived up to my responsibilities. I swore to him I would care for my mother and sisters and keep his legacy intact. The line has done well enough under my hand . . . at least until the war started. But even with that, we've fared better than most shipping concerns."

Aurora wasn't certain she wanted to see this admirable, appealing side of Nicholas—the quiet, thoughtful man revealing his innermost feelings, opening himself to her. Yet it helped her understand what drove him. "That was why you were so determined to see Raven settled, even to the extent of wedding a stranger."

"Yes." He smiled. "Nothing else could have forced me to the altar."

She, on the other hand, had known her whole life long that the altar was waiting for her. Aurora fell silent, contemplating how different their lives had been. Nicholas had rebelled and set off on a wild life of adventure, while she had remained dutifully complacent, obeying her father's every wish—except his last. Until her marriage to Nicholas, she had always conducted herself precisely as expected of her. And until now, she had never allowed herself to admit how much she resented it.

"What are you thinking?" Nicholas asked, watching her.

"That wedding you was the first time I ever defied my father."

"That isn't what Raven says," he said quietly. "She claims you were forced to defy him regularly to protect your servants."

Aurora looked away. She didn't like to think about her father's violent rages. It was too disturbing, too humiliating.

"Raven saw your father threaten you, Aurora. I gather he struck you often."

"Not often," she said reluctantly, wanting to be fair. "And it was a small price to pay. I was the only one who could stand up to him, and he would . . ." She shut her eyes, remembering her father's physical assaults on his defenseless servants.

"He wasn't always so bad," she finally said. "My mother could manage him, but after she died, he took to drinking more heavily. His moods were so . . . unpredictable. One day he would be amiable, the next he would fly into a rage at the slightest provocation. I could usually calm him if I didn't confront him directly, if I placated him. But I grew to dread even being near him. . . ." Her voice dropped to a whisper. "It's terrible to say, but I think I hated him."

"No."

"It is shameful to hate your own father."

"Not if he deserves it. Any man who would strike a—" Nicholas bit off the comment, his tone grim. "I would very much like to meet your father."

Aurora winced at the mere thought of that confrontation.

"I think he affected you more than you realize," Nicholas observed after a moment.

He was right, she knew, nodding slowly. "Perhaps so. All my life I lived in dread of his rages. They made me physically ill. I was always so powerless. . . . I learned to hate emotional turmoil." She gave an involuntary shudder.

She felt Nicholas's hand touch the small of her back, offering comfort, and drew a measured breath. Her father could not hurt her now—because of Nicholas.

"For the past two months I've known peace. I no longer wake up dreading having to face my father. I was grateful to you for that. Wedding you allowed me to escape him."

"Why didn't you tell me?"

"Tell you?"

"About the risk you were taking by marrying me."

"What good would it have done? You were not in a position to accept a refusal."

"I didn't realize the danger I was putting you in."

"It was my choice, Nicholas. And besides . . ." She smiled faintly down at him. "You allowed me to escape Halford, too. I would have had to endure that marriage." She shuddered again. "Truly, being widowed has allowed me far more freedom than I've ever known before, and I cherish it."

Nicholas considered her claim for a long moment. When he spoke, his tone was quiet, contemplative. "The bit of freedom you've carved out for yourself has barely scratched the surface, Aurora."

She gave him a questioning look. "What are you suggesting I do? I have already pressed the limits of decorum as far as I dare, setting up my own household and living on my own."

"You could dare a great deal more. You are still letting yourself be smothered, trying to conform to society's rigid rules, your father's expectations."

He was right again, Aurora thought, gazing out at the silvery lake. She did feel smothered. She had felt so her whole life long. Perhaps that was why the journal had struck such a deep chord inside her. That beautiful yet terrible tale of passion fascinated her more than she would have believed possible—a sheltered woman finding freedom in the very chains of slavery that bound her. . . .

Aurora pressed her lips together in denial. She certainly had no desire for such drastic liberation. But perhaps she *should* take more risks, as Nicholas was suggesting. Perhaps she should dare to be bolder. . . .

"You have a hunger for living, Aurora, beneath all those proper inhibitions." His tone was low and vibrant. "You want to feel alive. Yet you don't know how."

She felt his gaze probing her, as if he were seeing inside her and uncovering all her secrets. Somehow Nicholas understood the yearning she had always hidden in the deepest part of her, the part that was wild and restless and questing. The longing for some nameless fulfillment. Something elusive she could only imagine.

"And I suppose you are offering to teach me?" she said finally.

"I want to, very much." His rough-velvet voice resonated through her. "I could show you a world you've never seen before, one brilliant and vibrant with color. You aren't happy now in your dull gray world, alone in your cold, lonely bed."

At his implication that he warm her bed, her breath caught. "You are not responsible for my happiness, Nicholas," she managed to murmur.

"Perhaps not, but you need liberating. And I intend to be the one to do it."

"How? By wearing down my resistance?"

"By becoming your lover."

In the night's silence she could hear the hammering of her heart. "I have no intention of being intimate with you again. What if I should conceive? I could never live down the scandal."

"You read the journal. There are myriad ways to experience carnal relations that don't result in conception. We have a vast array of methods of arousal yet to explore. Of touching and caressing and enjoying each other."

It was true; the journal described in exquisite detail many different forms of sensual pleasure. Aurora looked down at Nicholas. He was watching her intently, a primal gaze of sensuality incarnate.

His voice dropped to a husky murmur. "Doesn't your heart race a little faster at the thought of making love to me? Can you deny my touch excites you?"

No, she couldn't deny it at all. This man was her husband. He had been her first lover. Her only lover. She wanted him.

She was suddenly filled with intense awareness. Of the

night. Of the tingling in her veins. Of Nicholas. Of the rich, disturbing promise of his mouth.

The air between them seemed to throb with pulses of anticipation and warning as she stared at him. There was something wild and savage singing through her blood, a whispering voice urging her to yield to abandon, to give in to the lush sensation he promised.

Yet another conflicting voice exhorted her to keep her defenses strong. Nicholas lusted after her because he wanted what he could not have.

But . . . what if she gave him what he wanted? If she yielded to him, he would soon tire of the chase, for the thrill would be gone. Surely he would end his maddening pursuit then.

There might even be a way to hasten his decision: she could take the offensive herself. She was weary of being his quarry, of defending herself, of endlessly having to keep up her guard.

He reminded her of her father in that respect. Whether intentionally or not, Nicholas was trying to intimidate her, to make her accede his demands, to control her. Yet after standing up to her father for so many years, she should be able to stand up to Nicholas.

It would be gratifying to turn the tables on him and make *him* the hunted for a change. If she pursued him, he might very well turn tail and run—all the way back to America. And if she could manage to ease his powerful carnal needs, he would no longer be driven by his fierce lust. . . .

"Perhaps you are right," Aurora said slowly, hoping she wasn't making an irrevocable mistake. "Perhaps we should become lovers."

When he had no response, she realized she had surprised him into silence. He had clearly not expected her acquiescence.

He would not expect her to take the first step, either.

Aurora drew a measured breath, wondering if she had

the courage to follow through with her wild plan. But what choice had he left her? She couldn't allow things to continue this way, with Nicholas driving her slowly mad. He wouldn't stop until she yielded, so the sooner she did so, the sooner their bizarre relationship would end.

She had scarce experience in carnal matters, but the journal had given her remarkable insights, teaching her the secrets of a man's body, how to excite his desire—an invaluable lesson, Aurora knew. A woman could wield great power if she controlled a man's desire.

Her wedding night, too, had helped her shed her virginal ignorance as well as her inhibitions. Nicholas himself had taught her about hunger and arousal. . . .

Holding his gaze, Aurora gathered her courage and slowly bent down to touch his warm lips with her own.

Nicholas remained frozen, as if startled into immobility. "Are you really serious?" he asked finally.

She answered with false calmness. "Quite serious. You said I should take more risks. Well, I intend to, beginning now. Will you lie back, please?"

When she reached out to press him down, he grasped her hand, holding it away from his body.

With a nervous laugh, Aurora straightened. "You aren't afraid of me, are you, Nicholas?" she murmured in a low voice that was intentionally challenging.

He narrowed his heated eyes. "Just what do you plan to do?"

"Ease your lust." Her hand pressed again on his chest. "And perhaps enjoy a taste of revenge. You delight in tormenting me. Well, it is my turn to torment you. Turnabout is fair play, after all. Now lie back."

He did as ordered, but his husky voice held a warning. "Aurora, I am not a saint. If you don't want to make love, then I strongly suggest you end this game right now."

She let her lips curl in a smile as she unfastened the buttons of his coat, even though she felt clumsy with nerves.

"A *saint* is the last thing I would call you, Nicholas. And I want to play this game. . . . Only I set the rules."

She slowly undid his waistcoat buttons and pushed aside the lapels. She could feel his heartbeat beneath the fine cambric of his shirt; warmth, life lay under her fingertips, reassuring as well as arousing. "The first rule is that you aren't to touch me."

"What if I don't want to play by your rules?"

"Oh, I think you will."

Her hand moved lower, to his hard abdomen. She hesitated a moment. Then clutching his shirt, she loosened the hem from the waistband of his breeches and drew it up till his stomach was completely bare.

When Nicholas shifted his weight uneasily, Aurora frowned in warning. "Lie still."

He obliged as she lightly stroked his taut belly, his skin hot beneath her palm. But when she slid her fingers into his waistband, his entire body tensed. Her courage swelled.

"Does this hurt?" she asked, slightly taunting.

"You know it doesn't, witch," he ground out.

She withdrew her hand, but she could tell he was already aroused; she could feel the enormous bulge under his breeches as her fingers worked the buttons.

"If you expect me to be still while you touch me like that," he said hoarsely, "you should think again."

"If you move, I shall stop," Aurora replied serenely.

He gritted his teeth as she opened his breeches and moved on to the buttons of his drawers. When a moment later she parted the fabric, his quivering length sprang from the dark gold curls of his groin.

Aurora felt her breath catch. He was stunning, with the moonlight silvering the hard planes and muscles of his body.

She might have little experience, but she knew what would happen when she touched him. How a soft caress would make his muscles bunch and tighten. How the lightest brush of her fingertips across his belly would make him quiver. How his skin would flush with heat and his male flesh grow rigid . . .

I stroke the thickening swell of your hardness and feel no shame. You have taught me desires of the flesh, sensitized my body to pleasure, burning away all inhibition.

She knew.

She kept her gaze trained on his manhood, at the shaft that was already thickly engorged, yet she wasn't as tranquil as she pretended. Her heart was pounding as she ran her hand lightly down his torso, following the feathery trail of hair over his belly, caressing him the way he'd taught her on their wedding night.

It fascinated her, the contrasts beneath her fingers—the sinewy hardness of his stomach . . . the velvet steel of his manhood . . . the downy softness of the sacs beneath. He jerked slightly when she touched him there, the heavy testicles tightening as she cupped him lightly.

"Aurora . . ." he rasped.

Enthralled by his response, she extended her exploration. With trembling fingers she moved upward, rimming the engorged crest of his arousal, teasing the sensitive ridge. When he shivered at her touch, she grew bolder, tracing the sleek contours, stroking the throbbing length, so swollen with heat.

Eventually her fingers folded completely around his manhood, enclosing the velvet-sheathed hardness and squeezing lightly. The thick length surged in her hand, swelling to fit her grasp. With rising confidence, she drew her hand slowly downward, then up again, creating an exquisite friction.

"Where did you learn to do that?" Nicholas asked in a strangled voice moments later.

"I had an excellent tutor," Aurora murmured.

"I don't recall teaching you that."

"Not that specifically, perhaps. But you taught me not to fear a man's body. You taught me about pleasure and arousal. The journal suggested the rest."

He was so hard under the hot, silky skin, so magnificently erect. Yet what amazed her was how simply touching him could affect her so strongly, how stroking him could stroke her own desire. She felt hot all over; her nerves, her skin, her pulse felt incredibly alive, while a sweet ache had begun throbbing between her thighs.

Her gaze locked with his, the clamor of her heart echoing his unspoken question.

Shivering with anticipation, she pushed back the hood of her cloak and bent her head to taste the male shaft that could give so much pleasure. It was shameless, brazen, yet thrilling to have this strong, vibrant man at her mercy.

When her mouth touched the distended tip, he seemed to stop breathing altogether, and her sense of power swelled. She glanced up to see that Nicholas's eyes had closed. Holding the base of his rigid length, she slid her tongue gently around the pulsing head. She felt his body clench.

"Am I doing this right?" she whispered.

His response was a strangled groan. "Exquisitely right. Don't stop."

She had no intention of stopping. Exploring the forbidden delights of his body was too sensuously exciting.

He felt the same excitement, Aurora knew, despite her lack of experience. She felt his hand touch her hair, guiding her lightly as her tongue circled the smooth, glistening crest, but his powerful body had gone rigid, his hips straining to keep from moving as she explored him with her mouth and tongue.

Letting her feminine instincts take over, she took him fully in her mouth, enveloping the thick bulbous tip with her lips. The shocking pleasure of it left her weak. He was scalding hot, pulsing with life, and her gentle suckling made him surge even larger and longer.

She heard him groan and looked up to see his hard virile face taut and rapt with ecstasy. Aurora felt a thrill of pleasure. She wanted to make him groan, wanted him writhing with need.

Almost eagerly she bent to him again, her hair spilling

around him, over his stomach and groin as she renewed her
sensual assault. His body clenched harder, and he arched
against the blanket as his hands moved to clutch her hair.

He was actually shaking, Aurora realized. Excitement
coursed through her, heightening the hungry longing in
her own loins. Her own desire was burgeoning, her secret
flesh wet and pulsing.

Fire beating through her senses, she feverishly stepped
up her assault, her fingers fondling his stiffened sacs as she
tormented him with suckling caresses.

His breathing turned harsh and ragged. He was nearing
climax, she knew. She could feel him shuddering deep in
her throat.

His self-control broke a moment later. With a low guttural sound, Nicholas pulled back abruptly. Turning on his
side away from her, he spent himself, his body convulsing
in an explosion of need, his shaft lifting and jerking helplessly as his seed gushed hot and milky onto the grass.

Aurora watched his wrenching, powerful release in awe,
exhilarated by her own power to make such a strong man
so helpless.

Drained, limp, he slowly rolled onto his back. But it was
a long moment before he opened his eyes. "It seems I owe
the journal a debt of gratitude."

Aurora felt herself flush at the heated intensity of his
gaze—and at his brazenness. He made no move to cover
his nakedness. She was suddenly unaccountably embarrassed by her own wanton behavior. She looked away.

"You don't mean to turn shy, siren?" Nicholas murmured. "Not now, when it is my turn to pleasure you."

He took her hand and brought it to his lips, pressing a
kiss into her palm. Aurora felt herself shudder at the intense heat that simple gesture aroused in her. Reluctantly,
she drew her hand away. "I think perhaps I have been
daring enough for one evening."

"There is only one trouble. A taste of you only makes

me want more. I want to spend the rest of the night making love to you."

Her breath faltered. "You cannot."

"Why not?" He reached up, beneath her cloak, to caress her breast. She winced when he found the sensitive peaked nipple beneath the thin muslin of her gown. "You're highly aroused, Aurora. You want me. Your body is eager for release, for pleasure."

She couldn't reply. Her instinctive wariness had returned with a vengeance, along with the warning voice clamoring in her head, urging her to beware his sensual blandishments.

When she didn't answer, Nicholas sat up. Lifting his fingers to her lips, he brushed them with the lightest of pressure. Aurora shut her eyes as a dizzying wave of need rushed through her. Her desire for him was a physical ache, throbbing and urgent.

She feared the strength of that desire, and yet the simple truth was she couldn't deny herself the pleasure of his touch.

When he started to draw her into his arms, she stopped him with a hand on his chest. Glancing around, she realized how revealing the moonlit darkness was. Though largely concealed by willows, they were still too visible for Aurora's comfort. "Not here, Nicholas . . ."

"You're right. We should find a bed. Where do you want to go?"

She took a deep breath, throwing prudence and caution to the wind. "Take me home."

"Gladly."

With a faint smile, he rearranged his clothing and fastened the buttons of his various garments. Then getting to his feet, he held his hand down to her. She took it with trembling fingers.

Scooping up the blanket, Nicholas led her to the curricle and handed her up. When he settled himself beside her and took up the reins, he gave one last look at the shore of the shining lake.

"After this evening," he murmured without any trace of amusement, "I will never see this place in quite the same way."

Nor would she, Aurora thought. From this point forward, whenever she visited the park, she would always remember this moment with Nicholas.

They were mostly silent on their way home. Aurora felt her heart hammering in conflict as she questioned the wisdom of her decision. Inviting Nicholas into her bed was like unleashing a caged tiger: she was very likely to be wounded.

Already her emotions were greatly at risk. And becoming even more intimate with him would blatantly endanger the serenity she'd striven so hard to find.

Yet she had taken this course and would see it through to the conclusion. She only hoped that her calculations had been right. That once he claimed her as a conquest, he would abandon the chase. And that he would tire of his pursuit before she was too badly hurt.

When she reached home, however, worries about her plan were driven out of her head as they turned into the drive at the rear of the house. She could see lights blazing from many of the rooms.

"Something has happened," Aurora murmured, trying to stem her alarm.

The moment Nicholas drew the curricle to a halt, Aurora scrambled down and ran up the back steps. Nicholas's tiger, who had been waiting patiently for their return, came to hold the horses, leaving Nicholas to follow her inside the house.

She was met in the hallway by her butler, who looked as if he'd been roused from sleep. Danby wore a dressing gown over his nightshirt and a cap over his gray hair, while his elderly face sported a grave expression.

"My lady, is aught amiss? We were concerned for you when we could not find you anywhere in the house."

Aurora lifted her chin, determined to brazen out her actions. She had no reason to cower before her servants in shame. "I went for a drive. What has happened, Danby? Why is the entire household awake?"

"The Earl of March has arrived, my lady."

For a moment Aurora's heart seemed to stop. Geoffrey could not have called, for he had perished at sea nearly a year ago. Then she remembered that his ten-year-old brother, Harry, had inherited the title.

"Harry is here? In London?"

"Yes, my lady. He is currently in the kitchens. He was . . . er . . . hungry after his travels."

"His travels? What do you mean? Did his mother bring him?"

"No, my lady. Only young Lord March—"

Just then a blond-haired boy came bounding into the hall from the stairway that led to the kitchens. He was dressed in breeches and jacket, but his hair was mussed and his young face that looked so much like Geoffrey's was actually dirty.

"Rory, am I ever so glad to see you—" When he spied Nicholas, the boy came to a halt. Much to her surprise, his hands curled into fists, and he stood there glowering at Nicholas. "Who are you?" he demanded angrily.

"Harry," Aurora said sharply in protest. "Where are your manners?"

"I am Lady Aurora's cousin by marriage, Brandon Deverill," Nicholas said mildly.

"You have no right to be here!" the boy nearly growled.

"Harry, this gentleman is a guest in my house. You will mind your tongue."

Still scowling, he cast Aurora an accusing look. "You cannot have forgotten my brother already? It has been only a year since he died. One year exactly today."

Aurora winced. She hadn't remembered that today was the anniversary of the tragic shipwreck. "No," she said guiltily. "The date may have slipped my mind, but I could never forget Geoffrey."

"Then what is *he* doing here, calling at this time of night?"

She took a measured breath. "You have no authority to ask such questions, my young lordling. Furthermore, as a relation, Nic— Mr. Deverill has every right to call here. Now it is your turn to give me some answers. What are you doing here in London? Especially at this hour of night?"

For the first time, Harry's scowl faded to uncertainty. "I've run away from home, Rory. Mama has become insufferable. Please, you must allow me to stay with you."

Chapter Fourteen

He touched me with startling tenderness, as if even my heart belonged to him.

"So tell me, Harry, how did you manage to find your way to London?" Aurora asked a short while later as she and Nicholas sat with the boy at the servants' table in the kitchen. To her exasperation, Nicholas had remained without invitation and simply made himself at home, and she hadn't wanted to argue with him in front of her unexpected young guest.

Harry looked up from munching on a meal of cold chicken and scones and apples. "The stage. It was ever so much fun. I rode on top first and then in the box. That was famous! The coachman let me take the reins, but only for a moment because some of the passengers complained about my driving."

"You traveled all the way from Sussex alone?" Aurora said, dismayed. "Don't you realize how dangerous that was? You could have been robbed or—"

"Oh, the stage was not dangerous in the least. It was only when I arrived at the posting inn that I almost landed in the briars. It was quite crowded, and I had to inquire about directions, and there were three fellows who looked like footpads. But when they tried to detain me, I showed them my fives and ran away."

Aurora shuddered to think what might have happened to a child alone at night on the London streets.

"I am not a complete gudgeon, Rory," he said when he saw her expression. "I can take care of myself. They stole my bundle, though." Harry suddenly looked glum. "It had my favorite ship in it."

"Ship?" Nicholas asked curiously.

The boy gave him a wary look, as if debating whether to trust him. "Admiral Nelson's flagship, the *Victory*. It was made of tin. My brother gave it to me." As if remembering Geoffrey, the boy suddenly sent Aurora an accusing look. "Danby did not want to let me in. He would not believe that I was Lord March, since I was in leading strings the last time he saw me. And you were not here to vouch for me."

She fought the urge to squirm, knowing she must look like a wanton. She had removed her cloak, and her hair was in disarray, tumbling down her back. "Does your mother know you've run away?" she asked, deliberately changing the subject.

Harry grinned impishly. "By now, she does. But I did leave her a note, telling her I intended to live with you."

"Harry, your mother will be frantic with worry."

"I know. That is why I ran away. She is in a quake all the time. She is *smothering* me, Rory. And this past week, it was even worse than usual, because Geoffrey passed on one year ago."

"She would be understandably upset," Aurora said patiently. "You are her only child now, Harry—"

"I *know*. Mama is muttonheaded when it comes to Geoff. But she raises a dust if I even leave the house! She means to keep me in leading strings till I am full grown, Rory. It is ever so plaguey."

Aurora frowned. "Where did you learn such vulgar cant?"

"From Tom, the groundskeeper. Do you mean to ring a peal over me, Rory? If so, then go ahead, but I shan't go home again, so there is no use trying to make me. If you will not let me live with you, I will just have to find someone else who will take me in."

Aurora hesitated to answer. She was eager to help Harry,

not only because she was extremely fond of him, but also because she wanted to appease her guilt. She had neglected the boy dreadfully this past year. He'd lost a brother he idolized and then had been forced to endure his mama's protective smothering. Lady March was not generally the scatterbrained sort, but she had been devastated at her elder son's death and was determined that nothing would befall her younger son. Aurora could well understand why Harry would finally rebel and seek refuge with someone he considered a friend. Yet she didn't want to encourage or abet his rebellion.

Before she could express her reservations, however, Harry spoke again.

"It will not be for long, for I mean to join the navy and fight the Frogs, like Geoffrey."

"You mean to do *what*?"

"I am going to run away to sea. I want to have *real* adventures, but Mama will never let me. She will not even permit me to fish in our own streams. I cannot go near water because she is afraid I will drown like Geoffrey did."

"I know something about running off to sea," Nicholas interjected mildly.

"You do?" Harry's look became interested. "You sound like a Colonial."

"I am American. But I have some experience with the British navy. There are numerous sailors on my ships who were impressed illegally by your country and forced to serve."

"You are a ship's captain?" His eyes lit up.

"Not a captain. Owner. I have a fleet of merchant ships."

"A *fleet*? That is capital!"

Nicholas smiled. "If you knew the hardships you would face in your navy, you would not want to join, believe me. The life of a tar is remarkably unpleasant compared to the one you're accustomed to. You would do much better to apprentice in the merchant marine."

Aurora gave Nicholas a quelling look, annoyed that he

would encourage the boy in such wild fantasies. "Harry is going to join neither."

Harry's jaw set mutinously as he clutched his drumstick. "I *am*, Rory."

Nicholas shook his head. "Well, this is not the way to go about it. Not only would you distress your mother, but you are ill-prepared to begin your venture. I'll wager you don't even have a letter of introduction."

"I must have a letter?"

"If you want to be more than a scullery, you do. You need someone in a position of authority to vouchsafe your character, and you will need money to outfit your sea chest."

"I have money. I am quite rich."

"Then instead of becoming a tar, you might consider buying your own ship and becoming the employer. Trust me, that would be far more agreeable than swabbing decks from morning till night."

Harry grinned broadly, obviously keen on this new idea.

Nicholas returned a slow grin of his own. Watching his irresistible smile, Aurora felt a knife of longing twist inside her. She should have known he could relate to a rebellious boy. The encounter gave her a glimpse of what Nicholas must have been like at that age. And yet she was dismayed to see him using his ruthless charm to wrap Harry around his thumb.

Waving the drumstick, the boy went off on another fantasy. "If I had my own ship, I could go to France and spy on the Frogs, like Geoffrey."

"What do you mean, like Geoffrey?" Aurora asked.

"He was on a secret mission when his yacht sank—" Harry glanced around him surreptitiously. "Oh, I should not have said that. Geoffrey made me promise not to tell."

Aurora put no credence in Harry's comment. She could not possibly conceive of bookish Geoffrey dashing off to France to spy. Perhaps Harry simply had concocted that tale to give meaning to his brother's senseless death at sea.

Evidently he was even more in need of a friend than she first suspected.

There was no question that she would be that friend. She felt a strong duty toward the boy. Harry had been underfoot much of the time when he was growing up, even when Geoffrey was officially courting her. Harry was horse mad and had wanted any excuse to visit the Eversley stables. And he had trusted her judgment in horseflesh more than his brother's. She, rather than Geoffrey, had chosen his first pony.

She had always thought of him as a younger brother, and he *would* have been her brother by marriage had not fate so callously intervened. Moreover, she well knew what it was like to want to escape a domineering parent. So despite her qualms about abetting his rebellion, she would allow Harry to remain with her for now. At least until she could persuade him to give up his nonsense about running off to sea in search of adventure.

When he yawned hugely, Aurora realized he was exhausted. "You should be in bed," she said gently. "I'm certain we can sort this out in the morning."

"You won't send me home?"

"Not immediately, although I shall write your mother directly in the morning and let her know you have arrived safely, and ask her permission to let you stay with me for a visit."

"You are a grand sport, Rory!" Getting up from the table, he ran around to her side and threw his arms around her neck.

Aurora couldn't help but smile. "Did you say you had lost your clothing? We shall have to find you a suitable nightshirt."

Danby, who was hovering discreetly just outside the door, appeared as if summoned. Aurora extricated herself from the boy's bear hug. "Would you please see Lord March settled in the green bedchamber, Danby?"

"As you wish, my lady."

When Harry started to follow the butler, Aurora stopped him. "One moment, my young lordling. I believe you owe Mr. Deverill an apology."

Harry turned to Nicholas with reluctant contrition. "I am very sorry if I was rude, sir. Will you please forgive me?"

"You're forgiven," Nicholas said easily.

"And if I promise to behave, will you tell me about your ships?"

Nicholas smiled. "I would be happy to."

"Thank you." Harry glanced at Aurora. "He is not as bad as I feared, Rory."

When the boy was gone, Aurora felt Nicholas's gaze settle on her.

"He calls you Rory?"

"Harry could not pronounce my name when he was young, so I have always been Rory to him. I apologize for his earlier outburst. He really is a delightful boy."

"I can see that." Nicholas paused. "You handled him well. You would make a good mother."

Their eyes met, and she wondered if he was thinking the same thought she was. What would their children have been like had their marriage been real and lasting?

Mentally Aurora chastised herself. She would be a fool to let herself dream of a true union with Nicholas. He wasn't the kind of man to give his heart to one woman. Love was a game to him, an adventure. He would satisfy a woman's carnal desires beyond her wildest imaginings, she had absolutely no doubt. But he would feel nothing deeper.

And with no stronger emotions to bind him, how long would it be before his restless urge to roam overtook him? Before the siren call of danger lured him from her side? Before he left her alone and heartbroken?

No, Aurora reminded herself as an ache of sadness twisted in her chest. There was no possibility of having children with Nicholas. . . .

She suddenly caught her breath, remembering the unfinished matter between them. Nicholas was here, in her kitchen, because she had invited him to share her bed. Sweet heaven . . .

All at once the moment was filled with a new kind of tension. When his eyes caressed her, Aurora shifted in her seat, uneasy under his dark perusal.

Her resolve to keep him at a distance had nearly shattered this evening. She was suddenly grateful Harry had arrived when he had. Although he presented a problem—and was another unexpected male in her life—he had saved her from making a dreadful mistake.

"I think you should go," she murmured, her voice suddenly hoarse.

"You didn't feel that way an hour ago."

"An hour ago I was suffering from a touch of moon madness. And I did not know Harry would run away from home and seek refuge here."

"So you mean to hide behind him." It was not a question. "To use him as a convenient excuse to deny the desire you feel for me."

"No, Nicholas—"

"Yes. You're fooling yourself, Aurora. Deceiving yourself about what you really want."

"That isn't true. I was inexcusably rash this evening—" Aurora shook her head. "I have to think of my responsibilities. I have a duty toward Harry. His brother is gone, and Geoffrey would have wanted me to watch over him."

When Nicholas stared at her steadily, she added defensively, "It would be disloyal to Geoffrey's memory for me to be intimate with you tonight. I should never have forgotten that today is the anniversary of his death. It was unforgivable of me."

Nicholas's mouth tightened. "What is unforgivable is you burying yourself alive in the past. You have to forget your former betrothed, Aurora, and move on with your life."

She averted her gaze. "It is not so easy to forget the death of someone you love." Her voice dropped to a low murmur. "You cannot conceive what it was like for me to lose Geoffrey. He was more than my betrothed. He was a dear friend, someone I had loved nearly from the cradle. And after losing my mother—" Abruptly she bit off the sentence, her throat tightening at the memory. Nicholas wouldn't understand the rage of loss, the desolate feeling of helplessness, the unbearable loneliness she had felt at losing Geoffrey, too.

She had been devastated when her beloved mother had succumbed to an influenza epidemic. Geoffrey had been her solace, had comforted her and helped ease her anguish. And then he had died as well. It was so unfair that he had been cut down in the prime of life. But then . . . she had learned how useless it was to rail against fate.

Forcing back the pain as she always did, Aurora rose abruptly. "I don't intend to argue with you about this, Nicholas. I trust you can show yourself out."

She turned to leave but his soft voice stopped her. "Aurora."

She wouldn't look at him. She heard him scrape back his chair, felt his nearness as he came up behind her. His arms encircled her, holding her lightly.

"Don't push me away," he said into her hair.

Her throat constricted. Heat pulsed through her, while need rose up in her like the pressure of tears.

As he drew her back against his hard, muscular form, she was reminded all over again why it was dangerous to have anything to do with Nicholas. The fierce desire she felt for him was a fiery ache inside her. She didn't want him to leave, didn't want to push him away, and yet a desperate need for self-preservation was clamoring within her, warning her to save herself.

"I was mistaken to have invited you here," she whispered. "I don't want to become intimate with you again. I can't."

"Why not?" His hand rose to shape the curve of her breast, the mound filling his palm. "We are husband and wife. We need no more license than that to become lovers."

"To what end?" Her voice was raw. "A momentary pleasure?"

He hesitated a long moment. "What is so wrong with a momentary pleasure?"

She shut her eyes. She could feel his warm breath on her cheek, feel his palm erotically cupping her breast, and she had to force back a moan.

"You, Nicholas," she said raggedly. "You are what is wrong. You are the last man I would ever willingly choose as my lover. I could not bear to form an attachment to a man who risks death for the sheer sport of it. I have had enough of death. First my mother, then Geoffrey . . . I won't open myself to that kind of hurt again."

"I am not asking you to."

"You *are*. You have accused me of hiding from my feelings. Perhaps I do, but it is less painful that way."

"Less painful, yes, but infinitely less fulfilling." His own voice was a rough whisper. "Do you really want to go through life missing the joys, the triumphs? What point is there in living if you wall yourself from everything that gives meaning to life? From excitement, from desire, from passion?"

When she didn't answer, he pressed his mouth against her hair. "Can you really hold yourself so aloof, Aurora? Can you deny your own wild yearning? Are you that strong?"

He was speaking to every forbidden impulse she had ever had. Desperately Aurora shook her head. She had to resist, had to fight her traitorous need for him. Surrendering to her desire would be madness, would lead only to hurt. Already she had come to feel too deeply for him. Already Nicholas had caught her in his powerful spell. . . .

She had to end it now, before she was too late.

"You are wrong," she said, almost pleading. "I don't want passion. I want only to be left alone."

"I don't believe that. I remember the captivating woman

you were in our marriage bed. I won't let you forget the passionate lover you were that night."

"Nicholas, please . . . just . . . go."

In answer he turned her slowly to face him, his arms at her waist lightly holding her captive, his searching eyes dark and intent. She stood helplessly looking up at him, drowning in his gaze.

"Aurora . . ." The word was a sensual husk of a whisper. Then he bent his head.

Aurora gave a soft moan of protest as she pressed her hands against his chest. She didn't want his kiss . . . didn't want to feel his warm lips moving upon hers, to open to him and take his breath into her mouth. Didn't want to lift her arms and entwine her fingers in his hair, to feel this wild, throbbing hunger that he alone could rouse in her . . .

His kiss deepened, becoming heated and urgent, while his arms tightened around her. Aurora made a soft whimpering sound of need. She was keenly aware of his hard body, the rigid evidence of his mounting desire pressing against her. She heard his breath become more ragged as his devouring mouth plundered her own.

Excitement flared through her senses at the promise of the unbearable pleasure he offered. He wanted her. And heaven help her, she wanted him. . . .

At that moment she heard a footfall on the steps leading to the kitchen. Alarm rippled through Aurora, giving her the strength to pull away from his forbidden embrace.

She was safely across the room, her heart thrumming erratically, her body still vibrating with riotous sensations, when Danby appeared.

"Young Lord March is being attended to, my lady," the butler informed her. "Is there anything else you wish?"

Aurora struggled for command of her passion-hazed senses. "Yes, Danby," she managed in a shaky voice. "Will you see Mr. . . . Deverill out? He was just leaving."

Without another glance at Nicholas, she fled.

Watching her, Nick locked his jaw, willing himself not

to follow. He sure as hell hadn't wanted to let her go. Yet maybe it was fortunate they had been interrupted, for he might not have stopped kissing Aurora until he was sheathed deep within her. He'd been so blinded with need, he could have taken her right there, in her kitchen.

It was only when he was driving his curricle back to his hotel, however, that Nicholas had time to consider his ravenous craving.

He was hard pressed to explain the power Aurora held over him. He had never met another woman whose touch produced such a blaze of desire in him. What was it about her that made her so damned tempting?

She was beautiful, true. She possessed a spellbinding combination of beauty and wit, intelligence and grace, that he'd rarely found in any other woman. Her resistance to his wooing, too, made her unique among her sex.

Unquestionably, he was driven by the challenge she presented. Not only did his competitive nature compel him to try to win the battle of wills between them, but having her so near, yet untouchable, was a sweet, sexual hell that roused his every primal male instinct.

But what he felt went far deeper than mere competitiveness or lust. Without realizing it, he'd become caught up in desire. The desire to claim her fully as his.

He was playing with fire, he knew, but never before had he been so willing to be burned.

Nick's mouth twisted in a dark smile. His friends and family would be amazed to find him so enamored of a woman—certainly of his own wife. But whether he wanted Aurora so intensely because she'd bewitched him or because she continued to deny him, he was less inclined than ever simply to walk away.

What had begun as a practical resolve to fulfill an obligation to his father and make the best of an unwanted marriage had somehow become a vital need. The more he came to know Aurora, the more certain he was that he wanted her for his wife.

He wasn't wrong about her. She had a wild spirit inside her that longed to be free. Her exquisite ministrations earlier in the park had proven that. Her momentary daring had startled and delighted him, giving him a savage release that had left him temporarily sated.

His triumph had been short-lived, though.

Remembering, Nicholas cursed. To see her retreat back into her self-protective cocoon afterward had infuriated him. He had wanted to shake some sense into her. And when she had spoken so tenderly of her love for her late betrothed, he had wanted to hit something.

Fierce possessiveness flooded Nick at the memory. *He was jealous of a dead man.* Her idolization of the late, great Geoffrey, Lord March, was enraging. But until she got over her memories of March, she would never be able to move on with her life . . . or give herself freely to anyone else. To him.

Nick set his jaw grimly. He was accustomed to rescuing damsels in distress, but usually the peril came from a physical threat. This time, however, he would save Aurora from herself.

He would claim her for his wife . . . and he would make her forget that she had ever loved another man.

Chapter Fifteen

He made his intent clear; he was determined to have me, body and soul.

Contrary to Aurora's hopes, young Harry's arrival in London did little to solve her dilemma: how to avoid her persistent, unwanted husband. Rather Harry's visit merely gave Nicholas further pretext for intimacy. He called at her house frequently, ostensibly to entertain Harry and take him to see the sights of London.

Their almost instant camaraderie greatly dismayed Aurora. Nicholas had won over the boy with his tales of ships and seafaring, along with liberal doses of charm. Yet she was reluctant to disappoint her newest young charge by refusing Nicholas entry to her home.

Frequently she was even grateful for his intervention. It was no small task, keeping an energetic ten-year-old occupied. She took Harry on her morning rides in the park, but that hardly scratched the surface of his adventurous itch. He wanted to see the world, beginning with every inch of London.

Fortunately—or unfortunately for convention's sake— Raven befriended him, and the two could often be found racing through the park like wild Indians. Aurora could hardly scold, since she had instigated the morning gallops in the first place.

Even wild gallops, however, could not compete with the entertainments Nicholas offered. Harry came home wide-eyed and excited when they visited Exeter 'Change to see the tigers and Egyptian Hall in Piccadilly, which boasted curiosities from Africa and the Americas. Three days later

he suffered a stomachache from eating too much ginger-
bread when they attended a local fair with conjurers and
tumblers and rope dancers.

When Aurora fretted that Nicholas was overindulging
the boy, he brushed off her concerns and told her not to
worry.

"Of course I worry," she responded. "I am responsible
for him."

"I won't allow him to come to any harm, I promise you."

She had to be content with that, but there was no question Nicholas was encouraging Harry to test his wings, or
that the boy had contracted a feverish case of hero-worship.

Raven accompanied them to Astley's Royal Amphi-
theater for a spectacle of acrobatics on horseback. The next
day Harry attempted one of the feats of horsemanship
and fell off his mount, skinning his knees and bloodying
his chin.

Aurora was alarmed, but Nicholas reminded her that
skinned knees were a rite of boyhood. When she would
have continued protesting, he warned her not to try to rein
the boy in too tightly, or he would think she was smothering him as his mother did.

Still, she didn't like it that Nicholas was aiding and
abetting Harry's rebellion.

The final straw was Burford's Panorama in Castle Street,
which offered murals of, among other things, the naval
victories of Admiral Nelson on the Nile. All Harry could
talk about afterward was going to sea.

"I think perhaps it's best if you cease taking him to any
more entertainments," Aurora told Nicholas during their
morning ride the following day.

"Why?"

"Because Harry is an impressionable young boy. I dread
to think what wild notions he is picking up from you."

"I would hardly call an exhibit of Egyptian hiero-
glyphics wild."

"It is not the entertainment but your company that concerns me. You are scarcely the best influence, Nicholas."

"Brandon, please, my love."

Aurora raised her eyes to the sky. "It disturbs me that Harry is becoming so attached to you. I don't like to consider how disappointed he will be when you must leave." *Or how she herself would feel.* "He sees you as a hero because of all your adventures."

"From all reports, I don't hold a candle to his late brother for adventures. According to Harry, your Geoffrey was a spy."

Aurora shook her head. "Harry is quite mistaken. Geoffrey was the last man who would ever become involved in spying."

"Why do you say so?"

"He was far too intellectual. He always had his nose in a book."

"He sounds deadly dull."

The accusation irked her, yet Aurora found herself averting her gaze in chagrin. She had scarcely thought of Geoffrey in the fortnight since Nicholas's arrival in England.

A sharp ache filled her at the realization, along with a profound surge of guilt. How could she be so disloyal to Geoffrey's memory? She had known him all her life, but she could barely remember him now, his image was so eclipsed by Nicholas's vital presence.

Compared to Nicholas, he was only a shadow.

Aurora pressed her lips together, determined to conquer her disloyalty. "Geoffrey was a proper gentleman, yes," she replied curtly, "and a *gentle* man. He would never leave his home and family and risk his life simply for the thrill of it. Unlike some others I know," she added pointedly.

"Like I said . . . *dull.*"

When Aurora bristled, Nicholas only grinned and gestured with his head toward a grove of trees beside the Serpentine. "I'll wager your dear Geoffrey would never have thought of bringing you here, or that you would ever have serviced him so delightfully if he had."

She realized they were passing the spot where Nicholas had brought her for a moonlit interlude, and she flushed. When she looked at him, though, the devilish light in his eyes faded, and so did the rest of the world.

Aurora froze, ensnared by the silent intensity of Nicholas's gaze. The raw tension that had lain simmering beneath the surface had returned in a heartbeat with the force of a blow . . . along with another dangerous emotion.

Desire. It flared up in her, swiftly, uncontrollably, at a single glance.

For the past two weeks she'd done her utmost to pretend indifference, to ignore the fierce longing Nicholas roused in her, but it was still keenly alive, smoldering between them.

At some point she would have to face it, Aurora realized. Unwilling, however, to deal with the issue just then, she forced her gaze away.

Yet she knew the volatile situation between them could not continue very much longer.

Even with Harry to shield her, Nicholas's pursuit of her showed no sign of abating, and it kept Aurora in a constant state of conflict. He was turning her life upside down, just as she feared, destroying her hard-won equanimity. It dismayed her, how vulnerable she was to him.

It was more dismaying to remember the danger he faced. The following afternoon, Aurora was rudely reminded just how precarious Nicholas's situation was: she received a letter from her cousin Percy in St. Kitts, wondering if she had heard from Nicholas.

Aurora feverishly devoured the contents, which implied that at least one earlier missive had gone astray.

Since I last wrote you, I have concluded that the rumors of Nicholas's survival must be true. Not only are

*there reports he was seen in the Caribbean since his
presumed drowning, but yesterday I was questioned by
naval officers searching for the pirate Captain Saber.*

*If Nicholas is indeed alive, my dear, you should pre-
pare yourself for scandal, for legally you will still be his
wedded wife. I now can only regret my part in arranging
your marriage. . . .*

Percy also apologized for deceiving her about the
hanging.

*Nick thought it best to spare you the trauma of
watching him die. And knowing the pain you had recently suffered with the loss of your betrothed, I agreed.*

It was not Percy's deception, however, that alarmed Aurora. It was knowing that before long the world would
realize the condemned criminal she had wed was still a
fugitive from British naval justice.

Her fingers clenched the letter. She couldn't let this
situation go on. It terrified her that Nicholas was risking
capture and death to pursue her. She had to make him see
reason, to convince him to leave England.

She made an earnest attempt the next day during their
morning ride. She'd gotten a later start than usual because
Harry's mount had gone lame from a stone bruise and had
to be replaced. When Aurora and Harry finally arrived, the
park was already filling with governesses and their young
charges.

Aurora joined Nicholas and Raven for a sedate ride
along Rotten Row, while Harry spurred his mount on, with
her groom following close behind. Raven, for once, chose
decorum over excitement, so Aurora was forced to hold
her tongue and wait for a private word with Nicholas.

Shortly they encountered an open barouche, where an
elegant couple was descending with a very young child.

Aurora tensed in alarm when she recognized the Baron and Baroness Sinclair. Damien Sinclair, once known as "Lord Sin," had been a premier rake of England and a prime leader of the Hellfire League before his marriage. There was every possibility, she knew, that he could identify Nicholas.

Aurora hoped to ride quietly past. She greatly admired Lord Sinclair's wife, Vanessa, for they had struck up a friendship during Aurora's come-out a few years earlier, but she had no desire to be seen just then.

As they passed the barouche, however, Vanessa Sinclair spied her and greeted her warmly. Unable to avoid acknowledging the acquaintance, Aurora drew rein.

Lord and Lady Sinclair made a striking couple. Their young daughter, Catherine, was perhaps eighteen months old and just as striking, with her father's raven hair and mother's dark eyes.

With great reluctance, Aurora introduced her party and felt apprehensive when Sinclair eyed Nicholas curiously. She was relieved for the distraction when the toddler squirmed in her father's arms and pointed toward the lake, exclaiming, "Duck! Duck!"

"We are teaching her to feed the ducks," Vanessa said, laughing.

"If you will please excuse us," Sinclair said with the sensual smile that had broken half the female hearts in England. "I've learned it is better never to leave an impatient lady waiting."

Before Vanessa turned away, she apologized to Aurora for not calling recently. "We have been in the country this past fortnight. But if you are free one afternoon this week, I would very much like to come for a visit."

"I would enjoy that immensely, and I hope you will bring Catherine."

Vanessa smiled at this interest in her daughter. "Of course. It was a pleasure meeting you, Mr. Deverill."

"And you, my lady," Nicholas replied, tipping his beaver hat.

Aurora breathed more easily when they were gone, but gave Nicholas an accusing look. "Sinclair seemed to know you."

"That isn't surprising. I met him briefly several years ago before he married, during a weekend of shooting in the country."

"I hear he was quite the rake," Raven said thoughtfully.

"He was," Nicholas acknowleged. "But according to Clune, Sinclair is very much in love with his wife now."

"I could tell by the way he looked at her," Raven replied softly.

Aurora caught the wistful note in her voice, and so apparently did Nicholas, for he gave his half sister a measuring look. "It is not too late to reconsider your marital aspirations, puss. You don't have to wed for financial considerations. You can afford the luxury of a love match."

Raven shook her head adamantly. "I will be quite content with a title. Speaking of which . . . there is Halford."

Raven adopted a brilliant smile and urged her horse forward to intercept Aurora's former suitor, the Duke of Halford.

Aurora tensed at his appearance and watched as he gave a start of surprise at Raven's bold greeting. Then he glanced Aurora's way, and his look turned icy.

Involuntarily Aurora winced, shuddering to think of her narrow escape. If not for her marriage to Nicholas, she would have been planning her nuptials to Halford by now.

His grace's frigid glance swept past her to include Nicholas, who met his stiffness with cool amusement.

"I am honored," Nicholas murmured to Aurora in an undertone, "that you chose me over him."

Before she could think of a fitting reply, Halford turned his attention back to Raven. His supercilious expression softened, and whatever he said made her laugh.

Aurora frowned to hear her friend's charming laugh. She

didn't like to see Raven on such good terms with the duke, for he was still looking for a wife.

"She knows her own mind," Nicholas said, as if reading her thoughts.

Aurora shook her head. Most young ladies of marriageable age would consider Halford prime husband material, but she didn't care to think what his coldness would do to someone with Raven's lively spirit. "They would not be the least compatible."

"But then you might not be the best qualified to judge suitors, considering the state of your own marriage."

Nicholas was watching her, Aurora realized, his amusement suddenly gone.

His solemnity made her recall the urgency of his situation and what she had meant to say to him.

"I heard from Percy yesterday," she remarked. "The entire Caribbean knows you escaped hanging."

"I expected as much."

"Nicholas . . ." She took a deep breath, striving for patience. "It is only a matter of time before someone in authority discerns your true identity. Please, won't you stop risking your life and return to America, where you will be safe?"

"I would consider it, certainly."

"You would?" Her eyes searched his.

"Yes," Nicholas replied slowly. "I would leave tomorrow under the right circumstances."

"And what are those?"

"If you agree to come with me. As my wife."

She stared at him a long moment. He was all seriousness now; the charming rogue was gone. Instead he emanated the keen intensity she had noticed about him when they had first met, when his life was at stake.

"I thought we had settled this," she responded uneasily.

"No, we never settled anything. We agreed to live separate lives for the time being. But since then, I have come to reconsider."

This was precisely what she had feared, Aurora thought, dismayed. "I have no desire to discuss our marriage," she murmured, wishing she had never begun this conversation.

"Ignoring it won't make it go away," he said just as quietly.

Aurora shut her eyes, knowing it was hopeless to try to argue with Nicholas in public. "Very well, we will discuss it."

"When?"

She averted her gaze from his potent one. "Tonight. Come to my house."

"Your bedchamber?"

She nodded reluctantly. "That is the only place where we can be private. I will leave the window open."

Wanting to escape, Aurora urged her horse forward, intending to intervene in Raven's ill-advised flirtation, but her thoughts remained on Nicholas and his dismaying revelation.

Aurora paced her bedchamber, every nerve ending she possessed alert and on edge. Another glance at the mantel clock showed the hour was nearing midnight, and still Nicholas didn't come.

She had tried reading, first a magazine and then the journal, but she was too restless to concentrate. Her mind was churning, preparing arguments to use in their forthcoming dispute. She had to convince Nicholas that she didn't wish to be his wife, that she deplored the very thought of living under the thumb of a dominating, forceful husband. Only recently had she even gained a measure of control over her life, over her fate. And now he was threatening to take that from her.

She would not accept defeat. She had to put an end to the constant state of turmoil that had afflicted her since his arrival in England.

She had no illusions that it would be easy; nothing with Nicholas was ever easy. It would take all her willpower to resist his influence and to persuade him to return to America without her.

And if her arguments failed?

Catching sight of herself in the cheval glass, Aurora came to a halt.

Then she would give him what he wanted. Her body.

Troubled, she stared at herself in the mirror. In the dim lamplight, the woman there was almost a stranger, her complexion flushed, her fair hair falling around her shoulders in casual dishevelment, but it was her attire that seemed foreign to her. She wore a dressing gown of deep blue brocade and nothing more.

She could feel the fabric pressing against her naked breasts, creating an erotic friction. Perhaps this was a mistake . . .

Aurora gave a start when she heard a soft scrape of sound behind her. Her nerves clanging, she turned to find Nicholas in her bedchamber. He stood just inside the window, observing her, his expression inscrutable.

When his gaze raked her dressing gown, lingering on her bosom, she nervously drew the lapels closer together.

"I am not sure there is any point to this discussion, Nicholas," Aurora began, gathering her courage. "I told you weeks ago I had no wish for a permanent marriage."

Moving farther into the room, he leaned a shoulder against the bedpost. "Weeks ago you were still reeling from the shock of my being alive. I didn't press you then because I thought you needed more time to consider."

"Well, I have considered. And my feelings have not changed."

"Mine have," he said softly.

"I cannot imagine why."

"Because I've come to know you better."

She turned away from the sensual look in his dark eyes and began to pace again.

"I think our marriage could work," Nicholas finally said, watching her restlessness.

"I don't see how."

"Aurora . . . why are you so opposed even to considering being my wife?"

"There are so many reasons, I don't know where to begin."

"Name one."

"Very well. For the first time in my life, I am free to live as I choose. Why would I wish to give that up?"

"Because you might find something better."

She gave him a searching glance. "Better? What could be better than independence?"

His mouth twisted in a wry smile. He had once felt the same way. "If you really wanted independence, love, you wouldn't hesitate to come with me to America. You will have far more freedom there than here in your rigid, upper-class society."

"Not as your wife, Nicholas. A wife has no rights whatsoever, not here or in America, either. I lived under my father's domination all my life. I won't endure that again."

He frowned at that, not liking the comparison. "I don't believe I am anything like your father."

"No? You are just as forceful as he is. And I think you might be just as ruthless. You would do anything to get your way—"

"I have no intention of trying to rule you. If I did, I would have demanded you return with me at once. I would never have given you a choice about our marriage."

"You don't seem to be giving me a choice now."

"Of course I am. I won't force you to be my wife."

She let out her breath in obvious relief.

Nick hesitated, at a loss about how to reassure her. "I think you have an impossibly dark vision of how it would be between us. Your fear seems almost irrational."

That made her stop her pacing. "It isn't irrational in the least. If I accompany you to America, I would have only you to rely upon. I would be completely dependent on you. What happens when you find life with me too tame? When the urge to wander strikes you? I would be alone in a strange country."

"I told you, I intend to settle down."

"And how long will your good intentions last? How long before you're lured away by the promise of adventure and danger? What would I do then?" She turned to face him directly, her gaze imploring. "You are asking me to risk *everything* to come with you, Nicholas. How can I trust you that much?"

The question made Nicholas wince, and he could only stare back at her. Her blue eyes were wide and dark like the ocean.

"You are focusing only on the possible disadvantages," he said finally. "Perhaps instead you should consider the advantages."

"I *have* considered them—and there is no contest. My life here may be dull, but at least I know what to expect." Aurora shook her head. "Besides, even if I wanted to go with you, I have responsibilities. Raven . . . Harry . . ."

"I have two sisters who could benefit from your guidance."

"What of your mother? She might not welcome another woman in her house."

That concern was unfounded Nick knew. "My mother would be no problem. In the first place, I have my own house, which I built to get out from underfoot of my family. And in the second, she would be delighted to have a new daughter, since she's despaired of ever seeing me wed." When Aurora had no response, he added truthfully, "If you're worried about leaving your horses behind, we have excellent horseflesh in Virginia. I can buy you a stableful of horses. And I have hundreds of acres where you can race to your heart's content."

Lifting her hand, Aurora rubbed her temple as if in pain. "This is not really even about me. This is about you. About the kind of man you are. Don't you see what you are doing? You are trying to rescue me from what you perceive as my discontent. You want to save me because it's so much part of your nature. You can't help yourself."

"There is far more to it than my nature," Nick replied.

"Is there? I think your nature is the heart of the problem." She hesitated. "Do you intend to be faithful to me, Nicholas?"

He didn't immediately answer.

Her smile was faint. "It is a reasonable question. How do I know you won't find someone else who arouses your interest? You desire me now, but how can you guarantee you will want me two years from now, or even two days?"

Averting his gaze, Nicholas considered the question. She was asking for more than fidelity in the marriage bed, he knew; she was asking him to remain by her side for always.

Was he willing to make that kind of commitment to Aurora? Essentially to give over his life to her?

"You don't love me," she said softly into the silence. "I'm not even certain you know what the word means."

"And you do?"

"Yes, I know. Love is kind and gentle and giving. It's laughing together, being comfortable and familiar. Sharing thoughts, common interests. It is a warm feeling in your heart. . . . You cannot claim to feel that for me."

"You forgot passion."

"Perhaps, but passion is a weak foundation upon which to base a marriage. I don't doubt you feel desire for me, but it is purely carnal. Love is not desire."

He met her gaze directly. "You're saying you could never care for me?"

She hesitated. "I am saying I would be a fool to let myself care. I don't want to mourn you again, to grieve when you die. And it's entirely too likely that one day I will be forced to, that you will set out on one of your adventures and never come home."

"I cannot promise that I won't die, Aurora. No one can promise that."

"No. But you could try to keep yourself safe. You insist on risking your life and won't listen when I implore you to leave England." She searched his face. "Will you leave, Nicholas?"

His silence told her clearly enough his answer.

Aurora took a deep breath. "Very well, then. I will give you what you want."

Her fingers moved to the sash at her waist. When she hesitated, their gazes fused. Loosening the tie, she let the robe fall from her shoulders.

She heard Nicholas's sharp intake of breath as she stood there naked in the dim glow of lamplight.

"What are you doing, Aurora?" he asked, his voice not entirely steady.

"Letting you win. If I give you my body, then maybe you will leave me alone."

He clenched his jaw, looking like a man in pain. "I didn't come here for this."

"Didn't you? Isn't this what you have wanted for weeks? A momentary pleasure?"

"What I want is you, as my wife." His faint smile never reached his eyes. "If all I wanted was sex, I could find it countless places."

His dark gaze remained solemn as he moved to stand before her. "I want more than lovemaking from you, Aurora. I want you willing, hungry for me. I want you to give me your body because you can't bear not to. Not because you feel you must placate me or bribe me."

Her breath faltered as she stared up at him. "I . . . don't want you, Nicholas," she lied.

"No?"

Lifting his hand, he touched the column of her throat, then drew his finger slowly downward. Her heart beat wildly as he deliberately brushed a taut, aching nipple.

"You aren't as indifferent as you pretend," he murmured softly.

He turned away then and went to the window. Without

another word, he disappeared into the night, leaving her standing there, stunned.

Nicholas had managed to confound her once again.

Trembling, Aurora reached down for her robe and covered her nakedness, then moved over to the bed and weakly sat down. She had lost again.

Nicholas was right. She was not indifferent to him. Not at all. The intense feelings he stirred in her were frightening. The wild restlessness alarming. He had only to touch her to prove his power over her.

Aurora shivered. He had asked if she could ever care for him. She would care too much, that was the trouble.

That reason alone was enough to fear having him for a husband, even aside from the issues of control or the vast differences between them. It would be unforgivably foolish to allow herself to love a man who was at risk of dying any moment.

Her sorrow when she'd thought Nicholas dead had been deep and cutting—and he had been virtually a stranger to her then. How much more devastated would she be once she learned to care for him? Once she learned to crave his touch?

And what if he left her? He hadn't been able to promise her fidelity just now; he hadn't answered her question at all.

Nicholas was a passionate man. It was quite possible he could develop a craving for some other woman, as his father had done. He would leave her to follow his heart—or, if he did honor his marriage vows, he would resent her for shackling him. He would be just like his father, entangled in the same misery.

Aurora winced at the thought. She couldn't do that to Nicholas, or to herself. No, her fear wasn't irrational in the least.

Her gaze fell on the journal, which she had left on the bedside table. Seeing it, Aurora felt her resolve strengthen. Most emphatically, she did not want to endure the Frenchwoman's fate, the kind of heartbreaking pain of losing the man she loved. She always wept over the final pages of the journal, for the tale did not end happily.

Nor had the affair between Raven's mother and Nicholas's father. Aurora could understand now why Elizabeth Kendrick had read the journal till the pages were worn; she had identified so deeply with the star-crossed lovers. Their passion was so powerful, their grief so devastating when they were ripped apart. . . .

Aurora bit her lip hard. She would have to be stronger than either of those two tragic women had been, she vowed. The journal was an unintentional warning about the madness of desire, and she would do well to take heed. She had to zealously guard her heart from Nicholas, or the result would be disastrous.

Chapter Sixteen

I struggled fiercely against the dark turmoil of emotions he unleashed in me, but was I fighting him—or myself?

Aurora was very much on Nick's mind that evening when, at Lord Clune's invitation, he attended a very private performance of a troupe of opera dancers. Their lovely charms held the all-male audience enthralled, but Nicholas remained uninspired and excused himself early.

He was surprised, however, when Clune followed him outside.

"You needn't interrupt your pleasure on my account, Dare," Nicholas said as they descended the front steps of the unassuming house in the theater district.

"I did not find the performance much of a pleasure, I'm afraid," Clune replied. "Truthfully, it has been ages since any entertainment has held me enthralled." He nodded toward his carriage, which awaited him a few paces along the darkened street. "May I offer you a lift back to your hotel? Or some other destination? A gaming club, perhaps?"

"I am returning to my hotel, but I planned to walk. You are welcome to join me, if you care to."

"Walk?" Clune said in amusement. "On foot? What a novel idea."

Patting his belly, Nick forced a grin. "This indolent life of a privileged gentleman is turning me shiftless and lazy."

"And restless, it seems."

"Ah, no, that is nothing new."

"You realize, of course, that you are taking your life in your hands, walking alone this near Covent Garden."

Nicholas raised his walking stick, which concealed a

deadly rapier. "I could use some excitement to enliven the evening."

Clune cocked his head thoughtfully. "I share your ennui, if not your restlessness. Perhaps I will join you."

"Be my guest, but I warn you, I may not be the best of company just now."

"Then we will be well matched."

Nicholas sent him a penetrating glance. "Any particular reason you say so?"

"Nothing of consequence," Clune answered lightly. "Perhaps I'm merely growing jaded in my waning years. I suppose even a dedicated libertine can begin to tire of a life of sin and debauchery."

Tactfully Nicholas refrained from comment. Clune's age was hardly an issue—he was still in his early thirties at most—but the years of hard living were evidently taking a toll on his soul.

The earl dismissed his carriage and fell into step beside Nicholas. A moment later Clune spoke, sounding surprisingly serious. "To be honest, my dark mood is probably due to my grandfather."

"I hear Wolverton is faring poorly."

"Quite. He isn't expected to live out the month."

"Are you close?"

"Not in the least. He's a bloody tyrant. We haven't spoken in years, even though I'm his heir." Clune's jaw hardened. "I won't weep when the old bastard breathes his last."

"You'll be a marquess then?"

"Yes, regrettably."

Nick waited for an explanation.

"I have no desire to assume the responsibilities that go with the title." Clune let out his breath in a sigh. "But I suppose we all must leave our youth behind at some point."

"True," Nicholas agreed, understanding that lament all too well.

For a while, each man was occupied by his own brooding thoughts. Eventually, however, Clune interrupted the silence again. "I take it your courtship of your wife is at an impasse?"

Nick's mouth twisted grimly. "Whatever gave you that notion?"

Clune smiled at the sardonic reply. "Something about the way you resemble a caged jungle cat, perhaps. Forgive me for prying, but it seems to me that drastic measures are called for."

"How drastic?"

"Have you considered abduction?"

Nicholas raised an eyebrow. "You're not proposing I emulate *you*, I trust. If I recall, Dare, the last abduction you engaged in landed you in a duel and caused you to shoot your closest friend."

With a rueful laugh, Clune shook his head. "That was clearly a mistake, one I infinitely regret. But I am not advocating anything illegal, or even immoral. Carrying your wife off for a passionate interlude would be well within the law and your rights as a husband."

"You have my curiosity aroused," Nicholas replied cautiously. "What are you suggesting?"

"A quiet love nest where you can persuade your bride to your way of thinking. At the very least, Lady Aurora would find it . . . stimulating."

"And I suppose you have a specific nest in mind?"

"In fact, I do. I have a house in Berkshire that would prove ideal for your purposes—completely secluded and well-staffed with discreet servants. I have yet to meet a woman who was not captivated by its exotic . . . ah . . . charms."

When Nicholas didn't immediately respond, his lordship brought up another point. "It would have the further benefit of removing you from London for a time. It wouldn't hurt for you to make yourself scarce just now, my friend. Damien Sinclair asked about you this afternoon.

He noticed the resemblance between you and the American who was a guest at our gathering of the Hellfire League three years ago."

"I thought perhaps he might have remembered me."

"You are taking a risk by remaining here, Nick."

"I know," he said thoughtfully.

It was indeed risky, chancing discovery by staying in London to be near Aurora, especially when he was making so little progress.

Nicholas grimaced. That reckless urge of his to defy fate was one of Aurora's chief complaints, and it had been the biggest bone of contention with his father as well. They had fought over it until the last, when the older man lay dying. Nicholas had never quite overcome his guilt for being such a disappointment to his father. He'd sworn then that he would settle down and fulfill his responsibilities—yet here he was, neglecting his shipping business and risking his life for a possibly hopeless cause.

Aurora was still fiercely resisting his pursuit, in part because she deplored his recklessness. She would be happier if he simply left England. . . .

Frowning, Nicholas turned that reflection over in his mind. Perhaps he could use that argument with her—that it would be safer for him to leave town. . . .

"I would be more than pleased to put my house at your disposal," Clune offered, interrupting his thoughts.

"That is extremely generous of you," Nick answered. "Let me consider it."

He did intend to give the idea serious thought. Having time alone with Aurora, without the strict constraints of society to dictate her every action, could indeed break the impasse between them, as well as give them a chance for intimacy that could lead to deeper feelings. . . .

It would also lessen the risk of discovery, Nicholas reminded himself. And his well-honed instincts for danger told him that time was running out.

He would have to act in regards to Aurora, and soon.

* * *

The impasse broke the following day, in a manner neither of them expected.

Raven was having a final fitting for the gowns she would wear while visiting her grandfather this summer, and she wanted Aurora's guidance. Knowing Harry wouldn't be comfortable in Lady Dalrymple's home and that Raven's aunt wouldn't welcome a rambunctious ten-year-old boy, Aurora left Harry in her butler's charge. Nicholas planned to call that morning to keep Harry occupied with a game of chess.

It was late afternoon by the time Aurora arrived home. When she heard strange sounds emanating from the drawing room, she gave Danby a puzzled glance.

"I believe Mr. Deverill and his young lordship are practicing fisticuffs," the butler informed her as he relieved her of her veiled bonnet.

Her heart leaping to her throat, Aurora moved swiftly past him. When she reached the drawing room door, she came up short. Some of the furnishings had been pushed aside to clear a space in the center of the room, and both Nicholas and Harry were in their shirtsleeves, brandishing their bare fists.

"Yes," Nicholas was saying. "Keep your hands up, even when you attack. Like this . . ." He demonstrated, assailing an imaginary opponent with a flurry of jabs.

Aurora went cold. Fear squeezed her heart, along with a fierce anger. "What in God's name are you doing?" she demanded hoarsely—and unnecessarily. Quite clearly he was teaching Harry to fight.

Nicholas straightened and turned to face her, as did Harry. The boy's young face was bright with excitement. "Rory, come and see what I have learned," Harry began.

Her irate gaze remained riveted on Nicholas. "I asked what you are doing."

"I heard you the first time," he replied mildly. "I am

teaching him the basics of self-defense, although he could use a qualified instructor."

"How dare you," Aurora said through gritted teeth.

"There is no cause for alarm. It isn't dangerous—"

"Of course there is cause for alarm. He could be *hurt*. Harry is just a child, and you are teaching him violence."

"He is old enough to learn to defend himself."

Her jaw locked with anger. "Get out, Nicholas," she grated out. "You are not welcome here. I don't wish you to see Harry again."

She ignored the boy's startled, bewildered look. She had called Nicholas by his real name, but she was too furious to care. "From now on, you will keep away from him, do you understand me? I forbid you even to speak to him."

"But Rory," the boy began plaintively. "I asked Mr. Deverill—"

"Harry, go to your room, please."

"Rory . . ."

"Now, at once!"

The boy gave her an accusing glance, his lower lip trembling. But surprisingly he didn't argue further. Instead, he stiffened his skinny shoulders and glanced at Nicholas, then marched past her out the door.

"You handled that well," Nicholas remarked sardonically, reaching for his coat.

Her chin rose regally. "How I deal with Harry is no concern of yours."

"I'm sorry I didn't consult you first, Aurora. But I didn't realize you would object so strongly."

"Of course I object. You are teaching him how to assault people!"

"It isn't at all the same thing. Don't you think you are overreacting just a bit?"

"Not in the least. I am protecting him from your influence. You will end up getting him injured or even killed."

A muscle in his jaw tightened. "Just because you live in fear doesn't mean that you should force young Harry to."

Aurora glared. "Get out, Nicholas! Get out of this house before I have you thrown out."

His eyes narrowed. "Some day you will have to face your fear, sweetheart. You're afraid of life, so afraid you've buried yourself alive. But you cannot just stop living simply because you might be hurt."

She was too angry to acknowledge the truth in his accusation. "I told you to go!" Quivering with fury, she pointed commandingly at the door.

Nicholas strode past her, but instead of leaving, he swung the door shut. When he turned to her, she felt as if she might melt from the blistering heat of his eyes. "Listen to me—" Crossing to her, he grasped her by the shoulders.

She recoiled from him, struggling. "Don't touch me. . . ." She tried to pull away, but he wouldn't release her. Enraged, she drew back her hand and struck his face with her open palm.

His head jerked back, while his face went so dark that she instinctively stepped back.

Aurora stared, horrified by what she had done. She had never struck anyone in her life. Dear God, she was no better than her father. . . . And Nicholas . . . He looked as if he might strike her in return.

"I . . . I'm sorry . . ." she stammered, her heart pounding as she waited for his expected explosion.

It never came.

"You're sorry?" he asked softly. His expression had suddenly changed.

Moving slowly, inexorably, toward her, he backed her to the wall, pinning her with his body. His eyes were ablaze, astonishingly not with anger, but with a fierce tenderness.

"Don't be sorry, Aurora," he goaded, his grasp a velvet manacle on her wrist. "I would rather have you lashing out at me than keeping your rage bottled up. Strike me again, if you want."

Her heart slammed against her ribs as she stared at him. His thighs burned into hers; his breath seared her lips. His expression was hard and sensual, his eyes dark with arousal. He was going to kiss her, she knew.

"Don't . . ." she protested in a shaking undertone. "I don't want you to touch me."

"No? Then why are you quivering? Why is your pulse so wild?"

Reaching down, he lifted her skirts and slid his hand under them and up her thigh, his hard, warm palm shocking on her bare skin. She went rigid, then gasped when his fingers found her feminine cleft.

He laughed, a low, taunting sound, deliberately inciting her. "Your body tells a different story, Aurora. You're so responsive, I have only to touch you and you grow wet." He stroked her slowly, making her throb.

Her hands rose to his shoulders, half clinging, half pushing, as she struggled to break free. "Stop . . . !" she gasped as his fingers slid deeper into her slick warmth.

"You want me, sweeting. You want me moving between your legs, filling you."

"I don't. . . ." she denied, but her protests were lies. Her entire body ached for him, her blood was on fire.

Nicholas felt the same fire. Just touching her had made him harden in the space of a breath. He was aching enough to burst. He clenched his teeth, wanting to seize and possess and consume.

He could feel her resistance, but no fear. Had he sensed that, he would have stopped at once, but she wasn't afraid of him. And he wouldn't back down this time. He *wanted* a fight from Aurora, wanted her fury. Fury was a short step from passion, and he wanted her passion more than he'd ever wanted anything in his life. He wanted to destroy her rigid control, to release her rage, to show her that fierce emotion wasn't such a terrible thing.

He stared into her blue, blue eyes. Each time he touched her, she responded like a woman desperate to live, desperate to love, but she wouldn't let go unless he drove her to it.

Purposefully he bent his head.

The hard kiss robbed her of breath. Expert, ruthless, he crushed her mouth with his, until a quickening, blinding throb of raw sensation caught her in its grasp. Feeling her shuddering response, Nicholas drew back, his own eyes hard and filled with a low, dangerous flame.

Aurora froze, shaking, as she read his intent. Before she could stop him, he had unfastened his breeches. Open lust burned in his narrowed eyes as his thighs spread hers, pressing her back against the wall. The thrill of it made her tremble.

She drew a shattered breath. "God, Nicholas . . . not here."

"Yes, *here*."

His hands clasping her waist, he lifted her up and lowered her onto his engorged erection, entering her with one smooth, powerful thrust. Her eyes widened in shock as she felt his hot penetration; her breath fled at the feeling of being stretched, filled by his swollen flesh.

His breathing turned harsh as he held himself still, sheathed tightly in her. A heartbeat later, he withdrew, only to drive into her deeply again. Huge and hot and urgent, he forced her legs wide open as he plunged his shaft hard into her.

She moaned helplessly, and suddenly her body could not remain still. She arched her hips against him, clinging as he took her with a savage rhythm. She had never known desire could be so primitive, so raw and angry. So fierce. It was madness.

She felt the fire in her veins, in every nerve. Her body burned. She had never felt more alive in her life. Alive with passion, with hunger, with need.

He moved relentlessly inside her, scalding her, making her wild. She gave a sob with each rocking jolt, each tumultuous sensation, until without warning, ecstasy burst upon her and she came in a savage explosion.

He captured her cry with his mouth as her body spasmed

in a wrenching shudder. Moments later he gave a low, rough groan and erupted in his own harsh climax, his powerful body clenching in convulsions of fierce release.

In the shattering aftermath Aurora sagged against him, almost too drained to feel the exquisite waves of pleasure ripple through her. For long minutes there was silence, the only sound the mingling of their jagged breaths. She couldn't speak. Her throat was parched, her flesh still sweetly pulsing, aching erotically between her thighs.

Finally, though, Nicholas cursed, a low dangerous sound.

Dazed, Aurora opened her eyes to find him watching her, his dark gaze intense, searching. When she saw his look, realization suddenly returned full force. Dear God, what had she done?

"Let me go," she whispered.

"Aurora . . ." Nicholas began, but she cut him off.

"Let me go!" she demanded, her voice stronger.

Obligingly he eased himself from her and lowered her to the floor, but she could barely stand, her limbs were so weak. His expression was enigmatic, remote, as he stepped back to fasten his breeches.

Aurora closed her eyes in despair, stunned by her wantonness. They had mated like animals. She had let Nicholas take her in her drawing room, where any of her servants could see. Where Harry could have returned to find them . . .

"How dare you?" she murmured raggedly. "How dare you treat me like a common trollop?"

Nicholas went still. "You are wrong, sweetheart. I treated you like a woman. A passionate woman who isn't afraid to feel fire in her blood."

He had struck a nerve, he could see it in her bruised expression, hear it in her furious undertone when she replied.

"Get out. I never want to see you again."

His jaw hardened. "I am still your husband, Aurora," he said softly. "I can take you any time, any place I choose."

She gave him a scathing look. "I told you to go."

Clenching his jaw, Nicholas stared at her, at her defiant, icy eyes, her quivering mouth still damp and reddened from his kiss. Even after his powerful release, he still wanted her. He could count each pulse of his heartbeat in the rigid flesh of his new erection. Yet he didn't dare touch her again. If he did, he wasn't certain he could control his lust, or his own anger.

"You are lying to yourself," he replied, his voice tightly controlled. "You want me. There's a hunger in you that you can't fill."

He saw the raw pain in her blue eyes, but when he took a step toward her, she flinched.

"Don't touch me."

His jaw set rigidly, he turned away, but when he reached the door, Nicholas hesitated. His laugh was short, harsh, almost inaudible. "Can you credit it? When I first met you, I thought you were one of the bravest women I had ever known. I was wrong. You're a coward. It takes courage to face yourself, to admit your fears and deal with them." He paused. "When you think you're woman enough to do that, Aurora, let me know."

Without a backward glance, he let himself from the room.

Aurora shut her eyes. She was shaking with fury, with relief, with fear.

The ache in the pit of her stomach was fear. Nicholas was right, she knew. She was a coward. She was terrified of him. Of the intense emotions he made her feel. Of the stranger she became whenever he touched her.

Damn him to Hades. Why did his touch make her forget everything except how much she wanted him? His caresses had set her on fire, had turned her into a creature of lust, frenzied and wild. In his arms she became someone she no longer knew.

Shaking her head in denial, Aurora stirred weakly, then gave a soft moan of dismay. Her back was still pressed against the wall, yet when she'd straightened, she felt his warm, wet seed slip down her thigh.

Her hand stole to her abdomen. Dear heaven, how could she have allowed him to make love to her like that? How could she forget him now? She could still feel the powerful thrust of Nicholas inside her, the searing fire he ignited in her. . . .

She took a deep, shuddering breath. She had to crush her feelings for him. She couldn't let him near her again. She could not.

A deep and lonely ache twisted like a knife inside her at the thought of never seeing Nicholas again, never feeling his sensual touch. Yet she had no choice.

She had thought her father domineering and controlling, but Nicholas would be a hundred times worse. He would own her. If she surrendered to him, her soul would no longer be her own. He would rule her, would totally consume her in his blazing passion. And her heart would be seared to ashes in the fire.

Chapter Seventeen

His arms enfolded me; his lips soft on my face eased my tears.

Nick lay staring at the dimly lit ceiling of his hotel room, cursing himself and his handling of Aurora this afternoon. It was inexcusable, the way he had treated her.

He hadn't meant for their argument to go so far, to erupt in a blaze of raw, unbridled desire. But her fury had ignited his resolve, while kissing her had driven him beyond the reach of reason. The instant he touched her, he had been wild to get inside her.

He shut his eyes, remembering Aurora's stunned look as he plunged himself inside her, her flushed face as she became swept up in the flame of frenzied passion. He had taken her against a wall, without preliminaries, without regard to where they were or who might see them. Like any whore. And she had loved it, responding with all the fire he knew was within her.

He didn't regret shattering her icy control. What he regretted was the dark anger that now lay between them. After weeks of carefully wooing her, of aching for her, he had destroyed the fragile balance of trust and growing desire in a blinding flash of heat.

Clenching his teeth, Nick ran a hand raggedly through his dark hair. He wasn't sure now how to salvage the tattered bonds of their relationship—or even if he wanted to salvage them. He couldn't understand the violence of his feelings for her.

Hell and damnation, he was getting in too deep. He'd never before felt such driving, desperate, mind-blotting need for anyone. His vulnerability staggered him. With just a look, Aurora could set his blood on fire faster, make his loins burn hotter, than any woman he'd ever known. He was panting after her like some lust-crazed, heartsick schoolboy. . . .

He swore again, savagely. Perhaps he should walk away, before he made a worse fool of himself. He shouldn't have stayed so long in England as it was.

He was obviously bent on torturing himself. It was looking more and more likely that she would never accept him as her husband or set free the passionate woman she had encased in ice.

Just then he heard a soft rap on the door. Puzzled, Nicholas sat up, wondering who could be calling at this time of the evening. The hour was not yet ten o'clock, and he had turned down Clune's offer for a night of carousing on the town.

The rap came again, more insistently this time. Easing himself from the bed, he went to open the door.

His heart gave a jolt of surprise when he saw the woman who stood there. She was veiled and wore a concealing cloak, but he would have recognized Aurora in any disguise.

He felt himself scowl. She had come to his hotel at night alone, risking scandal, after vowing she never wanted to see him again. But then he realized she would never take such a bold step without good reason. . . .

"What is wrong?" he demanded, his expression softening.

"Harry . . ." Aurora answered in a trembling voice. "He's gone."

"What do you mean, gone?"

"He ran away. Please, Nicholas, you must help me find him."

His jaw flexed grimly. He didn't point out the obvious incongruity of her plea coming so soon after ordering him to keep away from her. Instead, he drew her from the very public hallway into the privacy of his room.

"How long has he been gone?" he asked, shutting the door.

"I don't know. Hours." She raised her veil, her blue eyes imploring. "I found this note when he was late for supper. He left it on his pillow." She handed him a scrap of paper that had obviously been well perused.

> *Rory, I have gone to seek my fortune. Please do not worry.*

Nicholas frowned thoughtfully. "Do you have any idea where he might be?"

"No. My servants have looked everywhere. Please," Aurora repeated urgently. "Will you help me?"

He gave her a look of reproach. "Can you possibly doubt it?" Turning away, he began stripping off his fine cambric shirt.

"What are you doing?" she asked, momentarily startled out of her dismay.

"Changing clothes. I don't want to call undue attention to myself. A fine gentleman would be out of place searching the places Harry is likely to be. Sit down. I will be only a moment."

As he rummaged through the clothespress, she glanced at the comfortable settee to one side of the room. But apparently she was too distraught to obey, for she turned to pace the floor.

"This is my fault," she said in an anguished voice. "I drove Harry away. If I hadn't lost my temper, he would never have behaved so foolishly."

Nicholas shook his head as he shrugged on an old brown coat. "Your temper had little to do with it. Harry has been chomping at the bit to begin his adventures. The only surprise was that you persuaded him to wait this long." When she remained painfully silent, an aching wave of protectiveness hit him. "Don't despair, Aurora. I will find him."

She took a deep, shuddering breath, making a visible

effort to control herself. "Where will you even begin searching?"

"The docks. That is the most likely place he would go to look for a berth on a sailing ship. He never gave up his aspirations to sail to France."

Nick traded his shiny Hessian boots for a rougher pair and fished out a slouch hat. When he tucked a pair of pistols in his belt and a knife in his boot, Aurora's blue eyes filled with distress. He resembled the violent pirate she deplored, he knew. Yet she didn't protest. She simply watched him, her dread for Harry evident.

Nicholas could not blame her. In the past he had accused her of being overly fearful, but this time her fear was warranted. A youth of Harry's tender age and sheltered upbringing would be prey for all the miscreants and misfits in London. Nick didn't like to think of the danger the boy faced.

Grimly he slipped a heavy set of brass knuckles in his coat pocket and hefted a walking stick that doubled as a sword. He intended to be prepared for any kind of trouble. When he was ready, he took Aurora by the elbow and steered her toward the door.

"How did you come here?" he asked as he ushered her from the room.

"My carriage. Danby is waiting below for me."

"Have him take you home."

She halted, gazing up at Nicholas pleadingly. "But I want to come with you."

"No, sweetheart. I don't want to have to worry about your safety as well as Harry's."

Aurora clenched her hands into fists, obviously torn. Taking her lightly by the shoulders, Nicholas touched his lips briefly to her forehead in a gentle kiss meant to reassure her. "Go home, Aurora. I will find him, I promise you."

When still she hesitated, he reached up to stroke her cheek. "I am good at rescues, remember? Trust me a little."

She gave him a tremulous smile. "I do trust you, Nicholas," she whispered.

That brave smile tore at his heart.

As he turned her toward the stairs, Nicholas prayed silently that he would be able to keep his promise. For if real harm came to the boy, Nick knew instinctively he would forfeit any hope of prying Aurora from her fear of losing everyone she cared for.

Nicholas went first to the ship he had docked at the wharves. He kept a skeleton crew there on the schooner in the event he needed to make a swift getaway.

With a few of his roughest seamen, Nick combed the waterfront, looking for the runaway boy.

The night was teeming with humanity, sailors and bawds and cutpurses, while a din of drunken revelry issued from the taprooms and public houses. Nearest the docks, swirls of fog rose from the River Thames, bringing the damp odors of tar and rotting fish and half concealing the hundreds of bare-masted ships lying at anchor along the wharves.

The fog made the search more difficult, misting the cobblestones and making ghostly images of the crates and barrels and drays that occupied nearly every square inch of waterfront.

Yet the fog was the least of Nick's concerns. He was acquainted enough with London's underworld to have developed a healthy respect for it. The thieves' kitchens, the brothels, the opium dens here were some of the most dangerous in the world. Accordingly Nicholas adopted the low language of the waterfront, pretending to be a sailor in search of a runaway cabin boy for his master and even offering a small reward. But no one had seen a fugitive golden-haired boy.

The constricted feeling in his chest grew as the night wore on. Harry could be anywhere—abducted and forced into labor onboard a ship, or apprenticed as a pickpocket or a ragged chimney sweep, or taken into one of the sporting houses whose clientele craved the tender flesh of young boys, or lying in a dark alley, carved up for fishbait.

Or he might be miles away, having set out in a different direction entirely, Nicholas reminded himself. He'd only been relying on gut instinct when he began the search here. Although his gut was rarely wrong, he could have been mistaken. If so, then Harry could pay a costly price. . . .

He set his jaw and continued the search. There was no way in hell he would return to face Aurora without finding the boy.

It was nearing the darkest hours of night when he met up with two of his men as they exited a tavern.

"No luck, guv'nor," one of them confided. "There's nary a sign of the young toff."

"Keep looking," Nick commanded. "When you reach the end of the quay, start boarding vessels and questioning the crews. We won't stop until we find him."

He had started to turn away when he heard a sound that raised the hairs on the back of his neck.

"Devil . . ."

The raw whisper came from behind a stack of crates, but it wasn't an oath or an invocation of Satan, Nicholas realized. It was a plea for "Deverill," his assumed name.

Giving a low shout to alert his men, he threaded his way through the maze of crates. His heart went cold when he saw the pale shape huddled on the ground.

"Harry?" Nicholas said urgently, kneeling beside him.

The boy groaned and lifted his head. In the darkness, Nicholas could just make out his gold hair.

Nearly naked, he was clutching his stomach and shivering in the damp night air. Stripped of his clothing, he wore only his underdrawers, which stank of urine, no doubt because he had wet himself out of fear.

"Where are you hurt?" Nicholas asked, gently probing the boy's face and limbs.

"My . . . belly. They hit me. . . ."

Nicholas could feel no blood, but Harry's ribs were tender, as evidenced by his sharp winces. Nick suspected, however, that they were only bruised, not broken.

"You'll live," he said tersely, hiding his sympathy. "Tell me what happened."

Haltingly Harry's story came tumbling out: how he had made his way here shortly before dark, how he'd been chased off a brigantine he tried to board, then set upon by a gang of young pickpockets. He seemed most ashamed of his fear.

"I was so afraid," he mumbled, his voice ending in a whisper.

Nicholas didn't mince words. "You damn well should have been afraid. You're fortunate you were only bruised and battered. You could have been gutted and left to die."

"I prayed you would come."

"Count yourself lucky that I don't wring your neck. You frightened Lady Aurora witless."

"I . . . I am sorry. Will you tell her for me?"

"You'll tell her yourself—in the morning. For now, let's see what we can do to get you cleaned up."

Bending, he lifted the boy carefully in his arms. "I'll take you to my ship first," Nicholas added, rising. "I don't dare present you to her looking like this."

When he had Harry safely on board the *Talon*, however, Nicholas changed his mind about taking the boy home to Aurora. Harry was exhausted, as well as bruised and battered, but even more than rest, he needed a lesson about the harsh realities of life to underscore the one he'd learned tonight about the dangers.

When the boy was cleaned up and sound asleep in the first mate's bunk, Nicholas retreated to his own cabin, where he composed a message for Aurora. The note was brief, saying simply that Harry was safe and essentially unharmed, but that he would remain on the schooner for a time, to be taught a lesson.

That would undoubtedly rouse her protective instincts, Nick knew, and bring her running. Yet for what he wished to say to her, he needed privacy, which her house with its loyal staff of servants couldn't offer. He sent the message by three of his roughest crew members, trusting that they could protect her when she journeyed to the docks.

His plan worked as expected. In less than an hour, before dawn had even begun to appear, Nicholas heard the clatter of carriage wheels on cobblestone.

Standing at the foredeck railing, he watched as Aurora swiftly descended from the carriage and hurried toward the ship's gangway. He could feel the powerful thudding of his heart, knowing the next few moments could change his life forever.

When she reached the top of the gangway, he moved to help her step onto the deck, grasping her elbow for support.

"What have you done with Harry?" she demanded even before she was on board, her voice hoarse with strain. "Did you hurt him?"

"No, of course I didn't hurt him. He's sound asleep."

Abruptly she pulled away from Nick's grasp. Her gaze riveted on his face, fear and anger evident on her beautiful features in the lantern light. "What did you mean, you want to teach him a lesson?" she said in a fierce undertone. "He should be safe at home in bed."

"He is safe, Aurora."

"You said you intend to keep him on board your ship—"

"Let's not argue here," Nicholas replied warningly, gesturing with his head toward his crewmen, who were climbing the ladder after her.

With a visible effort to control her agitation, she allowed him to lead her. Taking up a lantern, he escorted her belowdeck to the mate's cabin. Quietly opening the door, he stepped aside to allow her entrance.

Harry was curled up in the bunk, fast asleep. Aurora approached him cautiously, afraid of what she would find. The pitiful sight was even more shocking than she anticipated. In the dim glow of lantern light, she could see his battered face—the bruise forming under one eye, the split lip. . . .

A sob caught in her throat, while a surge of nausea rose up to choke her; she had to press her hand to her mouth to stifle it.

This was what violence had done to him, she thought despairingly, fighting the storm of fury and helplessness that raged inside her. Yet Harry was alive, that was what mattered most. She had not been able to protect him, but he was *alive*.

Needing that reassurance, she reached down to touch his face. The boy stirred in his sleep, but didn't awaken. She drew a shuddering breath.

"Come," Nicholas murmured softly behind her. "He needs to rest after his ordeal."

Reluctant to leave, she tenderly brushed a disheveled lock of hair from the boy's forehead, then forced herself to turn away. After the strain and terror of the past hours, she suddenly felt drained, empty.

She hardly noticed where Nicholas was taking her, but found herself in a small but well-appointed cabin. She didn't resist when he led her to the bunk and pressed her to sit down.

He went straight to a cabinet and poured her a finger of brandy, then returned to her.

"Here, drink," he said, holding the glass to her lips.

The potent liquor burned like fire. Aurora shuddered as she swallowed, then pushed it away. Bending her head, she covered her face with her hands.

"I told you he was safe," Nicholas finally said.

Her shoulders quivered with involuntary trembles. "I know. I was just so afraid. . . ."

"You didn't truly think I would harm him?"

Mutely, Aurora shook her head. She knew Nicholas wouldn't hurt even a strand of Harry's blond hair, yet he

was the worst kind of influence on an impressionable
boy. . . .

"You said you meant to teach him a lesson," she said,
her muffled reply more a question than accusation.

"I do. In the morning I intend to put him to work swabbing decks and checking rigging."

"Why?"

"Because he needs to learn just how difficult life at sea
can be."

Lifting her head, she stared at him. "Harry cannot possibly become a sailor, Nicholas. It is too dangerous. By
keeping him on your ship, you will only be abetting his
ambition—"

"It is far more dangerous to leave him to strike out on
his own." Putting down the brandy glass, Nicholas sat
beside her on the bunk. "The boy has a fever, Aurora. A
burning desire that won't be quenched. Believe me, I know.
I was just like him when I was that age. Perhaps it's hard
for you to understand since you've never experienced anything like it, but Harry will have to pursue his ambition
until either it burns out or it's satisfied. Either way, you
cannot cure his fever by sheltering him from life. He will
only resent you for it—the way he now resents his mother.
The way I did my father."

"But I am responsible for him."

"And certainly you want to protect him. But he needs
the guidance of a man, Aurora. I can give him that."

"He doesn't need the kind of guidance you could provide. You will only teach him violence. I abhor violence,
Nicholas. After seeing all the terrible things my father
did—"

"I have no intention of teaching Harry to be violent,
sweetheart," he said gently. "Only to stand up for himself."
When she was silent, Nicholas added more forcefully, "You
cannot keep him wrapped in cotton wool forever, Aurora.
Certainly not by keeping him imprisoned in the safe little
sanctuary you've built for yourself."

Her throat tightening in despair, she looked away. "But . . . he is just a boy. I couldn't bear it if something happened to him and I was to blame."

"Then you should allow me to determine the safest way for him to explore his ambition."

When she wouldn't reply, Nicholas tilted her face back to his with a light touch of his fingers. "You said you trusted me."

She returned his gaze helplessly. His eyes were deep and quiet and searching, the strong planes of his face intent.

Aurora swallowed convulsively as pain congealed in her chest like a deep bruise. "I do trust you," she whispered.

His face softened, while his thumb brushed her lower lip with a featherlight pressure. At his gentleness, she blinked, and a tear slid down her cheek.

Closing her eyes, she brushed her cheek with the back of her hand. Crying never solved anything. Tears were useless in stopping the pain.

And yet she couldn't help herself. A sob escaped her, followed by another. And suddenly she couldn't stop.

When she felt Nicholas's arms come around her, she turned her face to his shoulder and wept as all the tension of the past day—indeed, all the dark emotions of the past year, fear, grief, loss—came pouring out.

Her body shook in racking sobs while the tears came. Nicholas simply held her, cradling her trembling body in his arms.

When finally her tears subsided, Aurora realized she was lying on the bunk with him, her head pressed into the curve of his neck. His hand gently stroked her hair as she clung to him, and she could feel the night stubble on his jaw grazing the softer skin of her cheek.

Eventually she took a deep, quavering breath. "I am sorry . . ." she murmured, her voice husky from crying.

"Don't be." His lips brushed against her temple. "Here."

He drew a snowy handkerchief from his pocket and used it to wipe away the dampness from her face.

Aurora lay unresisting for his ministrations, like a child. She hadn't the energy or the will to move.

"You were right," she murmured. "I am a coward."

"No," Nicholas replied softly. "But you've let fear rule you for too long."

She sighed when his warm lips touched her eyelids. She wanted to lie like this forever, safe in Nicholas's arms, pressed against his hardness, his warmth, sheltered and protected and cherished.

The intimacy of their embrace, however, had a starkly different effect on Nick. When Aurora nestled closer, he went still, his heartbeat quickening and deepening. Awareness of her flooded his senses, while a wave of longing hit him, colliding with the breath he was trying to take.

He wanted to comfort her. Wanted to ease her fear, her sadness, to erase that anguish and despair from her beautiful face. But even more, he wanted *her*.

Almost involuntarily, his lips began moving upon her flushed face, savoring the velvety texture of her soft skin. When she stirred against him, an ache started deep in his groin like a lick of fire.

Nicholas drew a steadying breath, struggling for control as hunger shuddered through his body. How had it happened, this deep and powerful need of her? He couldn't deny it any longer. . . .

Urgently he molded her soft lips to fit his, desire flaring through his senses as he took her mouth. She gave a soft murmur of protest at his sudden move, yet he kept up his tender assault and felt a surge of triumph when her mouth turned hot and pliant under his.

Then suddenly she drew back, her palms pressing against his chest. Her breath came in soft pants as she regarded him, her blue eyes wide with dismay.

Nicholas drew a sharp breath, struggling to check his

savage need. She wanted him, he knew. When he touched her throat, he could feel the wildness of her pulse.

"I intend to make love to you, Aurora," he warned hoarsely, his voice raw with desire. "If you want me to stop, then tell me now."

He lay still, waiting, drawn as tight as a bowstring. His loins were full and aching for her, his heartbeat like an anvil in his chest. Yet it had to be her decision this time.

Aurora stared into his eyes, drowning in the sheer intensity of the dark depths. She didn't want his lovemaking, his passion, and yet she couldn't fight his tenderness, the stirring kisses that were so sweet and so fierce. She no longer had any defenses against him.

Mutely she shook her head, knowing the sweet torment of defeat. A desperate longing welled up within her, the need to touch him, to feel him deep inside her.

"I don't want you to stop," she whispered. Reaching up, her fingers curled in the waving thickness of his silky hair.

"Please," she added helplessly. "Make love to me, Nicholas."

Chapter Eighteen

*He offered the haunting promise of paradise, if I but had
the courage to grasp it.*

He undressed her slowly, wanting her with a need so
powerful it made him shake. She was still shy about her
body, and he ached with the effort to be gentle.

When Aurora stood naked before him, he pulled the
pins from her hair one by one, and let the shining mass
cascade down over her bare shoulders. Her nipples were
erect, her skin pale gold in the flickering lamplight, her
legs long and slender.

She seemed to have no idea how beautiful she was, Nicholas thought reverently, or how exquisitely sensual. Her features mirrored the wanting, the longing, he felt; her blue
eyes were dark with yearning.

"Aurora," he murmured hoarsely as he took her mouth.
Hunger ran rampant through him as he kissed her, a slow,
deep, claiming kiss, parting her lips and thrusting his tongue
within her welcoming warmth, searching out her secrets.
Exultation filled him when he felt a shiver of desire surge
through her. He wanted her hot and wild, burning for him . . .
and yet he forced himself to restrain his dire urgency. This
was a moment to savor. He intended to love her slowly, completely. To make it last.

Steeling himself, he broke off the kiss and stepped back
to shed his own clothing.

Watching, Aurora drew a sharp breath at the magnificence of Nicholas's aroused body. He was so intensely
male, his form sculptured and shadowed with bronze in
the lamplight. But it was his gaze that held her spellbound.

She saw stark longing in his eyes; she saw need, raw and bold, as he came to her. His fingers glided gently over her bare shoulders, then lower, over the curve of her rib cage, her waist. Then his hands slid down over her hips, pulling her against him. She felt his hot, throbbing maleness against her.

"See what you do to me?" he asked softly. "Can you feel the fire raging in my loins?"

Not letting her answer, he bent to her breast, and the coolness of the night air against her bare skin gave way to the scorching heat of his mouth.

At the softest lash of his tongue, she quivered. When he suckled gently, her fingers dug into his shoulders and clung.

Her soft whimper only aroused him more fully. Nick clenched his jaw, remembering his violence when he'd taken her yesterday. His need was no longer so frantic this time. The frenzied, explosive desire had tempered. Instead he was filled with the longing to share tenderness, to express it.

He sank to his knees before her, rubbing a whiskered cheek on the inside of her thigh. Aurora went rigid as he inhaled her scent.

Ignoring her quiet gasp of protest, he bent forward to probe the delicate, petal-like folds of her womanness, letting his tongue find her ripeness.

Her knees nearly buckling beneath her, she clutched at his hair, but he had no intention of stopping. His hands held her hips still for the unrelenting caress of his tongue. Her hair tumbled in gold tangles around them as he continued savoring, exploring, claiming in long, slow strokes.

Aurora moaned with longing, arching against his clever mouth. It was torture, his infinite tenderness slaking one hunger, his sensuality creating another.

"Nicholas, please . . ." she pleaded.

Obliging, his lips pressed against her fully as his tongue

delved deep. A jolt of flame ran from him into her body, searing her, and she quaked in fierce need.

His hoarse whisper seemed far away. "Yes, be on fire for me . . ."

Another racking shudder convulsed her, and then she couldn't remain still. Shaking, she cried out as the tremors overtook her. Her legs gave way bonelessly, and she would have fallen had Nicholas not risen and caught her trembling body.

"Enough . . ." she murmured helplessly.

Desire was bold in his eyes, and so was dark intensity as he replied huskily. "No, angel. We've only just begun."

He kissed her as if he'd found something fragile, precious, then turned with her to the bed. His mouth still covered hers when he bore her down to the mattress.

Primal awareness shimmered through Aurora as he knelt above her and began his sensual assault all over again. His touch was warm, his mouth magical as it moved over her body, kissing her everywhere. She gave herself up to the sensations his touch elicited. She had never felt such sweet, aching tenderness, such intimate beauty.

He was so strong and so gentle, his caresses so soft. He held his power under careful control, his lips skilled and slow, and she could feel his caring.

She stirred beneath him, feeling a fierce, restless, feminine need. His touch was possessive and adoring, soothing and arousing, offering comfort and torment at the same time.

A feverish sound escaped her throat. She was drowning in desire. . . .

She pleaded with him again, but it seemed an eternity before he at last seemed to hear her.

His eyes fierce with tenderness and intent, he covered her with his body. Urgently Aurora raised her arms to draw him closer to her, reveling in the feel of him, of his weight pressing her down, of his maleness, hard and aroused between them.

He checked himself there for a moment, though, his

arms holding his weight lightly above her as he gazed down into her eyes. "Do you know how many times I've dreamed of this?" he demanded, his whisper wild and low. "Having you in my arms again, all beauty and fire."

His eyes were passion-black, waiting.

"I have dreamed of you, too," Aurora whispered shakily.

It was all the answer Nicholas seemed to need. He slid slowly, deeply within her, into the clenching tightness of her. Aurora gave a ragged sigh at the relief of having him finally part of her.

He paused for a moment, letting her grow accustomed to the swollen, rigid fullness. Her flesh throbbed as he slowly withdrew.

The second strong thrust of his hips forced him so deeply inside her, she gasped. Smiling tenderly, Nicholas reached down, pulling her hips up higher so that he could fill her even more completely. It was the most exquisite sensation she had ever experienced—being one with him.

Aurora's head fell back on the pillow. She couldn't think, she could only feel. The desire he'd awakened with his touch was so alive, so vibrant, like a flame burning in-side her.

He began to move then, with quiet haste, as if he felt the same flame. Her hands moved blindly over his hard-muscled body as he increased the rhythm, burying him-self deeper and harder into her welcoming body. Pleasure sharpened, and sharpened still more, swelling to a bursting point.

Nicholas found himself seared by the same urgency as she, the same primitive, powerful need. His breath quick-ened against her throat as his hips thrust even more force-fully. He tried to remember to be gentle, but the thought faded along with his control as the silken wave of desire gripping Aurora swept over him.

The explosion, when it came, dragged them both under. He caught her moans of ecstasy with his mouth as the

pulsing spasms shaking his body rippled into hers, along
with his release.

When he collapsed against her, tenderness was such an
ache within him, he trembled with it. At length, he weakly
rolled to his side and folded her against his chest.

For a long while, Nick lay there shaken, still pulsing with
the powerful aftershocks, his thoughts in turmoil. There
was a name for the fierce and overwhelming tenderness he
was feeling, he realized. *Love.* He loved Aurora. Sweet
heaven . . .

Nicholas squeezed his eyes shut, torn between wanting
to curse and pray.

It was a staggering acknowledgment. Love had never
entered his calculations in any other relationship. Always
before he had been able to leave with no regrets, to walk
away heart-whole. He'd never been in danger of succumbing to love, never been even remotely tempted by the possibility. He'd thought himself impervious to the soul-deep
kind of emotion his father had once experienced.

Yet that was before he met Aurora. Her lush loveliness
had entranced him from the first—but her appeal went far
beyond mere beauty or sensual allure. From the beginning,
her kindness, her quiet strength, her fierce protectiveness
had won his respect, and his feelings had only grown from
there. The more he knew her, the more he'd wanted her.
She'd given him tantalizing glimpses of the captivating,
passionate woman she kept hidden from the world. It was
that unforgettable woman who made him burn, who set his
blood and heart afire. . . .

"Are you all right?" he asked after a while.

Her answer was a murmured sigh of pleasure.

Reaching for the blanket at the foot of the bunk, Nicholas drew it up to cover their nakedness. Then absently he
pressed a kiss against her silken hair and gathered her closer,
his senses distracted by the wonderful, frightening refrain
ringing in his head. *I love her. I love her.* . . .

Again and again he turned the stunning thought over in

his mind, before finally allowing himself another reflection. *So what in hell's name am I to do about it?* How did he convince Aurora to be his wife when she had fought him every step of the way?

One night would never be enough to satisfy the hunger in his soul. He wanted Aurora for his wife. She belonged in his bed, in his life. Their unlikely marriage had been forged by a twist of fate, but he wanted it to be real.

He wanted the right to acknowledge the passion he felt for her. He wanted to lose himself in the hot silk of her body each night and wake up beside her each morning. He wanted to build a future with her, to have children. . . .

Nicholas went very still, wondering if his seed had taken root. Twice in as many days he had loved her without taking any measures to prevent conception. If he'd given her a child, then Aurora would have no choice but to accept their marriage, for she wouldn't be able to weather the scandal alone.

Mentally, Nick shook his head. The thought of Aurora bearing his child filled him with wonder and delight, but the choice had to be hers. He fervently wanted her as his wife, but she had to come willingly. Because she loved him. Because she wanted to spend the rest of her life with him. Not because she was forced to. The next time they made love, he vowed, he had to be certain to take precautions.

Yet would there even be a next time? He knew what he wanted, but what did Aurora want?

She didn't return his feelings, he knew that well enough. He was the antithesis of what she considered an ideal husband. And she was still in love with a damned ghost. Given enough time, perhaps he could change her affections, but he was running out of time.

That was what he needed—time. Time alone with Aurora. Time to break through her defenses. To convince her to give their marriage a chance. To show her that the desire they shared could ripen into something real and lasting. To kindle her passion until her feelings were so fierce and overwhelming, she could deny them no longer.

That was the only way he knew to reach her, through physical intimacy. Each time they touched, her defenses crumbled a little more, the hunger he aroused in her grew stronger.

And physical passion could lead to love. It had happened in the Frenchwoman's journal. It could happen with Aurora. No, it *would* happen, Nicholas vowed.

He didn't intend to give up his pursuit without doing everything in his power to win her. His father had lost the love of his life, and Nick refused to spend the rest of his days yearning for what might have been.

He raised a hand to touch her cheek with the lightest of pressures. "Are you awake?"

Stirring, she tilted her face to gaze up at him. "Yes," she murmured, her blue eyes slumberous and sensual.

Tenderly he brushed back the cloud of hair from her flushed face. She was so hauntingly beautiful. . . . He wanted her again, more powerfully than before, a craving that went beyond the physical.

Still, he couldn't simply blurt out his feelings. He doubted Aurora would believe any sudden confessions of love—indeed, he had difficulty believing it himself. His uncertainty left him feeling uncommonly vulnerable.

He couldn't tell her yet. He would have to bide his time, would have to *show* her how deeply he felt, with more than mere words.

"There is something I need to discuss with you," he said finally, struggling to keep his tone casual. "I am considering whether or not to leave London."

He felt her body tense. "What do you mean, leave?"

"I thought I would go to the country for a time. You're right. After encountering so many people who recognize me, the risk of discovery is too great. Clune has offered me the use of his house in Berkshire." Nicholas paused, taking a deep breath. "I want you to come with me, Aurora."

She sat up slowly, clutching the blanket to her breasts. "Come with you?" she repeated faintly.

"Yes. I want us to be together."

The troubled look was back in her eyes as she gazed down at him. "We are together now."

"Not the way we should be. As things are now, I'm relegated to acting the thief, stealing a few private moments alone with you, having to skulk around to enjoy any intimacy with my wife. I want to be able to kiss you without worrying about creating a scandal. To hold you and make love to you and wake up with you in my arms."

"Nicholas . . . we have been over this before. I don't want to be your wife."

He held her gaze steadily. "You cannot deny that you want me, not after the passion we just shared."

The distress in her eyes was evident. "That doesn't change anything. We are still completely wrong for each other."

"How can you be so sure? We have never truly put the question to the test. Our marriage was never given a fair chance to succeed. I want that chance, Aurora. And you owe it to yourself if not to me."

When she made no reply, he went on in a low voice. "We have very little time left. I cannot stay in England much longer. But before I leave, I have to be certain that we are not right for each other. We should prove it to ourselves, one way or the other."

"What . . . are you proposing?"

"Come to Berkshire with me—as my wife." He reached up to brush her bare arm with his thumb. "Give me a fortnight. Two weeks to persuade you that we belong together. At the end of that time, if you still want to sever our marriage and the solemn vows we took, I will agree. I'll leave England and take myself out of your life forever."

She stared at him. "Forever?"

"Yes," he agreed softly. "I'll return to America without you. You will never have to see me again. You can live your life here, independently, just as you wish."

Aurora raised a hand to her forehead, rubbing it distractedly. "I cannot leave London just now. What about Harry? What of Raven?"

He couldn't condemn her fierce streak of loyalty. Aurora was passionately dedicated to the people she cared for; it was one of the things he loved about her.

"Raven will do well enough on her own," Nicholas answered truthfully. "And I will deal with Harry. After his hazardous encounter tonight, I doubt he'll be eager to strike out on his own again. And I intend to make very certain he realizes that a seafaring life is not the glamorous adventure he's dreamed of. I wouldn't be surprised if he decides very soon to return home to his mama."

"I cannot leave him here, Nicholas."

"I promise that won't be necessary. What other objections do you have?"

She had a great number of objections, Aurora thought. The chief of which was Nicholas himself. He was a risk beyond anything she'd ever imagined: He threatened everything she had ever known of safety or sense. The emotions he created in her were intense and terrifying, as was his fierce, consuming passion. . . .

But if she refused to go with him? She would be letting her fear rule her. She would be acting the coward, just as he'd accused her of doing. She didn't want to live her life in fear.

Worse, if he remained in London and was discovered, he would be arrested and hanged. Sweet heaven, she couldn't bear it if he were to die. At least away from London he would be safer. . . .

Did she dare agree to what he was asking of her? Did she have any choice?

She stared back at him, caught in the spell of his intense gaze. Two weeks. A handful of days, alone with Nicholas. They would be lovers. It would be paradise; it would be torment.

Could she possibly manage to keep her emotional de-

fenses intact for so long? Two weeks would seem an eternity.
And the enforced intimacy would only bring her greater
agony when they had to part.

But if she could endure it, he would leave England and
return to America for good. Aurora swallowed the sudden
ache in her throat. Wasn't that what she desperately wanted?
To be free of Nicholas and his overwhelming passion?

She forced away the sharp feeling of desolation that
thought engendered. She wanted desperately for him to
go, before he tore her heart to shreds. . . .

"Will you give me that chance, sweetheart?" he asked,
his voice soft as velvet. "Will you come with me?"

"Yes," Aurora whispered, gazing down at Nicholas. "I
will come."

There was such fire in his eyes that her heart stopped.
Unable to bear that look, Aurora shut her own eyes, hoping with all her might that she was not making a dreadful
mistake.

PART III

A Passion of the Heart

Chapter Nineteen

He drew from me my heart's most intimate secrets.

"How much longer till we arrive?" Harry asked for the third time, twisting in his seat to look out the coach window at the Sussex countryside.

Aurora couldn't help but smile at the boy's eagerness to be home. They had been traveling only a few hours since leaving London early that morning, but Harry could scarcely contain his impatience. "Not long."

"You will speak to Mama, will you not, Rory? You won't let her scold?"

"Yes, of course. I promised I would. But I don't think you need worry. She will be too relieved to have you safely home to do much scolding."

Just then Harry spied Nicholas, who rode beside the carriage. "I wish I could have ridden like Mr. Deverill, instead of being shut up in this carriage."

"You said your ribs were still too tender to endure such a long ride on horseback, remember?"

The boy shuddered, as if recalling his ordeal—a reaction that Aurora noted with silent gratification. After his beating on the quay, Harry had sworn faithfully never to run away again, displaying a sincerity she thought was genuine. And much to her vast relief, two days of sweat and blisters and aching muscles had convinced him that he would not enjoy the hard life of a seaman.

Those two days seemed an eternity to Aurora, but she had promised Nicholas she wouldn't interfere with his harsh methods. And just as Nicholas predicted, Harry had abandoned his dream of joining the merchant marine, although not happily.

When she gently reminded him that upon reaching his majority, he would be wealthy enough to buy a fleet of his own ships, he had brightened considerably and decided that he would, after all, prefer to spend the intervening years in Sussex with his mama—that he missed her greatly and perhaps her smothering was not really so unendurable.

Aurora was taking the boy home now, while Nicholas provided escort. She, too, wished she could have ridden on the beautiful summer day and avoided the warmth and dust inside the carriage. But not only did she need to keep Harry company, she knew it was wiser to maintain the discreet pretense of Nicholas as a family friend and not advertise their actual plan. Upon delivering Harry to his mama, they would start back toward London but detour to Berkshire, where they would spend a fortnight together, as Aurora had agreed.

Until now she had managed to quell her reservations, but as they moved deeper into the East Sussex countryside of her childhood, she was glad to have Harry's chatter to distract her from her misgivings and from her feelings of sadness. This was the first time in nearly a year that she had been home. After Geoffrey's death, she had preferred to live in London, for there it was easier to avoid the painful reminders of her loss. She'd distanced herself even farther when she sailed for the Caribbean with her cousin and his wife.

How her life had changed since then, Aurora reflected pensively. She had been wed and widowed and then unwidowed. . . . She had become fully a woman, learning carnal knowledge at the hands of an expert lover who was the very opposite of the gentle man she had admired and cared for so much of her life.

This journey home roused sad memories of Geoffrey, and other ones as well.

Aurora stirred uncomfortably. She had tried not to think

about her father or the darker feelings he engendered. The March and Eversley estates were close, merely a few miles apart, but she had no reason even to call on the duke, since he had washed his hands of her and banished her from his property.

She couldn't forget, however, his threat to whip her through the streets if she exceeded the bounds of propriety. And she would soon be exceeding those bounds with a vengeance. Her father would be outraged if he learned of her intention to spend two intimate weeks alone with Nicholas. Even now she was skirting the edge. She had eschewed a maid on the flimsy grounds that the trip was of short duration.

At least one worry was unfounded; she wasn't with child after her rash intimacies with Nicholas. Her courses had come and gone this past week. And from now on, whenever they were together, they would take the kind of precautions the journal had described.

"So," she said to Harry, making an attempt at cheerfulness as she drew out a deck of cards from her reticule. "What game shall we play?"

It was nearly an hour later when the coach turned onto the smooth gravel drive of the March estate, and by then Harry was squirming in his seat. His mother, Lady March, came out to meet them as soon as the carriage drew to a halt before the impressive brick mansion.

She embraced her son fervently, then greeted Aurora with almost as much fondness. Lady March had been a friend to Aurora since her mother's death, and they had shared the sorrow of Geoffrey's death. With Nicholas watching her, though, she willed herself to shrug off her sadness and made the introductions.

Lady March was effusive in her greeting to Nicholas as well, clasping his hand in gratitude with both of hers. "Harry's letters have been full of you, Mr. Deverill. I cannot thank you enough."

"It was nothing, my lady," Nicholas replied mildly.

"Oh, but it was. Harry has not had a man to guide him in . . ." She swallowed her sudden tears and pasted on a bright smile. "Will you be staying the night?" she asked Aurora.

"Thank you, but we must be getting back."

"You must at least have luncheon. And you must tell me all the gossip from London. I rarely get there these days, you know. Come into the house. Harry, you will join us. . . ."

They settled in the drawing room until luncheon was served. Lady March kept Harry at her side, as if afraid he would disappear, but the moment the meal was through, Harry asked to be excused so he could go to the stables and visit his horses, barely waiting for permission before scrambling from his chair.

His mother stopped him from racing out the door, calling him to task for his ungentlemanlike behavior in front of guests.

"Pah, Rory is not a guest, Mama," Harry declared.

"Nevertheless you will apologize to her and to Mr. Deverill."

"Beg pardon," Harry said with an unrepentant grin.

"And I have yet to hear you thank her for her generous hospitality to you these past weeks," Lady March added sternly.

"Thank you, Rory." Returning to the table, he gave Aurora a fierce hug, shook Nicholas's hand, then dashed off.

Shaking her head in exasperation, Lady March sighed. "Sometimes I believe he is a changeling. He is so different from his brother Geoffrey. . . ." She gave a start and glanced at Nicholas. "Now it is my turn to apologize, Mr. Deverill. I don't mean to be melancholy, but it is hard for a mother to lose a son. Or for a woman to lose her betrothed," she added, including Aurora in her rueful look.

Nick gave a sympathetic nod, but he wasn't as sanguine as he appeared. He wasn't at all happy with this visit, for it stirred up too many memories of his chief rival in Aurora's mind and heart. She had elevated the late Lord March onto a pedestal, and it would be difficult to knock him off.

He couldn't fight such a paragon, Nicholas knew. He could only try to make her forget—which he would do his damnedest to make happen if he could ever get her away from here.

Another event occurred, however, to raise more painful memories for Aurora and interfere with the continuation of their journey. They were about to take their leave when Lady March asked Aurora if she had heard from her father lately.

"No," she replied. "I'm afraid we have not been on the best of terms since my marriage."

"I understand he isn't faring too well," Lady March admitted. "Since you left, he has found it difficult to retain any servants. But I suppose it serves him right since he drove them all away with his vile temper."

Nicholas saw the fleeting emotions that ran across Aurora's beautiful face; clearly she was disturbed by what she had heard. She was silent, however, until Nicholas started to hand her into the carriage. Then she touched his arm.

"Before we leave," she said in a low voice, "I would like to call on my father."

Nick gave her a narrow look. "What do you expect to accomplish? You can't really wish to see him after the way he treated you."

"I don't *wish* to see him. But he is still my father."

"And you have an overdeveloped sense of duty," Nicholas said disapprovingly.

Aurora gave him a rueful smile. "I expect so."

"You don't owe him anything, Aurora. He's forfeited any right to your allegiance."

"Perhaps he has. But my conscience would always plague me if I left without making certain he is all right. You don't have to come with me if you don't wish to."

"Oh, no," Nick said with a dangerous smile of his own.

"I would very much like the chance to meet the illustrious duke."

A short while later they arrived at the Eversley estate. The magnificent park had been badly neglected since she had last been there, Aurora saw with dismay. The gravel drive was rutted and unswept, while the unkempt lawns and ragged shrubbery looked a bit wild.

Her stomach was churning as she climbed the front steps with Nicholas, yet facing her father was something she had to do. She knew there was little chance for a reconciliation between them, nor did she really want one. But even though he had disowned her, he was her father, her flesh and blood. Whether he deserved compassion or not, she couldn't bring herself to turn her back on him. Not without making one last effort. She would never be able to close this chapter of her life, otherwise. She was very glad, however, to have Nicholas at her side.

When he applied the brass knocker, the thud sounded hollow, as if no one was home. Long minutes passed before the door was opened by a footman whose livery was soiled and disheveled. Not recognizing him, Aurora asked to see the duke.

"The duke ain't 'ome" was the sullen response.

"He is not at home, or he is not receiving visitors?"

" 'e ain't receiving."

"I should like to see him, nonetheless."

"And 'oo might you 'appen to be?"

Aurora lifted her chin regally, staring the man down. "I might 'happen' to be the duke's daughter, and I wish to speak to my father. You will please tell him I am here."

He glanced at Nicholas, as if sizing him up. Apparently deciding the visitor was both taller and stronger, the footman scowled and shuffled off.

Aurora glanced around her sadly. "When my mother was alive, this house was beautiful," she murmured.

She felt Nicholas's fingers brush her nape, a subtle display of sympathy and support. He didn't speak, but she felt him lending her strength, and she was grateful.

The servant finally returned. As sullen as ever, he gestured with his thumb over his shoulder. " 'is grace is in 'is study."

"I know the way," Aurora said coolly, moving past him.

Her footsteps slowed, however, when she neared the study door. Perhaps she *was* foolish to have come here. She pressed a hand to her stomach, reluctant to face the pain she knew she was about to bring on herself.

Bracing her shoulders, she stepped inside his study.

The sight of him was more shocking than she expected, even after Lady March's warning. The once noble Duke of Eversley was sprawled in a chair, his clothing as unkempt as his disreputable footman's, his blue eyes bleary and bloodshot as he scowled at her.

He had obviously been drinking, for his words were slurred when he spoke. "What the devil are you doing here? I told you I never wanted to set eyes on you again."

"Hello, Father," she said steadily. "Lady March said you were faring poorly."

"It is none of your business how I fare, you ungrateful wretch." Morosely, he lifted his glass of port wine to his lips and tossed off the remainder of the contents. "You are no daughter of mine. You defied my wishes, wedding a criminal on the gallows, shaming me . . . I should have taken my whip to you."

"Be very glad you didn't," Nicholas said chillingly beside her.

The duke's glance shifted to him. "Who the devil are you?"

Nicholas's smile did not reach his eyes. "The criminal's cousin, Brandon Deverill."

"Get out—and take her with you." Eversley raised his hand and pointed toward the door. "I won't have that whore in my house."

Aurora drew back as if slapped, but when Nicholas took

a step forward, she laid a restraining hand on his arm. Rather than wounding her, her father's attack had only angered and saddened her.

"*I* shamed *you*, Father?" Her lips twisted in an ironic smile. "That is rich. What of the countless times you shamed me? The whole of my life I had to watch the despicable way you treated everyone around you. You ruled by fear, beating innocents and flying into rages for no other reason than that your porridge was cold or a speck of dust was left on your boots. Well, you should be quite happy now. You no longer must endure your servants' transgressions. You drove them all away."

His face mottled with rage, Eversley slammed down his glass and rose threateningly to his feet.

But Aurora stood her ground. "I feel sorry for you, Father. I truly do. I thought you had more pride. I never would have expected you to sink to this pathetic level."

"How dare you . . ." Belying his drunkenness, Eversley cursed and lunged for her, his hand poised to strike.

Nicholas moved like lightning. In an instant, he hauled the duke up by his cravat, spun him around, twisted his arm behind his back, then forced him forward till his face was mashed against the far wall.

Eversley gave a strangled cry of pain.

Nicholas's voice was low and harsh in response. "I've been itching to do this ever since I heard what a bullying brute you are."

"Get your . . . damned hands . . . off me!" Eversley exclaimed, gasping for breath.

"What? You don't like getting a taste of your own medicine?"

"Damn you . . . I will have you horsewhipped! I will have you arrested . . . for assaulting a peer."

"You are welcome to try. But I'm giving you fair warning. If you ever lay a finger on your daughter, I'll slit your gullet. You harm so much as a hair of hers, and I'll hunt you down like the scum you are. You won't live to see your next sunrise. Do I make myself clear?"

Weakly the duke nodded, but Nicholas still wasn't satisfied.

"Keep out of her life, do you understand me? I don't want to hear that you've spoken even a whisper against her."

"Yes! All right!" He nearly sank to his knees when Nicholas released his savage grip.

Aurora had watched the exchange with her heart pounding, forcing herself not to intervene. When her father's malevolent glance found her, she lifted her chin and returned his gaze, dry eyed. She deplored violence, yet she couldn't be sorry for this clash. The duke had finally met his match—someone who couldn't be intimidated or made to cower in fear from his rages. Nicholas wasn't terrified in the least by his threats.

Nicholas turned then and offered her his arm, and she went willingly. Neither of them spoke as he escorted her from the house and outside to the waiting carriage.

Instead of riding, he tied his horse to the rear and joined her inside, yet Aurora scarcely noticed. As the coach drew away, she stared unseeingly out the window at the fading view of her home.

She was still trembling, but her strongest emotion was a vast feeling of release. She was free of her father, after years of living under his oppressive thumb. She had broken his hateful hold over her. She couldn't help him, she finally acknowledged. No longer was she constrained by filial duty; she needn't feel any responsibility toward him at all. With his violent repudiation of her, he had relinquished any right even to her compassion.

Surprisingly she felt no guilt, only a deep sadness that it had to end this way, with the severing of blood ties.

It was a few moments before she realized that Nicholas was watching her with a hooded gaze.

"You are well rid of him," he said finally.

"Yes." She shook her head, amazed that she had endured his tyranny for so long. "All my life he has been like a shadow hovering over me . . . dark and menacing. He made my life a misery. . . . He was always so hateful, so violent."

Nicholas's dark gaze intensified, yet held a touch of wariness. "I regret you had to witness that, but sometimes a bully can be stopped only by force."

"Perhaps so." She glanced down at Nicholas's hands. He had strong, beautiful hands, capable of violence and yet . . . Not all men were angry and brutal as her father was.

She gave him a fragile smile. "Thank you for what you did. I might not have found the courage to break free of him if not for you."

Nicholas felt her soft smile curl inside him and wanted to shout in triumph. She had dealt with one invidious relationship in her past. Now what remained was the ghost of her former love.

At the thought, Nick set his jaw. It would be far more difficult to free Aurora from that powerful influence. But he was determined to succeed. He would make her feel the same love for him that she once had harbored for her dead love. She would be his wife in every way.

The trouble was, he had only two weeks in which to do it.

They arrived well after dark at an elegant mansion hidden in a dense beechwood forest of the Chiltern Hills. At school, Aurora had heard whispered rumors about the pleasure houses wicked noblemen kept tucked away for their sinful purposes, but she had never envisioned anything quite so decadent. The chateau of honey-colored stone more closely resembled a miniature palace than an English manor, while the richly appointed interior had a distinctly exotic cast, with its tapestries and statuary and portraits of nudes.

They were greeted by a small staff and shown to separate rooms. Aurora found herself in a scented, dimly lit chamber hung with silks and brilliant paintings.

A low, wide bed stood against one wall, scattered with tasseled cushions in the Eastern manner. Near the divan, a table was set for a late supper. Along the opposite wall, marble arches led to a walled courtyard paved with brightly colored tiles.

Lured by the quiet splash of a fountain, she went to stand beneath one of the arches, staring out at the dark night. She could almost imagine herself stepping into Desiree's journal, a prisoner in the sandalwood splendor of a palace harem.

But she was no prisoner, Aurora reminded herself. Desiree had been enslaved and carried off to a strange land as a concubine, while she was here of her own free will. And yet she feared that like Desiree, she would be vulnerable to her master's exotic temptations and sweet seduction.

She sensed Nicholas before she heard his soft footfall. Wordlessly he slipped his arms around her from behind and drew her body back against his. Aurora sighed with pleasure at his warmth, his hardness. He was already hotly aroused, and yet they had barely touched. She shivered with anticipation of the night to come.

For a moment they simply stood there together in the hushed silence. She could hear the beating of her heart, feel the strong beat of his.

"Regrets?" he murmured finally against her ear.

He was asking if she was sorry to be here with him. She wasn't. She had qualms, but no regrets. The danger was very real, Aurora knew. It would require all the willpower she possessed to shield her heart from this powerful, vital man and the emotional firestorm he kindled inside her. Yet his promise of paradise was one no flesh-and-blood woman could ever refuse.

"No, no regrets."

"Good," Nicholas said softly.

Somewhere in the darkness came the musical trill of a nightingale.

"Then I have something to ask of you, sweetheart," he added quietly. "I want to renew the pact we made on our wedding night. For these next two weeks we live only for the present. While we're here, we have no past, no future, no discord . . . no inhibitions. We are lovers, simply that. This will be a time of forgetting, of sharing, of exploring. We can indulge in any fantasy we wish."

Aurora shut her eyes at the vision of heaven he offered. For these next two weeks, she could abandon herself in his arms, could completely indulge her passion for Nicholas. Perhaps then she could appease the hunger that was a constant ache inside her.

And then he would leave her, and her life would finally be at peace.

"Will you do that for me?" he prompted, his lips nuzzling her ear.

"Yes." She couldn't deny him anything he asked; she couldn't deny herself. She needed his kisses, his embrace, his passion. Needed them desperately . . .

Murmuring his name, Aurora turned in his arms, seeking his mouth. Nicholas was wrong, though. This would not be a time of forgetting, but of remembering.

She had to store up memories of him to cherish after he was gone. Enough memories to last a lifetime.

Chapter Twenty

He led me on an odyssey, into the fiery heart of passion.

His mouth was magical, his sensual heat creating a storm of sensation within Aurora. She felt want, yearning, need all rioting through her as they undressed each other with a feverish urgency. She was on fire, she was soaring, she was falling. . . .

No, not falling. Nicholas had swept her up in his arms, his hot mouth still drinking deeply of hers. He carried her inside to the low couch, where he followed her down amid the silk cushions. She wrapped her arms around him, hot and feverish, wanting him desperately—

She barely heard the soft, intrusive rap on the door, but Nicholas gave a sudden shudder, as if striving for control.

"Wait, angel . . ." He took a deep breath and tried to untangle himself from her. "That will be supper. I asked that it be served here."

Reluctantly Aurora released him, missing his warmth already. He stood up fluidly, unfolding his nude body in a movement that was purely sensual, and with a final heated glance at her, let the gauzy bed curtain fall to conceal the divan where she lay.

Aurora drew the silk sheet up to cover her nakedness and waited impatiently. She could hear Nicholas admitting the servants and ordering the trays to be set on the table. Then the door shut quietly, leaving a hushed silence. A moment later Nicholas drew the curtain aside.

Aurora could feel her heartbeat quicken as she took in the sight of his magnificent body.

"Are you hungry?" he murmured.

"No . . . Yes . . . for you," she answered almost shyly.

His dark eyes met hers, shadowed flame. "You can satisfy your appetite, love, for as long as you wish."

Surprisingly, though, Nicholas turned away and went to
the low table where supper had been laid out. Aurora
watched as he inspected a bottle of champagne and poured
some of the fizzing spirits into a dish.

His back was to her, and she found herself admiring the
powerful, sinewed lines of his nude body. He was like the
sensual prince in Desiree's journal—indeed, this entire
room resembled the silk and sandalwood seraglio described
in the journal, Aurora thought, her glance moving around
the exotic bedchamber. Especially this low divan with its
luxurious cushions and filmy curtains. She could almost
imagine herself in the Frenchwoman's place, waiting for her
lover. Nicholas was her magnificent master, and she his
captive, meant only for his heathen pleasures.

"The decor here," Aurora remarked curiously, striving
for calm, "is very much like the palace harem in the
journal."

"That isn't entirely coincidence," Nicholas replied. "I
asked that we be given these rooms once I learned of their
Eastern motif. You seem so taken with the journal."

He returned to her then and sat beside her on the divan,
presenting the dish for her inspection. It held several small
sponges soaked in champagne.

"Do you remember what the journal said about preventing conception?"

"Yes." She was strangely disquieted by their purpose—
preventing a man's seed from taking root—even though
she couldn't possibly risk letting Nicholas get her with
child.

"May I?" he asked.

"Yes."

The clamor of her heart echoed in the quiet of the room

as Nicholas drew down the sheet to bare her body to his warm gaze. When he slid a wet sponge between her thighs, Aurora caught her breath at the chill sensation.

With a murmur of apology, he gently parted her legs and pressed the sponge into her pulsing cleft, then farther still, until it was sheathed deep within her body. Aurora shivered, but then his mouth followed his fingers, warming her cool flesh.

Aurora gasped at the fierce jolt of desire Nicholas created, and arched against him. It was ice and fire. . . . But it wasn't enough.

"Nicholas," she pleaded, her urgency suddenly returning. "Come inside me." Eagerly she stretched out her arms to him in welcome, wanting him with all the willingness of her ripe woman's body. She wanted his hot skin against her, his heat, his power. She wanted him filling her.

He understood her craving, for without hesitation, he stretched out to cover her body with his. Pleasure darkened his eyes as he eased her legs open, his lean, hair-dusted thighs brushing abrasively against hers.

"Yes," he whispered hoarsely. "I want to be part of you all night, Aurora. I want to fall asleep deep inside you and wake up with the taste of you. . . ."

He kissed her again, urgently, and entered her in one long, slow thrust. Breathless, Aurora closed her eyes as hardness and softness melded into one ravishing sensation.

Nicholas began to move then, his rhythm quickening luxuriously. His thighs pressing hers wider, he claimed her in hot, slick strokes, penetrating deeper and deeper each time.

Her senses on fire, Aurora wrapped her legs around his hips and arched up in welcome. He wasn't gentle, but she didn't want gentle. The incredible, exquisite, painful hunger was building, until her arousal was as intense as his own. They were man and woman, filled with primal need. She could not get close enough.

He plunged into her, driving her to a place of wanton

delight, filled with bright, hot pleasure. She wanted to weep
with the beauty of it.

Their coupling grew rough, wilder, till the fiery, claw-
ing need became unbearable. They strained together, insatiable, in a mating of raw, animal passion. He demanded
her surrender, demanded abandon, and she gave him both.
She writhed beneath him. Her fingernails raked his back as
he took her, her soft cries goading him to greater wildness.

Her frenzy at last ripped the last shred of restraint from
Nicholas. His rasping breath choked words against her
mouth as he drove into her. He shook with the pounding
need to pleasure her, to possess her, to brand her with his
passion. . . .

The inferno broke over them in a tumult that made them
both cry out. Aurora sobbed as her body erupted in a white-
hot climax, while Nicholas groaned, a harsh, raw sound.
Crushing her savagely close, he shattered in a searing explosion of emotion that had her name at the end of it.

In the heated aftermath, he collapsed against her. For a
long moment, he lay there, trembling from the force of his
thundering heart, the only movement his fingers clenching
and unclenching in her hair.

Their bonding had been fierce and primal, like nothing
he had ever felt before. He wanted to throw back his head
and howl in triumph. . . .

He had won this time. He had conquered Aurora's
rigid control for the moment, making her surrender to
overwhelming passion. But now came the far harder task:
binding her to him in love.

And he had only two short weeks in which to succeed.

That night was the first of many such passionate moments together.

Despite her many qualms, Aurora found her time with
Nicholas pure enchantment, a magical interlude in her life
like nothing she had ever experienced. As he'd asked, they

had no past, no future, no nationality. They were simply man and woman, lovers in a paradise of desire.

The opulent secluded mansion offered sinful entice-ments Aurora could never even have imagined, but it was Nicholas who made their time together pure bliss.

He showed her pleasure beyond her dreams, leading her into a realm of the flesh and of the senses. They spent long hours exploring the boundaries of erotic ecstasy. He taught her to please him and to openly express what pleased her. At his impetus, she cast away all inhibition or awkward-ness, shedding the stifling codes of proper society with wild abandon, willingly surrendering to his tantalizing touch and the fire in his seductive eyes.

Nicholas made her feel utterly wanted and desired. And yet he challenged her spirit and her mind as well as her body. His intelligence and wit were a constant delight, while the rapier-sharp edge of his sensual charm made mincemeat of her usual reserve.

He made her laugh, and he made her yearn. She had never felt so cherished. She had never felt so free. Here she could be as wild and wanton as she wished.

It disturbed her, however, to discern his purpose. Nicho-las was not only mirroring certain carnal elements of the journal; he was wooing her as the Turkish prince had wooed Desiree.

Aurora herself gave him an opening to discuss their court-ship one afternoon when he surprised her reading the jour-nal. Coming up behind her unaware as she sat in the garden, Nicholas bent to press a delicate kiss on her nape.

Aurora gave a start at the erotic sensation and glanced up.

"What holds you so fascinated that you didn't even no-tice me?"

"This."

She flushed as he took the jeweled volume from her and studied the page. *"My lover and I are as one,"* he murmured, quoting a sensual passage. *"All reserve between us, all secrets, gone."* Nicholas eyed her thoughtfully. "That is precisely what I want for us, Aurora."

"My reserve is diminishing," she replied in her own defense. "You have seen to that."

"True, but you still have a long way to go." He returned the journal to her, but continued to regard her. "You are very much like Desiree was in the beginning—afraid of her own desire."

More alike than she cared to admit, Aurora thought unwillingly. Desiree had been a sheltered young innocent awakened to stunning passion by a man who became her obsession. . . . "She had good reason to be afraid, Nicholas. As a concubine, she was completely powerless, totally at the mercy of a savage ruler."

"He proved not to be so savage. And eventually she came to wield a great deal of power over him." Moving around the bench, Nicholas sat beside her. "That's something else you have in common. You have no notion of your own power." He smiled tenderly. "I think you could rule me with very little effort."

When she made no response, Nicholas bent toward her. His mouth caught her earlobe, and she shivered again, violently.

"And another similarity," he breathed in her ear. "Desiree thought she wanted liberty, but she discovered something she valued more. Passion. She chose that over freedom."

Uneasily Aurora edged away from his tormenting attention. "You forget that her tale ended unhappily. That her passion resulted in misery."

"Our story won't end like that, Aurora." His lips found her neck again, moving softly on her skin, each caress spinning pleasure about them like some silken, invisible web. "You can have all the incredible passion Desiree found without the heartache. . . ."

"Nicholas, please . . ." She shook her head. "You said we wouldn't think about our future."

"So I did." His eyelids drooped sensually as he gazed at her. "Then kiss me, sweetheart, and make me forget. . . ."

Gratefully, Aurora moved into his arms and raised her mouth to his, giving herself over to his sensual passion.

To her relief Nicholas did not mention the journal again, allowing her to slip back into their fantasy.

They took long lingering walks together, wandering the grounds, absorbed in each other. The gardens were a delight, boasting elegant, erotic statuary and even a giant maze sculpted from topiary yews, while the surrounding woods were intriguing. The dense, green-gladed beechwood offered an enchanted world all its own, full of quiet paths and running streams with mossy banks, dappled with blinks of golden sunlight and cool shadow.

They rode as well as walked. Here in this secluded hideaway, Aurora could indulge her secret vice to her heart's content. One of her greatest pleasures was enjoying a wild gallop through a morning meadow with the wind in her face and Nicholas close on her heels.

Mostly, however, they made love. Nothing was forbidden, no place or time off limits. Nicholas was determined to shatter every last measure of her reserve. They made love in the bath, and at the supper table, and beside the reflecting pool, sheltered by the high courtyard walls. They fed each other honey-drenched sweetmeats and delicious fruits, and then drank from each other's lips. They made love on a bed of rose petals, whose fragrant perfume was almost dizzying, just as in the journal.

The journal guided Aurora in certain instruments of delight as well. Her favorite novelty was a pair of smooth silver balls, meant to be inserted deep between a woman's thighs and designed to titillate and arouse.

The first time Aurora wore them was a shock; she had never felt such awareness of her body, or of Nicholas's. The delicious sensations filled her with such excitement, she could scarcely keep her hands off him.

They explored the maze during an afternoon warm and lazy and golden with sunlight. Nicholas made the venture an exercise in eroticism, showering her with hot, slow kisses as he led her deeper into the winding labyrinth.

When they reached the very heart of the maze, Aurora was unsurprised to find a life-size marble statue of two lovers in the throes of passion, displayed like a shrine in a grassy, open-air temple. She had no trouble divining Nicholas's intent when he spread a quilt on the grass and tugged off his cravat. But when he reached for her, she tensed. The high yew hedges offered all the privacy she could wish for, yet she still wasn't completely comfortable at such licentiousness.

At her hesitation, Nicholas gave her a look that was a challenge. "No one can see us, sweeting, but if it really troubles you . . ."

"No," she replied, remembering all the wonderful pleasures she had discovered at his wanton urging. "It doesn't trouble me."

"I'm glad. I want you naked, love, with only hot skin between us. Come here."

He drew her into his embrace, his soft, persuasive lips caressing her face. Aurora responded helplessly, swaying closer to the solid strength of him.

She melted to his touch as he freed her warm skin to the sun and to his hands; she could feel her body softening, turning to warm, sweet honey.

When she finally stood nude before him, his eyes devoured her with a boldness that alone aroused her. The mere feel of his heated eyes on her naked breasts made them quiver with sensation. Her nipples were peeking out from beneath the burnished strands of her hair, and his index finger leisurely traced an aureole. Aurora caught her breath as he plucked it to a taut peak.

Hearing the soft sound, he raised both his hands to cover her lush breasts. "You have the most responsive nipples. One touch and they harden."

His warm palms rubbing the crested points, he watched her start and shiver under his touch.

"Nicholas . . ."

At her husky plea, he made a sympathetic sound. "Easy, sweet."

He kissed her mouth, not roughly but possessively, as if he meant to make her his, then slowly bore her down to the coverlet. He was still clothed, while she was completely naked, Aurora realized.

She stared up at him with a sharp sense of awareness. He returned her gaze boldly as he knelt above her, his hot eyes roaming over her. Aurora felt her breath catch in her throat. She lay completely exposed to the sun and to his heated gaze, and when he looked at her with such raw hunger, she felt deliciously sinful and desirable.

She reached for him, but he shook his head. "No. Just let me touch you."

She closed her eyes, feeling an erotic heat spread through her body that had nothing to do with the warmth of the sun. His hands were moving over her flesh, creating a sensation so piercing and sweet, she felt weak. Then he bent his head, his lips lowering to lovingly attend her breasts.

The heat within her intensified; every sensation was vividly magnified as his tongue worshiped her breasts with slow, languid strokes upon their throbbing peaks. Restlessly, Aurora clutched the coverlet with her fingers. When he blew on the nipple that was still glistening from his mouth, she moaned.

"Nicholas . . ." she exclaimed hoarsely, "I want you. . . ."

He drew back; his eyes caressed her bare breasts. "Yes, I know."

The tender half smile playing on his lips promised even greater delights as his hand moved down her body to slip between her thighs to cover her hot, pulsing feminine mound. She gasped aloud, and then gasped again at the luscious slide of his thumb against the moist and aching focus of sensation.

"You are already wet for me," he said in husky approval. "Maybe we should see if we can make you wetter."

Easing himself between her parted, shivering thighs, he bent down to taste her. Excitement pierced Aurora like a lightning bolt as she realized his brazen intent.

Holding her hips with his strong hands, Nicholas brushed a probing kiss against her feminine cleft. Aurora gave a strangled moan at the intimate caress. "Ohhhh."

"Yes, love, let me hear you. . . ." His lips faintly upturned in the quiet certainty of his power, he bent to her again.

A delicious shock flared through her body as he explored the yielding, warm folds of flesh with his erotic mouth. Shuddering uncontrollably, she gave herself over to his lavish sensuality.

Her head fell back in surrender as he savored her with his caressing lips and tongue. When she arched against him, he clasped her buttocks, giving her no opportunity to evade him. With exquisite skill he lapped at her slowly, thoroughly, his hot, rasping tongue stroking her in heated pulses, delighting the quivering, throbbing bud that was the center of her pleasure.

Her hands rose to his hair, desperately clutching. His mouth with its lazy suckling was driving her wild. "God . . . Nicholas . . . please."

"Oh, yes," he murmured against her hot flesh. "I will please you in every possible way."

He held her to him more firmly, his face pressed against her, his tongue delving inside her swollen cleft, sweetly ravishing.

Fire leapt from his mouth into her flesh, dragging a wrenching shudder from her. Her whole body was a hot screaming mass of desire. She writhed beneath him, whimpering mindlessly, until finally a shriek tore from her.

She climaxed again and again, a wild, rippling, seemingly never-ending series. Mercilessly he drew every last drop of excruciating pleasure from her quivering flesh, until she fell back, limp and helpless with exhaustion.

Satisfied, he stretched out beside her. After a long moment, he pressed a kiss against her temple. "You cannot fall asleep just yet," he murmured warmly against her ear. "We have only begun to obliterate your inhibitions."

Aurora stirred against him languorously, not wanting to move. It was scandalous, what he had done, but she couldn't bring herself to lament her wanton behavior. Instead she wanted more.

"I am not about to fall asleep," she returned in a voice still husky with passion. "I am simply being patient, waiting for you to undress. You have far too many clothes on."

His smile was so sensual, it made her heart turn over. "Your wish is my command, angel."

He started to undress, but Aurora took over. It was her turn to torment him.

Kneeling over him, she took off his garments, one by one, drawing out the moment. When he was nude, she sat back on her heels, marveling at his hard-muscled glory. His skin was golden in the sunlight, except for the paler flesh at his groin and upper thighs. He was brazen, naked male, all corded muscle and lithe strength. And he was boldly aroused.

"Now what do you mean to do with me?" he murmured, half taunting.

She returned her own taunting smile in answer. Holding his gaze, she reached for him, her hands cupping his hard, pulsing arousal.

His groan was soft and erotic in the quiet of the afternoon.

When he tried to pull her down to him, she released him abruptly and pressed her palms against his powerful chest. She intended to be the seducer this time. "No, Nicholas. You aren't to touch me. You aren't even to move."

Reluctantly he obeyed, holding his arms by his side.

Aurora leaned over him, feeling the strength of his muscles beneath her hands, his hot skin against her palms.

"You think you can make me burn?" he asked, his tone challenging.

"I know I can," she replied, feeling very, very powerful.

She bent to taste him, running her tongue over his silky, granite-hard flesh.

He arched against her mouth, as if in pain. "Aurora . . ."

"Be still."

She knelt there in the warm sunlight, attending to him, arousing him the way he had her. It was exciting, exhilarating. She was totally in control this time, driving Nicholas slowly mad with desire. In only a few moments, his breathing became erratic. She felt his hand clutch in her hair as he strove to remain still.

"Enough," he at last muttered roughly. "Have mercy. I surrender."

He caught her shoulders and drew her down to lie full length upon him. Her breasts lightly caressed his chest as she stared down into his pleasure-hazed eyes.

Aurora didn't protest as he lifted her up to settle her astride him. It was what she wanted, too. She drew a sharp breath as he lowered her onto his thick shaft, his slow, filling length impaling her, then sighed when she felt the heat of him inside her.

"Do you know how badly I want you?" he asked, his voice a hoarse rasp as he held her hips to draw her even closer, to push himself even deeper. "I want to bury myself completely inside you. . . ."

Aurora arched her back, totally aroused. He was huge and hard and hot and filling her to bursting. Helplessly, she began to move, no longer maintaining the slightest measure of control. She rode him wildly, gasping, quaking against him, while her hips undulated in a mindless rhythm.

As her aching moans filled the air, though, his rough excitement grew to match her own frenzy. He arched up, driving into her. Aurora erupted, crying out with abandon as he forced jolt after tormenting jolt from her.

Her explosive heat shattered the last of his control. He whispered her name, fierce and low, and then let himself go, his body contracting in a wrenching, tearing release. When it was over, Nicholas sagged weakly back, while Aurora collapsed upon him, totally drained.

She lay there contented, bliss convulsing her senses. Nicholas had been right all along, she thought dazedly. She did have a hidden fire buried deep inside her. He had kindled it from the moment they had met.

She had not realized the depths of her need until now. Until knowing Nicholas, she had merely existed, pretending she could escape feeling a woman's desires, a woman's wants. And now she couldn't deny them. He filled her with a yearning so powerful, she ached.

A line from the journal floated into her mind: *I belonged to him, a captive of his raw and untamed passion.* That was how she felt about Nicholas. She was prisoner of his desire. Her physical need for him was like a sickness. . . .

Aurora's contentment suddenly faded, while her throat tightened. Nicholas was doing everything in his power to bind her to him with chains of love, wooing her with his tenderness and his gentle-fierce lovemaking. He had made her a woman and now he was bent on capturing her heart.

Dear God, she didn't want to love him. Yet he was making it harder and harder to resist.

The constriction in her throat increased.

Before Nicholas, she had yearned for a passionless life. She had desperately wanted to avoid the pain of loving him and losing him.

Yet how could she wall herself off emotionally from him now, when he was so set on taking full possession of her heart? How could she withstand his vital force when he was so single-mindedly tearing away her defenses with his incredible passion?

How, she wondered desperately, could she quell her own relentless need and this painful, yearning ache inside her?

Their agreement to live only in the present held into their second week. During one of their morning rides in the forest, however, they ventured into a discussion that Aurora would have preferred to leave alone.

She had just set her mount at a huge log, an obstacle that even Nicholas was leery of. She cleared it with inches to spare but had him shaking his head in wonder at her bravado.

"Don't talk to me about the risks I take," he said dryly. "I would never be so suicidal as to hazard that fence riding sidesaddle."

She laughed, still feeling the exhilaration of her success, and patted her horse's neck fondly. "I don't believe you, Nicholas," she retorted as she resumed her place beside him. "From what I have seen, you aren't the least afraid of anything. You have no fear."

"Oh, no," Nicholas said with a twisting smile. "I have one very great fear."

"And what is that?"

"I'm afraid I will lose you."

Aurora fell silent, not wanting to tread such dangerous grounds. "You said we wouldn't speak of such things."

"Sorry," he said unrepentantly. "But you did ask. And we will have to broach the subject at some point before I leave for America."

Disquieted, she tried to raise her defensive walls. "Nicholas, our time together here has been . . . wonderful, but our relationship is merely pretense. Whatever feelings we share now are only temporary. They cannot last."

"I would like them to be permanent, Aurora."

She knew her dismay was written on her face, but then he made light of her alarm.

"Very well, I won't ask for your heart. Only your body."

His grin held such devil-may-care charm that she couldn't be certain he was even serious, yet unaccountably she felt a stab of pain at his nonchalance.

Aurora shook her head. "I am not the sort of woman you want for your life's mate."

"I vehemently dispute that, love. You're the perfect match for me. You have never had any trouble holding your own in our disputes or in any other arena. You are more than equal to any challenge I could throw at you."

A troubled frown darkened her brow. "Don't you understand, I do not *want* you to throw challenges at me. I am not like you, Nicholas. All you care about is danger and excitement and adventure. I'm not at all interested in such a wild life."

"Nor am I any longer. I've thought about the questions you put to me, Aurora. You asked if I was willing to be faithful to you. Well, I am. Completely."

She stared at him.

"I'm through wandering, I promise you. I'm through taking unnecessary risks. All I want is to settle down with you . . . to be your husband, perhaps raise a family."

"You would actually give up your adventurous life in order to raise children?" she asked with total skepticism.

He shrugged his broad shoulders. "I know, it sounds unlikely. But I've discovered something in the past few years. . . . Adventure begins to pall when you have no one to share it."

She met his dark gaze searchingly. "I'm not certain I believe you," Aurora said finally.

"Well, I don't believe you're as timid as you pretend," he replied, his tone turning light once more. "I think you like to be daring, like how it makes you feel." A wicked gleam shone in his eyes. "Come closer and I will prove it to you."

They were riding side by side now through the dense, silent beechwood, his knee nearly touching her mount's side.

"I cannot move any closer," Aurora pointed out warily.

His mouth slashed in a sinful male grin. "Yes, you can." Reaching out, he caught her around the waist and scooped her onto his horse to sit sideways in front of him.

Startled, Aurora clung to his arm for balance. "What in heaven's name are you *doing*?"

"Showing you how daring you can be. Now turn around and lean back against me. Put your leg over my horse's neck . . . that's right."

"Nicholas . . . this is *mad*. . . ."

Her protest was interrupted by a gasp as he drew down the bodice of her gown to expose her bare breasts. An arrow of heat shot through her as he cupped the lush swells. Involuntarily Aurora arched against him, even as she gasped out an objection. "Nicholas . . . anyone could see us!"

"No one is within miles of us."

She could feel her breasts trembling, peaking, straining to fill his hands as she quivered in his arms. "Damn you, why are you doing this?"

"Because," he whispered huskily in her ear, "I want you to remember me. For the rest of your days, whenever you ride, you'll think of me. Now hush and enjoy this. . . ."

Her nipples became velvet daggers against his palms as he lavished her with tantalizing caresses. No longer resisting, Aurora bit her lip and leaned back against him, giving herself over to his erotic ministrations.

When she was thoroughly pliant, his hand stole unerringly beneath her skirts and found the curls at the apex of her thighs. His bold caress sent a shock of pleasure surging up through her body.

"Open your legs to me, love," he murmured. Yet Aurora needed no further urging. She was so ready, so instantly aroused that she trembled.

She whimpered as his hand pressed wantonly against her starving flesh. There was a brazenness about it that thrilled her. Her breathing became harsh and ragged as he molded his fingers over her sex, stroking, teasing, finding a relentless rhythm that matched the steady rocking of his horse.

"God, you're so silky wet. . . ." he whispered encouragingly. "So wet and so hot, it makes me want to take you right here."

She groaned at the indescribable pleasure of that possessing hand, undulating her pelvis beneath his palm. The heat building inside her was like a raging fire.

When she climaxed, Nick held her trembling, shaking body as passion flared through him. This was how he wanted her, hungry and burning with desire for him. Yet there was a vital element still missing.

He pressed his lips against her sun-bright hair, his own desire tormenting him with what he wanted more than breath. He should have felt triumphant, seeing her swept up in the storm of carnal passion he had striven to create. Aurora couldn't deny her body's need any more than he could. But while he could demand sexual surrender from her, it was her love he wanted. His want had become craving, a feverish hunger.

He had lied a moment ago. He did intend to ask for her heart. He could claim her body, but it would not be enough.

He was wiser now. Since meeting Aurora, he had come to believe an elemental truth. Something his father had tried to tell him, what the journal so eloquently expressed. That for every man there was one woman who was destined to be his life's mate.

Aurora was his mate, his destiny; Nicholas knew it in his soul.

But he had yet to convince her of that. Hell, he hadn't even told her of his love. Perhaps that had been a mistake. When he'd first realized his true feelings, he had wanted the opportunity to show Aurora how he felt, to give her the chance for her own feelings to grow. He had hoped physical passion would lead to love, and it still might. . . . But he was swiftly running out of time.

Nicholas drew a steadying breath. This wasn't the right moment, but he would have to press the issue, and soon.

Chapter Twenty-one

His price was too dear: he demanded my heart.

Aurora stared without seeing at an open page of the journal. She sat alone on a stone bench within the walled courtyard, shaded by towering, scarlet-blossomed rhododendrons, yet her thoughts were far away, in another time and place. The quiet ripple of the fountain in the shallow reflecting pool serenaded her along with the echo of Desiree's words written nearly a century before.

How I ache with the struggle in my heart and the irrevocable choice he has given me. I long for freedom; I yearn to escape this strange, exotic world and return to the familiar, genteel life I once knew. Yet the chains of passion binding me are as strong as my yearning.

What am I to do? What future is there here for me? He can never wed me, not if he means to survive the political intrigues of the Turkish court. Acknowledging his love for a foreign woman, a Christian no less, would be viewed as fatally weak. I can remain only as his concubine, one of many. The children born of my body would belong to his savage world, never mine.

And love can so easily fade, passion more swiftly still. He desires me now, yet what of five years from now, or ten, or thirty? Will I still be beautiful in his eyes when my flesh has lost its firmness, when my white skin its smoothness, when younger beauties seek to gain his affections? He claims so . . . but can I believe professions made in the

*magical heat of passion? Can I believe the love that burns
in his dark eyes?*

*He says the choice is mine alone. Seeing my sadness in
captivity, he has offered me the power to break my chains.
He will set me free, if that is what I wish, because he desires my happiness above his own.*

*And so I struggle to decide what is truly in my heart. Do
I grasp at this chance for freedom, making my escape,
never to see him again, never to feel his sensual touch
again? Could I bear to live without him? Or do I remain
with him, a slave to passion, abandoning all thought of my
former life, my family, my friends, my very life, to be with
him for as long as he wants me?*

Sweet heaven, I do not know.

Aurora shut her eyes, torn by conflict as Desiree had been.
Like the Frenchwoman, she had an irrevocable choice to
make: to keep her heart safe and avoid the pain of an impossible love. Or to risk an uncertain future with a magnificent man.

What am I to do? She could no longer fight her passion
for Nicholas, or deny that her feelings for him were growing ever deeper. She trembled with the joy of being in his
arms; his presence brought her desperate happiness. But
to lose Nicholas after loving him would be devastating.

Even now it would be hard to let him go. Could she bear
to live without him when he left England?

Aurora shook her head in despair, feeling as lost as Desiree had felt.

"Aurora?"

With a start, she glanced up to see Nicholas standing
beside her.

Her stomach muscles clenched involuntarily. This was
her last day with him in their secret paradise. Until now
they had mostly avoided the main issue between them—
the matter of their marriage. But she could see in the sol-

emn depths of his eyes that the time had come to face truths she was still not quite ready to face.

He sat beside her on the stone bench. "Did you come here to escape me?"

"Not really," she murmured, avoiding meeting his penetrating gaze. "I was merely thinking."

He took her hand, entwining his warm fingers with hers. "Thinking about the choice you have to make?"

"Yes."

"Whether you will come with me when I leave England."

"Yes."

"And have you reached a decision?"

"No ... not yet." She raised her troubled gaze to his. "I've never been to America, Nicholas. I don't know a soul there."

"You know me."

"And what happens when you go off into the world seeking adventure?"

"I told you, I am done seeking adventure." His thumb stroked her palm absently. "Life with you would be adventurous enough. Each day with you seems fresh and new."

When she didn't answer, Nicholas smiled faintly. "There will be times I shall have to travel because of my shipping business, but I would like nothing more than to have you sail with me. If you prefer to remain home, though, you will have new friends to bear you company. I think you will like my mother and sisters, and I know they will love you. We could make it work, Aurora."

She searched his dark eyes. "I still find it hard to believe you would be willing to give up your freedom."

Nicholas shrugged. "Freedom is overrated, I've come to realize. There has never been anything in my life I cared enough about to make me want to give it up. Until you."

"You'll give it up until you tire of me."

He returned her gaze steadily. "That will never happen."

"How can you know?"

She heard him draw a measured breath. "Because . . . I've fallen in love with you."

Stunned, disbelieving, Aurora stared at him.

"It's true," Nicholas said with a crooked, masculine smile. "You captured my heart on the quay in St. Kitts. Only it took me some time to realize it."

"You don't really love me. . . ." she breathed.

"No?" She watched his dark eyes turn very deep and soft. "How could I not love you after what you did for me? You saved my life, Aurora. You came to my rescue like an avenging angel, sparing me the brutal pleasure of my guards. You wed me at great risk to yourself, when you knew your father would be outraged. You've cared for Raven as if she were your own sister."

"Nicholas, you are confusing love with gratitude."

"No, sweeting. I'm not. From the very first, I've felt a bond with you that I've never experienced with any other woman." His voice was low, vibrant. "On our wedding night, it seemed as if we were joined in spirit as well as the flesh. The next morning, severing that bond . . . Sending you away was the hardest thing I've ever done. And afterward, when I knew I would live, you haunted my dreams. You stole my heart and left me aching with desire."

Her own heart wrenched at his singular admission. Could she possibly believe what Nicholas was saying? Did he truly love her? Or was he only telling her what he thought she wanted to hear, so that she would remain his wife?

"Nicholas," she said finally, "a marriage needs more than carnal desire to sustain it throughout the years."

"We have much more than that, sweetheart."

"We have passion, I cannot dispute that. But how long will that last? Passion can fade so easily."

He gazed down at their entwined fingers. "Or it can grow into love."

Aurora followed his gaze to their clasped hands, myriad emotions welling in her—want, hope, wonder, need, doubt.

He leaned his forehead against hers. "Be my wife, Aurora," he said, his voice soft.

"Nicholas . . ." she murmured. She wanted so much to believe him. "I . . . need more time."

After a moment he drew back. "I understand. You're not yet ready to commit yourself." He kissed her gently on the mouth and stood, releasing her hand. "You don't have to decide just yet. We'll return to London tomorrow, but it will take a few days to prepare my ship to sail."

"So soon?" she asked with a sharply indrawn breath.

His handsome face was a study in solemnity as he gazed down at her. "I'm afraid so." He hesitated. "I want you to come with me to America, Aurora, but I won't compel you. You would only resent me for it. You have to come willingly, because you want to be with me. With all my soul I hope your answer is yes."

He turned away then, leaving her to herself. Aurora watched him go, her gaze blurring, her heart torn.

Did she dare risk believing him? Or was Nicholas still trying to rescue her from her passionless existence, embellishing his arguments with tempting beguilements and promises of love in order to persuade her? How could she be certain what he felt for her was truly love? How could she even be certain of her own heart?

After a long moment, she glanced down at the jeweled book in her lap. Fresh tears stung her eyes as she remembered the Frenchwoman's fate in the journal. Desiree's prince had promised her raptures of love more precious than treasure, but in the end had given her only pain; the tale had ended tragically with the death of her prince.

Desiree had made her choice—to remain with her lover—but in so doing, had become his greatest vulnerability. Betrayed by the schemes of a jealous concubine, she was stolen from the palace harem by his fiercest enemy and carried off to a remote mountain fortress. The prince had mounted a long siege, determined to rescue her, but while he had killed her abductor, he was mortally wounded himself.

Desiree had wept tears of agony as her lover lay dying in
her arms. Yet it was her anguished lament afterward that
still rang in Aurora's mind.

*Regret tastes like bitter poison on my tongue. Why, why
did I ever let myself love you?*

With trembling fingertips, Aurora reached up to wipe
her tears away, wondering with a sharp sense of desperation if she was succumbing to the same malady.

A pale sliver of moonlight fell across the bed where
Nick lay entwined with Aurora. He had never felt such a
sense of rightness—the simple contentment of watching a
woman sleep in his arms and knowing he wanted to be like
this forever. He might be giving up his adventurous life,
but loving her would be an even greater adventure. It
would be enough.

She was the only woman he had ever wanted this way,
fiercely, desperately, permanently. The only one who filled
the empty places in his soul. Every time he touched her,
he was swept up by an emotion so intense, it took his
breath away.

He loved her. *Love.* It was like a fire burning deep in his
heart. Nicholas drew her closer, pressing his face against
the intoxicating softness of her skin, wanting to absorb her
very essence.

She was wavering, he knew. For the first time, Aurora
was actually contemplating what it would be like to live in
America as his wife. For the first time, he could dare let
himself believe he might someday win her love.

For the first time he could feel an easing of the taut
knots of fear inside him.

Aurora still had made no decision the following day when
they returned to London. She was grateful Nicholas rode
beside the carriage instead of with her, for her thoughts

were in such turmoil, she desperately needed the time alone, without his compelling, vital presence to overwhelm her senses and her good sense.

When the carriage drew to a halt before her house, she was slow to descend, feeling a lingering reluctance to have their magical interlude end. Nicholas escorted her up the front steps, where they were admitted by her stately butler.

It was only after Aurora relinquished her shawl to Danby, however, that she noticed the strange expression on his face.

"Danby, what is it?" she asked. "Are you unwell?"

"Well enough, thank you, my lady." The elderly man cleared his throat. "But if I may be so bold, I fear you should brace yourself for some strange tidings." He paused, his mouth grim. "Lord March has returned."

"Harry?" Aurora replied, torn between alarm and exasperation. "He has run away from home again?"

"No, my lady, not young Harry. It is his brother, the elder Lord March."

Aurora felt a cold chill squeeze her heart. "Geoffrey?" she whispered, suddenly hoarse. "No, that is impossible."

She must have looked faint, for Nicholas's hand came up to support her arm. "You must be mistaken, Danby," she forced herself to say. "Geoffrey has been dead this past year. He perished at sea."

"So it was believed," Danby said solemnly. "But his body was never found. It seems his lordship survived the shipwreck and washed up on the shores of France. He was badly wounded, but he is in truth alive, my lady."

In a shocked daze, Aurora turned to stare up at Nicholas.

His dark eyes were hooded, his expression a mask of stone.

Chapter Twenty-two

I am that most miserable of creatures, a woman tormented by heartache.

Still shaken by the shocking revelation, Aurora mounted the front steps of the elegant London mansion belonging to the Earl of March. A knot of anticipation tightened her stomach at the thought of seeing her former betrothed again after he'd been presumed dead for more than a year.

At least she needn't concern herself with the impropriety of calling on him. According to Danby, Lady March was in residence, having accompanied her prodigal son to London three days ago, along with young Harry.

Aurora fiercely regretted not being in town for Geoffrey's return. She should have been there to greet him—and the subterfuge she'd engaged in to explain her two-week absence only compounded her feelings of guilt. She'd given out the tale that she was visiting the sickbed of a schoolhood friend in Berkshire, when in truth she had been indulging in a fortnight of erotic pleasure with Nicholas.

Briefly she shut her eyes, remembering Nicholas's face when he'd learned the news. His grim countenance had suggested very clearly that he didn't welcome March's revival.

She could scarcely believe this impossible turn of fate herself. It was incredible that the second of her betrotheds should return from the grave. . . .

Nicholas had volunteered to escort her here, but she needed to see Geoffrey alone, in private. She still had no idea what she would or could say to him, whether to tell him of her marriage and her growing passion for another man, but she knew their first meeting would be too personal, too emotional, for an audience.

Aurora was acquainted with the footman who admitted her, and when she asked to speak to his lordship, she was shown at once to a parlor. She braced herself for what she would find, but was surprised when Lady March rose to greet her.

The countess had been crying, quite clearly, but she dabbed at her eyes with a lace handkerchief before taking Aurora's hand.

"I hoped I would have the chance to speak with you before you saw Geoffrey. I . . . I am afraid you must prepare yourself, Aurora. He is not the same man you knew."

"Danby said he had been severely wounded."

"Yes, that is true. . . . He . . . he lost an arm." Fresh tears sprang to her eyes.

"Come, sit down," Aurora said solicitously. Leading the countess back to the settee, she sat beside the distraught woman and put a comforting arm around her shoulder.

"I am unclear about what happened," Aurora said, wanting to distract Lady March from her grief. "How did he even survive?"

Her ladyship drew an unsteady breath, struggling for composure. "When his yacht sank off the coast of France, Geoffrey washed ashore, badly injured and with no memory of his past or even his identity. He was taken in by a French family, where he remained in hiding from Napoleon's army, recovering his health. But his arm grew putrid and had to be . . ." She shuddered. "It is a miracle that he is even alive, and I am very grateful, truly, but . . . my poor son . . ." Her voice broke on a sob and she buried her face in her hands.

For a long moment she sat quietly weeping, while Aurora murmured consoling reassurances. Finally the countess's tears stopped and she recovered enough to use her kerchief to blot her eyes.

"Oh, Aurora, I am so glad you have come," she said, her

voice muffled by lace. "You are just what Geoffrey needs. I know you will stand by him—" Abruptly the countess raised her tear-streaked face in consternation. "You would not be put off by a missing arm . . . would you? That would not change your feelings for him?"

"No," Aurora said soothingly. "Of course not. My feelings for Geoffrey will never change."

Lady March nodded gratefully. "He seems despondent, Aurora. His memory still is not fully restored, and he is so very thin. I fear for him. But now that you are here . . ." She forced a smile. "Everything can return to the way it was. You can be married this summer, and become my daughter in truth."

Aurora's heart twisted, both at the hope she saw in her friend's eyes and the hurt she knew she would bring when she confessed that she couldn't marry Geoffrey. She started to reply, but then realized it would be fairer to tell Geoffrey first.

"I would like to see him, if I may," she said quietly.

"Yes, yes, of course . . . I believe he is in the library. I will have Starks show you there."

Aurora knew the way, for she'd spent many a pleasant hour in the March library. But it was better for her to be announced, to allow Geoffrey time to prepare himself—and time for herself to bring her own emotions under control.

Several minutes passed before she found herself at the library door, her heart beating painfully. Geoffrey stood at the window, his back to her. The right sleeve of his jacket was pinned up nearly to the shoulder.

"Geoffrey?" she said quietly.

He turned slowly to meet her gaze. Her first reaction was one of shock as they stared at each other across the room. His beloved face was lined with pain, and he was far thinner than before. But he gave her the same gentle smile.

It was all Aurora could do to hold back the ache of tears in her throat. She managed a smile, however, as she crossed to him. Needing to touch him, to feel that he was truly alive, she reached up to put her arms around him. "Welcome home," she said simply, pressing her face into his shoulder.

She held him that way in an embrace that was comforting rather than carnal. Hesitantly his one good arm slid around her shoulders to draw her closer.

After a moment, Geoffrey gave a soft laugh. "I should have realized you would know precisely the right thing to say."

Aurora drew back, searching his face. "I am so very glad to see you. I've missed you unbelievably."

His handsome mouth twisted in a bitter smile. "I fear I cannot express the same sentiment . . . About missing you, I mean. Until a few weeks ago, I had no memory of my past life. Only images . . ." He reached up to touch her cheek. "I saw your beautiful face, Aurora, but I never knew why. It was only when Wycliff found me that the images became stronger. I think he must have jogged something loose in my mind, for I've slowly been regaining my memory since then."

"Wycliff? The Earl of Wycliff found you in France?"

"Yes, Lucian rescued me. In truth, I owe you both a debt of gratitude. It's because of you that he spent the last two months scouring the French countryside, searching for me."

Aurora frowned, wondering what the earl would be doing in France when the two countries had been at war for years. "How is that possible? How could Wycliff avoid capture by Napoleon's forces for that long a period?"

"He was in disguise, actually."

"Disguise?"

Geoffrey looked ill at ease. "Aurora, I will tell you something in confidence. Wycliff is actually a spy. A damned good one, I understand."

"Spy?" She stared, suddenly remembering the wild tales his younger brother had told her about Geoffrey. "Harry claimed you were engaged in spying," she said slowly, "but I thought he was simply fabricating a fantasy."

Geoffrey hesitated a long moment. "I was on a mission for England when my ship went down."

Startled, she eyed him with disbelief. "I never understood why you were sailing so near the French coast. You were *spying*?"

"Not precisely. Nothing like what Wycliff's agents do. I had only to break the secret codes of various dispatches. I've always been good with ciphers and puzzles, you know."

"Why did you never tell me?"

"I didn't want you to worry. Harry learned about it only because he eavesdropped on a conversation." Geoffrey frowned. "He should never have mentioned it, for he was sworn to secrecy."

"I would indeed have worried." Aurora shook her head, still not quite believing what she was hearing. "I cannot understand why you would become involved in something so dangerous."

"Why?" His smile was fleeting. "Because I finally had a chance to make a worthwhile contribution, Aurora. I have been bookish all my life, but that doesn't mean I never had a secret yearning to slay dragons, to reach beyond the confining boundaries of my rank and social position. I wanted in some small way to help in the fight against Napoleon, to save the world from his tyranny. Even now, I would do it again."

"Even at the risk of your life?"

"The risk was not supposed to be very great. I was merely to meet a courier in France and pick up the dispatches—but then my ship encountered a storm. The next thing I knew, I was waking on a straw pallet in a barn, with no idea of who I was. I spent most of the last year as a man with no name or past."

She reached up to smooth a lock of his fair hair back from his forehead that was etched with pain. "But your memory has returned now?"

"Not completely. Each day something new comes to me. Aurora, I am not the same man you knew. . . . I still suffer excruciating headaches, and I walk with a limp, besides losing my arm. . . ."

Her heart ached for him. "Geoffrey, I am so sorry."

"I don't want your pity, Aurora. I survived, while many good men did not—my crew included."

"Then I won't give you pity. But I can offer sympathy, can I not?"

He smiled faintly. "I suppose so." Then his smile slowly faded as he seemed to notice her black gown for the first time. "I understand you were wed while I was away. To Wycliff's notorious American cousin."

She felt her throat suddenly tighten. "Geoffrey . . . I don't know quite what to say. My only excuse is that my father . . . He was pressing me to marry, and . . . well, I'm sorry. If I'd had any inkling you might still be alive, I would never have left England with Percy and Jane."

"Mother says you told her your marriage was made under duress."

"That's true. I desperately wanted to avoid marriage to Halford, and my father was adamant. . . ."

"I understand, Aurora. It would be difficult for you to defy your father's wishes. So you married a condemned criminal to escape his choice of husband?"

"Yes. The marriage was expected to last only a day or two at most."

"I understand you were widowed immediately afterward."

Aurora hesitated. This was the moment she had dreaded. How could she tell Geoffrey that her husband hadn't died? That she was still legally wed to another man? That she had just spent the most incredible two weeks of her life indulging her most passionate fantasies with her lover? That she was considering leaving England altogether to be someone else's wife?

She stared at Geoffrey as guilt raked her with razor-sharp claws. She had loved this man for most of her life. He was a dear, dear friend, and he had come close to death. He was injured, still suffering. . . . She couldn't deal him another blow by disclosing the truth so soon after he had just reclaimed his life.

And what of Nicholas? How could she divulge his existence without putting him in danger? She couldn't be certain how Geoffrey would react. If he loved his country so much that he would spy, what would he do upon learning that a convicted pirate was here on English soil, thumbing his nose at the British government? Particularly a pirate who was wed to the woman Geoffrey himself had been engaged to marry?

Exposing Nicholas now could very well mean his death. She had to protect him for as long as possible, until he was safely out of the country. She had to conceal the fact that he was here now, that she had seen him, been with him.

"Geoffrey, there is something I must tell you," she said slowly, knowing she had to walk a fine line between truth and lies. "I have recently received word . . . Percy wrote to tell me that . . . my husband escaped hanging. Nicholas Sabine is still alive."

He stared at her a long moment before understanding dawned on his face. "You are still wed to a *pirate*?"

"So it would seem."

"That cannot be," he responded with unexpected fierceness. When she made no reply, he scowled. "Can the marriage be annulled? There must be adequate grounds."

Aurora regarded Geoffrey quizzically. "Perhaps, but I doubt it would be easy."

"We must make it happen." Grimness had seized his features. "The marriage cannot be allowed to stand. You cannot remain wedded to a criminal."

His reaction wasn't quite what she had expected, but she should have realized Geoffrey would want to protect her.

"You can be assured I will stand by you, Aurora," Geoffrey vowed. "There is certain to be a scandal when the truth comes out, but I will not allow you to face it alone."

She couldn't dispute that a scandal was likely, Aurora reflected.

When she remained silent, Geoffrey searched her face. "Mother expects our marriage to take place shortly, but this complicates matters. But once an annulment is granted . . . I want you to know, Aurora, if you wish for our marriage to go forward, I . . . would be honored to be your husband."

She felt a pang of dismay. "Geoffrey, you don't have to make such a sacrifice for my sake."

His expression suddenly grew cool. "Perhaps it would be a sacrifice for you rather than me. It would be understandable if you didn't wish to marry a cripple."

"Geoffrey, don't . . . Please don't say that. You aren't a cripple."

"But neither am I a whole man."

"Of course you are a whole man. Losing an arm doesn't make you any less the dear person I've always cared for."

His expression remained strangely solemn.

Then suddenly he shut his eyes and raised his hand to his temple, as if in blinding pain. "These headaches . . ."

"Perhaps you should sit down," she said urgently, putting an arm around his waist.

"Yes." He allowed her to assist him over to a chair and sank down heavily.

"If you don't mind . . . I would like to rest." He sounded short of breath. "My stamina . . . fades after a very short time and leaves me weak as a mouse."

"Yes, of course. I will let you be alone. May I fetch you something before I go? A cool compress? Some wine? Laudanum?"

"Thank you, no. Laudanum only fogs my mind more."

"Very well, then . . ."

Before she could turn away, though, he took her hand in his, gazing up at her with his blue eyes. "I won't desert you, Aurora."

"Thank you, Geoffrey," she barely whispered. "But please . . . don't worry about this. Just concentrate on getting well. We can settle our future when you are feeling better."

Nodding, he leaned his head back and shut his eyes. With all her heart, Aurora wished there was something more she could do to comfort him.

Leaving the library, she walked slowly down the hall, dimly aware of a sweeping sense of desolation. She couldn't abandon Geoffrey now, she knew. It would be a final betrayal. No matter what her feelings were for Nicholas, she couldn't simply walk away from her childhood friend to start a new life in America with another man. She couldn't hurt Geoffrey that way. She would have to remain in England. She would have to ask Nicholas to seek an annulment. . . .

She was so preoccupied with her bleak thoughts that she didn't hear Harry racing down the stairs until he was almost upon her.

"Rory! Rory!" Ignoring her start, he came to a skidding halt on the checkered tile floor and flung his arms around her joyously. "Can you believe the glad news? Geoffrey is alive! Now you will be my sister and you will live with us and we can ride together every day."

Aurora managed a faint smile, but inside, she was aching. She had thought her choice was difficult before, but now, no matter what her decision, she would hurt one of the two men who claimed to love her.

"You have the Devil's own luck, Nick," Lucian Tremayne, Earl of Wycliff, said with amusement. "When I returned to London three days ago and read your message, saying you were alive and had assumed Brand's identity . . . well, I don't recall ever receiving a more pleasant shock. I can still scarcely believe my eyes. To think, even the British navy couldn't kill you."

"It was a near thing," Nicholas replied soberly as he stared down into his brandy glass.

"I regret I was out of the country when you arrived in England."

Nick shrugged. "I'll forgive you, Luce, if you'll forgive me for commandeering one of your schooners."

"Don't mention it. You would have done the same for me, had I found myself facing the hangman. We held a memorial service in your honor, were you aware? I invited half the ton and made all my stuffy relatives attend. Solely for appearance's sake, you understand. A public show of support for your widow. Now I'm sorry I went to all that expense for naught."

Hearing the affection in his cousin's jest, Nick glanced up. Lucian was tall and lithely built, with dark, curling hair and lean, aristocratic features that were barely saved from arrogance by a ready half smile. Usually Nicholas enjoyed their male camaraderie. In this instance, however, he was in no mood to match wits with Lucian or endure his cousin's good-natured ribbing.

Setting down his brandy glass, he rose and went to stand at the French window, staring out. By now Aurora would have spoken to her former betrothed. Had she come to any decision? It was possible—even likely—that seeing March again could sway her. . . .

Nicholas clenched his fists as tension raced through his veins like fire. He needed every ounce of control he possessed to clamp down on the turmoil of emotions inside him: jealousy, anger, fear. . . . In agitation, he turned to pace the carpet of his cousin's study once again.

"What is making you so on edge?" Lucian asked finally. "You're acting like a caged tiger. If I had to guess, I would say you are having woman trouble."

"You could say that," Nick answered tersely.

"Your wife, I take it?"

He paused long enough to rake a hand through his hair. "Aurora never wanted our marriage, but now that we're wed . . . I've asked her to return to America with me. She was leaning in my favor when she learned March had risen from the grave—" He pinned Lucian with a dark glance.

"I can't believe you are the one who found March. Whatever made you search for him in the first place? Was he working for you?"

"Not directly, no. He was decoding enemy dispatches for the Foreign Office, but we never crossed paths professionally. I only learned the particulars about his disappearance at sea after I began helping Lady Aurora become established as your widow. Then on my last trip to France, I heard a rumor. . . . Reportedly a fair-haired Englishman had been badly injured in a shipwreck and was in hiding near the coast. It seemed logical to wonder if it could possibly be March, since his body was never found—although I couldn't imagine why he wouldn't come forward. My best guess was that his memory had been impaired, and that turned out to be right. I'm sorry his return has proven such an inconvenience for you."

Nicholas shrugged. "I can't say I would rather you hadn't found him. I don't really wish the man dead."

"But you would prefer he had stayed away for a while longer?"

He smiled grimly. "A few more days would have been enough. A week at most."

Lucian took a sip of brandy as he contemplated his cousin. "She is your wife, Nick. You have the right to demand that she live with you."

"It isn't nearly that simple."

"No? Why not?"

"Because I don't want an unwilling wife. What joy would I find in our union if Aurora found only unhappiness? She saved my life, Luce. How can I repay her kindness by compelling her to live with me? No, the decision has to be hers."

"Your persuasive skills are better than any I've ever seen, including mine. If you want her, why don't you simply convince her that she wants you for her husband?"

"What the devil do you think I've been trying to do for the past month?"

"There is always abduction," Lucian suggested lightly. "That would buy you more time, at least."

"That isn't an option. I would be a fool to resort to physical force. It would only remind Aurora of her bastard of a father."

Pursing his lips, Lucian shook his head in feigned amazement. "What has happened to you, cuz? Did your near brush with death affect your mind? The Nicholas Sabine I know would never have refrained from even drastic action to get what he wanted."

A muscle flexed in Nick's jaw. "This isn't some game to be won, with Aurora the prize. I once thought so, but that was before I knew her."

"I suppose you fell in love."

"Yes. I fell in love," Nicholas said quietly. *With a woman whose heart was already taken.* His frustration surging anew, he went to stare out the window again.

There was a long silence while Lucian digested that intelligence. "So you will now just let her go?"

"I may have to," Nick replied grimly. "If she loves March and wants to be with him . . ."

"I can't imagine that you would simply allow her to choose another man over you."

"Laugh if you will, Luce, but her happiness means more to me than my own. I know that's hard for you to grasp, since you've never been in love—"

"I am not laughing, I assure you," Lucian said with surprising solemnity. "I've never had the misfortune of experiencing that malady, but I can understand its effects. To be truthful, I was considering entering the fickle lists of love myself. I've been thinking of taking a wife."

"You? The elusive Lord Wycliff?" Glancing over his shoulder, Nicholas eyed his cousin with skepticism. Lucian was the most sought after bachelor in the country, with the kind of titled wealth and striking good looks that made debutantes swoon. Matchmaking mamas had been laying traps for him for years—and he had avoided them all expertly. "Do I know the lady?"

"No. I haven't chosen her yet."

"But you're prepared to shackle yourself to a bride?"

"It isn't the bride that interests me. I just thought it time I sired myself an heir."

This time Nicholas really did stare.

Lucian grinned his charming half smile. "Don't look as if I've suddenly sprouted antlers. I am not particularly fond of my relatives, other than you and Brandon. If I die, I would like to leave some sort of legacy behind. The thought of having a son—my own flesh and blood—has lately been growing in appeal."

"If you die, Luce?" Nicholas said slowly. "Is there something you haven't told me?"

Lucian's eyes grew hooded. "I had a . . . fateful experience recently. A glimpse of my own mortality. It's surprising how an incident like that makes you reassess your priorities in life."

"It's not surprising in the least," Nicholas said grimly. "In fact, it's quite common. What happened?"

Lucian remained deep in thought for a moment, as if recalling a dark memory. Nick wasn't certain what his cousin would have replied, for just then the earl's majordomo appeared to announce a visitor. "Lord Clune to see Mr. Deverill, my lord."

Lucian glanced at Nicholas, who nodded. "Show him here, if you please," his lordship commanded.

Lord Clune greeted both men with an affable smile. "Isn't it a bit early for tippling?"

"We are toasting Nick's return from the dead," Lucian replied mildly.

"I will happily drink to that." Clune glanced at the crystal snifter in Lucian's hand. "Your prime stock, I trust?"

"Of course." Lucian gestured toward the decanter on the side table. "Help yourself. So what brings you here, Dare?"

"An interesting encounter at my club," he said, pouring himself a glass. "With an enemy of yours, Nick."

Turning from the window, Nicholas leaned against the frame, giving his friend his full attention. "Which one?"

Clune smiled. "You have so many that you need ask? Captain Richard Gerrod of His Majesty's navy."

Nicholas felt himself scowl.

"Gerrod?" Lucian repeated thoughtfully. "I seem to recall that someone named Gerrod left his card here yesterday when I was out. Do I know him?"

"He is the overeager patriot who captured Nick and sentenced him to hang for piracy. Gerrod is in London, and he is clearly after blood. Your blood, Nick. Reportedly when he learned of your escape from the hangman, he was livid."

"How ill-mannered of me to disappoint him," Nicholas replied sardonically.

"This is hardly the moment for levity," Clune commented coolly. "Gerrod considers you gallows bait and is quite anxious to remedy the mistake that was made in letting you slip away. Actually, he was making inquiries about your American cousin Deverill. I wouldn't be at all surprised if he suspects your impersonation."

"What if he does?"

"Then it makes your situation doubly precarious. I would play least in sight, if I were you. In fact, this might be an excellent time to take yourself back to the Colonies."

"Or it might be a good time to pay the zealous captain a visit."

"You cannot be serious," Clune said with a frown.

A muscle hardened in Nick's jaw, while a grim smile curved his lips.

"Devil take it, I know that look," Lucian observed. "You're spoiling for a fight, Nick—and I cannot blame you. But in this case, I agree with Dare. The odds are too much against you. It would be far wiser to relinquish your desire for retribution and get yourself safely away. There may come a point in the future when you can confront Gerrod, but on your own turf."

"Perhaps." Grimly Nicholas turned back to the window, the tension in his muscles screaming for release. He would indeed relish the exultation of a physical fight and the chance to lock horns again with Gerrod. But his cousin was right, Nick knew. It would be suicidal to act now with the entire British navy against him. There were smarter ways to fight his battle with Gerrod.

It was the battle for Aurora's heart that he didn't dare lose.

Nicholas locked his jaw against the cold wave of dread that swept through him. By rights he should be alarmed by the news of Gerrod's blood quest. But the captain wasn't the cause of the cloying fear in his chest.

What terrified him was Aurora and the choice she intended to make in husbands.

Chapter Twenty-three

The thought of never again knowing his touch, his fierce caress, is more than I can bear.

Her reflections bleak, Aurora entered her bedchamber to find the lamps had strangely been dimmed. *Nicholas.* She came to an abrupt halt, her heart leaping as she felt his presence.

"Oh, my lady, 'tis very dark here," her maid said from behind her.

"It's all right, Nell . . . I have changed my mind. I don't wish to prepare for bed just yet. I think I would prefer to sit quietly for a moment."

"Very well, my lady. Shall I turn up the lamp?"

"No, thank you. Please, seek your own bed. I won't require you this evening."

The maidservant curtsied and withdrew. Carefully bolting the door, Aurora turned around, her eyes searching the dim room. Nicholas sat in the shadows in the far corner, watching her.

She pressed a hand to her mouth, wondering for the thousandth time how she would ever tell him of her decision.

"So you spoke to him," he said finally, breaking the tense silence.

Slowly she nodded, struggling against the flood of tightness that closed around her throat. "Yes. Geoffrey still wants me for his wife."

For the span of several heartbeats, Nicholas made no reply. He simply watched her, his eyes dark and intense.

"I can't leave him, Nicholas. He has been hurt enough."

His voice was low and flat when he ventured to speak. "You want to sever our marriage."

"I . . . I have no choice. I cannot hurt him more than he has already been hurt. He has lost his arm, Nicholas. Can you imagine what it would be like to suffer such a fate? Geoffrey needs me to stand by him."

Time pulsed between them, dark and endless.

"What about your needs, Aurora?" Nicholas asked at last. "What of mine?"

Aurora shook her head. "My needs can't be allowed to matter. As for yours . . . You are far stronger than Geoffrey is."

Nicholas gave a mirthless laugh.

"I have known Geoffrey all my life, Nicholas," she said pleadingly, trying to make him understand. "He is part of my past . . . part of me . . ."

"And you love him." The words were stark, bleak.

She lowered her gaze. "I cannot abandon him. Can you not see that?"

"I see that you're trying to protect him. You're set on protecting everyone but yourself."

Hearing the sudden harshness of his tone, Aurora wrapped her arms around herself, as if to defend herself against his recriminations.

After a moment Nicholas drew a slow breath. "What do you want me to do?"

"I . . . I want you to try and seek an annulment."

He was silent and completely still. She moved closer, searching his expression in the shadows. He stared back at her, his face torn with a raw and agonizing emotion that mirrored her own.

"Very well," he said finally. "I'll try."

"You will try?"

"To have our marriage annulled. So you can be free to wed your true love."

She had expected fierce resistance, not this quiet resignation. Perhaps he didn't love her as much as he'd claimed. Despair coursed through Aurora at the thought.

"You will forget me in time, Nicholas," she said, aching. "You will find someone who can be the wife you want."

"You think so?"

He lunged to his feet suddenly, no longer resigned. Covering the short distance between them, he reached for her, his hands closing on her shoulders. His velvet grasp was inescapable as he held her in a soft, dangerous embrace. "You think I could ever forget you, sweetheart? That I could forget what we shared?"

"It was just passion. . . ."

"*No.* It was far more." His eyes blazed. "I love you, Aurora. Understand that. Taste it, breathe it . . ."

Without warning his mouth came down on hers. His kiss was fierce, demanding, harsh, as if to punish her. She was struggling for breath before he finally ended it.

When he drew back, the dark hunger in his eyes held a power and starkness that both frightened and compelled her.

She read the intent there, even before he swung her into his arms and carried her to the bed, letting her down none too gently.

Aurora tried to sit up but found herself pinned by his strong body. "Nicholas . . . we can't do this."

"We *can.*" His whisper was wild and low. "You need to remember what you are giving up."

Flattening his hand alongside her head, he held himself above her, staring down. His eyes were ablaze with angry fire, consuming fire. The gentleness she knew in him was gone.

"Can your precious Geoffrey make you feel what I do?" he demanded. Deliberately he reached beneath her skirts and swept his palm along her bare thigh. "Can he set your blood on fire with just a touch? Can he make your nipples tighten, your skin flush? Can he make you grow wet . . . like this . . . ?"

He found the center of her desire, hot and throbbing.

When he slid his finger into her, she gasped, straining against him.

It was all the invitation Nicholas needed. His eyes were fierce, naked in intent, as he fumbled with the buttons of his breeches.

"Nicholas . . ."

He kissed her again, to silence her protest. He had to make her feel the desire raking through his body, his fierce need.

He couldn't have anticipated the explosion of passion he unleashed from her. She gripped his head, her hands clutching his hair as she tried to draw his mouth closer, his tongue deeper.

When she frantically welcomed his devouring kiss, he shoved her skirts to her waist and moved over her. He could feel the pulse of fire lash through her as he sank into her, hard, deep, claiming her in a savage stroke of hunger.

It was like sliding into fire. She arched wildly beneath him and moaned into his mouth, a panicky, anguished sound of need. A sound that would haunt him forever.

Shuddering, he drove into her, feverish with intensity. She came almost at once, convulsing in his arms with a wild cry. Aurora sobbed his name as with one last strong plunge the peak burst on him, helplessly, savagely.

In the heated aftermath, the tortured sounds of their breathing filled the quiet room. Nicholas lay buried inside her, wondering if she could feel the desperation pulsing in hot waves through his body. He pressed his face into her shoulder, fighting the wildness inside him, the violent yearning.

Finally he lifted his head. "Don't do this, Aurora," he whispered, his voice raw and cracked.

Stirring, she opened her eyes to gaze back at him in agony. "I . . . have no choice."

He could see the torment in her eyes. She truly believed she was making the right decision. And perhaps she was.

He looked at her, aching and empty. He had lost.

Nicholas closed his eyes on the anguish and helplessness inside him. A man couldn't force love. He couldn't command a heart's surrender by sheer force of will.

Not trusting himself to speak, he rose from the bed and adjusted his clothing.

Grieving, Aurora remained totally still. Nicholas's vulnerability was infinitely more powerful than his anger. There was such bleakness in his face, she wanted to weep.

She sat up slowly, drawing her skirts down over her naked limbs. She was trembling.

"Nicholas . . . I am sorry," she whispered.

His dark eyes met hers. "I know."

Reaching for her, he cupped her face in his palms. He stood looking down at her for a long moment before slowly bending. When his lips brushed hers, heartbreakingly gentle, anguish clawed inside her.

Then he stepped back and drew a shuddering breath, as if fighting for control. His voice had no inflection when he spoke. "I intend to sail with the tide tomorrow night. If you change your mind, you know where to find me."

He turned and went to the window. A moment later, the shadows covered him and there was silence.

Aurora pressed her knuckles to her mouth and bit down hard. The pain was so raw, she felt as if a knife had sliced through her heart.

He was truly gone. She had sent him away.

Aurora covered her face with her hands and wept.

Chapter Twenty-four

It is true that passion of the flesh can beget passion of the heart. I am living proof.

Aurora stared blindly at Lady March's supper invitation. The countess begged Aurora to attend their private family gathering that evening, although it would entail bending the strict rules of mourning. She would be performing an act of Christian mercy, Lady March wrote, to help ease Geoffrey's reentry into society.

It would also permit them to show their support for Aurora during this trying period in her life, until her sham of a marriage was dissolved. Apparently the countess still wanted Aurora as her daughter.

Numbly Aurora set down the invitation and glanced at the ormolu clock on the mantel. Seven o'clock. The engagement was for eight. She should bestir herself to dress, and yet she didn't know if she could bear to see Geoffrey and his mother this evening. If she could find the willpower to feign a cheerful facade when her heart was breaking. In a few hours Nicholas would set sail without her.

A fresh wave of bleakness washed over her, leaving her cold, empty.

Despairing, she picked up the journal and turned to a well-worn page—the death of Desiree's prince.

My tears fall on your pale face as the lifeblood drains from your once powerful body. In desperation, I kiss your waxen lips, willing you to live. But my efforts are futile. Hopeless.

You open your eyes, your dark gaze so full of pain and

tenderness. No tears, *you whisper hoarsely.* Your tears are torment.

But what of my torment? My heart is ripping from my chest. Dear God, I cannot bear it.

Your trembling hand, so weak now, rises to caress my face. Be free, my beautiful Desiree.

With your last breath, you give me the freedom I yearned for. But merciful heaven, that price is far, far too dear. . . .

Aurora swallowed the burning ache of her own tears. Desiree had realized too late that freedom was nothing compared to love—

A quiet rap on her bedchamber door interrupted her dark thoughts.

"Miss Kendrick has called again," Danby informed her through the door.

"Please tell her I am indisposed," Aurora responded, closing the journal. She could not face Raven just now.

A few moments later, the knock was repeated, only this time much louder.

"Aurora?" Raven called out urgently. "I must speak with you."

With a resigned sigh, Aurora bid entrance. It would take more stamina than she possessed just now to fight Raven's determined assault.

Entering the bedchamber, the younger woman shut the door behind her and stood for a moment. Aurora was sitting before the empty hearth, feeling as cold as a winter's day, even though the July evening was quite pleasant.

"Are you really unwell," Raven asked, "or are you merely avoiding me because you know what I will say?"

"I have the headache," Aurora replied, not quite a lie. "But yes"—she smiled faintly—"I would rather avoid this conversation."

Undeterred, Raven moved across the room to stand

directly before Aurora. "Nicholas is leaving tonight, do you realize that?"

"Yes, I know."

"And you just mean to let him go?"

"Raven . . . it is for the best. England is my home. I belong here. And I must stay for Geoffrey's sake."

"My brother said that you mean to have your marriage annulled so you can wed Lord March. Is that true?"

"Yes."

Raven's blue eyes narrowed unhappily. "You are making a grave mistake, Aurora. You should go with Nicholas. He loves you."

"I . . . I'm not certain what Nicholas feels is love."

"I think it is." Raven fished in her reticule and withdrew a folded piece of vellum. "He asked me to give you this."

Opening the note, Aurora read feverishly.

Aurora, I realize you feel you must honor your obligation to March, but I cannot relinquish you to him without making certain you understand my true feelings. Last night you said I would forget you in time. I won't.

It is curious. I never understood my father, how a man could be so obsessed with a woman, letting his heart overcome his head. Certainly I never believed it could happen to me. I never wanted to find a love like that—a heart-deep passion. The kind that overwhelms you and makes you lose control. But I had no choice. Not once I met you.

I realize now that what my father believed was true. When you find your true mate, then second best isn't enough.

You are my heart, Aurora. You always will be.

Aurora felt her own heart twist in her chest. Nicholas truly loved her, she could doubt it no longer. He could never have made such a tender, intimate confession merely to win a conquest.

"Nicholas loves you, Aurora," Raven said with quiet fervency. "He has risked his *life* to be with you. What more proof do you need?"

It was true; Nicholas had risked capture and death to pursue her.

Gathering her control, Aurora clasped her hands together. "I cannot leave Geoffrey, Raven. He needs me to stand by him. He is too badly injured to face the future alone."

"He is not alone. He has family, friends, not to mention wealth and title— Oh, how I wish I could make you stop worrying about everyone but yourself." Raven gave her a beseeching look. "I cannot believe you would simply throw away this chance for true love."

Aurora winced at the unwavering intensity of her friend's gaze. "I thought you were the one who didn't believe in love."

"I believe in it. I just don't want it for myself. But you and Nicholas are different. You were meant for each other; even I can see that."

"Geoffrey is not the only reason I intend to remain, Raven. I have other responsibilities . . . to you, for one. I made a promise to see you safely settled."

"Which you have done admirably," Raven insisted. Taking a deep breath, she sat down in the other wing chair before the hearth. "You need not worry about me, Aurora. I didn't want to tell you yet, but . . . I have received an extremely advantageous proposal of marriage."

Aurora stared. "From whom?"

"The Duke of Halford. I am considering accepting."

"You *cannot* be serious."

"I knew you would not approve. But this should be my decision, Aurora. I am the one who must live with the consequences."

Aurora felt herself shudder. "Raven, you cannot wed Halford. He is controlling and dictatorial and cold—"

"He is not as bad as you think, not once you come to know him. He is reserved, true, and certainly a bit arrogant. And he likes having his way. But what lord does not? I believe I can manage him."

Reaching out earnestly, Aurora took her hand. "Raven, I understand this desire of yours to marry a title—you feel you must fulfill your mother's wishes. But I cannot help believing you would be far happier if you were to marry for love."

Just as earnestly, Raven leaned forward. "Do you love Lord March?"

"Yes, of course I do. I have loved him all my life."

"And do you love Nicholas?"

Aurora looked away, not wanting to face the answer to that question. Her love for Geoffrey had been sweet and tender, not this anguished yearning. What she felt for Nicholas was so complex . . . so disturbing . . . so painful . . .

"I know I am not experienced in matters of the heart," Raven said, "but I can't believe you are indifferent to my brother. I've seen the way you look at him. If that isn't love, then what is it?"

Passion, Aurora wanted to reply—yet even as she had the thought, Desiree's observation in the journal came back to her with poignant force. *Passion of the flesh can beget passion of the heart. I am living proof. . . .*

Passion could lead to love, Aurora acknowledged despairingly. It had happened to Desiree. It had happened to her as well.

The ache in her heart welled up to clutch at her throat. She had trouble speaking when she replied, "Whatever I feel for Nicholas cannot be allowed to matter."

Impatiently Raven rose from her chair and began to pace the room. "What does Lord March think of all this? Does the man have no heart? How could he demand such a sacrifice from you?"

"He doesn't know about my relationship with Nicholas.

Yesterday I told him only that I'd heard my husband was still alive."

Turning, Raven stared. "He doesn't know Nick is here in England?"

"I . . . I couldn't tell him. I couldn't deliver that kind of blow. And I was afraid of exposing Nicholas. I thought it better to wait until he was safely away."

"Forgive me for such bluntness, Aurora, but the Earl of March may not want a wife who has had a marriage annulled. He may not want to bring such a stain to his family name."

"Geoffrey isn't concerned about his family consequence. He's only determined to shield me from scandal. He is the one who proposed helping me gain an annulment. He wants me to have the protection of his name once I sever my marriage to a criminal."

"But if you tell him how you feel, that Nicholas is no criminal . . ."

Aurora squeezed her eyes shut, struggling against the rising anguish inside her. She couldn't tell Geoffrey that she loved another man. She couldn't hurt him that way. If he desired her for his wife, then she had no choice but to honor his wishes. She owed him that much loyalty.

"Shouldn't he be allowed to decide for himself?" Raven asked. "You should tell him the truth, Aurora. At least about your relationship with Nicholas. It would be unfair not to. And it could make all the difference."

"I cannot tell him anything," Aurora whispered. "Not until Nicholas is gone."

"But by then it may be too late! Aurora, don't you see—"

Another polite rap sounded on the door, causing Raven to break off her impassioned plea.

When wearily Aurora bid entrance, the door opened a crack to reveal Danby's grave face. "There is a gentleman to see you, my lady. A Captain Richard Gerrod. He says it is urgent that he speak to you about your husband."

Aurora felt the color drain from her face. Dear God.

Captain Gerrod was the naval officer who had apprehended Nicholas in the Caribbean. By now he would know his former prisoner was still alive. Did he realize Nicholas was in England? But why else would Gerrod have come to call on her if not to seek out Nicholas?

For the space of a dozen heartbeats, Aurora could not make a sound. It was left to Raven to answer Danby.

"Please tell the captain her ladyship will be down in a moment."

"As you wish," the elderly butler responded before withdrawing.

Still in shock, Aurora turned to stare at Raven. The younger woman looked pale and only marginally more composed than Aurora herself felt.

"You must speak to him, Aurora. Pretend to be taken completely by surprise when you learn your husband is still alive."

"How do you even know who Gerrod is?" Aurora asked in bewilderment.

"Nicholas warned me this morning when he came to say farewell."

"*Nicholas* warned you?"

"He knows Gerrod is searching for him. Why else would he consider it imperative to sail this evening?"

Aurora raised a hand to her temple. Last night when Nicholas had made love to her, he'd known he was in mortal danger, and yet he hadn't even hinted at it. Damn him . . .

"He never said a word," she murmured, torn between fear and anger at his keeping such a revelation to himself.

"Possibly because he didn't want you to worry," Raven said quickly. "I suspect he wanted you to make the decision whether to accompany him without any further duress."

Duress? Fear suddenly winning out over anger, Aurora rose to her feet. "I have to warn Nicholas—"

"No!" Raven objected. "I tell you, he already knows he is being pursued. If you want to protect him, you would do better to try to throw Gerrod off the scent. We should devise a plan, Aurora."

Aurora drew a shuddering breath, trying to gain control of her panic. Raven was right. If she wished to help Nicholas, she would have to fool the captain into believing she knew nothing about her husband's whereabouts.

Her blood had turned to ice in her veins by the time Aurora descended the stairs to the parlor where Gerrod awaited her.

"Captain," she said coldly, pausing in the doorway. "I am amazed that you have the gall to call upon me after what you did. I trust you have a good reason for being here?"

His expression was stern to the point of grimness as he searched her face. "I am seeking your husband, my lady."

"My husband is dead, sir," Aurora retorted frigidly, "as you very well know. You were the one who sent him to his death."

"Then you have not heard the news?" Gerrod asked skeptically.

"What news?"

"Nicholas Sabine is still very much alive."

Aurora stared at him, then carefully schooled her features to scorn. "Your jest is in exceedingly poor taste."

"It is no jest, my lady. The pirate, Captain Saber, made a bold escape while being transported to Barbados for execution."

"Why in heaven's name should I believe such a wild tale? You expect me simply to accept your word for it? The man who arrested my husband and ordered his execution?"

"I did not imagine you would require proof, my lady," the captain said stiffly. "I felt sure Sabine had visited you before now."

"I assure you he has not."

Gerrod scowled. "I have good reason to believe he is masquerading as his cousin, Mr. Brandon Deverill. And word is, you have been seen with Deverill."

"I don't deny my acquaintance with Mr. Deverill, Captain, but I think I would know my own husband," Aurora said with sarcasm.

"Perhaps he has fooled you."

"And perhaps you are the one who has been fooled."

When Gerrod clenched his jaw in frustration and anger, Aurora adopted a more conciliatory tone. "Even if my husband were alive—which I don't believe—whatever makes you think he would come here to England? His home is . . . was . . . in Virginia."

"If I had so lovely a wife, I would not hesitate to seek her out."

"If so, then surely he would have approached me before now. But he has not."

"You are absolutely certain?" Gerrod asked, staring at her.

"Captain . . ." she said, thinking furiously. "I am engaged to wed the Earl of March—even though no announcement will be made until my period of mourning is over. Do you actually think I would have entered into such an agreement if I still believed myself to be wed to another man?"

For the first time, the captain's expression showed serious doubt. But then he shook his head. "I think, my lady, that you are intent on protecting your husband."

Aurora let her features grow deliberately chill. "And I think you have convinced yourself of this fantasy out of vengeance or spite, I'm not sure which."

Gerrod's scowl returned. "If the man I seek truly is Deverill and not Sabine, then he can have nothing to fear from me."

She drew a measured breath, as if she were considering whether or not to help him. "It is my understanding Mr. Deverill left London a fortnight or so ago on a journey to Somerset . . . or was it Berkshire? Perhaps you should begin your search there."

His hard gaze held hers. "No doubt," Gerrod replied with renewed snideness, "you would be happy to send me on such a fool's errand. No, my lady, I believe you know of Sabine's whereabouts."

"Are you accusing me of *lying*, Captain Gerrod?" Aurora raised her chin regally. "You are offensive, sir. I must ask you to leave."

"Very well," Gerrod bit out. "But I will not give up. I will find Nicholas Sabine and bring him to justice."

Jamming his hat on his head, he brushed past her, heading for the front entrance. Aurora remained tensely silent until he was gone. Then she let out a shuddering sigh. She hoped her lies had convinced him, but she seriously doubted it.

Turning to pace the floor, she swore under her breath. There had to be something she could do to protect Nicholas. She couldn't bear just to remain idle, deploring her helplessness.

Sweet mercy, perhaps she should have concocted a better tale. Perhaps she hadn't been wise to claim she was betrothed to Lord March. She would have to persuade Geoffrey to go along with the pretense if Captain Gerrod asked . . .

Geoffrey! Aurora froze where she stood. He knew nothing about Nicholas being in England. Word would reach him, and then he would realize she hadn't told him the truth. He would feel hurt and betrayed. . . .

No, the revelation had to come from her, Aurora knew. She had to tell him herself. She owed him that.

Urgently she turned to summon her butler. But it wasn't Geoffrey she was thinking of when she asked Danby to order her carriage.

Please, Nicholas, she pleaded silently. *Please get away safely.* She couldn't bear it if Nicholas died, for a part of her would die with him.

Chapter Twenty-five

The heart will know its one true mate.

She found Lord March and his mother awaiting her arrival. Both rose to greet Aurora when she entered the elegant drawing room, and both registered surprise to see her muslin day gown and spencer. It was obvious from her attire that she did not intend to take supper with them.

"Is something amiss, my dear?" the countess asked with a worried frown.

Indeed there was something greatly amiss, Aurora thought dismally. She should be feeling joy to see the man with whom she intended to spend the rest of her life. Not this terrible hollowness.

"Forgive me, Lady March," Aurora replied, evading the question, "but I must speak to Geoffrey for a moment. Alone, if I may."

"Yes . . . of course," the countess said, puzzled. "I will just go fetch a wrap. I confess I was feeling a chill." She withdrew quietly, leaving Aurora alone with Geoffrey.

She saw the surprise in his eyes, but as always he acted the gentleman, offering her a seat without immediately pressing her for an explanation.

She was too agitated to sit, though. Her heart aching, she turned to pace the room.

Geoffrey was watching her, she realized, his brows drawn together with concern. "What is wrong, Aurora? You are obviously distressed."

Stiffening her shoulders as if preparing for a blow, she forced herself to turn and face him. "I . . . I fear I haven't been completely truthful, Geoffrey. There is something I failed to tell you."

"What is it, my dear?"

Her eyes burned. How could she bear to hurt this man? How could she not? She couldn't marry him. Not when she loved Nicholas so desperately . . .

She had been fooling herself all along. The signs had been so obvious: the joy she felt in Nicholas's presence, her grief at having to part, her terror at the possibility of him dying. . . .

Tonight, with the danger he faced, she had finally been forced to acknowledge the truth. She couldn't lose Nicholas. Even if he died tomorrow, she wanted to be with him for as long as she could.

"Aurora?" Geoffrey prodded when she stood silently.

With effort, she swallowed the ache in her throat. She had no choice. She couldn't let Nicholas go.

"You are bound to hear the truth," she began finally, "but I wanted it to come from me."

"Aurora, please," he said gently, "I hope you will end my suspense."

She nodded, taking a steadying breath. "I told you yesterday that my husband was alive, but . . . there is more. Nicholas Sabine is here, Geoffrey. In England."

There was a long silence while Geoffrey digested that intelligence. "Your husband is here?" he said slowly.

"Yes. He has been here these past six weeks."

"So long?"

She couldn't read the expression in Geoffrey's blue eyes. Shock? Dismay? Anger?

Despite her vow to control her emotions, Aurora found herself clenching her hands. "Geoffrey, I . . . I have been with him."

"He *forced* himself on you?" Definite anger laced his tone as his eyebrows snapped together in a scowl.

"No. He never forced me. I . . . welcomed him."

"I see." Geoffrey raised a hand to his temple. "Do you mind if I sit down?"

"Yes . . . no, of course I don't mind. . . ." Aurora took an agitated step toward him. "It was thoughtless of me to keep you standing."

He sank slowly onto the settee. "Why did you not tell me yesterday?" he finally asked.

"I couldn't. I didn't want to hurt you so shortly after you had returned home. I did mean to tell you . . . soon," Aurora finished lamely.

Compelling herself to meet his gaze, she came to sit beside him. "I hoped to give you time to adjust to being home before you had to learn of it, but . . . well . . . there have been complications. The British navy is searching for Nicholas. They came to me a short while ago, demanding to know his whereabouts."

Geoffrey still seemed to be considering the ramifications of her earlier disclosure. "Yesterday you led me to believe you wanted the marriage annulled."

"I thought I did." She took another shaky breath. "After you returned, I asked Nicholas to have our marriage annulled, and he agreed."

"You asked him to sever the marriage?"

"Yes."

"Why?"

"Why?" She searched Geoffrey's face. His blue eyes were solemn, penetrating.

"I am curious about your reasoning," he said slowly. "Whether you meant to end it for my sake, or because that is what you truly wanted."

Aurora looked down at her clasped hands, struggling to hide the despair welling in her eyes.

"You love him, don't you." It was not a question.

She felt her eyes blurring as she nodded. For weeks now she had fought admitting her love. She had thought she could save herself from heartbreak by pushing Nicholas away. But she knew now that her heart would break if she lost him.

"Yes, I love him." The hot tears behind her burning eyes finally spilled over. "Geoffrey, I am so sorry."

"Aurora . . . don't cry, please . . ."

Mutely she shook her head, torn at having to choose between loyalty and love. She had wanted to honor her pledge to marry Geoffrey, yet she knew she couldn't go through with it. She couldn't share her life with this man, no matter how much she cared for him. Not when her heart belonged so completely to Nicholas.

As she fought against her tears, Geoffrey sighed. "What a tangle fate has made of our lives," he murmured, his tone filled with irony. "Aurora . . . look at me, please . . ."

With a forefinger, he lifted her chin. "There is no reason for you to end your marriage." His smile was bittersweet. "I am honored you were prepared to sacrifice your future for me, my dear, but I couldn't let you make such a noble gesture. It wouldn't be fair to you, or to me, either. You would be miserable, and I would not be happy, knowing that you have feelings for another man. I want no ghosts in my marriage bed."

She swallowed convulsively, her heart twisting with hurt for him. "Can you ever forgive me?"

"Yes, of course I can forgive you, Aurora. We cannot choose whom we love."

"I do love you, Geoffrey. Just not the way you deserve." She forced herself to meet his gentle eyes. "You deserve true love, Geoffrey. Our betrothal . . . was always based more on friendship than love, on expedience rather than emotion. We never felt real passion for each other. Not the overpowering kind that starts wars and crumbles empires."

When Geoffrey took her hand, she wiped fiercely at her eyes, trying to regain control of her emotions. To her surprise, though, he no longer seemed troubled.

"I understand what you are trying to say, Aurora. True love is a fire in the heart. It is a joyous, wondrous feeling. A magnificent agony. It's being unable to eat or think or even breathe unless the object of your affection is near. It is not feeling whole without her. . . ."

Taken aback by his quiet admission, Aurora stared at him, wondering how he could describe her own feelings so eloquently. "You sound . . . as if you speak from experience."

He smiled faintly. "I do. I am afraid I haven't been entirely truthful either, my dear. While I was in France, I fell in love."

Aurora's lips parted, but she remained speechless.

"There was a girl—a young lady—on the farm where I was nursed back to health. Her family was in hiding—aristos who survived the Terror. The eldest daughter . . . she was so kind, Aurora. I couldn't help loving her."

"Why did you not tell me?"

"For the same reason you didn't tell me about your change of heart. I didn't wish to hurt you. Moreover, as a gentleman, I could not be the one to end our betrothal. It would not have been at all honorable."

Slowly her mouth curved with a misty smile as she felt dawning joy well inside her. "So we were both trying to be noble."

"Evidently. I confess relief to learn that you have given your heart to someone else. It means I can ask Simone to be my wife. Here, dry your eyes so I won't feel quite so much guilt."

Her quiet laughter was muffled by the lawn handkerchief he handed her. Geoffrey's expression, however, remained solemn as she wiped away the dampness on her cheeks.

"If this past year has taught me anything at all, Aurora, it is that no one's future is certain. If you are ever fortunate enough to find true love, you shouldn't risk letting it slip away."

She nodded in fervent agreement, even while chastising herself for coming to that realization so belatedly. If Nicholas died tomorrow, she would be devastated, yet she would rather have even a moment's blazing happiness with him than a lifetime of the dull, gray existence she'd known before coming to love him.

She had never told him of her love. Like Desiree with her prince, she had never disclosed her true feelings until— Sweet heaven, she hoped she was not too late. Aurora drew a sharp breath as her heart experienced a jolt.

"What is it?" Geoffrey asked.

For a moment she hesitated, wondering if she could risk telling Geoffrey what she meant to do. But he had been willing to sacrifice his love for her, possibly mire his family name in scandal just to stand by her, because he wanted her happiness. She could trust him. He wouldn't harm the man she loved. "Nicholas is leaving tonight for America."

"And you want to go with him?"

She searched his face. "I have to, Geoffrey. Can you understand?"

"Yes, my dear." The answer was soft as his lips touched her brow. "I do understand. And if it means anything, you have my full blessing."

"It means a great deal to me." Softly she smiled her thanks, but then her smile faded as a fresh urgency gripped her. "I only hope I am not too late. Nicholas meant to sail for the Caribbean at high tide."

"Then you have another hour or more. High tide will not come until close to ten o'clock. But you haven't much time to pack. You should go."

"Yes." She rose abruptly, her thoughts spinning feverishly as she tried to plan. She would return home long enough to gather some clothing and a few necessities for the weeks she would be at sea— Aurora stopped suddenly, remembering another obligation. "I should say farewell to Harry first and explain why I am leaving . . . although perhaps he won't mind excessively. He idolizes Nicholas."

"Harry is acquainted with him?" Geoffrey asked, puzzled.

Aurora returned an uncertain glance. "Nicholas has been posing as his American cousin, Brandon Deverill."

"Ah, Deverill," Geoffrey said wryly. "I heard an earful about the fellow when Harry recounted tales of his London excursion. My brother does indeed idolize him."

"Your mother won't be as forgiving, I imagine."

"Only because she doesn't yet know about my Simone. Once I tell her, she'll be more amenable to losing you. If you like," Geoffrey offered, "I shall escort you to your house and then to the docks. I take it that is where your Nicholas can be found?"

"Yes, but you needn't put yourself to such trouble."

"It is no trouble. And I confess I should like to meet the man who won your heart."

Aurora turned to go, her mind whirling with anticipation and anxiety. What if Nicholas had already sailed?

Then she would simply follow, a determined voice replied in her head. If he left without her, then she would hire a ship to take her to America. She would not let Nicholas get away.

He owned her heart and nothing else mattered.

Almost an hour had passed before Aurora found herself nearing the docks, feverishly searching for Nicholas's schooner, the *Talon*. The mist rising off the Thames obscured most of the ships alongside the wharf, but she remembered the general location from her last visit, and then she spied one vessel among the skeletal masts whose ghostly white sails had been raised.

The gangway was still in place for boarding, she saw with relief, although the crew was scurrying about, setting rigging and securing lines in preparation for casting off.

Geoffrey had some difficulty negotiating the gangway and winced when he stepped down onto the deck on his bad leg. They were immediately challenged by a seaman, who directed them to the captain. The captain, in turn, led them to the same cabin where Aurora had made love to Nicholas what seemed like a lifetime ago.

The cabin door was open, but at first she didn't see Nicholas. The man lounging on the bunk was his cousin, Lucian Tremayne, Lord Wycliff, while the nobleman sprawled elegantly in a wooden chair was Lord Clune.

Nicholas stood with his back to her, staring out the porthole window at the dark night. Aurora felt her heart wrench with love. Thank God she wasn't too late.

"Sir, you have visitors," the captain announced before making a polite bow and withdrawing.

She saw Nicholas go totally still, but the other two gentlemen rose to their feet.

"I do believe I've won our wager after all," Clune said in an amused drawl.

"So you have, Dare," Lucian replied. "But this is one wager I don't mind losing. Welcome, my lady. We were just bidding our American friend farewell."

Nicholas turned slowly, as if not daring to let himself hope. His gaze riveted on her face, his eyes dark and intense as he searched hers.

Aurora took a step inside the small cabin and halted, suddenly at a loss for words. How could she say all the things she wanted, needed, to say to Nicholas in front of an audience?

When she remained mute, his gaze dropped to her traveling suit, then moved beyond her to Geoffrey. Nicholas froze, his expression turning bleak.

"So you have come to say good-bye," he said tonelessly.

"No," she replied, her own voice hoarse.

Geoffrey intervened then.

"I don't believe we have met," he said, entering the cabin and taking a step past Aurora. "I am March." He offered his good arm to shake hands, but Nicholas made no attempt to accept.

"I understand why you would not welcome me," Geoffrey remarked lightly, not taking offense. "But you needn't

be concerned. I am not your rival any longer. Aurora and I
have reached an understanding."

"An understanding?" Nicholas replied warily, his face
still shuttered.

"Yes. I believe your wife has something to tell you."

His gaze shifted again to Aurora, intense, questioning.

"I am not here to say good-bye," she said, returning his
gaze steadily. "I am going with you."

For an instant she saw a blazing flash of what might be
joy. Then suddenly his expression darkened with anger. He
was looking beyond her at the doorway, Aurora realized.

Behind her she heard a voice she dreaded. "So, I wasn't
wrong," Captain Gerrod said tersely. "You are Nicholas
Sabine after all."

Her heart faltering, Aurora glanced over her shoulder.
Gerrod stood in the doorway, a deadly pistol trained directly at Nicholas's heart.

Chapter Twenty-six

Only now do I understand: Bonds of love are stronger than the mightiest chains. There is no escaping.

As he stared at the deadly pistol, Nick felt a jolt of emotion stab at his heart—not fear but fury. No way in blazes would he allow Gerrod to take him prisoner. Not now, when he could dare hope that heaven was within his grasp.

His fingers clenched around the crystal snifter in his hand. With his friends earlier tonight, he'd plowed halfway through a consoling bottle of brandy in an attempt to drown his sorrows, even knowing no amount of spirits could numb the pain of losing Aurora. But he'd sobered abruptly when she appeared like an angel sprung from his fevered imagination.

Then Gerrod had shown himself, evidently having followed her to the docks. Unless perhaps March had somehow arranged it in order to eliminate his chief rival . . . ? But this was no time to worry about how Gerrod had found him.

The captain pushed his way into the cabin, brushing past both Aurora and March. "In the name of the Crown," he intoned with no little satisfaction, "I am placing you under arrest, Sabine."

Nick's eyes narrowed as he measured the distance to the pistol. He could perhaps wrest the weapon away from Gerrod, but a struggle might well endanger Aurora. Was there a way other than physical violence? He wasn't certain he could count on his friends' intervention. They were British citizens, after all, and it would be treasonous to interfere with a naval officer in the execution of his duty. This was his fight, in any case.

When Nicholas remained silent, Gerrod took another step toward him. "What do you have to say for yourself, Saber?"

Nick smiled. "I say get the hell off my ship, Captain."

Gerrod scowled. "I have every right to apprehend you. You *will* accompany me—"

"Or what? You will shoot me in cold blood?"

"If you force me to. But I would rather see you dancing on the end of a rope. There are a half dozen of my men waiting on the dock to escort you to Newgate prison, where your sentence will be carried out."

Casually, without appearing to move, Nicholas balanced on the balls of his feet, preparing to spring. Just then, however, his cousin spoke up.

"It seems you are overzealous in your commitment to duty, Captain," Lucian remarked calmly. "You have mistaken this man's identity. I am fully prepared to vouch for Mr. Deverill."

"As am I," Dare added in an amused drawl.

"So you see, Captain, it will be your word against that of two peers of the realm."

"Three peers," Geoffrey said quietly.

Nick's gaze shot to March. The man was willing to risk his honor for a stranger? If so, it clearly was for Aurora's sake. But of course March would be under her spell. If he loved her, he would want her happiness above his own.

Nicholas felt another rush of searing emotions—including sympathy for his rival. He knew the agony of losing Aurora.

"You have my sincerest thanks, Lord March," Nicholas said solemnly.

"You must admit," Dare suggested to the captain, "those odds will be hard to beat."

Anger crossed Gerrod's features as he looked from one to the other of the lords. "You would lie to protect this . . . pirate? It is treason to abet a criminal."

"That is where you are wrong," Lucian replied. "This

man is no criminal. He is an American royalist who has been granted sanctuary on British soil. And you, Captain, are acting illegally in trying to apprehend him."

Gerrod's fury only escalated, and he raised the pistol higher, waving it at Nick. Out of the corner of his eye, Nicholas saw Aurora move, but he didn't dare take his attention from the weapon.

"By God," the captain vowed, "you will not escape this time—" His tirade was cut off in midstream by a dull thud. A dazed look claimed his expression before he slowly slumped to the ground.

Nicholas felt his heart lodge in his throat. Aurora stood over the captain's prone form, clutching a half-full brandy bottle in her hand. She had struck Gerrod over the head, Nick realized.

Her bold action had startled his friends as much as himself. They were staring at her with varying degrees of amazement.

Aurora clenched her jaw, looking calm but pale. "Did I . . . Is he dead?"

Nicholas bent over to relieve Gerrod of the pistol and pressed two fingers to the man's neck pulse. "No, just stunned."

His gaze lifted to Aurora. "Once again you surprise me, angel."

"You said sometimes violence was warranted," she declared, her tone defiant. "I considered this to be one of those times. He meant to shoot you."

"He did indeed." Rising to his feet, Nicholas handed the pistol to Dare, then went to Aurora. Taking the bottle from her, he set it and his glass on the nearby table and enfolded her in his arms.

"I couldn't let him hurt you," she said fiercely, gazing up at him.

"I am very glad, sweetheart," he returned with a smile.

Just then Gerrod stirred, although he didn't wake.

"Much as I regret having to interrupt you lovers, er . . .

Brandon," Dare drawled, "I believe we should decide what to do with our overeager friend."

"We should fetch some line to tie him," Lucian said. "I doubt he will be amenable otherwise."

"Tie him?" Dare asked, amused. "Your ingenuity amazes me."

Lucian flashed his wry half smile. "You might be surprised at the resourcefulness a man can develop when the stakes are high enough."

Releasing Aurora with reluctance, Nicholas turned to rummage in a locker and came back with a length of rope and a knife. His cousin did the honors, kneeling down to bind Gerrod's hands.

"I suppose you have a plan, Luce?" Dare remarked as Wycliff worked.

"I'll take him away and keep him hidden until our friend Brandon sails."

"What about his men?" March asked.

"I will simply order them to return to their posts. I doubt they will challenge me, especially if their captain is wearing a gag and cannot countermand me."

"Gerrod will be livid that you interfered with his duty."

"What of it? I am not about to let him deliver Nick to the hangman's noose."

"It may not come to hanging," Dare mused aloud. "Not if Nick petitions the Prince Regent for a pardon."

"Just what did you have in mind?" Nicholas asked with extreme interest.

"Buying a pardon. Pirate or not, you could no doubt convince Prinny of your innocence if you offer to fill his coffers."

"It is certainly worth a shot," Luce remarked.

He finished tying the knots just as Gerrod awakened.

Groaning, the captain raised his bound hands to his head and winced in pain. When he looked up dazedly, it was to find the Earl of Clune training his own pistol on him.

"You struck me . . ." Gerrod said in amazement. "You bastard . . . How dare you!"

"No," Aurora replied, staring down at him. "I am the one who struck you."

At the captain's astonished look, Nicholas couldn't repress a smile. "You should not have threatened me, Gerrod. My—" He stopped at the word *wife*, remembering the pretense he still had to maintain. "Lady Aurora is like a ti-gress when it comes to defending her loved ones."

If looks could kill, Nick knew he would have been skewered by Gerrod's malevolent glare.

Eventually the captain turned his angry focus to the other men in the room. "You obviously have been duped, my lords. I tell you, this man is not Brandon Deverill but a con-victed pirate—"

"This stale claim is beginning to bore me," Dare re-marked. "Would you like a gag for the good captain, Luce?" Drawing out a clean handkerchief, he handed it to Wycliff.

Gerrod recoiled in horror. "Damn you, you will pay for this!" he threatened. "I will charge you all with treason!"

"I doubt you'll succeed," Lucian said mildly. "You'll find that my word carries more weight with the Admiralty than yours. The navy owes me a few favors, in any case. And Lord March is considered a war hero."

Almost wildly Gerrod looked to Aurora. "You will re-gret it if you go with that criminal, my lady. You will be considered a fugitive in England. You will never be able to return."

She met Nicholas's gaze across the small cabin. "I don't care," she said staunchly, her blue eyes soft.

He felt joy well within him, and it was all he could do to refrain from lunging across the room and taking her in his arms.

Just then Wycliff raised the gag to the captain's mouth.

"You cannot do this!" Gerrod exclaimed, beginning to struggle.

Lucian simply grasped the captain by the throat and stared at him with narrowed eyes. "I hope you won't put me to the trouble of dispatching you to your Maker. You could easily find yourself alone at sea, with no rescue ship in sight."

Immediately Gerrod ceased his struggles.

Barbaric but effective, Nick thought with satisfaction.

Gerrod looked as if he had swallowed bile.

Lucian gagged the captain, then hauled him to his feet. "We should be on our way and leave you two to prepare to sail."

"Thank you, my lord," Aurora said to Wycliff, her smile including Clune as well. "Our thanks to you both."

Lucian raised an eyebrow. "For helping save his skin? You needn't thank me. I'm rather fond of the rogue. If you wish, I will make your apologies to your acquaintances for your sudden departure."

Nicholas saw Aurora's smile fade. "What is it, angel?"

"Raven . . . I wasn't able to say farewell. And I am apprehensive about leaving her alone in England."

He glanced at his cousin. "Will you look after Miss Kendrick for me, Luce?"

"I would be happy to."

"And I," Dare volunteered, "would be pleased to offer my services as well."

"Forgive me," Nicholas retorted, flashing a grin, "but asking you to safeguard a lady is like expecting a wolf to protect a flock of sheep."

"In this instance you have nothing to fear. I vow I will be as chaste as an elderly brother."

"If I hear anything to the contrary," Nick threatened, only half in jest, "I'll string you up by your thumbs."

"Point taken. Well then, farewell and good journey, my friend."

When the two noblemen had shepherded their prisoner from the cabin, only March was left. Nicholas watched as Aurora went to the earl and took his hand. With the softest of smiles, she raised her lips and planted a tender kiss on his cheek.

Nick found himself clenching his jaw . . . but he willed himself to endure it. He no longer had reason to be jealous of the nobleman, he told himself. Not when he was the one claiming Aurora as his wife.

March murmured a farewell and then fixed his gaze pointedly on Nicholas. "You had best take good care of her, Sabine, or you can be certain I will be paying you a visit in America."

"Be assured, I will guard her with my life," Nick vowed solemnly.

The earl returned his attention to Aurora. "I wish you all the happiness in the world, my dear."

"And I, you. Simone is a fortunate woman. Perhaps someday I may meet her."

Stepping back, March gave Aurora a final smile and then left, shutting the cabin door behind him.

Nick took a slow breath, trying to ease the brutal tension in his body. When Aurora turned to face him, his gaze riveted on hers. "I wasn't wrong, was I?" he breathed. "You love me?"

"Yes, Nicholas. I love you."

Joy hit him with such fierceness it made him shake. In two strides he had reached her and caught her up in his arms, the way he'd been longing to do since her arrival onboard the schooner. Aurora found her lips smothered beneath his passionate kiss.

Even when he had stolen her breath away, he wouldn't cease. His mouth moved over hers hungrily as if he were starved for the taste of her. Finally, however, Nicholas broke off the tender assault long enough to rasp hoarsely against her lips.

"Tell me again," he demanded.

She didn't misunderstand his urgency. "I love you," she managed to say before he cut off her declaration with another devastating kiss.

It was a long, long moment before Nick allowed her to speak again, although he still refused to let her go.

Breathless with desire and love, he pressed his forehead against hers. "What caused your change in heart?" he dared ask.

"I realized I couldn't live without you," Aurora said simply.

"Then you will be my wife?" He lifted his head, searching her face. Her eyes were bright with love; her lovely smile trapped his breath in his throat.

"Yes, Nicholas. I will . . . on one condition."

That finally gave him pause. He drew back to eye her warily. "What condition?"

"That you promise to make at least a small attempt to curb your recklessness."

"My recklessness?"

"Since I've known you, all you have ever done is deliberately court danger. I have no intention of becoming a widow again."

"I have no intention of letting you."

"You just said you intended to guard me with your life. And I saw you eyeing Gerrod's pistol as if you planned something rash. I felt sure you would have fought him for it if I hadn't acted."

"I would have found another way. I wouldn't have risked endangering you." Nick couldn't help but grin. "The look on Gerrod's face . . . He was so certain he had me in his grasp. He didn't count on having to deal with my beautiful, courageous wife."

"It was not courageous in the least. I was terrified he would shoot you." She shuddered. "I couldn't bear to lose you, Nicholas. I want your promise that you will try to keep yourself safe for my sake."

"I promise, sweetheart. My reckless days are over, I swear to you. I have too much at stake to risk losing you."

He gazed down into her azure eyes, still not quite believing his good fortune. "I want to spend the rest of my life with you, Aurora. I want to have children with you and grow old with you. I want to sleep with you and share dreams with you and wake up beside you. . . ."

Aurora thought she had never heard words more beautiful.

Just then she felt the movement of the ship as the anchor was weighed. Nicholas lifted his head for a moment, then bent again to nuzzle her lips. "We have a long journey ahead of us, do you realize that, my love?"

She felt her pulse quicken at the thought; the prospect of having weeks and weeks alone with Nicholas filled her with joy.

Deliberately she raised her arms to encircle his neck, gazing into his dark eyes that shone so fiercely with tenderness.

"Not long enough," Aurora whispered, wanting to sing with the fullness in her heart.

She was actually sailing to Virginia with Nicholas as his wife. The enormity of her decision no longer alarmed her. She could only contemplate her future with eagerness and excitement and hope.

Nicholas was her life. The only man she would ever love.

As her lips molded to his, a line from the journal came back to her: *He held my heart captive, with chains stronger than steel.*

She was Nicholas's captive, she reflected, but a completely willing one.

She sighed and gave herself up to his searing kiss. Nicholas owned her heart. And she knew with utter certainty they had touched only the beginning of something vast and beautiful. Their future lay ahead of them. A future bright with promise. Husband and wife, bound together by an irresistible passion known as love.

Epilogue

Journal entry, February 4, 1814

I see the truth so clearly now. All of my existence before you was nothing but a shadow of living. I kept life at a distance, never allowing myself to get close.

Only you freed me from my prison. Only you touched me deeply enough to find the core of passion inside me. Only you saw into my heart, baring the depth of my yearning.

You taught me passion and then taught me love—

Aurora paused in her writing, her gaze lifting to the door of the sitting room that adjoined the bedchamber. *Nicholas.* She had sensed his presence rather than heard him, they were so attuned to one another.

He stood casually leaning against the doorjamb, looking so irresistibly handsome that her heart skipped a beat. The bright winter light gleamed golden in his hair, which was no longer darkened to disguise his identity.

She smiled to see him, overcome with love and desire. "How long have you been standing there?"

"Not long."

"You seem to be developing a habit of watching me."

"True. It's one of my greatest pleasures, looking at my beautiful wife." Nicholas crossed the room to where Aurora sat at her writing desk. "Are you writing about me again?"

"About us," she contradicted.

She was writing her own journal, setting down her most intimate thoughts. She had wanted, needed, a means to express the depth of her feelings for Nicholas.

He was the only one who would ever see it. She had no secrets from him. He had led her on an odyssey of the heart, an odyssey that was still unfolding. Each day with him was a fresh wonder, each moment a joy.

"Forgive me for interrupting, dearheart," he said, handing her a rolled parchment, "but this just came from Lucian. It should please you."

Curious, Aurora set down her pen and opened the document. She gave a cry of delight to see the royal seal of England's Prince Regent. "You have been pardoned?" she exclaimed, reading feverishly.

"Yes. The price was exorbitant—two merchantmen and a schooner from the Sabine shipping line—but I can now return to England without a death warrant hanging over my head. And you can visit your homeland, sweetheart."

Aurora was elated, more for Nicholas's sake than her own. He was no longer a fugitive. She no longer had to live in terror that he would be apprehended like a criminal and sent to the gallows.

"If you like, we can plan a trip there as soon as the war ends," he offered.

She glanced up at him in contemplation. America's war with England was still raging—dangerously close to their own shores, in fact—which made travel across the Atlantic extremely hazardous.

Giving him a smile of gratitude, Aurora shook her head. "I have no urgent need to return to England," she said softly. "This is my home now, Nicholas. Everything I care most about is here. Except for Raven, of course . . . Did your cousin Wycliff send any word of her?"

"A brief mention. She's still the toast of London, apparently. Her betrothal to a duke only seems to have added to her allure."

A slight frown scored Aurora's brow. "I worry about

her, Nicholas. It disturbs me that she accepted Halford
when she had so many better choices of husband."

"I don't much care for her choice either, sweetheart, but
we have discussed this before. And we agreed I wouldn't
forbid the marriage."

"I know, but even so . . . I think we were right to send
her the journal. Perhaps it will help Raven reconsider before she commits to a life without passion or love. I want
her to understand what she is giving up and realize that the
joy of love is well worth the risk of pain."

"As Desiree discovered?"

"Yes." Aurora smiled faintly at her husband's superior
look. "You were right, I admit. In the end, Desiree had both
passion and love torn from her, but she didn't regret loving." Aurora gazed up at Nicholas soberly. "I only wish
Raven could see that she would be far happier to marry for
love."

"We didn't, remember? You took pity on a condemned
pirate and spared me a fate worse than death, never knowing your love."

Aurora gave a small shiver, recalling how close they had
come to missing their destiny.

Nicholas, however, evidently wasn't as disturbed by the
dark memories as she was, for his mouth curved up at one
corner. "As much as I dislike admitting it, we should be
grateful to Gerrod. If not for him, we never would have
met, let alone wed."

Perhaps she did owe the captain gratitude, Aurora grudgingly admitted. For the first time in her life, she was truly
happy. She had a wonderful husband who filled her heart,
and a completely new family as well. Nicholas's mother
and two sisters had welcomed her eagerly as his wife, becoming as close as any cherished blood relations. She still
couldn't think of Gerrod with equanimity, however, considering how he had sought Nicholas's death.

"Did Wycliff have any other news to relate?" she asked,
changing the subject. "How is he faring with his new bride?"

"His letter didn't say." Nicholas's eyes lingered upon hers. "I can only hope he is half as fortunate as I am."

Smiling softly, Aurora rolled up the parchment and retied the ribbon. "Well, I would say a celebration is in order."

He bent to place a light kiss on her lips. "I can think of the perfect way to celebrate," he murmured warmly against her ear. "Indulging in another of my greatest pleasures . . . ravishing my beautiful wife."

"In the middle of the day?" she asked, feigning shock. "How very scandalous."

Nicholas's smile was pure, wicked magic. It made her blood sing and her nipples harden with the need for his touch. When he drew her to her feet, she went willingly. She ached for him, an ache only he could fill.

She felt the heat and strength of his body as his lips met hers. He kissed her tenderly, his taste deliciously familiar, the scent of his heated skin exquisitely tantalizing. Fever mounting, she wrapped her arms around him, letting the wild yearning rise up in her and overflow.

Wordlessly then, he led her into their bedchamber and shut the door behind him, closing them inside.

They undressed each other slowly, drawing out the moment, lingering to taste and touch. His dark eyes smoldered with desire as he laid her naked on the bed, while her heart leapt with the same desire at the magnificence of his aroused body. Rapt, she watched him come to her, sighing with pleasure as he joined her.

The smooth, hot flesh of his broad chest pressed against her sensitive nipples, the long sleek hardness of his thighs eased hers apart. Yet he was not prepared to give her completion, it seemed. Instead he wanted to torment her.

Aurora watched his eyes go smoky as he shifted his weight. Bending over her, he feathered light, erotic kisses over her skin, her tight nipples, her belly, moving ever lower, until his lips found the mound of her sex. She drew a sharp breath as he tasted her moist flesh, the hotter moistness of his tongue a delicious shock. She trembled under his erotic assault as talons of passion sank into her, raking her with need.

Finally, though, she could bear no more. Clutching at his dark gold hair, Aurora said his name in a raw, shaky voice, needing to feel the hot slide of his flesh into hers. "Nicholas, please . . ."

He wanted his possession as much as she did, she knew; his arousal thrust hard against her thigh, huge and impatient, as he covered her with his body.

His hands wound in her hair, and he kissed her hungrily, a slow, writhing kiss as he slowly entered her. A low groan sounded from his throat as her hot flesh tightly sheathed him.

Aurora welcomed him fully, arching beneath him as he filled her with melting fire. Her body was full of him, molten with him. She felt like weeping. Each time Nicholas touched her was so new and beautiful. . . .

He felt the same wonder, she was certain. A shudder rocked him, and he drew back only enough to meet her gaze, his eyes burning into hers. Then he thrust again, sinking deeply into her, so deeply she couldn't tell where he ended and she began.

She did weep moments later as blinding surges pulsed from the deepest center of her. Pulses that caught Nicholas in their wake.

They moved as one and shattered as one, splintering in shards of bright, hot light. It seemed as if their souls fragmented and slowly re-formed, fusing with unbearable sweetness.

They calmed slowly, small aftershocks of sensation rippling along nerve endings and prolonging the pleasure. Drowsy, sated with rapture, they held each other, limbs entwined.

"My life," Nicholas whispered against her temple, echoing her own thoughts. "My very soul."

Her heart unbearably full, Aurora sighed with contentment. Love had demanded an irrevocable choice from her, but she had absolutely no regrets. This sense of rightness between them was undeniable. They were fated to be together.

She pressed her face into the warm flesh of her husband's shoulder, thinking of Desiree's journal. *The heart will know its one true mate.*

It was true, Aurora reflected. Nicholas was her mate, now and forever. He had ignited her heart's hidden passion and brought her joy beyond imagining. He was her one true love, and she could not ask for more.

Read on for an exciting taste of

To Desire a Wicked Duke

by Nicole Jordan

Chapter One

❧

I have been off the Marriage Mart for a good while now, but I am quickly learning an indisputable rule of engagement with the opposite sex: When you play with fire, you are likely to be burned . . . and Rotham is the hottest sort of fire.
—DIARY ENTRY OF MISS TESS BLANCHARD

Richmond, England: October 1817

The kiss was amazingly insipid.

Disappointment surged through Tess Blanchard as Mr. Hennessy drew her more fully into his embrace. She had expected so much more when she acquiesced to his impulsive gesture.

More excitement, more pleasure, more *feeling*. In short, she had secretly longed to be swept away by romantic passion.

Instead she found herself logically analyzing the construction of his love-making. The precise pressure of his lips. The exact angle of his head. The unarousing feel of his arms around her.

There was no spark, no *fire* between them at all, Tess realized sorrowfully. The entire business left her remarkably cold.

Oh, Patrick Hennessy certainly *seemed* skilled in the art of kissing, she mused as his mouth plied hers with increased ardor. But surely a man who counted himself such an expert lover should have elicited a stronger response from her?

Not that she had much basis for comparison. This was only the second man she had ever romantically embraced in her three-and-twenty years.

It had happened purely on a whim. One moment they were laughing together over a line in the comic play Hennessy had written. The next, an arrested expression claimed his features as he gazed down at her. When he stepped closer and bent his head to capture her lips, Tess had no thought of stopping him. For too long she had let herself languish on the shelf in the game of love, refusing to open herself up to renewed heartbreak. But it was past time to reenter the lists.

Admittedly, in Mr. Hennessy she was drawn by both curiosity and the lure of the forbidden. She knew better, of course. A proper lady did not indulge in scandalous experiments with libertine actors behind the stage curtains. Hennessy was known as something of a Lothario among the London theater crowd, in addition to being a brilliant performer, a successful manager of his own troupe, and a budding playwright as well.

Then again, perhaps she was not giving him a fair chance.

Closing her eyes more tightly, Tess made a stronger

effort to enter into the spirit of the kiss. In response, Hennessy's hand stole lower down her back, over her derriere, to pull her closer. Despite her own lack of enthusiasm, she had evidently affected *him*, judging by the swelling hardness she felt pressing against her lower abdomen—

"Well, well, are you practicing to play the part of lovers in your production, Miss Blanchard?"

At the sharp-edged drawl, a startled Tess tore her mouth away from Hennessy's—and froze in mortification upon recognizing that sardonic male voice. Obviously she had failed to hear anyone enter the ballroom where their makeshift stage was erected.

Good Lord, what utterly dreadful timing, to have her transgression discovered by the arrogant, infuriating Duke of Rotham, elder cousin of her late betrothed. Rotham had stepped behind the stage curtains to find her locked in a clandestine embrace with the man she had hired to produce her amateur theatrical.

Scalding heat flooded Tess's cheeks as she pulled away from her partner in crime. Hennessy had also reacted to the duke's unexpected appearance by releasing her instantly. Yet the actor looked not only guilty but somewhat alarmed, as if he'd been caught in a hanging offense.

Squaring her shoulders, Tess turned to face Ian Sutherland, the tall, lithe Duke of Rotham. His handsome face was an enigmatic mask in the muted daylight seeping over the stage curtains from the ballroom windows, but his mouth held a tightness that signified displeasure.

He had no right to judge her, she told herself defiantly.

"You are mistaken, your grace," Tess murmured, striving to keep her voice calm as she responded to his mocking tone. "There are no lovers in Mr. Hennessy's play. It is merely a comedy of manners about a mischievous ghost."

"You were testing out a new role then?"

"What may I do for you, Rotham?" Tess asked, ignoring his jibe. "We have only just concluded the dress rehearsal and still have a great deal to accomplish before this evening's performance."

They had constructed a stage at one end of the ballroom of her godmother's country mansion for the theatrical—the crowning entertainment of the charitable benefit Tess had organized. Tess had engaged Hennessy and his troupe to put on the one-act play and direct the houseguests in their respective acting roles.

"I doubt your preparations entail kissing the hired help," Rotham drawled in that annoyingly cynical tone of his.

Tess stiffened. "It is hardly any of your business whom I kiss, your grace."

"I beg to differ."

Renewed ire rose in Tess. She would not allow him to dictate to her, as he was so fond of doing. Indeed, they had had similar arguments before. The Duke of Rotham was head of the family she would have married into had her betrothed not perished two years ago at the Battle of Waterloo. But they had no real blood ties, and Rotham was mistaken in thinking that he had any say over her affairs. Particularly her amorous affairs.

Shifting his attention, Rotham turned his penetrating gaze to Mr. Hennessy, who still seemed wary and on edge. "I expected better of you, Hennessy. You were supposed to be protecting her, not assaulting her. Is this how you fulfill your duties?"

The actor shot the duke a chagrined look of apology. "I beg your forgiveness, your grace. I fell down in my duties deplorably." Rather sheepishly, he turned to Tess. "A thousand pardons, Miss Blanchard. I was vastly out of line."

Tess started to respond, but Rotham interrupted her. "I'll thank you to leave us, Hennessy. I shall deal with you later."

Her jaw dropped at Rotham's arrogant dismissal, but before she could raise an objection, Hennessy gave her a brief bow, then pivoted with alacrity and disappeared through a part in the curtains.

She remained speechless as she listened to him bound down the stage steps and hurry away across the ballroom. It was hardly chivalrous of him to abandon her to the mercies of the duke, Tess thought resentfully. No doubt he preferred not to challenge a nobleman of Rotham's station and ruthless influence.

However, when she at last gathered her wits enough to protest, Rotham held up an imperious hand, forestalling her. "You should know better than to indulge in trysts with libertines such as Hennessy."

Prickling with indignation, Tess returned a mutinous look. The nerve of him, scolding her for a sin she had not even committed. "I was not indulging in any *tryst,* your grace. It was just a simple kiss."

The corner of Rotham's mouth curled. "It did not look at all *simple* to me. You were participating fully."

He sounded almost angry, although why he would be angry with her for returning the actor's kiss, she couldn't fathom.

"What if I *was* participating? It is no crime—"

Realizing how high-pitched and flustered her own voice sounded, Tess took a calming breath and forced a cool smile. "I truly cannot believe your gall, Rotham. How someone of your wicked character can deride another man for rakish behavior—or criticize me for something so innocent as a mere kiss—is the *height* of irony. Do you even recognize your hypocrisy?"

A hint of sardonic amusement tugged at his lips. "I acknowledge your point, Miss Blanchard. But I am not the only one concerned about your relationship with Hennessy. Lady Wingate is worried that you have become overly attached to him. In fact, she sent me to find you."

That gave Tess pause, as doubtless Rotham knew it would. Lady Wingate was not just Tess's godmother but chief patron for her various charities. She could not afford to offend the woman whose generosity impacted so many lives for the better.

"I have not become attached to Hennessy in the least," Tess finally replied. "He is a valued employee, nothing more."

"Do you go around kissing all your employees?" Rotham taunted. Before she could reply, he shook his head in reproach. "Lady Wingate will be severely disappointed in you. She arranged a lavish house party solely for your sake, so you could dun her guests for your various charities. And *this* is how you repay her?"

Unable to refute the charge, Tess regarded Rotham in frustration. Her godmother had long disapproved of her endeavors to promote her charitable organizations and had only recently relented and invited some four dozen wealthy guests to a week-long house party, thereby providing Tess with a captive audience. She'd spent the past week attempting to persuade each one of them to contribute to her causes.

"Do you mean to tattle to her?" she asked Rotham.

His answer, rife with mocking humor, disturbed her. "That depends."

"On what?"

"On whether or not you intend to continue your liaison with Hennessy."

"I tell you, I am *not* having a liaison with him! You have completely misconstrued the matter."

"Who initiated the kiss?"

"What does that matter?"

"If Hennessy took advantage of you, I will have to call him out."

"You cannot be serious!" Tess stared at him, appalled to think he might not be jesting. The last Duke of Rotham, Laurence Sutherland, had ended his licentious career when he was killed in a duel over a married woman by her jealous husband. His son Ian had followed a similar reckless path all through his youth, generating wild tales of gambling and womanizing. Ian Sutherland's scandalous endeavors had earned him the nickname "the devil duke" when he came into the title eight years ago. But surely he would not actually *shoot* Hennessy for the mere act of kissing her.

"You know very well that dueling is illegal," Tess objected, "in addition to being dangerous and possibly even lethal."

Rotham's mouth tightened again, as if he too had recalled his sire's ignominious end. "Indeed."

When he said nothing further, Tess suddenly recalled the confusing remark he'd made before ordering the actor from the ballroom. "What did you mean when you said Mr. Hennessy should have been 'protecting' me?"

Rotham waved a careless hand in dismissal. "It is of no import."

"I should like to know." Tess fixed him with a stubborn gaze, determined not to back down.

He must have sensed her resolve, for he gave a shrug of his broad shoulders. "When you began spending so much time at the Theatre Royal in Covent Garden in preparation for your last charity event, I charged Hennessy with keeping an eye on you. The theater district is a dangerous area, especially for an unescorted young lady."

Her eyebrows lifted in puzzlement. "So you asked him to look after me?"

"Yes. I paid him a significant sum, in fact."

So *that* explained why Hennessy always insisted on escorting her to and from her carriage, Tess realized, and why he had hovered around her whenever she attended rehearsals. She had thought it was because the actor was growing enamored of her company. Irrationally, she couldn't help feeling a prick to her self-esteem.

"My companion usually accompanies me to the theater," she pointed out to Rotham.

"Your companion is an aging spinster with all the substance of a butterfly. She would be no help whatsoever if you were confronted by trouble."

That much was true, Tess conceded. Mrs. Dorothy Croft was tiny and gentle and soft-spoken, as well as being a bit scatterbrained. The impoverished friend of Tess's late mother, Dorothy had needed somewhere to live after being widowed, so Tess had opened her home in Chiswick to her. The relationship had also benefitted Tess. With a genteel, elderly lady to lend her single state respectability, she had much more freedom to conduct her charitable endeavors.

"I have a sturdy coachman and footmen to provide me protection should I require it," Tess argued.

Rotham's gray gaze never faltered. "Even so, I thought it wise to ensure your safety. And you would not readily have accepted any edicts from me."

That was also certainly true. They had long been at odds—which is what made Rotham's current interest in her safety so startling. That he might be seriously concerned for her welfare had never crossed her mind.

"Well, you needn't worry about me, your grace. I am capable of providing for my own protection."

"Then you should refrain from kissing the likes of Hennessy. And he had best keep away from you. If he dares to touch you again, he will answer to me."

At the edge of possessiveness in the duke's tone,

Tess's eyebrows narrowed in disbelief. He could not possibly be jealous. No doubt he was merely angry at Hennessy for disobeying a direct order, and at her for daring to contradict him.

"Your transgressions are a thousand times worse, Rotham."

"But I am not an unmarried young lady, as you are."

"I am not so young any more," Tess rejoined.

Instead of replying, Rotham hesitated, as if suddenly aware how sharp his tone had become. Shaking his head, he seemed visibly to repress his emotions, as if distancing himself from their argument.

His succeeding laugh was soft and laced with real amusement. "You are hardly ancient, Miss Blanchard. You only just turned twenty-three today."

Tess eyed him with suspicion. "How did you know it was my birthday?"

"As head of the family, it is my business to know."

"You are not head of *my* family."

"For all practical purposes, I am."

There it was again, that ironic drawl that convinced her he was deliberately attempting to provoke her.

It was infuriating, how Rotham always seemed to get under her skin, Tess reflected. Particularly when she was normally serene and even-tempered.

She had always thought him vexing—and deplorably fascinating. Rotham not only had a wicked reputation, he even *looked* wicked. He had striking gray eyes fringed by dark lashes, with lean, aristocratic features that were handsome as sin. His hair was a rich brown shot with gold threads, several shades lighter than her own sable hue, and held a slight curl. He possessed the muscular build of a sportsman but with a lethal elegance that proclaimed his nobility.

Yet it was Rotham's powerful personality that made him utterly unforgettable.

At the moment his features were mainly in shadow, since it was barely noon on a gray, rainy autumn day and they were shrouded by stage curtains. Yet he still had the strange ability to affect her, Tess acknowledged.

She'd felt that same magnetic allure the first moment of meeting Rotham during her comeout four Seasons ago, when he'd deigned to dance with her. But shortly afterward, she'd fallen in love with his younger cousin Richard.

Ever since, she had felt guilty for her forbidden attraction to the Duke of Rotham. He was every inch the fallen angel. And lamentably even now, she felt his hypnotic pull as his gray gaze bored into her. . . . .